ALSO BY MEGAN MCANDREW

Going Topless

Dreaming in French

A NOVEL

Megan McAndrew

SCRIBNER
New York London Toronto Sydney

SCRIBNER

A Division of Simon & Schuster, Inc.
1230 Avenue of the Americas
New York, NY 10020

First Scribner hardcover edition September 2009

SCRIBNER and design are registered trademarks of The Gale Group, Inc.,
used under license by Simon & Schuster, Inc., the publisher of this work.

For information about special discounts for bulk purchases,
please contact Simon & Schuster Special Sales:
1-866-506-1949 or business@simonandschuster.com.

The Simon & Schuster Speakers Bureau
can bring authors to your live event. For more information or to book an
event contact the Simon & Schuster Speakers Bureau at 1-866-248-3049
or visit our website at www.simonspeakers.com.

Text set in Berling

Manufactured in the United States of America

1   3   5   7   9   10   8   6   4   2

Library of Congress Control Number: 2009002298

ISBN 978-1-4165-9972-2
ISBN 978-1-4391-0958-8 (ebook)

For my parents

1

ASTRID BECAME A MARXIST after it stopped being fashionable, even in France, but fashion, as she always told us, was for people without imagination. How a woman who shopped at Sonia Rykiel could have discovered within herself a sudden solidarity with the working classes was a matter for some perplexity, though not on the part of Lea, who expressed the view that our mother was unstable. At sixteen my older sister was cultivating cynicism. She had also just gone on the pill, which was easy to do in those days. All it took was a visit to the *clinique* on Rue Bonaparte, where the darkly handsome Docteur Bernard, who looked more like a hairdresser than a gynecologist, dispensed contraception to the young sirens of the Sixth Arrondissement after the most nominal of examinations and, it was rumored, occasionally seduced one, though Lea was disappointingly not among their number. Why Lea had sought birth control was in itself cause for speculation, since she didn't have a boyfriend. But, as she grimly told me, it was better to be prepared. Grimness was a sentiment that gripped Lea frequently. Like Vera in *War and Peace*, my older sister saw herself as the only dignified member of a ridiculous family. She bore our mother's idiosyncrasies stoically but, in her heart, my sister thought of herself as French, and French mothers did not go to ashrams in India, or march in demonstrations, or hire Maoist housepainters, or walk around the apartment wearing nothing but red nail polish.

We lived on the Rue de Seine, in an eighteenth-century *hôtel particulier* with a sober sandstone façade and a portal originally intended to accommodate horse-drawn coaches; the kind of place tourists walk by and, catching through a tall window a glimpse of a fresco or a chandelier, wonder who might inhabit such a splendid interior. It was a huge warren of an apartment with creaky floors and a salon intended for receiving, with so many *poutres apparentes* that, as my father joked, you could have hung pheasants from them. In the winter it was never quite warm enough, and in the summer, the smell of roses wafted up from the vast cobblestoned courtyard. When my parents first came to Paris, they had been shown, by a well-meaning real-estate agency used to dealing with Americans, various palatial dwellings in the Eighth and the Sixteenth, but Astrid was dead set on Saint-Germain. She wanted to live in a place with ghosts, and the Rue de Seine had plenty, from George Sand to Queen Margot, both women my mother admired, though Margot, with her tumultuous passions, was probably closer to her heart. On the day that Astrid declared herself a Marxist, my sister said, "Communists don't eat lunch at Lipp," a remark that impressed me with its sagacity, even as I found it a bit rich coming from someone who went on the pill without intending to have sex.

"Oh, darling, don't be such a grump," Astrid said, lighting a ciga-rette. She smoked Benson & Hedges, which came in long golden packs whose husks lay crumpled all over our home like fallen leaves. I rolled my eyes and she winked at me, our private signal of complic-ity, for Astrid knew that I didn't really mind the contradictions that drove Lea crazy, that I was content to adore her for having long sin-gled me out as her favorite.

"And they don't live in the Sixth," persisted Lea, who was so popular at school that her status at home left her indifferent.

Our mother dropped onto the sofa and kicked off her shoes, sending them skidding across the carpet. The shoes were green and high-heeled and terribly chic in the way that everything she put on became chic, even though she was from Kentucky. She was long and supple and taller than Frenchwomen, and she had to order her shoes from I. Magnin because her feet were too big for European sizes.

"In France they do," Astrid replied, stretching out her legs and inspecting her toenails. Usually she did them herself, having worked as a manicurist in her youth, but she'd gone to Elizabeth Arden that morning, and then had lunch with Grace de Lasnoy. A long lunch; it was almost four o'clock. "Besides, Communists are different from Marxists. Communists are dreadfully dull. Marxists are much sexier." Astrid sank back against the sofa's cushions, and as she exhaled a plume of smoke, a dreamy expression came into her eyes.

Grace was Astrid's best friend, and the source, as far as Lea was concerned, of her more questionable enthusiasms. The ashram had been Grace's idea, as had a jewelry-buying trip to Afghanistan (they were going to open a boutique) that had almost gotten them both arrested; there had been an episode involving a block of hash, which had so evolved over its many retellings that I now, as with all stories involving Grace, question its veracity. Grace was married to a Belgian count who had mistresses—according to Astrid, it was something you just had to accept if you married a European—and had the restless quality of a caged cat. She selected her lovers among the starving artists of the city, but they were a sorry lot, and one wondered sometimes, or at least Astrid wondered, why she bothered. At one of Grace's parties, there had been a professor from Jussieu, one of those magnetic, vaguely foreign-looking personalities with long hair and artfully rumpled jackets who were willing to socialize with Americans, and the next thing we knew, all of Grace's friends had become Marxists, including my mother, who had always had a weakness for revolutionaries.

When Lea announced at the dinner table, with a smirk, that Astrid had become a Communist, Frank raised his eyebrows and said, "Oh good, does that mean we can go to Tignes instead of Chamonix this year?"

Astrid smiled her lopsided smile. I remember that she seemed particularly mesmerizing that night, as if she were animated by electricity. My mother was not a classic beauty: Her features were irregular and her hair too red, but her imperfections conspired to make her unique. It was her spirit, however, that raised her above the

ranks of the merely lovely. Although she was named after Queen
Astrid of Belgium, Astrid never forgot that she was the daughter of
a waitress. Indeed, she found the notion of regality hilarious. She
hated snobs. She had a deep, throaty laugh, and the unabashed femininity of Southern women. When she talked to you, she looked you
straight in the eye. I was the one who looked like her, albeit in a sadly
vestigial form. Lea, who got Frank's genes, had the spooky beauty of
a Flemish Virgin.

It was the fall of 1979. Valéry Giscard d'Estaing was president
and the French economy was in crisis, as it always seemed to be,
though, as Frank quipped, you wouldn't have known it from trying
to get a restaurant reservation. Islamic clerics had taken over Iran,
and the Poles had begun to rebel against Communism. But even if
the whole world had been exploding around us, I probably wouldn't
have noticed, for I was consumed at the time with my own preoccu-
pations. That morning I had stood naked in front of the mirror, nar-
rowing my eyes until I thought I saw a womanly shape, though one
look at Astrid striding down the hallway in her naked glory was
enough to dispel this illusion. Clearly I, Charlotte Sanders, was
doomed to remain a runt. At fifteen and two months, I had failed
even to reach the milestone that monthly sent half my classmates
slinking to the bathroom with coyly secretive looks: While Lea had
bled triumphantly at eleven, my daily inspected underwear remained
as white as a vestal's, and even as I towered over her, I feared that a
witch had stood over my cradle at birth, casting a spell that would
leave me a child forever.

2

L EA AND I WENT TO the École Bilingue Colbert, which was
housed in a Second Empire palace on the Rue de Lisbonne,
and was popular with rich Americans and Arabs. It had a
renowned *cantine*, where we were served in courses by Portuguese
women, but most of us preferred the café across the street, which
was equipped with pinball machines and a jukebox from which
issued a steady diet of French pop interspersed with the Rolling
Stones and the Rubettes.

"Is that him?" Delphine hunched over and peered at me in an
agony of concentration. Over the summer she had become obsessed
with boys, and now she was officially in love, but I had the view of
the café door, which had just swung open to admit two classmates.

"No," I said. "It's just Cécile's brother and creepy whatsisface," I
added, trying to sound condescending when in fact I found creepy
whatsisface to be quite attractive in a brooding sort of way, and
knew his name, Patrice Fabre, perfectly well.

"Oh God, I could just *diiiiiie,*" moaned Delphine. Like many of
our schoolmates, my best friend had an American mother and a
French father, and her English had the deracinated quality peculiar
to that milieu. She had, however, just spent a month with her
cousins in New Jersey, and had returned with all the latest idioms
and fashions, teenagers in America being altogether a more evolved
species than those in Europe. To my alarm, she was transformed in
other ways as well, her hair inexplicably blonder (she claimed it was
bleached by the sun) and her suddenly impressive breasts molded
into a bra, its straps discernible under her T-shirt. The bra had been

purchased along with several other essential accessories during an expedition to Bloomingdale's with her cousin Sarah, a particularly highly evolved American teenager who lived in a mansion in Short Hills, and whose exploits had already been reported to me several times in minute detail, with particular emphasis on an escapade to Studio 54, where she and Delphine had gained entrance with fake IDs and had been offered cocaine in a back room, a proposition Delphine swore she had refused in shocked dismay, though the same couldn't be said for Sarah. I had received this account with a carefully neutral expression, unwilling to betray my unease at this gulf that had opened between us. I had never even set foot in a nightclub, and before her American sojourn, neither had Delphine.

Serge Lubomirski came in just then, and headed for the pinball machine. When I reported this to Delphine, she hid her face in her hands.

"Aren't you overdoing it?" I suggested. "He can't even see you." On the table before us, our Coke glasses stood empty. Delphine pulled a pack of cigarettes out of her bag and lit up. She had started smoking that summer in New Jersey, too, and though she didn't really like them, as betrayed the rather too-intent expression with which she inhaled, she thought they made her look sophisticated. I didn't smoke, though Lea did, a fact that Astrid halfheartedly deplored and Frank was kept in the dark about. From the jukebox came the first strains of "Daniel." Her equilibrium restored, Delphine rolled her eyes. "Elton John is so cheesy," she declared, *cheesy* being her current favorite word, brought back from the States along with a newfound contempt for Elton John. Alain, the café owner, came over and wiped our table with a dirty cloth.

"*Ça va, les filles?*"

"She's dying of love," I said with a smirk.

"Eh, it won't be the last time."

"What a creep," Delphine said when he was gone.

"I thought you liked Alain."

"He's always checking us out; it's disgusting."

I eyed her with undisguised shock. What was disgusting was that this thought would even enter Delphine's mind. Again I detected the influence of Sarah who, Delphine had reported with awe, went out with older men.

To distract myself, I glanced over at the object of her desire. He was standing with his back to us at the pinball machine, his hips twitching as he maneuvered the flippers. There was something about those narrow hips in their tight jeans that unsettled me. He hadn't seen us, and if he had, he wouldn't care, because he ran with a cool crowd and in his eyes we didn't even exist. I wished sometimes that Delphine had more sense.

"He's going to tilt it," I remarked, as the twitching turned to thrusts and the machine, which was adorned with big-breasted girls in Tarzan-inspired bikinis, responded by ominously flashing its lights.

"No he isn't."

"Yes he is."

The buzzer went off and Serge slammed his fist down on the glass; then, as if remembering himself, he nonchalantly made his way to the bar. After Alain had poured him a Coke, he turned around and surveyed the room with icy hauteur. When his eyes fell on us, I assumed they would move on, but instead a small smile came to his lips. He detached himself from the counter and headed in our direction. I shot Delphine an uneasy glance.

"He's coming this way."

"Omigod!"

"Would you stop it!" I snapped.

Delphine's choice of love objects puzzled me, focusing as it did on boys who were clearly and hopelessly unattainable. The first had been Dominique Lévy, whose father was a famous journalist married to an even more famous actress. At least Dominique was nice though—Serge Lubomirski was a snob. His father was supposed to be some kind of Polish prince, and Serge certainly acted as if he were issued from royalty. He had reached our table now, however, and to my dismay, dropped into a chair. Delphine scrabbled for another cigarette. With a smooth movement, Serge pulled out a lighter and flicked it on, reaching across the table to hold the flame before her. As I looked on in amazement, Delphine, her hair falling across her face like a curtain, lowered her eyes and then raised them to meet Serge's before exhaling a scrim of smoke. Serge transferred his glance to me. The glance said, *Don't you have something better to do?* I was going to blurt out something sarcastic when Lea entered the café, took in the startling tableau of me and Delphine sitting with Serge Lubomirski, and raised her eyebrows.

"Hey!" I called, waving her over. Delphine shot me a furious look but it was too late; Lea was on her way over. Serge lifted his eyelids as if they held the weight of the world and drawled, "*Salut.*"

"*Bonjour,*" Lea said crisply. She didn't sit down. Serge looked at me again. It must have only come to him at that moment that I was Lea Sanders's younger sister. It might have been my imagination, but he seemed to suddenly regard me with new respect. My sister hung around with a fancy French crowd from her riding club, most of whom went to Lycée Henri-IV—Astrid called them her hoity-toity friends—and she didn't normally concern herself with lesser mortals. She was also one class ahead of Serge, who had had to repeat a year. It was rumored that he had come to École Colbert after being kicked out of Saint-Louis. Since Lea wasn't budging, he slowly got up. "I'll see you around," he said, looking at Delphine.

"*Salut,*" Delphine said with her newly acquired poise. I felt like kicking her.

"What were you doing with *him?*" Lea asked.

Delphine gave her a challenging stare, which only made Lea laugh. "Oh, well," she said, "live and learn . . ."

"Your sister is a bitch," Delphine declared when Lea had gone away.

"No, she isn't."

Delphine shrugged. "Whatever . . ." Another new expression brought back from the States. I scrutinized her anxiously. She had started to wear mascara, though she had to apply it on the Metro and remove it before she got home, because her mother found it vulgar; and her hair, formerly blondish, had turned suspiciously yellow, but surely this was still the same old Delphine who had wept with me over the trials of Black Beauty and who had once called me at midnight to describe in sobbing detail the agony of a hamster's death.

"Can I copy your math homework?" she asked.

"Sure," I said with relief, for this was more like the Delphine I knew. I reached eagerly into my bag for my notebook and handed it to her.

"I don't know what I'd do without you," she asked.

"You'd fail math."

She fixed me with her round, reproachful blue eyes and, as if she had suddenly remembered something, got up. "I'll be right back," she said, heading toward the bathroom. I saw them in the embrasure of her bag as she walked by, the little blue box of tampons, nestled between her cigarettes and a pack of grape-flavored Bubble Yum.

3

ELPHINE'S FATHER WAS thirty years older than her mother. He had been a high official in Pompidou's government, and was retired but still kept an office that he went to every day. Delphine said all he did in the office was drink cognac and read the paper, but it seemed a fitting enough occupation for a man his age, and I didn't see why she had to sound so contemptuous about it. Delphine's mother fascinated me. Though she and Astrid were both Americans, they didn't frequent the same circles. Sylvia Fauché was involved in things like charities and the American Church, where Astrid said the sight of all those velvet hair bands gave her a headache. Grace said Sylvia was uppity, and it was true that, in her Chanel suits and pumps, she seemed a little formal, but I felt sorry for her, being married to such an old man, and in my eyes she was a romantic and rather melancholy figure.

"Oh, Charlotte," she said distractedly when she opened the door. She looked as though she might have been crying, and I felt embarrassed, as if I had caught her in an intimate moment. Before I could even say hello, though, Delphine appeared and shoved me out. "Let's go," she hissed, grabbing my arm and pulling me behind her down the stairs, evidently in such a hurry that she couldn't stand to wait for the elevator. It was only once we were outside on the Madeleine, the traffic roaring past, that I caught my breath to ask what was going on.

"I hate her!" she cried.

"Why?" I asked, for I couldn't understand how this sad, gentle woman could arouse such vicious emotions. But then Delphine was like that; she flew from one passion to the next. It was what both thrilled and terrified me about her.

"Because she won't let me go to Chiara Grzebine's party."

I gave her a puzzled look. She had never mentioned anything to me about Chiara Grzebine inviting her to a party. Growing impatient with my idiocy, she added, "Oh, for God's sake, for her birthday! It's in two weeks, at her parents' country place, and that *witch* won't let me go!"

"Since when are you friends with Chiara Grzebine?" I hazarded.

Delphine narrowed her eyes. "What's that supposed to mean?"

"Just what I said. I didn't know you even knew her. She's in Lea's class."

"So?" Delphine said truculently.

I shrugged. "So nothing." Chiara Grzebine hung around with Serge Lubomirski's crowd and was reputed to have posed naked for David Hamilton. She was two years older than us, and not exactly known for acts of social largesse.

"You're just angry that *you* weren't invited," Delphine said.

That wasn't true. I was hurt that my best friend would consider doing something without me, and I didn't like Chiara Grzebine. Lea had told me that she slept around, and, though we all pretended to be sophisticated about these things, there was something obscurely distasteful about the idea.

"Well," I said bluntly, "to tell you the truth, it surprises me that *you* were." The transformation that had occurred in Delphine over the summer was beginning to exhaust me. All of a sudden I remembered that we were supposed to be going to the movies. *Oliver's Story* had just come out, and since Delphine was madly in love with Ryan O'Neal, it seemed like the perfect distraction. "Come on," I said, "we're going to be late."

But Delphine wasn't budging. "I don't want to go to the movies," she said, and then, as if struck by an impulse, "Let's go have a Coke."

I wanted to go to the movies. I had read *Love Story* more times than I could count, weeping each time afresh when Jennifer died, and though I hadn't liked *Oliver's Story* as much, Delphine's strangeness made me yearn for anything familiar. But it clearly wasn't worth arguing with her. I followed her into the corner café. It was a place frequented by tourists, and I felt awkward sitting on the terrace, where everyone could see us. Delphine pulled a tube out of her pocket and slathered pink gloss all over her lips. It looked sticky and, like most of the cosmetics she had brought back from the States, smelled like bubble gum. I thought of her lovely mother, from whom emanated, like a wistful sigh, the melancholy smell of Diorissimo.

"What are you doing?"

She handed me the tube. "Try it, it's watermelon-flavored."

"No thanks."

"Whatever," she said, lighting a cigarette. She gazed moodily ahead as she exhaled. "*Your* mother would let you go."

She was right, Astrid would, but in my mind it wasn't something she should be commended for. In Delphine's opinion, the benign anarchy in which we were raised was sadly wasted on Lea and me. I sometimes wondered if Astrid wished we had more of her wild streak. Maybe the reason she spent so much time with Grace was that she found us boring. This unbidden thought made me queasy.

"I know. I'll tell her I'm spending the weekend with you."

I told myself I hadn't heard Delphine correctly, but of course, I had. "What did you say?"

"I'll tell my mother I'm staying at your place, that we have to study for a test."

"No."

A challenging look came into her eyes. "Why not?"

"Because it's a stupid idea."

"No, it isn't. It's brilliant. I'll bet Astrid would even go along with it," she added, as if this would somehow convince me. Instead I bristled. At this moment, Delphine's bandying my mother's name around struck me as the most glaring presumption.

"I'm not going to lie for you," I said.

She looked stunned. Then she mimicked me, twisting her face into a caricature of what I assumed was my expression. "*I'm not going to lie for you.* . . . Listen to Miss Goody Two-Shoes."

I was close to bursting into tears, but was saved from further ignominy by the arrival of the waiter, who had been held up by a table of Americans. Their loud, cheerful voices made me wish I was sitting with them. They had all ordered the kinds of big ice creams cafés put on the menu for tourists, and I decided I wanted one, too.

"*Pêche Melba,*" I said, because it looked the most extravagant.

"*Un* Schweppes," Delphine said coldly. I regarded her with surprise because she always ordered Cokes. Maybe she thought Schweppes was more grown up. As the waiter walked away, I realized I had forgotten to take any money with me, and I had just ordered the most expensive thing on the menu.

4

THE YEAR BEFORE, a new pope had been elected, a Polish priest with kind eyes. It wasn't the sort of event I normally would have paid attention to—Frank was Episcopalian and Astrid had been brought up Baptist—but Poland had been in the news because of the growing rebellion against the Communists, and all of a sudden everyone was interested in what was going on there. The new pope had caused the kind of excitement that the French press went into when they smelled revolution in the air, or so said Frank, who watched all the discussion shows on TV because he liked the way the French argued dispassionately about things, without getting all heated up as Americans did, though Astrid said it was all a bunch of hogwash and the French were as bloodthirsty as anyone, they still guillotined people for heaven's sake! I always enjoyed listening to my parents' banter at dinner and, even as I recognized them as such, marveled at the outrageous statements Astrid resorted to when logic failed her.

"The French will outlaw capital punishment before we do," Frank said with the amused, if sometimes a bit exasperated smile he often wore when debating a point with his wife. "Especially if the Socialists win."

"Oh, nonsense, darling, they just chopped the head off that poor man, whatsisname."

"Hamida Djandoubi. I seem to recall you attending a protest march. He was convicted for torture and murder, by the way."

It was true. During a brief period of political activism, Grace and Astrid had taken me—Lea had flatly refused to go—to two demonstrations, one against the death penalty, and the other in support of an Algerian girl called Daliyah, who had been imprisoned by her parents for eloping with her lover. We had marched to the Algerian embassy chanting "*Libérez Daliyah*," an exhortation that, by the end of the line, got mangled into "*Libérez Dalida*," affording passersby the curious spectacle of a gaggle of chic Left Bank women shouting for the release of the notoriously awful pop singer of that name whose hit "Gigi l'Amoroso" had recently highjacked the airwaves.

"Oh well," Astrid said grandly, "if we're going to trust the French legal system . . . Heavens, you're guilty until proven innocent in this country—we might as well be living in the Middle Ages."

"I do believe they've implemented a few reforms since," Frank said mildly. "Besides, when you think about it, the guillotine is a remarkably rational approach to institutionalized murder. From the point of view of design alone—" he began, assuming the abstracted expression he always took on when embarking on one of what Astrid termed his "divagations."

"Darling, you're upsetting the girls."

"I doubt it," Frank said, "They're cold-blooded little fiends."

As we were finishing dessert, Astrid rose and announced, "I'm off to Grace's; don't wait up for me."

Frank raised his eyebrows. "Isn't it a bit late, darling?"

My heart sank. Astrid didn't usually go out after dinner, and now she would be back even later. I had never told anyone this, but I couldn't sleep properly until my mother was home, the sound of every passing siren causing my chest to clench. It was only when I heard the click of the door, and the sound of her heels in the hallway that I would finally drift off, relief flooding through me like a narcotic.

"She's raising money for those Polish workers—I promised I'd at least show my face. Why don't you come along? You'd enjoy it."

Frank's expression made it clear how much he thought he would enjoy spending an evening at Grace's. He didn't like going out at night, unless it was to the opera, which Astrid hated. Except for

dinners with clients, and the parties Astrid hosted, he rarely social-
ized, preferring the company of his books and music.

"Since when is Grace interested in Polish labor unions?" he asked
with an amused smile.

"Oh, darling, you know Grace, she has to be part of everything.
There's someone coming from Warsaw—it's all terribly hush-hush,
they had to smuggle him out in a truck or something—and she's
having that journalist from *Le Monde*. . . ." Astrid rolled her eyes. "It
all sounds frightfully *serious*, I doubt I'll be long."

That night I was jolted from the restless sleep into which I had
finally fallen by the sound of the front door closing. When I looked
at the clock, I saw that it was three o'clock in the morning. I don't
know what made me get out of bed. Maybe I was just so relieved she
was back that I had to touch her. I crept out into the dark hallway.
At the far end, light spilled out from the living room where I could
hear Astrid walking around. My mother, though she was tall, always
wore heels. When I reached the living room, I stopped in the embrasure. In those days French people were throwing out their antiques
in favor of a spare, modern look, but Astrid wasn't one for minimal-
ism. Her salon was a profoundly feminine room, full of textures and
shadows and long, swooning drapes, the air heavy with the scent of
roses that stood in a corner in a fat blue vase. She was standing with
her back to me, and she hadn't heard me approach because she had
opened a window and was looking out. Paris is never completely
quiet, the din of the big boulevards always in the background, but in
the hours before dawn, a lull descends, as if the city were recharging
itself, and I thought she was maybe doing the same, drawing
strength from the night. It was still dark, and the way in which she
stood, framed by the black window, gave her the appearance of a
mysterious photograph. When a floorboard creaked under my bare
foot, she turned around.

"Oh, honey, you scared me!"

She didn't look scared; she looked alive and excited, her eyes
bright.

"Did you have a good time?" I asked. It seemed a stupid question, but I couldn't do what I really wanted, which was to rush into her arms. Ever since I was small, I had had an irrational fear that, like a genie in a bottle, she would vanish if I loved her too much.

"Oh, it was marvelous! We drank vodka and sang!"

I remember thinking that it didn't sound at all like the dull event she'd described.

"I thought you were going to a political meeting," I said.

"Oh, honey, you sound like the Grand Inquisitor. . . . It *was* a political meeting, but the Poles are mad, they have such passion!"

"Can we go to bed?"

"Yes, of course we can go to bed; come here you silly grouch." When she folded me in her arms, I smelled cigarettes and vodka and perfume, sweat and skin. Every pore of her body seemed alive both with her and the world that pulled her out of my grasp. I breathed her in and clung.

5

IN A WAY, my parents were both on the run, Astrid from Appalachia, and Frank from whatever it was in America that constrained his very being. My father came from a wealthy Connecticut family that expected its sons to be lawyers, and though Frank had loved music more than law, he had followed in his father's footsteps. I always wondered why he didn't rebel. In his mild-mannered way, he, too, had a wild streak—after all, he married Astrid—but he claimed he had no talent for music, and maybe that was true, though Astrid said he simply lacked the courage of his convictions.

Frank's mother didn't approve of Astrid. She found her wild and bohemian and, it was obscurely understood, lower class. She made overtures after they were married at City Hall, inviting them to lunch in Greenwich and presenting them with a punch bowl in a Tiffany box, but the damage was done and neither Astrid nor my father ever entirely forgave her. I had only met her twice, the second time when I was eight and we were returning to New York from my Kentucky grandmother's funeral. We drove up to Connecticut, where we sat through a formal lunch in a vast blue dining room, after which Lea and I were presented with identical leather-bound copies of the works of Laura Ingalls Wilder. I don't think Lea ever read hers, but I devoured *Little House in the Big Woods* on the plane. Though I barely knew her, I felt a little sorry for my Connecticut grandmother. Her Christmas and birthday presents always included a card expressing the wish that we could see each other more often, but when I pointed this out to Frank, he replied that there was nothing to prevent her from coming to France. She never did, though, and we rarely traveled to America. Our home was in Paris and Frank saw no reason to drag us back and forth across the ocean when there were so many more pleasant places in Europe to visit.

My parents met in New York, where Frank worked for a law firm and Astrid had come to be an actress, boarding a Greyhound bus in Louisville with ten dollars in one pocket and the address of Radio City Music Hall in the other. You would think that Astrid would have been a natural on the stage but, like most extravagant personalities, she was only good at playing herself. She did enjoy a moderate success as a chorus girl, because of her lovely, long legs, but she was too tall to be a leading lady, and by the time Frank came along, she was working as a coat-check girl at Shrafft's and wondering what had happened to her dreams.

She and Frank met on the Madison Avenue bus, where he sat on her hat. Astrid always believed that luck only comes to those who tempt it, and she had bought the hat at Bergdorf's with her last thirty dollars, a sum that equaled her monthly rent on Cornelia Street. The hat was sitting on the next seat, and when Frank came along, he didn't see the box and sat right on it, crushing it under his weight. Astrid let out a shriek. She was looking particularly fetching that day, in a cherry-red Claire McCardell dress with a yellow belt, and when she shrieked, Frank first thought she was mad and, then, after he got a look at her, realized she was the most striking woman he had ever seen. Astrid grandly refused to let him replace the hat, but accepted an invitation to dinner at Lutèce. That night, she entered another world, where waiters called her *Madame* and served her rich foods in creamy puddles. It was the first fancy meal she had ever had, and she reveled in every morsel, from the *quenelles de brochet sauce Nantua* to the *bombe glacée* that came for dessert, rimy and sumptuous on its silver platter. My mother always said that luxury is wasted on the rich, that you have to have been brought up on Velveeta and crackers in order to truly appreciate the fine things in life. Afterward, they took a carriage ride through

Central Park. It was a balmy spring night; the Japanese cherries around the reservoir were in bloom. By then they were just soft shapes in the dark, but their scent perfumed the air. Frank held her hand and asked her to marry him. She thought he was kidding, but then she looked in his eyes and realized he was serious. "Why don't you sleep on it?" she said.

He did, and in due course, Astrid moved in to his Gramercy Park apartment, to the dismay of his parents, and the delight of her sister, Maybelle, who stayed with them when she visited New York. Maybelle wasn't fat back then, and though she didn't have Astrid's sense of style, she was a flirt of the first order and quite turned the head of Frank's colleague Phil Atwater, who joined the ranks of the many rich men Maybelle might have married, if they'd only behaved like gentlemen. That spring, to make up for their City Hall wedding, Frank took Astrid to Paris on the *Queen Mary*. They traveled first class and Astrid wore a different cocktail dress every night. In those days she hadn't yet learned to flout convention, and she dressed like Audrey Hepburn in *Charade*. I have a picture of her standing on the deck in cat-eye sunglasses, her hair caught back in a scarf, and if you didn't know anything about her, you would think she had spent her life on ships, when the truth was that, until that day, she had never even seen the ocean.

My parents found themselves in Paris. There was something in them both that could only flourish in exile, like plants that do better in hothouses than in their natural habitat. They stayed at the Montalembert and strolled over to the Deux Magots every afternoon, where they sat on the terrace and Frank talked about the existentialists. In fact my father didn't care for Sartre and Camus; he found them depressing and boorish. His true loves were Balzac and Maupassant, whom he had studied at Yale. Back then, as she would have been the first to admit, Astrid couldn't have told one from the other, but, thirsty for culture, she soaked it all up like a sponge. The night before their return to New York, she wondered out loud why they had to go back. What was the point of having money if you couldn't do what you wanted with it? Frank was so seduced by this notion, which ran counter to all his family's precepts on thrift and prudence, that he agreed; though he insisted later that they go back to New York so he could get himself transferred to his firm's Paris office, prudence winning out in the end, as it usually did with my father.

It is said that Americans come to Paris to reinvent themselves, and my parents were no exception. Unmoored from his Yankee roots, Frank was finally able to become the gentleman scholar he had always wanted to be, devoting himself to his library and the collection of rare opera recordings that would in time consume most of his leisure. It was Astrid, however, who underwent the truly glorious transformation: The French love *caractère*, and my mother had *caractère* to burn, as well as the adaptive skills of a chameleon. Paris was her finishing school, the atelier in which, layer by layer, she acquired her polish, a process aided by the fact that, as she would have been the first to tell you, the French can't tell a Rockefeller from a hillbilly. She started with the usual stints at Alliance Française and Cordon Bleu, conjugating irregular verbs and making béchamel with the other American ladies, but as she told Frank, she hadn't come to Paris to become Betty Housewife. Then she met Grace, who explained that no one expects Americans to speak French, let alone cook.

After they returned from Afghanistan, Astrid had the apartment painted. She hired one of Grace's protégés, a Chilean Maoist on the run from the Pinochet regime. "We need a painter, not a terrorist," Frank objected, but she talked him into it in the end, assuring him that Armando had been trained as a housepainter. This turned out to be a slight exaggeration, but before my father could protest any further, Armando had moved into our *chambre de bonne*, his sole possessions a guitar and a Che Guevara poster that he affixed over the bed. Lea was sure he was going to murder us all in our sleep, but I was smitten.

"No more neutrals!" Astrid cried. "I want color!" Armando obliged

her with a shrug, as if he had long grown used to the caprices of rich
women. He painted the dining room cerise and the hallway lapis,
the living room the vibrant yellow of buttercups. I followed him
from room to room, making cow eyes and offering him Cokes.
Astrid kept cases of them in the fridge—it was the one thing she
missed about America—and he would gulp them down thirstily,
handing me back the empty bottle with a disdainful expression.
When he was finished, the apartment looked like a jewel box, and it
was generally felt that Astrid had pulled off a coup. "She has some
nerve, your mother," Grace said admiringly. Frank was the only one
who noticed that the corners were sloppy, and that Armando had
only done one coat in the hallway.

Armando hung around for a few more weeks. Frank, who
enjoyed a political debate, tried to engage him a couple times at the
dinner table, but Armando just frowned and changed the subject,
until Frank finally gave up. As he didn't seem like the type of person
who would blow things up, I assumed that he had done something
more intellectual, like write songs against the government or dis-
tribute leaflets, which people were always doing in Paris. Then one
day he disappeared, without even leaving a note. I thought he must
have had a reason. Pinochet's henchmen must have tracked him
down, maybe even kidnapped him. He was probably in danger. In
my bed at night, I played scenarios in my head where I saved him
and, in his gratitude, he pledged eternal love to me. Then Lea saw
him with a girl in the Luxembourg Gardens. Typical, she said, but I
was crushed, and I resolved to never love again.

6

I DON'T KNOW WHY I let Delphine talk me into covering for her. I suppose in the end she wore me down with her whining, or maybe she actually succeeded in convincing me that I was ruining her life. What I really hoped was that she would give up on the whole idea. The weekend party was going to take place at Chiara's parents' château in Normandy, though Lea, who knew the château set from her riding club, wondered by what standards the Grzebine place qualified as such since, to her knowledge, it was at best a glorified *manoir*, not to mention one that had been in the family for all of five years. My sister's grasp of these niceties mystified me; as Americans, and as Astrid's daughters, we weren't supposed to care about arcane class distinctions. Lea, however, could actually distinguish sterling from plate, and counts from barons, and could even have told you if they'd been ennobled by Napoleon, or had ancestors who had lugged their swords to Jerusalem in the twelfth century. When I told her that Delphine had been invited to Chiara's, she gave me a funny look. She had just come in from riding and, in her breeches and tall boots spattered with mud from the *bois*, looked the very picture of equestrian elegance.

"That's a pretty fast set," she remarked, bending down to pull off her boots.

"What do you mean?"

She glanced at me impatiently. "Don't be so dim, Charlotte. Drinking. Drugs. Sex." She went back to taking off her boots.

I made a snorting sound.

"What's so funny?" she muttered from her bent-over position.

"I'm sure that's exactly what Delphine is hoping for."

"Oh, you two are just so sophisticated," my sister said derisively.

In a way she was right. We were at once coolly conversant with the vocabulary of vice, and wholly innocent of its practice. It was a common condition among our peers, many of our parents having spent the last decade testing the limits of adult behavior. The truth was that the only person close to me with direct experience of sex, drinking, or drugs was my mother, who I knew had smoked hash with Grace, but even as this knowledge made me feel terribly grown up, the thought of her engaging in any of these activities mortified me, to the point that I sometimes actually found myself envying Delphine her prim and proper parents. It was, of course, these very qualities in her family that made Delphine thrilled to be associated with Chiara Grzebine, whose film producer father was known to be friends with Polanski, and who was regarded by Lea's friends as one of those Eastern European aristocrats of dubious provenance that our school was full of. Their ranks, coincidentally, included Serge Lubomirski, though, according to Lea, he really was an actual prince, in Poland anyway, a fact that in Delphine's eyes only increased his glamour.

It wasn't that I didn't understand about love. I was in love myself, with Patrice Fabre, whose brooding mien evoked images of Heathcliff on the moor. I hadn't told Delphine because I feared that, in her brittle new incarnation, she would only mock me. Besides, the difference in our love objects was so vast as to make me wonder if it did not bespeak other abysses between us. Serge Lubomirski was the most prosaic of officially sanctioned heart-throbs, while Patrice was mine alone, since I was surely the only girl in school to have seen beyond his unprepossessing exterior into what I imagined to be the fathomless depths of his soul. Since I could no longer confide in my best friend, I had begun keeping a diary, where I daily recorded the temperature of my passion, as well as my unrest over Delphine's small betrayals, and my growing anxiety over whether I would *ever* reach womanhood. I had just finished unburdening myself on this very topic, wondering if I should notify the *Guinness Book of Records*, for I was clearly well on my way to becoming a freak of nature, when Delphine barged into my room without knocking, a record under her arm and a by-now familiar belligerent expression on her face.

"I thought you had violin," I said, slipping the diary under my bed.

"I'm skipping."

"You'll get in trouble," I remarked. I wished I'd told Maria, our maid, to say I wasn't home, but it was too late now. Delphine stood in the middle of the floor, as if uncertain which tack to take with me next. The weekend of Chiara's party was drawing closer.

"Did you get a new record?"

"Yes," she said. "*Hunky Dory*, it's brilliant," and then, to my horror, the scowl dissolved and her chin began to tremble as she fixed great, blue pleading eyes on me. "*Pleeeeeeeeease.*"

"No."

"I'll die if I can't go!"

"No you won't. Nobody ever died from not going to a party."

"You're ruining my life!"

And so I relented, because she was my best friend, and I really didn't want to ruin her life, though I had a feeling she was perfectly capable of doing that on her own, and because I hoped that if I caved in, she would go back to her old self, even as I knew that she couldn't.

7

CHIARA WASN'T THE ONLY ONE having a party. Astrid's forty-fifth birthday was approaching, and preparations were underway for a celebration, largely spurred on by Grace who asserted that forty-five was a woman's Austerlitz. Even our normally reclusive father had been caught up in the whirl, entrusted by Grace with hiring a band, a perplexing assignment in Lea's and my opinion, unless it was a string quartet she had in mind. Frank, however, applied himself assiduously to the task, combing *Pariscope* for the obscure midwestern jazz ensembles that were always performing in Parisian bars and would undoubtedly be happy for a few thousand francs and a hot meal. The by-now exasperated catering director at Fauchon had already submitted three menus, only to have Grace decide that Fauchon was for old ladies, and that something fun and new was needed, the something fun and new being a Vietnamese caterer recently discovered by Candy de Bethune. The party was meant to be a surprise, and we all pretended that Astrid had no idea of what we were up to, just as we expected her to feign amazement when she arrived at Grace's on November 19 at eight o'clock in the evening to find seventy people and a jazz band from Pittsburgh massed in the salon.

Lea and I had been debating for weeks what to get Astrid for her birthday, and had finally found the perfect gift in a little shop on the Rue de l'Université run by one of those heavy-lidded women of indeterminable age who seemed to run all little shops in Paris. In the end we had decided on a glass necklace uncovered in a back recess of the store. Astrid was impossible to buy presents for because, though she loved baubles, her style was so very much her own; but this necklace, with its rough, uneven beads which, as the woman explained to us, were made of sea glass, seemed perfect in that it was as unique and quirkily beautiful as our mother. Wrapped in layers of tissue paper, it now lay in my sock drawer, waiting for the morning of Astrid's birthday, when we planned to present it to her along with breakfast in bed, our custom since we had been little girls.

Grace lived on the Place des Vosges, one of those iconic Parisian addresses that only foreigners could afford. She had summoned Lea and me to discuss unspecified *arrangements*, and I was making my way to her apartment alone, since Lea had flatly refused to accompany me, saying that she had better things to do than play errand girl for Grace. The *bac* loomed ahead, and since Lea intended to go to university in France, a decision that Frank deplored but had resigned himself to, she was determined to do well. I didn't understand her preoccupation, but *bac* hysteria was a peculiarly French phenomenon, and Lea, being more French than the French, wasn't going to miss out on this defining experience. I intended to go to college in America, where Frank said you actually were allowed to express opinions in class, as opposed to sitting in an auditorium listening to some old coot drone on from memory about the Napoleonic Code. Lea said Frank was anti-French, but that wasn't true. Like so many expatriates, he had, rather, simply become more attached to America, in a sentimental way that is only possible to achieve from a distance.

I was walking along the Rue des Rosiers, past the falafel stands and the sweet shops with the trays of poppy seed cake in the window, when I saw Chiara Grzebine coming out of Jo Goldenberg with a man I recognized from television but whose identity I couldn't quite place. That Chiara should be in the company of someone famous was no surprise, since her father was a film producer. What caught my attention was a certain intimate ease between them, discernible in the way his hand lingered on her forearm as he guided her out. I wouldn't have thought much of it, except that Chiara, when she saw me, looked right through me as if I didn't exist, and I wondered once again why Delphine would want to have anything to do with her. She had been going on all week about how Chiara had offered her a ride to the party, which was to take place that weekend, and had intimated that Serge would be joining them, this string of breathless confidences only quelled when I suggested that, in that case, she may not want to wear so much blue eye makeup as to be mistaken for Miss Piggy.

As I turned in to the Place des Vosges, I pushed these thoughts out of my mind. Uncharacteristically for early November, the sun was shining, and the cafés were full of tourists watching the children and their au pairs in the park. The au pairs were all Scandinavian. They came to Paris in the hopes of being preyed upon by Frenchmen, or so asserted Grace, whose husband, the count, was frequently to be found lurking in their vicinity. Although Grace irritated me, I didn't mind going to her apartment because I knew that, whatever wild-goose chase she intended to send me on, she would first bribe me lavishly with macaroons from Ladurée.

"Oh good, you're here!" she exclaimed when the maid let me in. Grace's maid was called Maria, as were Delphine's and ours. Grace's and Delphine's Marias, however, were young and pretty, and, because it seemed so sad that beautiful young women should have to work as servants, especially for someone like Grace, I had a fantasy that it was in fact a joke they played on their employers, that they were really called Esmeralda and Divina, and read poetry in bed at night, and went out on their days off in pearls and feathers to meet mysterious lovers.

"Have your *goûter* like a good girl," Grace said, "and then I need you to run out and pick up some ribbons."

In Grace's mind, I was stuck forever at the age of six, when she had first met me. She had no children herself, not because she couldn't, but because she didn't want them, a revelation that fascinated me, especially in the light of Lea's observation that, if you didn't want children, you should use birth control, and not get pregnant all the time and have to have abortions.

"You haven't breathed a word to Astrid, have you?" Grace now said as she loomed over me and hungrily watched me eat my macaroons. Another piece of information gleaned from Lea was that Grace took laxatives to stay thin, which made me wonder why she just didn't go ahead and eat all she wanted. She and Astrid had come back from Afghanistan with their bags full of tribal jewelry; grimy silver pendants studded with dusky stones, and heavy earrings that looked like they might rip through your flesh. Grace was wearing one of those pendants that day, over a black turtleneck and pants that made her look particularly cadaverous, and I was reminded of Astrid's dictum that, unless you were attending a funeral, you should wear bright colors after forty.

"No," I assured her with my mouth full. "She's completely in the dark." That morning Astrid had pulled me aside and said that, if I was going over to Grace's, please make sure she wasn't planning on inviting Candy de Bethune to the party, because if she had to listen to her sing "Blue Bayou" one more time in that Texas twang, she was going to throw up.

I was finishing my hot chocolate when a scruffy-looking man with piercing blue eyes came into the room, hesitating in the doorway as if he were surprised to find me there.

"Oh, it's you, Łukasz," Grace said. She pronounced it "Wookash," which made me wonder if maybe he was Norwegian. "Meet Charlotte, Astrid's younger daughter. Charlotte, honey, this is Łukasz; he's visiting from Warsaw," Grace added in a voice that suggested this information was freighted with significance. So he knew my mother. I wondered if he was one of the Polish workers she had drunk vodka and sung with, though he looked rather too serious for that. He certainly wasn't the kind of man you would expect to find in Grace's apartment. He hadn't shaved that morning, and his jacket looked like he'd slept in it, but he had a nice face, handsome in a distracted sort of way, which just now seemed troubled.

"Is something wrong?" Grace said, a little impatiently.

"They have taken over the American embassy in Tehran."

Grace gave him a blank look.

"Islamic radicals. They have taken hostages." He spoke good, if cautious English, and sounded like he might have spent some time in America.

"Oh my Lord," Grace exclaimed, hurrying into the next room, where the TV was on. We followed her and stood before the screen, which was filled with an unruly crowd brandishing a burning American flag. A correspondent was explaining that radical Islamic students had taken over the U.S. embassy in Tehran, and were holding the staff hostage. The students were chanting angrily and holding up pictures of the Ayatollah Khomeini, who looked like a sinister fairy-tale character in his beard and turban. I knew all about the Ayatollah Khomeini. Our school was full of Iranians, a fresh wave having arrived after the Shah had fled the country. They all seemed to be descended from royalty, and had beautiful, imperious profiles and fabulous wardrobes, especially the older girls, who Lea said all had nose jobs as well. The one I knew best was Nahid Farman-Farmian in Lea's class, who was picked up every day in a chauffeured Mercedes and whose father had rented out a whole disco for her sixteenth-birthday party, on the occasion of which all the girl guests were given diamond stud earrings. Lea had pronounced the whole thing unbelievably vulgar, but you could tell she was impressed, and she wore the earrings all the time. Nahid, according to my sister, was not only completely wild, but bisexual as well, and hung out at the Katmandou, the famous lesbian club off the Place Saint-Sulpice. Lea claimed that Iranian girls slept with each other to keep their virginity intact, though if they didn't, there was a plastic surgeon in the Eighth who could fix things.

The radicals shouting on the TV screen, however, bore little resemblance to Nahid or any other Iranian at our school. They just seemed angry and shrill, their malevolent leader glaring down over their heads.

"Of course," Grace said, "the French will blame it all on us."

I gathered that by *us*, she meant Americans. "But it has nothing to do with us!" I cried, feeling obscurely attacked.

"*That*," the Polish man mildly observed, "is completely beside the point." Though he made no effort to be friendly, he wasn't condescending like most adults. Frankly, he didn't seem at all like Grace's sort of person. I eyed him curiously.

"I am sorry, I must go to a meeting," he suddenly announced, and withdrew.

Grace turned to me. "Łukasz is a *very* important figure in the Polish opposition."

"You'd never know it," I remarked, attacking the final macaroon—caramel, my favorite, which I had saved till last.

She shook her head. "Mark my word, you'll be reading about him one day." She switched off the TV, banishing the angry mob. "Now, I really need you to go pick up those ribbons. I've ordered the flowers from Bertaud but the French have *no* imagination; I'm sure we'll have to spice them up."

Although she was married to a Belgian, Grace was a self-proclaimed authority on the French, and peppered her conversation with pronouncements on their quirks and proclivities, with particular emphasis on their belligerent anti-Americanism, and their enthusiastic collaboration with the Germans during World War Two. In truth she would have forgiven them anything if they had only accepted her as one of them. She was rummaging through her Hermès bag for money for the ribbons when the phone rang and she snatched it up. "Yes, we've been *glued* to the TV, isn't it *awful?*"

I recognized Astrid's voice on the other end.

"Those poor people!" Grace gushed and, after a pause. "No, darling, he just left. Yes, I'll tell him. I must run, *kiné* appointment—call you later! Huge kiss!"

She hung up the phone and turned to me with a conspiratorial expression. "I didn't want to say you were here, in case she might guess . . ."

"Might guess what?" I said.

"About the *party*, you silly goose! Now off you go. . . . And make sure they give you satin ribbon, not the nasty cheap stuff—oh, and on the way back, be a dear and pick me up some Elancyl at the pharmacy," she added, referring to a product that, in the face of common sense, women across France believed would melt the cellulite from their thighs.

8

ELPHINE HAD BEEN my best friend since we were ten, when her parents had moved her to the École Colbert because she was failing at her old school. Our school was known as something of an expensive dumping ground for rich foreigners and kids who couldn't make it in the French system, a fact that Lea frequently invoked to Frank in her quest to transfer to Henri-IV, to which Frank would blandly reply that the French would naturally have a problem with an institution that didn't turn out docile functionaries, and go back to reading the *Herald Tribune*. Delphine certainly wasn't bothered by the stigma, even though it had been made clear to her that the tuition would come out of her trust fund. It was common knowledge in Paris, or at least among Grace and Astrid's friends, that her father had married her mother for her money. He was from the kind of French family spoken of sympathetically as *aristocrates désargentés*, with whom American heiresses had always been exceedingly popular. French aristocrats weren't the least bit embarrassed about marrying for money. What they brought to the table, in the form of châteaus and furniture and knowing how to use a fish fork, was considered infinitely more valuable than tacky American lucre.

Delphine's trust fund came from her rich American grandmother, who lived in New York. She was called Gloria, and wore a leopard coat and huge sunglasses. She subsisted on filterless Pall Malls and consommé. When she came over for the couture shows, she always stayed at the Ritz, which had proper American-style water pressure, and she would let Delphine take endless baths in the huge tub, and order Cokes from room service. Delphine said that Gloria stayed at the Ritz because she hated her father, called him a freeloader, and though it was hard to imagine anyone falling in love with this stiff and dignified figure whom even Delphine addressed as *vous*, I thought Delphine's mother must have once, to marry him. She had certainly embraced his way of life. Unlike Grace, who wished she could be, or my parents, who didn't even try, Sylvia Fauché, from her Chanel suits to her Louis XV furniture, could easily have passed for French. She spoke English with an elusive but decidedly European accent, as if she had wanted to shed every last trace of her American identity, and she had converted to Catholicism, which struck me as ineffably romantic. I would sometimes be invited for the weekend to their family château, a gloomy old pile outside Bourges with turrets and threadbare tapestries, and in this evocative setting, it was easy to imagine her as a fairy-tale princess, the prisoner of a beast who, deep inside, maybe wasn't a beast at all.

But lately, Delphine hadn't wanted to go to the country. She said there was nothing to do there. When we were younger, we had had a secret garden, its entrance a gap in a lilac border. We would spend hours in its leafy recesses dreaming and making up stories in which we both died tragically young, all the boys who had secretly been in love with us weeping and throwing roses at our funeral procession, which wound for hours through the streets of Paris. Funerals were a particular obsession of Delphine's: Our garden was lined with the graves of several hamsters and a rabbit, for whom we had staged elaborate mortuary rites with the help of an old Bible and Delphine's First Communion crucifix, an object of ghoulish fascination to me with its emaciated Christ hanging from nails that we had bloodied with a bottle of filched Guerlain polish. Once we had gotten married, Delphine in an old white dress and lace tablecloth, and me in a dented top hat, with a cigar clenched between my teeth, and countless times, we had staged the suicide of Ophelia,

Delphine lying in her nightgown in the shallow end of the trout pond with flowers and leaves twined in her hair.

Of course I knew that we were too old now to play little girls' games, but over the summer it was as if Delphine had sprinted ahead of me and left me standing alone. These days all she wanted to do was fill out the Mad Libs her cousin Sarah sent her from New Jersey, or listen to Roxy Music, or talk about her undying passion for Serge Lubomirski, fuelled, as far as I could tell, by a couple glances and the whole three minutes he had spent at our table that afternoon at the café. Then she came back from Chiara's weekend party, and I might as well have stopped existing.

It wasn't her transformation that shocked me. Delphine had always been easily transported, and whatever happened at Chiara's, I had expected her to return full of implausible stories, unless she got caught, in which case she would just be grounded for the rest of the year, or, what she dreamed of, packed off to a boarding school in the States. Her mother, however, had obviously swallowed the story about her having spent the weekend at my house, because she never even called to check, a fact that made me feel both guilty and relieved. What shocked me about Delphine when I saw her in school the following Monday was the glassy look she gave me when I made eye contact in history class, as if she were visiting from another planet and couldn't quite adjust to her new surroundings. Back then, everyone in France was obsessed with drugs. The magazines were full of lurid stories about *drogués*, desperate souls from respectable middle-class families who ended up on the margins of society, stealing and even prostituting themselves to support a habit that, as with so many social ills, was perceived to have come from America.

Being fairly impressionable myself, when Delphine gave me that unfocused look, I imagined the worst. If anyone in our circle was likely to become addicted to drugs, it was surely Chiara with her wild friends and film-producer father. Just then the identity of the man I had seen her coming out of Jo Goldenberg with came to me:

it was Patrick Aubray, a pop singer whose marital infidelities had been exhaustively documented in the press. That clinched it in my mind: A girl who went to restaurants with married pop stars was capable of anything. What *anything* constituted was a bit vague, but it didn't take much imagination to picture Chiara's country house as the scene of the kind of untrammeled debauchery one was always reading about in *Paris Match*. By that point I had completely stopped paying attention to class, and when our teacher asked me pointedly why Francis the First had felt compelled to invade Italy, I regarded him with a blank look that must have eerily mirrored Delphine's.

I caught her afterward in the hallway. "Well?" I said, trying to keep the accusation out of my voice.

"Well, what?" she drawled, and it came to me, with the force of a blow, that the unfocused look I had seen in her eyes was not incipient drug addiction but boredom, boredom with me and our childish pursuits.

"I lied for you," I said, as if this entitled me to something.

"No, you didn't. I was the one who lied, and anyway, I really don't care."

I was humble now. "Did you have a good time?" I asked meekly.

Her eyes assumed again that dreamy, faraway look. "Oh God, it was amazing!"

I waited, but no more was forthcoming. "Was Serge there?" I asked stupidly.

"Oh." That was all she said, "Oh," but that "Oh" contained whole worlds. The bell rang.

"Meet me at the café?"

"Sure," she called back as she hurried off to Spanish. I had wanted her to take Latin with me but she said it was too hard with all those cases. Actually the cases weren't that difficult; even the ablative made sense once you got used to it, and as I recited *Caesar militibus urbam oppugnavit*, and let myself fall into the text's soothing rhythm, I fixed my eyes on the nape of Patrice Fabre two rows ahead, blanking out the dusting of dandruff that adorned his collar, and telling myself that if I were someday to know the ecstasies of love, it would surely be with the one boy in our grade who was taller than me.

Delphine met me at the café after school and, after some hesitation, ordered a Schweppes. I noisily sucked down the last of my Coke.

"Sorry I'm late," she said. "I ran into Chiara."

"I saw her coming out of a restaurant with Patrick Aubray," I sniggered. It was a given among us that all French pop music was awful, from the simpering Sheila et Ringo to the appalling Claude François, and although Patrick Aubray was more of an auteur, he was still no Bob Dylan.

I waited for Delphine to share in my derision, but instead she gushed, "Oh God, Chiara knows everyone. . . . Her father stopped by on Saturday with his girlfriend, you know, Sandrine Perrault, she was in that movie with Alain Delon, and she is *soooo* cool, she's like Chiara's best friend . . ." Delphine's voice trailed off, presumably as she transported herself back to this infinitely more appealing universe.

"There weren't any adults there?" I asked, sensing that my best defense was to act like a complete moron. Of course I knew who Sandrine Perrault was. I was reminded of Frank's deadpan comment when she was being hailed on TV as the next Mireille Darc: "Does the world really need another Mireille Darc?"

Delphine assumed a superior air. "Don't be dense, Charlotte. Chiara is almost seventeen. She doesn't need to be supervised."

"So what did you do all weekend?"

The faraway look descended again. "Oh, it was so great . . . Gaby Marchand was there, and Boris Sarkozy"—she enumerated, naming two of Serge's cohorts—"and Nahid Farman-Farmian."

"Nahid was there?"

"Yes, she's so sweet; she told us how her whole family had to flee when those horrible priests took over Iran—she's related to the Shah, did you know that?" Delphine added with big eyes.

Actually I knew, because Lea had told me, though she had also pointed out that this particular Shah was considered a parvenu by the *real* royal family of Iran, who went all the way back to the days of Alexander. "They're not priests; they're called mullahs."

"Whatever. They make women cover themselves in black table-cloths."

I was going to remark that I bet that wouldn't go over well with Nahid, whose cleavage was the envy of every girl at school, when she came in with Serge Lubomirski, wearing his usual superior smirk. Since I found Nahid entrancingly beautiful and madly stylish, I was willing to forgive her her poor taste in friends, especially since she was also a nice person and actually acknowledged my existence, unlike some of Lea's friends. She waved at us and I smiled back, pointedly not including Serge in my gaze. Delphine broke into an ecstatic smile, as if she had just seen God, but her expression faltered when Serge looked right through us, and when he passed our table without a glance, Delphine's eyes took on a sheen of such naked despair that I found myself thinking irritably that, in love or no, she really *was* overdoing it.

"I have to go," she stammered, rising unsteadily and fumbling for her book bag under the table.

"Whatever," I said, none too kindly. I was going to remind her that we had a math test the next day, when Patrice Fabre walked in, looking forlorn and alienated. As my new plan of seduction involved his seeing me absorbed in serious works of literature, I scrabbled in my bag for the copy of Baudelaire's *Les Fleurs du Mal* that I had taken from Lea's room for this express purpose. I far preferred Verlaine, whole verses of which Delphine and I had raptly memorized in our secret garden, but Baudelaire seemed somehow less soft, more decadent, and I assumed an air of entranced concentration as I held the book up in front of my nose.

Patrice didn't notice me, but Nahid did. "My, aren't we serious?" she purred, tweaking my shoulder and engulfing me in a wave of Opium. I looked up and smiled gratefully. She had Cleopatra eyes and thick, long, auburn-streaked hair that made you want to bury your face in it. I had a sudden impulse to confide in her: Surely Nahid knew how to make a boy fall in love with you. But Serge now appeared at her shoulder, reminding me of the anguish of being made to look like a fool. I thought that maybe he would ask where Delphine had gone, but he just observed me sardonically and said to Nahid, grabbing her possessively by the arm, "Come on, we'll be late." As I watched them leave the café together, I couldn't help but think that they made a stunning couple.

9

WHEN I GOT OUT OF BED the next morning and saw the stain on my nightgown, my first impulse was to run to Astrid, but she was still asleep. I barged into Lea's room instead, trying to keep the triumph out of my voice.

"I got it!" I crowed.

"Ever hear of knocking?" Lea grumbled, but then her eyes fell to my nightgown and she smirked. "About time, we were beginning to think there was something wrong with you."

I was stung. Surely she and Astrid hadn't been discussing me?

"Oh God," Lea said, "don't be such a dope. Did it get on the sheets?"

"No," I confessed, disappointed, for the buckets of gore I had anticipated, based on Delphine's lurid description of blood-soaked linens and gut-wrenching cramps, had failed to materialize, and all I had to show was the little brown stain on my nightshirt, which was emblazoned with a picture of Lucy saying something cutting in French to Charlie Brown.

My sister went to her drawer and pulled out a pack of tampons, which she handed me with a mocking bow. "Do you know what to do with them?"

"Please," I retorted with dignity, snatching the box and dashing to the bathroom.

"You can keep them," she called after me.

I was somewhat crushed to find Delphine absent from school that day, but when I got home and told Astrid my news, she teared up in the way she always did on momentous occasions and pressed me to her. "Oh, my baby girl," she cooed. "We must celebrate!"

Actually, my excitement had already been dampened by a completely uneventful day at school, where no one had seemed to take note of my frequent trips to the bathroom, especially Patrice Fabre, who had particularly failed to register my passage into womanhood. I was beginning to think that maybe it would be best to let the whole thing slide. Astrid, however, jumped up from the sofa. "Let's call Grace!"

"Oh God, no, please!"

"But, honey, this is a special day in your life—we must have a girls' night out! I know, we'll go to the Drugstore!"

My doubtful expression must have given her pause.

"How silly of me, you're all grown up now! I know, we'll go to Castel, show you off to all the old goats!"

"I have to study for a test," I prevaricated.

"Oh, honey, don't be such a party pooper!" And she dashed to the phone, but Grace, thank God, was busy, though she sent *heaps* of kisses, and after I had assured Astrid that I really didn't want to paint the town red, she relented, though not before clutching me again to her chest and wiping away another tear. That night I found a box on my pillow from a jewelry store on the Rue de l'Université. I opened it and there, cushioned in white satin, lay a delicate gold chain with an antique heart pendant. With some difficulty, because the clasp was so small, I fastened it around my neck. In my own private celebration, I had put on my favorite Laura Ashley nightgown, a frilly folly worthy of Marie Antoinette that Lea had pronounced the height of *mauvais goût* but that Astrid had bought me anyway on a shopping trip to London, retorting that good taste was for dullards. I knew all about wearing old underwear in my condition, but I hoped the nightgown would get stained, marked irrevocably with the symbol of my new status. I stood before the vanity and adjusted the chain so that the pendant nestled between my breasts, and all of a sudden, in the lamplight's long shadows, with my hair

falling to my shoulders and the golden bauble glinting dully in the
embrasure of my gown, I thought I could discern the adumbrations
of womanhood.

I wanted more than anything for Astrid to see me like this, and
was about to run to her when I remembered that she had gone out
to a reading, something to do with Poland again, and wouldn't be
back until late. I repressed the sick feeling that threatened to engulf
me and told myself sternly that grown women don't sit up all night
waiting for their mother. Firm in my new resolve, I went instead to
say good night to Frank, who was reading in his study as he always
did after dinner. I wondered if he missed her as much as I did, but he
looked peaceful and content in his armchair, absorbed in his book.

"Hi there," he said when I came in, putting the book down and
smiling. I knew Astrid had told him, because she always told everyone everything. I also knew that, unlike Astrid, he wouldn't embar-
rass me.

"What are you reading?" I asked.

"*L'Assommoir*, in French," he added with a grimace. My father
was the first to admit that he would have found it easier to read Zola
in translation, but, as he was always saying, one should not confuse
ease with pleasure.

"We read that in school last year," I said.

"I should hope so—I must be paying for *something*."

I shrugged and grinned. "I can tell you what it's about," I said
slyly.

Frank look scandalized. "What, and deprive me of the agony of
plowing through it myself?"

"It doesn't end happily," I warned him. I didn't really like Zola,
though he was considered a Great and Serious writer for exposing
the social ills of his age. Though I felt for poor Gervaise, the truth
was that the world of the Rougon-Macquarts was as foreign to me
as that of the Iranian mullahs on TV, and I was much more at home
with Claudine, or Cécile, in *Bonjour Tristesse*, in whom I recognized
troubling echoes of myself.

"What a surprise," Frank said. "A French nineteenth-century novel that ends in disaster!"

"Don't stay up too late," I said, for Frank often fell asleep on the leather sofa in his study, where we would find him in the morning, his glasses askew on his nose and a book splayed across his chest as if he had dozed off in the middle of a sentence.

"I liked you fine as a girl," he said a little awkwardly, as if it had just come out.

"I know," I said, and I bent to kiss him good night.

10

DELPHINE WASN'T IN SCHOOL the next day, either, and when I called her apartment, her mother, sounding worried and exasperated exclaimed, "I don't know what's wrong with her. The doctor says it's nerves—*nerves!* Only a French doctor would allow a perfectly healthy girl to stay in bed for two days; he even gave her a tranquilizer!"

This outburst was so unlike her that I was at loss for a response. I knew what was wrong with Delphine: She was being Natasha in *War and Peace* and, as usual, was taking the histrionics a step too far. After all, it wasn't as if anything had actually happened. "Maybe you could come and see her," Sylvia said, and I promised to, the following day after school, at which time I fully intended to set Delphine straight.

But something *had* happened, at Chiara's party. Lea told me that afternoon. As I might have guessed, Chiara had had an ulterior motive in inviting Delphine. Having observed with great amusement her infatuation with Serge, she had an idea: Why not ask Delphine to the party and have Serge seduce her? The word soon spread among their crowd, and since Serge was wavering, Boris Sarkozy upped the ante to five hundred francs if he could get Delphine into bed. As Lea recounted the details, a sick feeling came over me. I remembered Delphine's ecstatic trance the day after the party, and her reaction when Serge looked right through her.

"Does Delphine know?"

"Half the school knows," my sister said breezily—"Hard to imagine it wouldn't have gotten to her by now."

"You're horrible!" I cried.

Lea shrugged. "I wasn't even there. If I had been, I might have stopped her from making an ass of herself."

I regarded Lea with disbelief. Was that really all it amounted to in her mind? I wanted to protest that Delphine was in love with Serge, that it wasn't fair, that it was Serge and Chiara who should be pilloried. I wanted to say that there was honor in passion, even if it was misguided, and yet, even as I pitied her, I had to agree that my best friend was a fool.

"I warned you about Chiara," Lea said dismissively.

But I wasn't going to let her off that easily. "How can you be friends with someone like that?!"

"How can you be friends with someone who takes advantage of you?"

Since I had no answer, I stalked off, slamming the front door behind me. I walked down the Rue de Seine until I reached the gate of the Luxembourg Gardens. We had been brought there as children by a succession of au pairs, for puppet shows or pony rides, and for the damp, chilly air that is deemed essential to the proper development of Parisian children, and its gravel paths were as fixed in my mind as the inscrutable expressions on the faces of the queens of France who gazed down from their stone pedestals around the boat basin. On this bleak November afternoon, though, the gardens were empty, the carousel and concession stand boarded up, and my only company as I circled the basin were two art students, their easels aimed at Marie de Medici's palace, and an old lady grimly walking her dog. I, too, felt grim, or rather steeped in sorrow, for it struck me suddenly that Delphine had taken an irrevocable step. For all that we were fascinated with sex, and talked about it endlessly, it remained an inviolable frontier, both the mystery that opened the gate to adulthood and the path to unfathomable disasters. The mere thought of Delphine *having* sex, when I had never even properly kissed a boy (I wasn't counting the compulsory lip-mashing sessions we were all subjected to at parties when "Shine on

You Crazy Diamond" came on), was so troubling that I had to block it from my mind. All of a sudden I was gripped by a horrible thought: What if she tried to kill herself?

I had to go to her. I was the only person who could save her. Galvanized, I ran out of the park and sprinted toward the Rennes station, where there was a direct line to the Madeleine. As I waited on the platform, I envisioned bursting into her room where she lay, pale as a ghost, on the pink bed where we used to sprawl all afternoon reading *Spirou* and *Lucky Luke*. At first, she refuses to speak to me, but I assure her that all will be well, that I will stand by her. I take her hand and look deep into her eyes, which are burning with shame and remorse, and she smiles, gratefully, and—suddenly an entirely more alarming thought struck me: What if her mother found out? She would be sent to boarding school, not in the States but to some bleak Catholic *pensionnat* near the Belgian border, like Cécile Matthews who had been caught shoplifting, or Amande Liebeskind, who, it was rumored, had gotten pregnant.

Pregnant. It was such a preposterous notion as to be frankly Gothic. Of course Delphine wasn't pregnant! I had heard somewhere that you couldn't get pregnant the first time, something about your tubes not being ready, and in any case we all knew about contraception, though presumably so had Amande, who, it was also rumored, had had an abortion at a private clinic in Neuilly before being sent into exile. As the ever-pragmatic Lea was fond of pointing out, most things could be fixed, unless you killed someone. By then I had reached the Madeleine. I hurried out of the metro and crossed over to Delphine's building, impatiently punching the code at the door. Truth be told, a part of me was enjoying the drama, redolent as it was with opportunities to remind Delphine of my loyalty and her faithlessness, and, as I rode up in the elevator, I couldn't resist the smug thought that none of this would have happened if she had listened to me.

Her mother met me at the door, looking Frenchly elegant in navy cashmere and gray wool pants. She seemed awfully happy to see me, which only fuelled my swelling sense of self-importance.

"Oh, Charlotte, I'm so glad you came. Maybe you can talk some sense into her."

"I'll try," I said gravely.

"I don't care what that doctor says, she's going back to school tomorrow."

I made a soothing sound and headed down the corridor to Delphine's room, the door of which was shut. I opened it without knocking and entered, a stern look on my face. The room was done in the same muted pastels as the rest of the apartment, which was full of spindly Louis XV chairs and eighteenth-century portraits, but Delphine had papered the walls with David Bowie posters, and a huge portrait of Jim Morrison that loomed over her bed, and contrasted rather oddly with her bookcase full of Bibliothèque Rose volumes. Delphine was curled up in bed, the sheets pulled up to her chin and her eyes squeezed shut. I wasn't fooled.

"We have a history test on Monday," I announced. "And a ton of math homework."

No response.

"I know you're not asleep."

Her eyelids fluttered. "I know what happened at the party," I said loudly. "It's really not such a big deal."

Except that it *was* a big deal, we both knew that. Somehow my best friend had managed, in the space of a weekend, to cross the gulf between nice girl and slut, which was what people were going to call her, even as they admired Serge's panache. No wonder she didn't want to get out of bed, I thought with pity, as I contemplated her childish form under the rose satin cover.

"What was going through your head?" I blurted out.

She opened her eyes and let out a wail. "I thought he was in love with me!"

"Oh come on," I snapped. Even Delphine wasn't that stupid.

But Delphine had dissolved into hiccupping sobs. I came over and sat on the bed, where I awkwardly patted her back and tried to curb the ghoulish curiosity that made me want to ask her what it had been like. Had it hurt? Had there been blood on the sheets? Lea said the boys always enjoyed it more, and most girls faked orgasms. Had Delphine had an orgasm? Had she sighed and moaned and tossed around like Linda Blair in *The Exorcist?* The image was at once repulsive and fascinating.

"I'm finished," she keened.

"No you're not. Something else will happen and everyone will forget about it."

"I can't bear to show my face in school!"

"You'll have to," I said. "You don't have an alternative."

"Yes I do, I can run away."

"To where?" I said impatiently. As the dramatic possibilities of the situation receded, my practical side began to kick in. "You're just going to have to tough it out. Chiara is a complete tart and no one minds," I said, surprised at this insight. "It's all about attitude," I firmly concluded.

Delphine actually seemed intrigued, until she remembered, or so I surmised because the same thought came to me at that moment, that she wasn't Chiara and never would be, that a different set of rules applied to the Chiaras and Serges of this world. Her face crumpled again.

"It's useless! I wish I were dead!"

"That's not going to solve anything," I remarked and pressed her hand. I really did feel sorry for her. Not only did it not escape me that my fast-accruing wisdom came at the expense of her experience, I knew what tormented Delphine: the cruel discovery that she was not so much tragic as ridiculous.

"Come on," I said. "I brought you the math homework. You can copy it."

Delphine blinked uncertainly. I knew her well enough to understand that even she was getting bored with her own misery, would indeed leap at any chance to forget about it. Lea was right: Most things could be fixed. It was a comforting thought, and if I wondered if it was altogether true, this was no time to share my doubts with Delphine, who, with a final, and not totally convincing whimper, pushed herself up and said, "I don't feel like doing math; let's go to the movies." I was happy to oblige her.

11

PREPARATIONS HAD NOW BEGUN IN EARNEST for Astrid's birthday party, and I was at Grace's beck and call, dispatched to far-flung corners of Paris to collect party hats and streamers ("We're certainly not going to be *grown up* about it") and the ranch dressing to accompany the buffalo wings that were Astrid's favorite party food because, as she maliciously explained, it was so much fun to watch French people try to eat them.

Astrid didn't disappoint us. When she walked into Grace's living room on Saturday evening, clutching a bag from Lolita Lempicka as if she had just been shopping in the neighborhood, and the band struck up "Unforgettable," her hands flew to her face and she burst into tears, and I wondered if I was the only one who noticed that she was dressed rather extravagantly for what had been billed as a quiet dinner *en famille*.

"Oh, you wicked things!" she cried, hugging Grace and then Frank, who looked foolishly pleased even though he hated parties, before wrapping me and Lea in a fragrant embrace. I was wearing a red dress from Dorothée Bis, of which I was particularly proud, and I had even put on a bit of eye shadow, which Lea said made me look like a child prostitute. Ignoring her, I tapped my foot to the music and hoped everyone noticed how sophisticated I looked. It soon became clear though, that people were only talking to me to be kind, as opposed to Lea who, in her black dress and pearls, was attracting the attention of men twice her age. I went in search of Frank, who I knew would be happy for my company.

I was surprised to find my father not skulking miserably in a corner but absorbed in conversation with Grace's houseguest, the
Polish dissident, who looked out of place in his worn jacket and
cheap shoes amid the raffish beau monde crowded into Grace's
Deco salon. I wondered what he was doing at the party, but Grace
prided herself on her eclectic tastes, and maybe she hoped he would
add some intellectual gravitas to the occasion, or at least remind
people that she followed world events.

Before I could even say hello, she swooped down on us in a way
that made my father blink in alarm. "Oh good," she said to Frank,
"you've met Łukasz—he's terribly serious, I'm sure you'll find tons
to talk about," and she clamped her bony hand around my arm and
hustled me to the kitchen where she shut the door and leaned back
against it as if to ward off some impending calamity.

"Is there something wrong?" I asked.

"The sculpture," she moaned. She was wearing charcoal eye
shadow that made her cheeks look even more sunken than usual,
and her collarbone jutted over the neckline of her Kenzo sheath.
Astrid was thin, too, but she had a womanly figure, while Grace
looked like she would rattle if you shook her. At first I had no idea
what she was talking about, but then I remembered that she'd
ordered a sugar sculpture in Astrid's likeness to be placed atop the
croquembouche, an insanely sweet confection of which I was particularly fond. I had thought it was a corny idea, not to mention
fraught with potential for disaster, but I hadn't seen it yet, and was
in fact curious as to how it had come off. The kitchen, which was
normally never used, was a hive of activity that night, with waiters
from the catering service bustling about and giving Grace the disdainful looks that hysterical American women tend to elicit from
French underlings. The object of all the commotion was standing in
a box on the counter. I went over and had a look, and had to agree
with Grace that it looked pretty stupid. She had given them a photograph to work on, but the *pâtissier* must have used poetic license,

because my mother, rendered in sugar, looked like one of those cheap wedding figures you sometimes see in the windows of pastry shops, her breasts enlarged by about three bra sizes, and a tawdry come-hither smile etched on her pink lips.

"Oh," I said.

"Those boobs," Grace moaned.

"*Elle est tout à fait bien,*" the headwaiter opined with a subtle leer, prompting Grace to issue in his direction a withering look meant to put him in his place, but that in fact had the opposite effect.

"I hate the French," she muttered under her breath.

The waiter shrugged and turned his back on us, muttering something to himself. The *croquembouche* looked delicious at any rate, towering over the trays of hors d'oeuvres in its spun-sugar casing, and appetizing odors issued from the oven where a Vietnamese woman in a black dress and apron was checking the duck. I hungrily eyed the canapés on the table, but had a feeling that Grace would lose it altogether if I took one.

"Just don't use it," I said. "The cake looks fine without it."

"Oh God, that's not the point!" she snapped, though what *was* the point would remain a mystery for just then her husband came in and eyed us coolly from the doorway.

"What is all the fuss?" he said, making me wonder if one of the waiters had ratted on Grace. Grace assumed an air of icy politeness. Everyone knew she and her husband didn't get along, and even I had to admit that there was something humorless and off-putting about Hubert de Lasnoy, a mean look about his eyes that suggested a sadistic nature. A lot of people thought he had married Grace for her money, but she was from Brooklyn and not rich at all, and he had plenty of his own from his family's breweries in Belgium. Astrid said he had found Grace amusing, and that he had wanted to make his parents angry by marrying a Jew, which not many people knew, either, because, as Grace put it, "It's bad enough in this country just being an American." Predictably, though, the amusement had worn off, and they had lived for years now in a state of edgy

détente, occupying separate wings of the apartment and only meeting at the few social functions that they attended together. I was a
little surprised to find him there that evening, but I knew that he
liked Astrid, probably for the same reasons that he had once liked
his wife.

"He thinks I don't know his tart is here," Grace hissed after he
had gone, making me wish, as I frequently did, that she would culti-
vate discretion. It mystified me why she would even get angry, when
her own lover, a sad-eyed painter called Vladimir whose work she
was always trying to foist on people, was out there for all to see,
gloomily haunting the bar. It sometimes seemed to me that my parents were the only ones in Paris who didn't cheat on each other,
though I didn't think Delphine's did either. At the thought of my
best friend, languishing in her room as I cavorted in my new red
dress, guilt gripped me, and I thought I might invoke the pretext of
needing to call her to get away from Grace.

"You're right; we'll just have to do without it!" she exclaimed,
and she grabbed the box with the sculpture and tossed it grandly in
the trash, under the scandalized eyes of the waiters, who all knew
how much it had cost.

I slipped out and headed for Grace's study in the back of the
apartment, where there was a phone. In a prior incarnation it had
been the office out of which she had run a relocation service for
Americans, until she had become disenchanted with hunting for
oversized showerheads, and explaining why you couldn't hail a cab
in Paris. The door to the study was ajar, and when I opened it, I saw
my mother standing by the desk with the Polish man, Łukasz. They
had obviously been deep in conversation, and seemed surprised to
see me.

"Oh, honey! I didn't hear you!" Astrid exclaimed. She was wearing a turquoise Fortuny dress, the kind you had to keep crinkled up
in a bag, and the necklace we had given her, and with her red hair
streaming down her back, she looked like some marvelous sea creature, washed ashore in a spray of iridescent foam. There was no

shortage of glamorous mothers in Paris, but I was sometimes amazed that I could have sprung from such a fantastic being, like the off-spring of one of those goddesses in the Greek myths who had care-lessly mated with a mortal. Normally I would have had to repress the urge to run to her, but I was feeling guilty for neglecting Delphine, whom I'd promised to check in on.

"Have you met Łukasz?" Astrid said.

I said I had, and was about to go in search of another phone, but she stopped me. "Don't go, sweetheart; Łukasz was just telling me he has to go back to Warsaw tomorrow."

I regarded her quizzically.

Her voice turned reproachful. "Do you have any idea what's happening in Poland?"

I did have an idea, since it was on TV all the time, but at that moment I couldn't have cared less, and even Łukasz had the good grace to look embarrassed, as if he understood perfectly well why I might not want to listen just then to a lecture on world events. Besides, wasn't Astrid supposed to be a Communist—exactly the type of person Łukasz and his cohorts were trying to get rid of?

Astrid turned to him and said apologetically, "I'm afraid she's been rather spoiled."

I gaped at her, stung to the core, and even shot Łukasz a glance, hoping he would come to my aid, but he seemed as perplexed as I was, not to mention a little bored. "I must go pack," he said uncom-fortably.

"Oh no," Astrid cried, and then, as if she realized she was acting ridiculous, she broke into her lovely, crooked smile and wrapped her arm around my shoulder. "Doesn't she look gorgeous?" she asked, squeezing me to her.

Although Łukasz clearly hadn't given any thought to my appear-ance before that moment, he said I looked very nice, but he really did have to go pack.

"Of course you do," Astrid murmured, and then, to me, "Come on, sweetie, let's go back to the party." We parted with Łukasz at the

door, where Astrid made him promise he would come and say good-
bye, and then she and I walked back down the hall, her arm still
around me.

"Isn't he marvelous?" she said, in the conspiratorial tone she
always employed in talking of some great new discovery.

I shrugged. "I guess," I said with ill grace. I was still angry about
her comment: spoiled indeed! As if I were the one who spent my
days shopping and getting manicures. . . . Frankly, although I was
used to her loopy causes, I didn't understand at all what she and
Grace saw in Łukasz. He acted more like a professor than a revolu-
tionary, and Poland didn't seem like the kind of place they would be
interested in, especially Grace, whose passion for the world's downtrodden was aroused in direct proportion with their ability to pro-
duce tribal jewelry or hand-woven carpets.

We had reached the salon by then, though, where Astrid's arrival
was enthusiastically greeted with cries of "Speech! Speech!" and she
squeezed me one last time before whispering in my ear, "I love you
so much." I stood in the doorway and watched the crowd engulf her.
She was mine, but she was theirs, too, and how could I begrudge
them their adoration, when I myself was helpless before her?

12

D ELPHINE'S ORDEAL lasted a week, the worst moment being when Frédéric Pierson pulled her aside on the way out of math class and asked her if it was true that she'd been playing *à la jambe en l'air*. I stood by her through the leers and sniggers, casting dirty looks at her tormentors, and maybe the fact that I was considered a bit of a priss actually helped, because by the end of the week, people were clearly getting bored with humiliating her. Then Chiara Grzebine was caught in a hotel room with Patrick Aubray, the pop singer, and this event was deemed infinitely more newsworthy than poor Delphine's trampled virtue, especially as it was his wife who caught them, and the story ended up in the tabloids. Lea, meanwhile, had a stern talk with Nahid, who felt so bad that she offered up the name of the famous doctor who did the patch-up jobs, and life resumed its normal course. Until the day Patrice Fabre noticed me.

We were reading *Huis Clos* for French, and I had put it off till the last minute. I was cramming it in in the café before class when Patrice dropped into the chair opposite me and tossed his copy on the table.

"Existentialism is such crap," he announced.

Actually I held the same view as my father on the existentialists. But I was so startled that I just gaped, which didn't seem to please Patrice.

"I guess you find it profound," he said disdainfully, motioning at my open book.

"No," I said. And then, more firmly, "No, I don't at all. I find Sartre dreary and misanthropic. Camus, too," I added for good measure.

"You read poetry," he said.

So he'd noticed me reading Baudelaire. What else had he noticed? That I might not be entirely devoid of womanly charms? As my eyes fell on my chewed, ink-stained nails, I realized that I had better rely on my wits. I smiled with what I hoped was bewitching allure.

"Sometimes," I allowed.

"Who do you like?"

"Verlaine," I said, which was true.

He smiled, too, now. Maybe he was just shy. He *did* spend an awful lot of time alone, reading or chewing his nails, like me, though his were so thoroughly gnawed that they appeared to grow inward, as if seeking shelter from his teeth.

"*Les sanglots longs des violons de l'automne . . .*"

"*Blessent mon coeur d'une langueur monotone,*" I finished. Everyone knew that one.

He didn't exactly look impressed, but he didn't look disgusted, either. And anyway, I reminded myself, he was the one who had sat down.

"I prefer Rimbaud," he said.

That didn't surprise me, boys always preferred Rimbaud. But I kept my mouth shut. Boys didn't like smart alecks, either, according to my all-knowing sister. I smiled encouragingly, my abandoned book pushed aside. I wished that I smoked.

"Want to cut class?" he said.

I looked at him uncomprehendingly. Was he seriously suggesting that we not go back to school? Apparently he was, because he added, "There's a Godard festival at the Cinémathèque. If we hurry, we can make the two o'clock screening."

My mind was racing. It wasn't so much that I had moral objections to cutting class, but I didn't want to get in trouble, even though

I knew that I wouldn't, since Astrid would undoubtedly let me off with a wink if I played hooky to go to the movies with a boy. Frank, though, would be disappointed.

"Okay," I said, though it didn't feel okay at all, but then he broke into a real smile, one that quite altered his face, and my reservations evaporated. I gathered up my things and followed him out. I still worried that we might get caught but, as luck would have it, I had gone to the less-frequented café around the corner from school, and no one saw us sneak into the metro. From behind, Patrice looked even ganglier, his head bobbing on his long neck as he loped down the stairs. Delphine thought he was strange-looking, and there was no denying that he was, but he had beautiful, soulful eyes, and the ascetic features of a medieval saint. The metro was empty at this time of day. We stood by the door, rocking with the motion of the train, and as I watched our reflection in the glass, I realized with a shock that we looked like we belonged together. Trocadéro was only a few stops away. We got to the Palais de Chaillot in plenty of time and, after he had bought our tickets, we went over to watch the skateboarders, who were executing their gravity-defying maneuvers under the rheumy December sky. I watched them, mesmerized, as they hurtled down the ramp, until Patrice said, "These guys are complete amateurs."

"They look pretty good to me," I objected. In my eyes, the skateboarders possessed all the grace I lacked.

"If you want to see real skateboarding, you should go to New York."

"Have you been there?" I asked. I had, with Astrid, but just for shopping. It seemed a thrilling, dangerous city to me, a place where only brave people would live. We had stayed at the Plaza, like Eloise, though Eloise had never mentioned that you could get mugged in Central Park, as Frank once had.

"My dad lives there. I spend the summers with him."

"Oh," I said. "Is he American?" We tended to break down our school in terms of nationalities, and I had never thought of Patrice as

part of the American contingent—he looked, well, just too *French* in his black velvet blazer and loafers.

"Yes, but he has a weakness for Frenchwomen, with the exception of my mother," he added wryly.

"Are your parents divorced?" I asked.

"Aren't everyone's?"

I was going to say that my parents weren't, but it seemed impolitic. We turned away from the skateboarders and headed back to the Cinémathèque. I had heard about it, of course, but had never actually been there. I wasn't interested in cinema in that way, unlike Patrice, who told me on the metro that he spent whole afternoons there. The movie was *À Bout de Souffle*, with a very young Jean-Paul Belmondo. I wondered if Patrice had picked on purpose a movie about a Frenchman falling in love with an American girl, and when he leaned over and kissed me, I was both startled and not surprised at all. It seemed so natural to have your first kiss in a dark cinema on a December afternoon that I just closed my eyes and let myself enjoy the sensation of everything falling into place, from the first contact of our tongues to his clumsy attempts to unhook my bra, a pale blue Huit that Astrid had bought me at Galeries Lafayette.

How easily we slip into whole new worlds that, just a day ago, were unfathomable. When Patrice and I walked out of the cinema holding hands, it seemed like something we had been doing forever, as if I had been rehearsing this moment so long that, when it came, it just seemed like habit.

"Let's go get a hot chocolate," he said, after we had stopped again to kiss, and I smiled happily, because even this seemed preordained, that we both would prefer hot chocolate to coffee. It was an unfamiliar neighborhood to me, the Eiffel Tower looming across the river like a prop on a movie set, one of those monumental stretches of Paris that were always full of tour buses and emptied out by evening. Patrice steered us to a *tabac* on the Avenue d'Iéna where they seemed to know him because the man behind the bar nodded when we came in. We sat at a table by the window and watched the

darkling street, and he kept his arm around me as we sipped our chocolate and talked, not about the movie, which neither one of us had seen much of, but about our lives, in the terribly serious way of adolescents. His father was a photographer and lived in Greenwich Village with his latest girlfriend, who was only a few years older than Patrice. His parents had only been married for two years, just long enough to have him, and now he divided his time between the two of them, spending the summers in New York and the school year in Paris with his mother, who resented his trips to America.

"Then why do you go?" I asked.

"Because it's not my fault that they don't get along. I don't mind my father. My mother thinks he's a shit, but he's no worse than most guys. And I like staying with him; he leaves me alone. What I hate is the first week after I come back. My mother goes on and on about how we'd be better off if he sent her money, instead of subsidizing transatlantic vacations. He took me to Mexico once for Christmas, and it was months before I heard the end of it. Sometimes I think she's jealous."

I nodded sympathetically, though in fact I had little experience of his situation. I imagined his mother must be one of those embittered divorced women that Grace and Astrid talked about, their plight somehow evoking more contempt than compassion. What would it be like for a boy to grow up alone with an angry mother? I pictured the two of them eating dinner together, Patrice helping afterward with the dishes. In their diminished circumstances, they probably wouldn't have a maid.

I was so absorbed in the pleasure of listening to him that I only half registered the door opening at the *tabac* end, admitting my mother and Łukasz. They headed for the counter where I heard Astrid, in her idiosyncratic French, order a pack of Benson & Hedges, before turning to Łukasz and saying, in English, "Darling, do you want something?"

I froze. Patrice shot me an inquiring look, but I motioned him to be quiet. Astrid had obviously not seen me, and both her and Łukasz's

backs were now turned to us. She paid for the cigarettes and they left quickly, the doorbell tinkling behind them.

"What's wrong?" Patrice asked.

"Nothing. I thought I recognized someone."

"You're so pretty," he said, leaning into me.

"No I'm not," I said irritably. What was Łukasz doing back in Paris? He was supposed to be in Warsaw. And if he had come back, why hadn't Astrid mentioned it? Not that there was any reason she should. It just seemed strange that they should be together in this out-of-the-way neighborhood, swallowed up like thieves by the night.

Patrice's wounded expression stopped me. I pushed away all thoughts of my mother and took his hand, tracing his red knuckles with my finger. *I'm here*, I reminded myself. "I'm sorry," I said. Astrid called everyone darling. It didn't mean anything.

"I've been watching you," he said, looking at me with his big serious eyes. "You're smart. You observe things. And you have eyes the color of rain."

He actually said *gris comme la pluie*, which sounded a lot better, as things often do in French. I wasn't used to being paid compliments. Lea's most frequent terms of endearment for me were Fatty, though I was painfully thin, and Dork, and although Astrid was always telling me how pretty I was, I didn't really believe her. I knew I was too tall, and had a nose like a potato. My best feature was my hair, inherited from Astrid along with her big, full-lipped mouth, though it was not as red as hers, or as extravagantly curly.

"You're a Modigliani," he said.

I blushed. "Why didn't you ever speak to me?"

His expression turned disdainful. "You're always stuck to that dopey blonde."

I waited for him to say something about Serge Lubomirski, but he didn't. Was it possible that he hadn't heard the story? My feeling of disloyalty was only aggravated by the fact that, suddenly, I found Delphine dopey, too.

"Delphine isn't all that bad," I said. "You just have to get to know her."

"No thanks."

Night had fallen, the way it abruptly does in Paris in winter. I looked at my watch, and saw that it was nearly six o'clock.

"I should be getting home," I said regretfully.

He looked disappointed. Maybe no one cared when he got home, not that anyone was checking on me. But I found myself longing suddenly for Lea, and for my father, though neither would be in the apartment when I got there. Patrice paid for our drinks and we left, the door chime tinkling behind us as it had behind Astrid and Łukasz earlier, and we headed for the metro like all lovers on a chilly night, huddled together, warding off till the last possible second the final kiss good-bye.

13

ONE DAY I WAS JUST ME, and the next I was in love, my moony expression betraying me instantly to Lea, who asked if I was suffering from gas. Astrid noticed, too. "What's his name?" she whispered conspiratorially, pulling me aside after he called and I spent a half hour hunched in a corner over the phone.

I blushed with embarrassed pleasure. "Patrice."

"Oh, isn't that lovely . . ." Her eyes lit up: We were going to have a secret. "Is he nice?"

"Yes," I said, still blushing.

"Of course he is, you wouldn't pick a mean one." She gathered me in her arms and sighed. "My little girl, in love!"

"Is Łukasz back in town?" I asked after she had released me.

She looked surprised. "Why do you ask?"

"I thought I saw him on the street."

Her voice dropped. "You mustn't breathe a word about it to anyone. He's here to raise money."

"Is he staying with Grace?"

Astrid laughed. "Oh dear, no, she kept trying to have cocktail parties for him and he's supposed to be keeping a low profile. You know Grace: If she can't make a party of it, it's not worth the bother. He's staying with some terribly fancy Polish count, Lumabirski or something . . ."

"Lubomirski?"

"Yes, that's it—I must say, quite the most devastatingly handsome man I've ever met! He's been giving them loads of money, he really believes they're going to succeed in toppling the Communists—no doubt out of self-interest: I expect he's hoping to get his estates back."

I was sure she was talking about Serge's father. Nahid had told Lea that he was involved in some top-secret political activity, possibly espionage, and I didn't doubt that he was as good-looking as his son, who had recently, much to my disgust, taken a shine to my sister.

"His son has a crush on Lea," I said. "He goes to our school." I left out Serge's more opprobrious claim to fame, not that I wasn't tempted to tell, but Delphine would never forgive me if she found out.

"Oh *really*? She never said anything to me. . . ."

"Well, you know how she gets. But she doesn't like him; he's a real creep." I was putting words in my sister's mouth: Lea had never actually said that she didn't like Serge; she just found him beneath her, as she did most boys. In fact, she had sounded rather amused at his sudden interest in her, no doubt because it tickled her vanity.

"With that lovely father? Hard to believe."

So that explained what Astrid had been doing on the Right Bank. I knew that Serge lived in the Sixteenth; she must have gone over to meet Łukasz. Although my mother's infatuation with the Polish opposition continued to baffle me, there was a noble part of her that sided with the downtrodden. She was always bringing home strays: Irish girls she found on the street, lost backpackers who couldn't afford a hotel, surly Armando, whom I had actually thought I was in love with—how foolish I had been! It seemed impossible that I could ever have loved anyone but Patrice, who now exclusively occupied my thoughts, much to the dismay of Delphine, who acted as if I had betrayed her.

"But he's so . . . *weird*" was all she had found to say.

"No he isn't; he's just different."

"Yeah, different as in 'weird.'"

The worst of her humiliation over, Delphine had retreated

behind a permanent sulk that seemed part defiance, part resignation. I knew she resented me for not spending all my time with her anymore. The truth was, I had stopped enjoying her company. I got enough sarcasm at home from Lea, who was a lot better at it, and when I did make an effort to spend time with Delphine, she was gloomy and uncommunicative. She must have known that Serge now had designs on my sister, and though I might have reassured her that Lea thought much too highly of herself to even acknowledge his existence, let alone his sudden ardor, there seemed no way to do so without making Delphine even more miserable. So I said nothing.

Christmas was coming, and I was in love, a concurrence so dizzying that it left me slightly breathless. We took Christmas seriously in our family—Astrid couldn't understand how French people got by with a sprig of holly and a couple of candles. Our tree was nine feet tall and laden with forty years' worth of accumulated ornaments that dated back to her childhood, each of which had a story attached to it. My favorites were Elmer the blinking plastic reindeer, a present from my aunt Maybelle, who had a genius for unearthing oddities in the back of dime stores, and the crystal snowflakes from a fancy shop on Fifth Avenue that Frank had bought Astrid their first Christmas Eve together, only to leave them in the cab. The driver had turned up just before midnight, explaining that he had looked inside the card for an address, and when he'd read *"To the most beautiful girl in the world,"* had felt duty-bound to deliver the package at the end of his shift.

Our crèche had a cast of thousands, including a flock of sheep and a rather disconcerted-looking penguin (also from Maybelle), and we flung tinsel and blinking lights about with such abandon that the living room glittered from mid-December to mid-January like a cross between a Woolworth's and Ali Baba's cave, its gaudy illumination greeting us every evening as we turned off the boulevard, and causing much wonderment on the part of the concierge, who, until we came along, had never experienced American yuletide exuberance. It was my job to line up Astrid's angel collection along the top of the fireplace, while Lea, who possessed more attention to detail, oversaw the production of hundreds of cookies that coated the air for days with their buttery fragrance. Even Grace came over to lend a hand, having a deft touch with a paintbrush and colored icing. Her husband, like most French people, was sadly deficient in holiday spirit, and limited his revels to the consumption of oysters and langouste in a restaurant, in the company of his mistress.

Americans in Paris really came together at Christmas and Thanksgiving, trading hard-to-find cranberry sightings and addresses of *volaille* vendors, and for those who happened to be coming back from the States, filling their suitcases with marshmallows and candy canes and, in one famous instance, a frozen Butterball turkey that Candy de Bethune had thought would defrost over the Atlantic, but which instead leaked all over her sweaters, only to be apprehended and confiscated by the *douane*. We pitied the poor French kids who, instead of a capacious stocking, had to content themselves with a shoe. Delphine, with her French father and might-as-well-be-French mother, was one of these unfortunates. Over the holidays, she was often to be found at our apartment, helping to string popcorn and cranberries and to mix the eggnog that Astrid swore had only the *teensiest* drop of bourbon in it. This year, though, she only came over once, on the day we made our gingerbread house, and Astrid remarked that she looked awfully sulky, which was a shame, considering what a pretty girl she'd become.

Patrice came to see the tree. I had tried to time his arrival for when Astrid wouldn't be home, because I was afraid she might make him feel even worse about his bitter mother, but was foiled when she came tripping in laden with packages right as I was introducing him to Frank, who sweetly pretended to have no idea who he was. Not so Astrid, who dropped all her bags on the floor with a thud and came rushing forward with her arms outspread, causing Lea, whom I had also hoped would not be home, to roll her eyes, and me to cringe with embarrassment, even as I hoped he would find her as marvelous as I did.

I needn't have worried: Patrice proved helpless before her charms. He accepted a cup of eggnog with the teensiest bit of bourbon in it and listened attentively while she recounted the provenance of some of the more curious ornaments on our tree, rather unnecessarily, in my opinion, dwelling on the big-breasted angels she had picked up one year in Bucharest, *the* most depressing place on earth, which naturally led to the story of how she and Grace had ended up in Bucharest at Christmas in the first place, a much retold saga involving missed train connections and a Turkish carpet. By the time she asked him if he could stay for dinner, I was beginning to wonder if this had been such a good idea. Lea elbowed me.

"There goes the boyfriend . . ."

I elbowed her back. "At least I *have* one," I hissed, though we both knew that Lea could have anyone she wanted. So far, however, the only boy she had deemed worthy of her attention was Gauthier de Montfort from her riding club, a pompous boob in gray flannel pants and ascot who slicked back his hair and had never deigned to say more than two words to me, though he had been quite chummy with Astrid. He had hung around for several weeks and then mysteriously vanished, all enquiries on the subject eliciting only a tight-lipped scowl from Lea. "Maybe he tried to touch her," Astrid had joked, and even as I had felt that she shouldn't be making fun of her daughter, I knew exactly what she meant.

I *wanted* to be touched. Ever since that first kiss in the cinema, I felt like I existed on two parallel planes: one just me, going to school and doing homework, and the other the welter of confused sensation into which I tumbled every time Patrice slid his tongue into my mouth. We had spent two Saturday afternoons kissing on his bed, only to be interrupted by his mother just at the point where I wondered what was next. She didn't seem to like me very much. Patrice swore it wasn't true, that she was just tired from work, but how tired could you get teaching French in a lycée? Their apartment, in a new building in the Fifth, was much smaller than ours, with no nooks and corners to hide in, the rooms strangely barren except for Patrice's, which was papered with movie posters, and I had been dying to bring him to my house, where at least we would get some privacy.

At dinner, Patrice and Frank talked about Montaigne, whom we were reading in school. "Pascal thought he was a sissy," Frank said, and I hoped that Patrice was duly impressed that my father had read both Pascal *and* Montaigne, and could joke about them. I don't think Patrice was used to formal family dinners. When he complimented Astrid on the food, he seemed surprised when she laughed and said, "Oh darling, I'd love to take the credit but I just heated it up."

Afterward, in my room, he asked, "Who cooked the dinner?" and I had to confess that Maria had made it before leaving because, though Astrid thought a family should sit down to eat together, she couldn't cook to save her life.

"So you have a maid *and* a cook," he remarked, with his old smirk.

"No," I said, feeling suddenly uncomfortable. Money didn't often come up at our school, since everyone had it, and, for all the small apartment and his mother having to work, someone, his father I assumed, must have been paying Patrice's tuition. "Astrid pays Maria extra to make dinner, that's all." I could have explained what I knew perfectly well, that what might have been construed as her patrician indolence was actually rooted in my mother's having grown up eating bologna sandwiches, but I didn't like being put on the spot.

"Why do you call your mother Astrid?" he asked.

"What do you mean?"

"It's a little precious, don't you think?"

"We've always called her Astrid," I said, no doubt sounding as defensive as I felt. It didn't seem worth explaining to him, that when

I was little I'd called her *Mommy*, and I still addressed her as *Mom*—
it was in speaking *of* her that she became Astrid, because *Mother* was
somehow too pedestrian.

As if in atonement, he ran his fingers through my hair. We were
lying entwined on my bed, me slightly breathless from one of those
long, probing kisses that left me swollen and disoriented. "You're a
spoiled brat," he said, though he seemed to rather like the idea, and
before I could object, he swung his leg over and straddled me. I
knew that what I felt pushing against my groin was his erection. He
moved against me and I couldn't repress a gasp of surprise.

"You like that?"

"Yes," I said, though *like* seemed a weak word for the ache that
rippled through me.

"You do," he said. "I can tell," and he started unbuttoning my
shirt. I knew no one would bother us. Astrid wouldn't dream of
barging into my room, and though the same couldn't be said of Lea,
she was busy just then studying for a test. And yet, for a confused
second, I found myself half wishing that one of them would come
down the hallway. Not Frank though. I hoped Frank had no idea
what I was up to.

"Don't be scared," Patrice whispered. And I wasn't; I wasn't
scared. It wasn't that. I wanted him, desperately, but everything I
knew about what lay ahead came from books and movies and the
not exactly edifying experience of Delphine. Only recently, Lea,
who was awfully well versed on these matters for a presumed virgin,
had offered the information that boys would do anything to stick it
in you, though the nice ones would butter you up first with cun-
nilingus, which was said by Nahid to be divine, and which Lea help-
fully explained consisted of a boy licking your private parts, a
prospect so embarrassing that I had actually turned beet red. Also
from Nahid had come the information that it was best to do it the
first time with a boy who didn't have a huge penis (how were you
supposed to tell?), which would hurt.

None of this was foremost in my mind at that moment though.

Foremost in my mind was Astrid's admonition, offered shortly after I had got my period. "Don't give yourself away cheaply, honey," she had said over lunch at Allard, where we had finally gone, *sans* Grace, to celebrate my passage to womanhood. We had feasted on foie gras and cassoulet, followed by slabs of *charlotte au chocolat* awash in custard. Afterward, she allowed me to light her cigarette, an honor Lea and I used to fight over, and I was feeling a little drunk from the champagne kir I'd ordered for *apéritif,* and the half bottle of Meursault we had shared with our meal.

"Don't worry, Mom," I squirmed. "I *know.*"

"No one ever told me; I had to figure it out for myself—but you're such a bright girl," and she had gripped my hand in that special way that said, *We understand each other,* though I wasn't entirely sure at that moment that we did, and I wished she wouldn't tear up, because I was sure people were staring at us.

Now, however, as Patrice ran his palms over my breasts, my aplomb deserted me. I knew what was next, and I wasn't ready. I didn't want his mouth down there. I hadn't even taken a bath that day. And what if he bragged about it in school? Not that I believed he would, but all of a sudden, the ghost of uncertainty rose between us. Maybe I was a prig, but I wanted to linger just a little bit longer in this nimbus of half-realized longings, where I could be a girl and a woman at the same time.

Patrice brushed his fingers over my nipples, barely touching them, and then delicately but insistently, he pinched them, so startling me that I let out a moan. I closed my eyes, and when Lea hollered through the closed door, "Phone for you, Fatty!" I actually wished she'd said I wasn't home.

14

MAYBELLE WAS COMING FOR CHRISTMAS and Astrid and I went to meet her at the airport. Astrid insisted on driving, though Frank had urged us to use the chauffeured company car. "I'm not picking up my sister in a limo," Astrid declared, although the car was in fact a Peugeot, and I for one would have been perfectly happy to take him up on his offer. Driving on the *périphérique* with my mother required nerves of steel. Although she railed against Parisian drivers, Astrid united all their worst traits with the gunslinging bravado that the French were always mocking in Americans. Paradoxically, it was her very prowess at the wheel— she'd been driving since she was fourteen—that made her so terrifying. Being utterly at ease, she had no fear, and it was left to her passengers to apprehend alone the certainty of impending death. Morning rush hour was over, and the denuded landscape of the *banlieue* flashed by as we hurtled along, the windshield wipers swiping at the December drizzle. A car that was going even faster than we were pulled up behind us and switched on its high beams. Muttering imprecations, Astrid swerved into the next lane.

"Slow down," I pleaded.

"Don't be silly, darling, we're miles below the speed limit," Astrid cheerfully replied. She was always in high spirits before Maybelle's arrival, a mood that would last only until their first argument. Although Astrid was two years older, Maybelle had a bossy streak, and wasn't shy about expressing her opinions, especially on sensitive subjects like child rearing, which she didn't feel Astrid did nearly enough of. These spirited discussions, as Maybelle called them, were the main reason Frank spent most of her visits in his study, absorbed in nebulous cases that suddenly required his utmost attention.

When Maybelle emerged, huge and clad in bright pink behind a towering cart of luggage, we hurled ourselves at her as if she had just disembarked from the *Titanic*. These antics caused many a head to turn, a reaction that Maybelle took as a tribute to her immense personal elegance for, in the belief that every flight might be her last, she always dressed to the nines to cross the Atlantic.

"Mah word, Charlotte, you've grown as tall as a beanpole!" she cried, clasping me to her chest. The scent of Coty's Emeraude rolled off her in great, syrupy waves. She lugged a big bottle of it everywhere, its eponymous green the exact same color, as Lea was fond of pointing out, of Lux dishwashing detergent. Astrid had tried in vain over the years to seduce her with gifts of Chanel and Dior, but the bottles just gathered dust in Maybelle's medicine cabinet, their contents eventually turning dark from spoilage.

"Jeezuhs," cried Astrid. "You smell lahk a dahme store toilet." My mother's Southern accent had long subsided to a sultry drawl, but in her sister's presence, it came flaring back, redolent of all the long, hot afternoons they had spent together on the porch of their Louisville house, popping gum and scratching mosquito bites, and presumably insulting each other, as they still did today, though Astrid insisted it was only in jest.

"Better a dahme store toilet than a French whorehouse," Maybelle grandly replied as she slipped me one of those giant Toblerone bars that they sold at the duty-free.

Astrid shot me a look. Maybelle always made a big deal about how thin Lea and I were, though we looked like any girls our age in Paris. "The car's right outside," she said, picking up one of the three Samsonite suitcases that contained Maybelle's carefully selected wardrobe for the next two weeks, and beginning to drag it toward the exit. It was with some difficulty that we squeezed the luggage into the back of the Peugeot, but we finally got it all in. As she lowered herself into the passenger seat, Maybelle asked, "Has this car gotten smaller?"

"No," Astrid said, "yer bottom's gotten bigger."

"Mah bottom is exactly the same size it was last year."

"Well then, ah guess the car must've shrunk," Astrid said, and she winked at me in the rearview mirror.

I hadn't expected anyone to be home when we got back, so when I opened the door and found Serge Lubomirski standing in the vestibule, I thought for a second that I had the wrong apartment. But not many people had a foyer the color of ripe tomatoes, and there was our umbrella stand in the corner, the dark stain on the sisal carpet where Astrid had spilled a glass of wine, and Frank's collection of old anatomical prints on the wall. As for Serge, he seemed quite at home. "Hello," he said, coming hastily forward to take Maybelle's bag.

"And who is *this* fahn young gentleman?" Maybelle coyly enquired.

Lea emerged just then from the hallway. "Oh, hi, Auntie M," she said, coming over to peck her on the cheek. She and Serge were both dressed for riding, and Lea was clearly determined to pretend that there was nothing the least bit unusual about his presence in our home. "This is Serge," she said distractedly. "My mother, my aunt Maybelle, and my sister, Charlotte."

As I watched, dumbstruck, Serge kissed Astrid's hand, and then swooped down on Maybelle, who giggled like a schoolgirl. I was afraid I was in for the same treatment, but he just smiled at me pleasantly and said, "Of course I know Charlotte."

"No you don't!" I wanted to protest, but was stopped by a warning look from my sister.

"We're going riding," she sweetly informed us.

Serge held her jacket for her and, with effortless grace, she shrugged it on before turning to adjust her riding hat in the mirror.

"Who was *that*?" Astrid asked after the door had shut behind them.

I scowled. "Serge Lubomirski, from school."

"Really? I thought you said he wasn't nice."

"He isn't."

"Darling, anyone that good-looking is bound to be a bit spoiled. I thought he was perfectly charming."

"He sure charmed the pants off me," Maybelle roguishly cut in.

I sighed in disgust, but just then, Maria put her head around the kitchen door, and said, "Your young man called."

"Hello, Maria," Maybelle sang out, only to be rewarded with a stiff nod. Maybelle thought it was our fault Maria was so surly, that we acted high and mighty with her, and there was no convincing her that this was in fact Maria's decision, that she just wasn't a friendly person, which didn't prevent her, as Frank often remarked to tease Maybelle, from being an excellent servant.

But as I hurried to the phone, I banished all thoughts of Maybelle and what Frank called her misguided populism, or my sister's sudden baffling tolerance of Serge Lubomirski, or anything else that might distract me from the only person in my life who, it was rapidly becoming clear to me, was not completely ridiculous.

15

GRACE ALWAYS CAME OVER FOR CHRISTMAS EVE, and the champagne had been on ice for an hour, prompting Maybelle to observe that it was just like Her Royal Highness to keep everyone waiting, a remark that caused Astrid to raise her eyes to the ceiling and Frank to propose that we watch the news. He was just about to switch on the TV when the doorbell rang. Astrid hurried out to the hallway as, with an exaggerated sigh, Maybelle struggled out of her armchair and went to fetch the glasses. I knew that Astrid was worried about Maybelle's weight. It couldn't be healthy to be that fat, especially for someone so small-boned, though Maybelle's reputed small-bonedness was one of those family legends that had to be taken on faith. In deference to the holiday, she wore earrings shaped like miniature Christmas ornaments, and they bobbed gaily as she made her way to the table, where the glasses were lined up next to a tray of hors d'oeuvres from Fauchon. She and I had spent the afternoon wrapping presents, and I had finally had a chance to relate the thrilling developments of the past month, as well as the news that Patrice would be dropping by on the day after Christmas, so she would actually get to meet him.

Lea only had selected friends over when our aunt was around, people like Nahid, who had plenty of outrageous relatives of her own, some of whom were even in jail. I didn't care how fat Maybelle was, or how tacky, in fact I almost liked her better for it. I didn't trust perfection. That was why I fell in love with boys like Patrice and not Serge, with his Greek-god looks and supercilious smirk that Lea now asserted existed only in my imagination. Lea loved Maybelle, too, but I loved her unreservedly, while my sister could never entirely mask her dismay at our aunt's gargantuan appearance. Earlier we'd gone to Ladurée, which, with its Grande Époque bombast and decadent sweets, was Maybelle's favorite place in Paris. When she'd ordered a large macaroon in every flavor, with a dish of strawberry ice cream on the side, Lea had nervously glanced around, clearly hoping no one would associate her with this fat American lady in the garish outfit perched so precariously atop her slender gilt chair. I was surprised that she'd let Serge into her presence, until I remembered that it had been an accident. I was even more surprised that Serge had been so *charmant*. He must, I realized, be trying really hard to get into her pants. This was just the kind of thought that I had lately become a prey to, its coarseness at once thrilling and disconcerting, and I made my face a blank, though I couldn't help the small smile that twitched briefly on my lips.

As Maybelle poured the champagne, she cast a mock despairing glance at the exquisite canapés, topped with smoked salmon slivers and dustings of caviar and chopped egg, and whispered loudly in my ear that she'd slipped a couple bags of Fritos into her luggage. With a conspiratorial giggle, I lifted the tray, the bubbles popping merrily in the slender flutes, and turned to find Astrid in the doorway, her face pale.

"Łukasz has been arrested," she blurted out. Grace, now visible behind her, edged her gently forward.

"Who?" Maybelle asked.

Astrid didn't reply. She just stood there with a stricken look on her face until Grace nudged her to sit down. "I just found out," Grace informed us with the self-important air of one delivering momentous news. "Adam Lubomirski called to tell me. That's why I was late," she added gratuitously, since Grace had never been on time in her life. At the mention of Serge's father's name, I shot a glance at Lea, but she had turned inscrutable.

"Might we ask," Frank said, "who Łukasz is?"

Grace gave him a look of contemptuous disbelief. Astrid laid a hand on her arm. "Darling, you met him at Grace's party," she said wearily. "You talked for hours."

Frank nodded in his abstracted way. "Ah, yes, your Polish friend. That's a shame."

The same outraged look crossed Grace's face again, and I had to control myself from snapping that that was just the way Frank was, that he didn't wear his emotions on his sleeve, like some people I knew, or blurt out any stupid thing that came into his head. Lea's expression by now made it quite clear that she'd had enough of Grace's and Astrid's antics. She looked as if she were about to get up and leave the room, though I knew she wouldn't, because it would just create more drama.

"How could they?" Astrid cried. "On Christmas Eve!"

"They've been counting too much on that pope of theirs," Frank mildly observed. "The Russians were bound to come down on them sooner or later." And he shook his head, as if to say, well, that's how it goes.

I wasn't entirely sure what he was talking about, but it seemed clear that Łukasz had gotten arrested for some political reason in his wintry, far-off country. While this news undeniably increased his glamour—in France, getting arrested still carried a certain cachet— I resented its intrusion into an evening I had been looking forward to, one of the two times a year I was allowed, at least as far as Frank was aware, to drink champagne, though this rule, as every other rule in our house, was enforced with characteristic laxity.

"Well," Frank said, rising from his chair, "perhaps we should have some champagne," and I realized that I had been standing there all along with the tray in my hands. Frank plucked up two flutes and took them over to Astrid and Grace, who accepted them absent-mindedly. When we had all been served, he raised his glass. His hair had started to thin in the past few years and he wore it brushed back from his forehead, which gave him, I thought, an air of subtle distinction. I admired that, like some men, he didn't try to hide his baldness. He wasn't an imposing man, like Grace's husband, or a haughty one like Delphine's father. He possessed neither European arrogance nor American boldness—there was, in fact, an almost delicate quality to him—but to me, at that moment, he radiated calm and authority.

"On this evening, we count our blessings, and thank Providence for our good fortune. Speaking for myself, I remain humbly grateful for my beautiful and accomplished daughters"—he bowed in our direction—"our friends and family who have traveled from afar to be with us, and," he concluded, raising his glass again to Astrid, "my wife who, I might add, looks particularly ravishing tonight."

"Oh, honey," Astrid murmured, and she rose to kiss him, followed closely by Maybelle, who engulfed him in a huge, lip-smacking smooch that left him looking a bit dazed. Lea and I came next, then Grace, who dispensed her customary bird peck, blithely ignoring Lea's disgusted look as she bore down on her.

"Well then," Frank said, adjusting his glasses. "Shall we proceed with the festivities?"

Astrid was clearly making an effort to look cheerful, but I could tell she was distraught, and even I felt a little guilty at the thought of poor Łukasz, who had been nice to me, languishing in some Communist jail cell while we feasted on langouste and oysters. Nobody mentioned him again, though, and by the time we sat down to dinner, Astrid had returned to herself. She was wearing a long crushed-velvet dress the color of a forest, her hair a coppery halo in the candlelight, and I thought of my father's words, of being grateful for our good fortune, and felt a surge of pride and happiness. Patrice and I had exchanged presents the day before, and the small package he had handed me waited under my pillow. He was spending Christmas alone with his mother, as he usually did, and though I wished he could have been with us, I loved him all the more for his selfless devotion to this sour, disillusioned woman who so inexplicably disliked me.

It was chilly in the dining room, which only had one radiator, and Astrid asked me to fetch her shawl. We didn't open presents until morning, and when I went to her closet, I found it full of gaily wrapped boxes, my mother being a firm subscriber to the belief that presentation is as important as content. Many would have my name on them, but this year, the prospect of tearing through tissue paper and ribbon to uncover the lovely things within left me curiously unmoved, the only present I really cared about being the one from Patrice. I got the shawl and retraced my steps down the hallway, and was about to go back into the dining room when I heard voices in the kitchen. Astrid and Grace were standing by the sink, talking. Astrid looked devastated.

"I just can't believe there's nothing anyone can do," she cried, and then looked up to find me standing in the doorway. A strange look passed over Grace's face. She laid her hand on Astrid's arm, and a visceral wave of dislike for her welled up within me.

Astrid's eyes were red. She held out her arms and said, "Oh, baby, I'm just so worried."

I was surprised at the harshness of my voice. "You need to come back to the table," I said. "Everyone's waiting for you."

She looked stunned. Grace's expression turned disapproving. "You may not realize it," she said, "but Łukasz is a key figure in the Polish opposition, and his arrest is nothing short of a tragedy."

"I live in France," I said coldly.

"Well, there's a whole world out there beyond your nose, young lady," Grace snapped. "It's about time you found out."

It was my turn to look stunned. I was going to retort that she had some nerve lecturing me on the state of the world, and other things as well, when Astrid sighed and, pulling herself away from the sink, said, "Stop it, you two. It's just frustrating to feel so helpless."

"Adam is trying to apply pressure through the French diplomatic channels," Grace said, "but you know how they are . . ."

I assumed she meant Serge Lubomirski's father, whom I hadn't realized Grace was so close to, though I suspected that, because he was evidently an important person, she was making it sound like they were better friends than they actually were. She lit a cigarette and sucked in, and there was something rapacious about the way her neck muscles tensed, and the smoke streamed out through her flared nostrils. *No one loves you,* I thought.

"Let's go back to the table," Astrid said. Grace crushed her cigarette in the sink and, in a gesture that both disgusted me and aroused my reluctant pity, pulled her lipstick out of her bag and touched up her mouth, baring her teeth to check them in her compact for stains.

16

WHEN I AWOKE ON CHRISTMAS MORNING, I reached under my pillow and pulled out Patrice's present. It was wrapped in blue paper scattered with little golden stars, and I carefully undid the wrapping, peeling back the tape with surgical precision so as not to mar a single detail of a talisman that I intended to preserve forever. Inside the box was a silver bracelet. I removed it and slipped it on my wrist, the touch of the metal cool against my skin. Feeling light with happiness, I put on my bathrobe and went down the hall where I collided with Lea.

"Merry Christmas, Fatty," she said. I yanked at her braid and broke into a run and she came galloping after me, only catching up at the entrance to the living room, where she locked me in an iron grip that reminded me that she was a more accomplished athlete than I.

"Let go!" I pleaded.

"Not until you've begged for mercy."

"Cow!"

"Dork!"

"Really, girls" came Astrid's voice behind us. "You'll wake the whole building."

"What's that on your wrist?" Lea asked, but just then Maybelle appeared in the doorway, draped in a vast purple velour garment with a zipper up the front, her head bristling with curlers. She looked like some sort of ancient fertility goddess in a ritual head-dress.

"I don't know how you sleep in those things," Lea said.

"Same way you do, except I don't snore like a trucker."

"I do *not* snore," Lea replied indignantly.

"Yes you do, I could hear you raght through the door when I got up to go to the bathroom."

"Oh, stop it, you two," Astrid cut in, ushering us into the living room to open our stockings.

They were full, as always, of lovely baubles: scarves and bangles and rings and gloves, and little marzipan fruits that I would devour before breakfast, the thick, almondy paste clinging to my tongue. Lea, though she was trying to be grown up, squealed with delight when she opened the lumbering package that took up half her pile to find a new saddle. I hadn't asked for anything in particular, but Astrid had divined that what I needed to make my life complete was one of those puffy down jackets that everyone at school had been sporting since autumn. Maybelle had given me a diary with a lock, "against prying eyes," she winked with a nod at Lea, who haughtily declined to respond. Frank appeared just as Astrid was opening a box from Hermès. It contained a handbag that Lea eyed approvingly, but then Lea approved of anything that came from Hermès.

"Darling, it's lovely," Astrid murmured, and went over to kiss him, leaving the handbag in its box. Her present to him was, oddly enough, also from Hermès: a silk scarf, two ties, and a wallet that Frank said was just what he needed, though Lea and I had given him one for his birthday.

When Grace arrived for dinner, Maybelle shot me a look. I knew she hoped as I did that Grace would keep to herself whatever unfortunate tidings she had become privy to in the few hours since we last saw her. In typical Grace fashion, however, she seemed to have completely forgotten about poor Łukasz and his troubles. She was all charm and smiles, dispensing expensive and unsuitable presents, at least in the opinion of Frank who could not entirely hide a look of dismay when I opened a pink box from a notorious lingerie store in the Eighth to find a minute pink *soutien-gorge* and panty set that made Lea snigger gleefully, even though she had received the same item in blue, the bra admittedly two sizes larger. When the conversation turned to the Berlin Film Festival, which Grace and Astrid were going to attend, Grace having received an invitation from Vassily Grzebine, whose latest film, *Outrage*, was rumored to be a front-runner for an award, Frank wondered when Astrid had become interested in cinema.

"I've always been interested in movies," Astrid replied a bit shortly.

Frank raised an eyebrow. "Berlin is a fascinating city," he said after a pause, helping himself to the canned cranberry sauce that Maybelle had brought from Kentucky. "You'll have to cross over to the East."

"Why on earth would we do that?"

"It's where all the museums are."

"Oh, darling," Astrid said, "you know I can't bear museums . . ."

"Of course," Frank said. "How silly of me to forget."

17

A S HAPPY AS SHE WAS that I had a boyfriend, I could tell
Maybelle was disappointed that I wasn't spending as
much time with her as I used to, going to the movies or
playing Scrabble, or standing in line for ice cream at Berthillon,
where the tininess of the scoops never failed to arouse her indignation. As her official favorite, I had always felt responsible for
entertaining her, and until then I had never minded because not
only was Maybelle a lot of fun, I, unlike my sister or my mother,
had plenty of time on my hands. Astrid had long impressed upon
me that Maybelle had to scrape and save for months on her
nurse's salary to come to Paris. I was never to let her pay for anything, which was easier said than done since Maybelle's generosity
was exceeded only by her pride. The chocolate éclairs and ice
creams and boat trips up the Seine became our little secret, and I
kept to myself the guilty knowledge that she often used a credit
card. I kept other things to myself as well: Although she presented
an unfailingly cheerful face to the world, Maybelle had many
regrets. She would have liked to get married and have her own
children, but things just hadn't worked out, and, though she
laughed about it, she hated being fat. She once told me, "We both
know what it's like to live in our sister's shadow." Another time
she said, "That's just the way life is; you have the worker bees and
the queens. You and me, we're worker bees."

But when Maybelle finally met Patrice, I was embarrassed. She
went right into her jolly fat-lady act, turning up the Kentucky
accent and carrying on like Mae West and, though I understood why

she was doing this, I suddenly saw her through his eyes, and wished he could see the Maybelle I knew, the one who had introduced me to the Brontës and Jane Austen, and who believed that Elizabeth Bennett had thrown herself away on stodgy Darcy. It was one of those bleak and endless winter vacation afternoons. Astrid and Lea were out shopping, and Frank was at work. I knew I should be doing something with Maybelle, but the pull of Patrice, who headed to my room after saying hello, fully expecting that I would follow, proved stronger. I was growing tired of being the good girl, and though I wished that Patrice had made more of an effort to be sociable, I hurried after him, telling myself I would be right back. As he closed the door and kissed me, I repressed the guilty thought that he had barely noticed Maybelle, that he had been rather rude in fact, and that it was because he knew he could get away with it. Maybelle was right: There were worker bees, and there were queens, and without intending to, I had crossed the divide.

And so, when Patrice said as he unclasped my bra—the one that Grace had given me, though he didn't notice its exquisite design— "I can't believe that fat lady and your mother are related," I kissed him greedily into silence. We still hadn't had proper sex. I knew he wanted to, and I appreciated his delicacy, even as I suspected it was rooted in the knowledge that I would soon be giving in.

It was already dark when, having let Patrice out, I heard Maybelle's voice in the study as I crept back, still disheveled, to my room.

"You do know what they're doing in there, don't you?"

I froze and shrank back. I hadn't even heard Astrid and Lea come in.

"Oh Lord," Astrid replied in a bored voice. "They're doing what everyone does at their age, it's perfectly natural."

"In France, maybe. Back home we don't let fifteen-year-old girls lock themselves in all afternoon with their boyfriends."

"Charlotte is almost sixteen, and Patrice is a perfectly nice boy."

"So I guess you don't think there's any heavy petting going on?"

Astrid burst out laughing. "*Heavy petting?* Good Lord, I haven't heard that one in years!"

"Maybe it's time you remembered—I seem to recall it got *you* in plenty of trouble."

I felt nauseated, at the grotesque expression, at Maybelle's insinuations, and, most of all, at her betrayal. Nothing Patrice and I had done had ever made me feel as dirty as I did at that moment lurking in the hallway. I wished I could run away, and yet I remained glued to the spot.

"And what exactly do you mean by that?" Astrid said sharply. She and Maybelle argued all the time—about us, about Grace, who Maybelle thought was a bad influence, even about politics, which neither of them cared about, but I had never heard her use that tone with her.

"You know perfectly well what I mean."

"What I know is that you're insinuating things about my daughter—"

It was Maybelle who snapped now. "You're a damn fool, Astrid, always have been. Lea, I'm not worried about, but Charlotte, she's like a ripe fruit waiting to be picked—"

"Oh, *please* . . ."

"No, you listen to me. You make your way through the world taking whatever you want, and your older daughter may be just like you, but Charlotte—"

"Oh, and who's Charlotte like? You? I don't think she'll be a spinster at forty. *My* daughters are normal."

"*Your* daughters are gonna get in the same trouble you did if you don't start keeping an eye on them."

"I'm not going to keep an eye on anyone!" Astrid spat furiously.

"Right, 'cause it might keep you out of mischief yourself. Don't think I don't know what you've been up to—"

"You watch out, Maybelle!"

"I'll say my piece!"

I couldn't take any more. I crept away, my face burning, and ran smack into Lea who had just come out of the bathroom.

"What's wrong with you?"

"Nothing," I mumbled, ducking into my room and closing the door. My eyes fell on the musical jewelry box Maybelle had given me years ago for my birthday, lined in pink satin with a little ballerina that revolved to the tinkling sound of "Für Elise" when you opened the lid. Hatred rose within me like bile. I wanted to hurl the box against the wall and smash it to pieces, but I contented myself with slamming the lid shut so hard that the rings and bracelets rattled within. In the pitiless light of anger, I saw Maybelle for what she was: a fat, unhappy woman who'd never gotten married, a maiden aunt, a freak. She had always been jealous of Astrid, and now that I was in love, she was jealous of me, too. Well, I didn't need her. None of us did. I touched the bracelet on my wrist. That was what being a woman was about, being wanted and admired, being loved, basking like a cat in the deliciously agonizing sensations that Maybelle, who could only dream of them, distorted with ugly names.

But already I could feel pity supplanting rage. As one of the blessed, I should show compassion. Maybelle would be leaving soon, and since Patrice was going to Rome to meet his father for the New Year, I could afford to be magnanimous. We had been planning to go to the Doll Museum the next day, and though the dolls in their overwrought dresses and kitschy backdrops, of which Maybelle never tired, had long ceased to excite me, I resolved to be kind. It was a kindness that felt rather hollow though, since it was tinged with cruelty, and in my heart, I knew that something had been destroyed.

18

WE USUALLY STAYED HOME for New Year's Eve. Astrid thought New Year's parties were dreadful, and Maybelle, who was leaving the next day, wanted to get to bed before dawn. By then I had sunk into a pleasantly claustrophobic holiday torpor, a state that had made it all the more easy to forgive and forget, and I was looking forward to the Scrabble tournament with which we planned to ring in the New Year, one that Frank would undoubtedly win, though Maybelle would give him a run for his money. The only one of us going out was Lea, who was attending her riding club's Saint Sylvester Ball. This affair involved the most rarefied strata of Parisian society and was preceded by hours of agonized shopping trips and phone consultations, culminating in a frantic depilatory session that kept the bathroom off-limits for an hour. In the end, Lea had settled on a simple silver gown that made me wonder as usual what all the fuss had been about. Astrid lent her her pearls, which she never wore because she found them boring, and when Lea emerged for inspection, we all agreed that she looked ravishing, and that no one would ever guess that, only hours before, she had been running around like a madwoman in Frank's old bathrobe with a mud mask all over her face, screaming at me to *immediately* reveal the location of her eyebrow tweezers.

When the doorbell rang at nine, I assumed it would be Lea's friends from the club coming to pick her up. The last person I had expected to see Frank usher in was Serge Lubomirski, in full evening dress and bearing, to my disgust, a bunch of roses that he offered with a bow to Astrid. Frank poured him a glass of champagne and he took a seat directly opposite me, affording me the opportunity to glare at him unseen. Or so I thought. After they finally left, Astrid turned to me.

"Charlotte, do you really think Serge didn't notice you making gargoyle faces at him?"

"I don't care if he did," I sulked.

Maybelle laughed. "That's my girl, Miss Congeniality."

Astrid sighed and stung me by saying, "I wish sometimes that you would grow up." She had seemed out of sorts for the past couple of days, but when I had mentioned this to Lea, she dismissed it as holiday grumps. Just as we had finished setting up the board, the phone rang, and Astrid went out to the hallway to answer. I pored gloomily over my letters, all consonants, as Maybelle let out a gleeful cackle.

"Her Royal Highness, I'll bet," she said with a pointed look at the door, when Astrid had failed to reappear after a few minutes. Frank frowned and rearranged his letters.

"Actually I believe she's a countess," he said with a half smile.

"Countess, my foot; she's as much of a countess as I am!"

"A little more so, I'm afraid, since she married a count."

"Well *ah* could have married a prince," Maybelle grandly retorted, "if I'd wanted to spend my life locked up in a harem."

This, as with many of the details of Maybelle's romantic past, was a slight exaggeration. She *had* once dated a charming Pakistani called Hassan, but his royal title had existed only in his imagination, though his wife, who, to be fair, Maybelle hadn't known about, had been very real indeed.

"It's the concubines they put in the harem, not the wives," I pointed out.

"Oh, really?" Maybelle said, "and what makes *you* such an expert on the subject?"

"She goes to school with half the Iranian community in exile."

Maybelle assumed a sentimental expression. "I dated an Iranian gentleman once. . . ."

Frank and I exchanged mirthful glances. Maybelle's fatal attraction to Southeast Asian and Middle Eastern men, who were in turn transfixed by her blond amplitude, was an old family joke. The problem was that her exotic beaus usually turned out to be married, to conservatively minded ladies who took a dim view of infidel seductresses with a weakness for dark mustaches.

"*Where* is Astrid?"

"I'll go see," I said, getting a little irritated myself. Surely whatever fresh drama had befallen Grace could wait until morning. I went out to the hall, but found it empty. "Mom?" I called. Thinking that she might have gone to get something in her room, I headed down the corridor in that direction. The light was on in Frank's study, and as I drew closer I heard a sound like a whimper. "Mom?" I called again.

She was standing at the window, but at the sound of my voice, she started and turned around. She must have hastily wiped her eyes. Her mascara was smudged, giving her an almost comical appearance.

"Mom?" I said again. "What's wrong?"

She smiled in the forced way people do when they don't mean it. "Oh, honey . . . it's nothing, just—life just seems so sad sometimes."

I looked at her blankly. Of course life was sad, but not *our* life.

She must have sensed my incomprehension, because she smiled again, more convincingly this time and said, "Hubert is off with his mistress again, and Grace is alone and feeling rather sorry for herself and—oh, it's just . . . I don't know what came over me, maybe the futility of it all."

"She could have come over here," I said. "She does all the time anyway."

"Oh, honey, don't be mean. . . ."

"I'm not being mean," I said impatiently. "We're all waiting for you to play Scrabble."

Her face grew serious. "Charlotte, you mustn't be so judgmental; people are weak."

"That's one way to put it."

"Honey, don't scowl, you'll get wrinkles. You're right, I'm being silly. I'll go wash my face and I'll be right there, okay?"

"We're waiting," I repeated, and turned on my heel.

When she rejoined us a few minutes later, you never would have guessed that she had just been crying. We played three rounds of Scrabble, two of which Maybelle won, and clinked glasses at midnight. "I love you," Astrid whispered into my ear, and it seemed to me that she held me just a little longer, though it could have been my imagination.

I heard Lea come in at four o'clock in the morning, presumably with Serge because there was laughing and whispering in the hallway. Lea never brought boys home. I strained to hear whether they would go into her bedroom, and when their muffled voices came again through the wall, I wondered what had happened to make her lower her standards. Could it be that Serge had seduced my ice-queen sister the same way he had seduced Delphine? Was she going to sleep with him? I felt compelled to cough loudly in protest at this shocking breach of my sister's principles. A silence fell, followed by the sound of the door closing softly, and then more laughter. I lay in the darkness waiting, but the night hung heavy on me and I drifted off. In the morning Serge was gone and Lea was as composed as ever, so that I had to wonder if I hadn't made the whole thing up, until I saw the flushed mark on her neck, like a mosquito bite, and a secret and rather self-satisfied look that I recognized instinctively, having worn it myself.

19

MAYBELLE WENT BACK TO THE STATES, Patrice came back from Rome, school started again, and life resumed its course, with one startling development: Over the holidays, and presumably as a result of their midnight tryst, Lea started officially going out with Serge Lubomirski. Apart from my indignation, the only real consequence this had for me was that Delphine, undoubtedly feeling that I had had a hand in the affair, stopped speaking to me. Not that I could have explained my sister's behavior if she hadn't. I had approached Lea myself, only to be smartly rebuffed.

"I hate to break this to you, but your opinion on this matter is of no consequence."

"But," I blurted out, "you *know* about the bet!"

"If Delphine was silly enough to throw herself at the *premier venu*, it's not my affair," my sister coolly replied.

I stared at her, dumbfounded. "And what are *you* doing?"

"I'm not throwing myself at anyone."

As it turned out, there *was* an explanation of sorts for her behavior. Serge was a fanatic rider. His ancestors had bred Arabians in Poland for centuries, and he himself owned two, which he kept at his father's place in the country. He and Lea had collided in this equestrian universe, a parallel world governed by its own rules and logic, and quite incomprehensible to anyone who couldn't tell a bridle from a stirrup. All the same, I felt duty-bound to try to reason with her.

"He's a cad," I reminded her.

Lea burst out laughing. "You know, you're really very funny sometimes."

But I didn't feel funny at all. I had always known that Lea and I were different, but it was a difference rooted in common reference. Now it seemed an inexorable process had set in that was slowly peeling us apart. At that moment I had my first glimmer of the woman Lea would become, and I felt a slight chill, as if I had already begun to lose her. She must have sensed this, because she ruffled my hair. "I know what I'm doing," she said.

And clearly she did. Overnight, the haughty Serge was transformed into a lapdog. When he wasn't picking Lea up on his motorcycle to go to the stables, he was escorting her to the movies, or obstructing the phone line and preventing Patrice from getting through. Lea, however, betrayed no signs of the passionate ardor that gripped me at the mere sound of my beloved's voice. She seemed to take Serge's attentions as her due, the manifestation of his fundamental good taste. Even Astrid regarded her with wonder, as if marveling at this foreign creature she had spawned.

"Lea's got quite a future ahead of her," she remarked one evening, as the door shut behind them.

Frank looked up from his newspaper. "Hmmm, what did you say?"

I thought I saw Astrid repress an irritated frown. "Has it escaped your attention, darling, that your daughter is dating a prince?"

"I should think they'd be a dime a dozen at their school," Frank said.

"Doesn't *anything* ever impress you?" Astrid snapped. We both regarded her with surprise.

She looked baffled herself. Maybe it had come back to her that she couldn't have cared less about princes. "I'm sorry, I've got a terrible headache."

"Maybe you should put off your departure," Frank mildly observed, for Astrid and Grace were leaving for Berlin the next day.

Astrid regarded him with disbelief. "Are you kidding? The tickets are already booked, and we had a hell of a time with the visas."

"Visas?"

"The transit visas, through East Germany."

"I don't see why you couldn't have just flown," Frank said. "Surely they have an airport in Berlin."

Astrid made a face. "Oh, you know Grace; she thought it would be more romantic to take the train, like Anna Karenina. . . ."

"Anna Karenina indeed," Frank said with an inscrutable expression, returning to his paper.

"Help me pack?" Astrid said to me.

I followed her to her room, a little mournfully. Patrice and I had planned to go to the movies that evening, but his mother had asked him to stay home and help her paint the kitchen. When I had said, without thinking, "Why don't you just hire someone to do it?" he had given me a funny look. Now I hated myself.

"What's wrong, pumpkin?" Astrid said once we were in her bedroom. "You look all out of sorts."

I told her what had happened.

She laughed. "Is that all? Don't worry, baby; men don't expect women to be reasonable."

"Lea is reasonable," I said.

"No she isn't; she just sets herself a high standard, and sticks to it. You're more like me."

Not only was I not sure what she meant, I didn't find this declaration comforting. Astrid opened her armoire, and her clothes exhaled her perfume into the air. She contemplated the trailing silks and cashmeres, a doubtful expression on her face.

"I hate packing," she said.

"Then don't go."

"I have to, silly. Besides, I won't be gone long."

"It always feels like forever," I said, without thinking, and she turned to me, her eyes suddenly serious.

"You mustn't love me so hard," she said.

"But you're my mother."

She smiled, a little sadly. "What about Patrice?"

"It's not the same."

"Oh, sweetie, it's never the same." She stood before the closet with her hand on the door, as if she'd forgotten why she'd opened it. "It seems so terribly important at the time, and then, years later, you wonder what on earth it was that made you think you couldn't live without them."

My face must have betrayed my anguish, because she reached out and stroked my hair and said, her voice light, "I'm just teasing, honey. Of course he'll always be a part of you."

It was only later, after she was gone, that I realized she'd misunderstood me.

20

PATRICE'S MOTHER WAS AWAY, too, on a *stage* in the Dordogne, and we started going to his apartment after school. It felt strangely grown up to be alone together, making ourselves tea and doing homework, before retreating to his room where he would put on Pink Floyd or Genesis and shut the blinds before guiding me onto the batik-covered mattress that served as his bed. Increasingly our embraces had taken on a sense of purpose, as if we had mastered a new language and were ready to move on. I was, but the faintest thread still held me back, the need for an occasion to mark the moment. I had fixed on such an occasion, Patrice's birthday a week away, when I intended to offer him my virginity. The idea seemed at once corny and solemn, but I clung to it nonetheless, and hoped it was the latter that would impress him. I knew it was time. I had touched by then every inch of his body, marveling at the way it responded to my clumsy caresses, and I had shuddered as his fingers entered me, his tongue flicking parts of me that no one else had ever even seen. Lea, in her clinical manner, had instructed me in all the ways of gratifying a man, and what she had missed I had gleaned from giggly readings of *Call Me Madam*, but there was a difference between theory and practice. The first time I closed my lips around his penis, Patrice's moan of pleasure made me both feel acutely conscious of my powers, and vaguely ridiculous at my reticence to proceed to an act that seemed infinitely less intimate. Thus, because I had by then already made up my mind, I was annoyed when a wheedling tone I had never heard before crept into his voice as he whispered, "I want to make love to you," tenderly at first, and then with mounting urgency. I wanted him somehow to have guessed my intentions. Wasn't that what was supposed to happen when you were in love?

"Soon," I said. I didn't even care anymore about losing my virginity—in truth, half the girls in school had, and no one thought the worse of you for it, unless you ended up a laughingstock like poor Delphine. All the same, it was only mine to offer once.

"I love you," he said, and though I luxuriated in the knowledge, I clung to my resolution.

"It won't hurt."

"What makes you so sure?"

"I've done it."

"You have?" I said, unable to entirely mask the pain in my voice. He stroked my hair. "Just once. It didn't mean anything."

I was amazed he couldn't discern that I would not find this reassuring. So there had been others before me. Who? Had he told her he loved her? I was too proud to ask, but the question lingered in my mind.

"Soon," I promised.

And I hurried home through the rain-slicked streets.

Astrid had been gone four days when the phone rang one evening as I came in. I could tell Frank wasn't home yet, because his overcoat wasn't hanging on its hook, nor the fedora he wore in winter to protect his bald spot from Paris's damp cold. I picked up the receiver. I heard the burr of static and then Grace's voice, high-pitched and frantic.

"Charlotte, is that you?"

"Yes?"

She inhaled sharply and cried, "Thank God!"

"What's wrong?" I said warily.

"It's Astrid. She's been arrested!"

"What?"

"Charlotte, you have to listen to me. She's been arrested, in Warsaw."

I felt as if the blood had drained from my body, but I still managed to say, in an even voice, "I thought you were in Berlin."

"I *am* in Berlin—Astrid went to Poland."

"Why?" I said, my voice now eerily calm.

"To see Łukasz. She was meeting with some friends of his, and the police raided the apartment. Some dreadful man from the American embassy called me!" Grace broke into sobs. I stared mutely at one of Frank's anatomical prints on the wall, an arm, the veins blue tributaries, the muscles and tendons labeled in Latin. "Think of them as maps," he always said when someone commented on the ghoulishness of his collection. Maps of the body.

"I don't understand."

Her voice turned shrill. "Charlotte, don't play stupid with me!"

"I'm not playing stupid," I said numbly. "I don't understand what she's doing in Warsaw." But I did. All of a sudden it was very clear.

"You mustn't tell your father!"

I was beginning to feel sick. I pressed a clammy hand against the wall to steady myself. "What am I supposed to do?" I said.

"Call the embassy. The man I spoke with is called Roger McCormick," and she read me off a long number. "I don't know anything about him. I'd try someone in Paris but I'm afraid it'll get back to your father. Frankly, I'm not even sure you should say anything to Lea."

"Why me?" I pleaded.

But she didn't answer.

I walked down the hallway in a trance and went into the bathroom, where I threw up. Having unburdened myself of the sour contents of my stomach, I went to my room and, still panting, closed the door. In my hand was the piece of paper with the phone number Grace had dictated to me. I smoothed it out and scrutinized the figures, transcribed in my neat, good-girl handwriting. Except that I wasn't a good girl; I was a fraud, a monster. I had known all along about my mother and Łukasz, and because I had done nothing about it, it was now up to me to fix everything. Suddenly exhausted, I lay on my bed. I must have fallen asleep, because I was woken by Lea.

"What's wrong? You look awful."

I opened my eyes and burst into tears.

21

LEA GAZED AT ME BLANKLY. "What was she doing in Poland? She was supposed to be in Berlin."

"She thought she could help Łukasz."

"She said she was going to Berlin," Lea obtusely repeated.

"She must have changed her mind," I said, and as the words left my lips, I wondered at my overpowering instinct to defend her. "It's not that far away."

"You can't just *go* to Poland. It's behind the Iron Curtain, you have to get visas. It takes planning." Lea's voice was preternaturally steady. "He's her lover, isn't he? She'd planned this all along."

I lowered my eyes. Hadn't she known as I did, without knowing? But Lea's voice had turned icy with contempt.

"How could she do this to us?" I had never seen the look in her eyes: cold, clear, and pitiless. All of a sudden I was terrified.

"Lea, she's in jail."

"It's where she belongs."

"Lea!"

"How long do you think she's been cheating on Dad?"

"It's not like that—"

"It isn't? Then what *is* it like?"

"I—she must be in love with him," I whispered. Because I knew she was, it was the only explanation. Whatever we suffered, it would be a million times worse for her. Why couldn't Lea see that?

She laughed harshly, making an ugly, barking sound. "In *love*? Oh well, then, that excuses everything. I'm sure Dad will understand."

I grabbed her arm. "You can't tell him!"

She stared at me incredulously. "You're not thinking of keeping this from him, are you?"

Shamefaced, I lowered my eyes again.

"I can't believe you're defending her," she said.

But she didn't tell him. I could tell by her face at dinner that she had decided to simply remove herself from the whole situation. Frank glanced at me enquiringly a couple of times as he served the cold roast and salad Maria had left us and, having no doubt concluded that I was brooding over some private concern, steered the conversation to a production of *Platée* that was being lauded in the press. He had asked his secretary, Inge, a statuesque blonde whom Astrid called the Swedish Sex Bomb, to get tickets. Normally we would have made some dumb joke, about how maybe he should go with the Swedish Sex Bomb, who Astrid swore was always making cow eyes at him, but that night we just stared at our plates.

"I don't suppose your mother will want to go," Frank continued unperturbed, "but I got the extra just in case. You can always ask one of those boys who seem to be constantly hovering about of late," he added. "Charlotte, are you feeling all right?"

"I—I'm a little tired," I mumbled, knowing that Frank would be too discreet to persist. Still, it seemed like hours before I could escape again to my room, where I tossed and turned all night, the little sleep I got riven with nightmares.

I called the number Grace had given me the next morning, feeling like a thief, from a phone booth outside school. It took me several attempts to get through, and I was afraid I would run out of coins, but finally, I heard a series of clicks, and a nasal American voice said, "Roger McCormick."

My name clearly meant nothing to him, so I added, my voice thick with humiliation, "Astrid Sanders's daughter."

There was a pause. "Oh, right. Hang on." There was another click, the fuzz of static, and then the same voice again, clearer this time. I thought of spy movies. Was I being taped? "Well, I won't

mince words with you. Your mother's gotten herself into one hell of
a mess."

"I'm sorry," I whispered.

"Yeah, I'll bet she is, too." My cheeks were burning. Didn't he
realize I was just a child?

"Where is she?" I asked, trying to keep my voice level.

"She's being held at the central precinct downtown. Could be
worse, I guess they've decided to show her some consideration—
Polish gallantry, you know?" He made a sound as if he were popping gum.

Astrid in jail. I couldn't even summon an image in my mind.
"Have you seen her?"

"Sure, I went over as soon as I found out. Look, they've got nothing on her, they'll have to let her go eventually."

"There's nothing you can do?"

"Nope. Just sit and wait. Does she have a husband?"

I blinked back tears. "Yes, but he's—away."

"Well, when he comes back, I'd suggest he get on a plane. . . ."
Roger McCormick must have heard my voice catch, because he
said, a little less gruffly, "Look, kid, get your dad to call me when he
gets back, okay? We'll get her out."

I picked up my bag and looked longingly toward school, where
a group of my classmates was gathered at the entrance, smoking
before the bell. A gulf now seemed to divide us. I walked blindly
down the Rue Rembrandt until I reached the Parc Monceau,
whose mossy pyramid Lea and I had loved as children. I had
always preferred the Monceau's artful abandon to the Luxembourg's prissy flower beds, but on this January morning, it was as
bleak and gray as Warsaw was year-round in my imagination. I felt
utterly bereft.

When the phone rang as I let myself into the apartment, I
snatched it up, knowing it would be Grace.

"Did you talk to Roger McCormick?"

"Yes," I whispered.

"I just got off the phone with him. He was hoping they might just let her go, but it seems it's more complicated."

"What do you mean?"

"We're going to have to tell your father," she said. "She needs a lawyer."

"No!"

"Charlotte, listen to me! I'm going to Warsaw tomorrow. I want you to meet me there."

My brain had slowed to a crawl. "How?" I said numbly. "How am I supposed to get there?"

"For God's sake, Charlotte!" Grace's voice was rising hysterically. "Go to a travel agency and buy a ticket. You'll need a visa, but they can probably arrange it for you."

"I don't have any money," I said. It was true. When I needed money, Frank gave it to me. I'd never had any reason to hoard it.

"Then borrow some, or steal it! I'll call you this evening." She hung up.

I was amazed to find that it was only four o'clock. The smell of fried onions wafted out of the kitchen, where Maria was cooking our dinner. Lea was still in school. I went and lay down on Astrid's bed, where I buried my face in the pillows that still held her scent, and fell into an exhausted sleep.

The moment Frank walked in that evening, I knew that Grace had told him. She didn't believe I would come to her rescue, and she was right: I had failed. Wordlessly, Frank went to his study and shut the door. I went to my room and waited. The phone rang twice, but no one answered. Patrice probably, worried about me, but the thought of talking to him was unbearable. When Frank finally summoned me, I was flooded with relief: He was going to take charge. That was what fathers and husbands did. He would be disappointed of course, and hurt, but he would forgive her. You forgave the people you loved, and my father was a man of principle, everyone said that about him. But when I came in, he didn't get up, just gazed at me coldly from behind his desk. Since he didn't ask me to sit down, I remained standing.

"I understand you are aware of your mother's predicament. Under the pretext of attending the Berlin Film Festival, she went to Poland, to see her lover, a certain Łukasz Baran, whom I understand you've met. In the process of trying to reach him, she was arrested by the authorities."

I could feel my eyes growing huge, the moisture draining from them. My father spoke in a mild, dry tone, pronouncing Łukasz's name with punctilious exactitude, as if he were concerned he might not get it right.

"I'm sure you will understand that I do not intend to lift a finger to help her."

I didn't recognize the voice that issued from me. It was the pleading keen of a supplicant.

"Please."

But he was unmoved. His eyes looked right through me, and at that moment, a terrible understanding dawned: By betraying him, Astrid had breached my father's core. There would be no compromise, no mercy, because that would constitute another betrayal, of the very principles that lay at the heart of his being. She had, quite simply, gone too far, and now, faith destroyed, the only relief he would find would be in correctness. The surge of hatred that traveled through me in that instant so disoriented me that I winced, as if struck by a blow. Frank must have felt the force of it, because he finally met my gaze. For a second, I thought I read bewilderment in his eyes, but when he spoke, they had grown cold again.

"Some things," he said, "are unforgivable," and I knew then why I had been summoned alone: I was to share in her shame. Because I had known and done nothing, and because I carried her hunger.

22

THE NEXT MORNING, Lea came into my room. I must have fallen asleep at some point, because I was conscious of having awoken, from a leaden, oppressed stupor that had brought no rest.

"We're going to Warsaw," she said.

I stared at her uncomprehendingly. Was she really going to help? Suddenly I realized that Grace had never called back. Or had I been supposed to call her? "Grace is on her way there," I said, because it was the only fact I could muster from the exhausted welter in my mind.

"No she isn't. I told her to stay out of it; she'll only make matters worse."

So Lea had taken control. I gazed at her with a mute gratitude that only seemed to enrage her.

"I neither condone nor even begin to understand. In fact, to tell you the truth, I'm entirely on Dad's side." She threw me a challenging look, but I knew better than to ask why she'd come around, her motives no doubt rooted in some chivalric notion of family honor. The important thing was that she was going to help. I was no longer alone.

"I've told Serge that we have to go to England for a funeral, and I expect you to tell Patrice the same."

"We don't know anyone in England," I objected.

"Yes we do," Lea snapped. "Dad has an aunt there. We'll work out the details later. How much money do you have?"

"None," I confessed. "No, there's the hundred dollars Maybelle gave me for Christmas."

"Good, I still have mine, too. That'll cover the tickets—we'll have to take the train, flying's too expensive. And we'll need money for visas and hotels." Lea had lapsed into her practical manner, which was what she always did under stress. I followed her lead eagerly: As bad as the situation was, once you broke it down into rational components, it became just another problem to be solved.

"Dad keeps cash in his desk," I said, without thinking, but her eyes had already turned contemptuous.

"Are you proposing we take it?"

"No," I said meekly, though I would have.

"I'll think of something," she said, and walked out.

That afternoon, we went to the Polish embassy, which was near the Invalides. The building was set back from the street in a small park, and we waited at the gate to be buzzed in, glancing uneasily over our shoulders in case someone should see us. Inside, a dreary little man in a cardigan escorted us down a hallway, his feet padding silently along the floor. There didn't seem to be anyone around, and I wondered if there were people watching us through peepholes, or lurking behind the ugly maroon curtains that obscured the windows. In the consular section, we were handed visa forms by a blond woman with incurious eyes who was seated behind a glass partition. While not exactly friendly, she didn't seem suspicious of our desire to visit her inhospitable land in the middle of winter, and even volunteered, when she saw our dismay at the news that the paperwork took two weeks that, for an extra fee, we could obtain a visa in forty-eight hours. We hastily agreed.

We had exchanged Maybelle's money into francs, and they had indeed just covered the cost of the tickets. The cheapest hotel the agent had found in Warsaw was surprisingly expensive for a place you would think no one would want to go to. I had thought of asking Maybelle for more, but I knew she didn't have it, though my scruples could easily have been surmounted. Even so, I would have had to tell her why, and the conversation I had overheard between them made me realize that Astrid couldn't bear to have Maybelle be the one to save her. Then Lea remembered Nahid's earrings. We took them to a pawnshop, like girls in a Balzac story, and though they didn't bring as much as we had hoped, we had enough.

It was a relief to have something to do. Between getting photographed for the visas, and making all the travel arrangements, the day crawled by. Frank didn't come home for dinner, though I thought I heard the front door close late at night. Patrice called to ask why I wasn't in school, and hadn't returned his calls. I told him that our aunt had died and we had to go to England for the funeral.

"You mean the fat lady?" he said, surprised.

"No, another aunt."

I was sure he didn't believe me. I was a lousy liar, unlike Lea, who gave Serge the story over the phone with seamless aplomb.

"I'll call you when I get there," I said.

"Sure." I knew that sarcastic tone; I'd just never been its object.

I felt as if I were moving in a dream, my limbs thick, the air around me like water. When we went to pick up our visas the next day, I thought the reality would finally sink in, but I might as well have been watching a movie. Our train left from the Gare du Nord at six in the evening. Although it didn't seem so far on the map, it would take twenty-eight hours to reach Warsaw. It had never taken me so long to get anywhere in my life.

I wondered if we should bring anything for Astrid, who had packed for a film festival, but then I remembered with a pang that she knew she was going to Poland all along. All the same, I went into her room and, from among her ski clothes, the only practical clothing she owned, selected warm sweaters and socks, which I stuffed with my own things into a backpack. The only person home when we left was Maria, humming to herself in the kitchen. Although she seemed surprised at our backpacks, she didn't ask any questions, and I assumed that she had guessed at our troubles and preferred not to know. Her scrupulous formality had never bothered me before, but I now found myself wishing desperately that she would ask where we were going. She just said *bonsoir*, however, as if she expected to see us in the morning, and it was then it hit me, like a dull blow, that there would be no one to bid us farewell.

I've always hated the Gare du Nord: its dank, chilly vastness and toilet smells, the trains like slumbering beasts snaking out into the night. As we made our way to the train, two ladies in fur hats and shearling coats pushed past us, talking loudly in what sounded like Russian. On the track, the guttural foreign syllables echoed everywhere, from stout men in leather jackets unloading towering luggage carts and passing their contents in through the windows, to the women already inside, exhorting them, presumably, to be careful. The train itself was an old model of the kind that the SNCF had long since retired, dark green and filthy, its windows opaque with dirt. The plaques on the cars said Paris–Moscow, in both Latin script and Cyrillic, and I glanced apprehensively at Lea, but she just stared grimly ahead, here eyes scanning the wagon numbers. I knew the train went on to Russia, but it seemed an outlandish and sinister destination, though the loud, fur-hatted ladies appeared eager to embark, clambering up the metals steps as if they were off on a wonderful holiday. Finally we reached our car, a burgundy-colored one bearing the reassuringly familiar emblem of the Compagnie Internationale des Wagons-Lits. Lea, ever practical, had taken sleeping berths.

Three people sat in our compartment: two women and a man in an ill-fitting, liver-colored suit who leaped up as we came in. They all stared at us, not in an unfriendly manner, thinking perhaps that we had gotten on the wrong train. Their luggage, which included two barrels of Omo laundry detergent and several bulging pink bags from the Tati store in Pigalle, was crammed into every inch of the overhead rack, and piled on the seats beside them, and a lively and incomprehensible discussion broke out as they began to shift parcels to make room for us. The compartment smelled musty and overheated, and for a moment Lea looked so wan that I thought she might pass out. In due course, the ladies cleared two spaces, and gestured eagerly for us to sit down. We did, still clutching our backpacks until the man pried them away from us and squeezed them into the rack overhead. Then we all sat smiling helplessly at one another until the train shuddered into motion and began to pull out of the station.

Much of my childhood had been spent traversing Europe's darkened landscapes, morning finding us in the Alps' icy air, or the torpid heat of Nice or Cannes. This time I had no idea of our destination, and as Paris receded behind us, I had an awful premonition that we would never come back. Lea's presence brought little comfort. As soon as we were moving, she pulled out a book and immured herself in it, her face a blank mask. Though the past two days had revolved around her, we hadn't spoken a word about Astrid, and clearly, Lea was determined to maintain this silence. I lacked her resolve. As miserable as I felt, a small, no doubt ignominious part of me had begun to rebel at the constant weight of oppression. My own book abandoned on my knees, I smiled timidly at the motherly lady opposite, who grinned back reassuringly. After a few seconds of this silent exchange, she pulled a candy bar from her purse and offered it to me. I accepted, thanking her in both French and English, though she clearly spoke neither. There was something curiously soothing about this unbridgeable language barrier, which precluded any prospect of explanation. For the first time in days, I let myself relax, and, lulled by the compartment's stuffy heat, I nodded off.

When I awoke to unfamiliar stillness, it was two in the morning. The train had stopped, seemingly in the middle of nowhere. Voices and footsteps sounded in the corridor, and then the lights blinked on, their sallow fluorescence flooding the compartment. When I looked down, the Polish ladies were sitting on their berths, discussing something in hushed tones. They motioned for me to wake Lea. "*Polizei*," one of them whispered, and then, as I gazed at her blankly, *"Paszport kontrole."* The door was yanked open and a soldier stood in the embrasure. A metal box hung on a strap from his neck, and, had it not been for the expression on his face, I would have thought it looked rather silly, the kind of thing a child would carry.

"Ausweisskontrole!" he barked, as the Polish ladies hurriedly handed over their papers. He spent a long time scrutinizing them, his narrowed glance passing back and forth between the women and their photographs, until, seemingly satisfied, he pulled a stamp from his box and slammed it down with a thunk. Lea by then was awake, and when he looked at her, she handed him our documents with a haughty expression that made me nervous. With a small smile, the man examined our passports.

"Amerikanerinen," he observed. The Polish ladies, I noticed from my perch, had fallen anxiously silent.

I wished Lea would smile, so he wouldn't think her rude, but she just coolly returned his gaze. He called to another soldier and they passed our passports back and forth between them, conferring the whole time in German. Outside, on the platform, I heard a dog barking. A sick feeling took hold of me as the soldiers disappeared, still holding our passports, and were replaced by two others, one wielding a powerful flashlight and the other a mirror at the end of a pole, which he swept under the lower bunks. Their search completed, they, too, departed, and we were left alone, the Polish ladies and I exchanging nervous glances as Lea stared stonily at the wall. It seemed like the soldiers were gone with our passports for hours, but finally they returned, handing them back to us with what seemed like a sardonic flourish, and the enormity of my relief made me realize how scared I'd been. At length, the train started again, and continued its progress through the night.

We reached Poland at dawn, the stone-faced Germans coming through once more, with, in their wake, a group of far more loquacious Polish soldiers who, although they carried guns, smiled and chatted with the ladies. After they had left we all exchanged glances, and the look on the Poles' faces seemed to say, "See, that wasn't so bad." Outside, a pale morning light illuminated a flat landscape of brown and gray fields. A sour smell, of yesterday's meal and sleeping bodies, had insinuated itself into the compartment's close air, and I wished I could open a window. The train was stopping more frequently now, in desolate stations with names composed of dizzying strings of consonants, and where it seemed no one ever got off. The wagon attendant came by with coffee in glasses. I accepted one, only to regret my eagerness, for when I brought the hot, murky liquid to my lips, I found myself swallowing a mouthful of grounds that stuck to my teeth and left an acrid taste.

Somehow the day passed, and by the time we reached Warsaw that evening, I was numb and exhausted, even the prospect of getting off the train bringing no relief. As if through someone else's eyes, I registered the gradual change in the landscape, premonitory of the approaching city: warehouses and buildings and ever more concentrated clusters of light, the tracks widening and splitting like arteries as we approached the station. Suddenly the train plunged underground, and a general momentum set in, the corridor filling with passengers and luggage. The Polish ladies put on their hats and applied lipstick in the grimy mirror, and the man helped them gather their bags and parcels from the rack. I smiled at them again, but Lea said brusquely, "Come on," and with a curt nod, moved into the corridor. Regretfully miming my good-byes, I followed her.

The platform was full of expectant-looking people, many clutching flowers, and as we hurried past them and made our way to the escalator ahead, I realized with a sharp pang that no one knew we were here. We could die, we could be kidnapped, and no one would ever know. There were soldiers everywhere in olive uniforms, barely out of their teens, their eyes following us with a furtive hunger. An unpleasant smell of grease and dirt hung in the air. I had expected cupolas and izbas, something to signify the East, but the subterranean station was merely vast and ugly, and eerily empty once we had left the track. The travel agent in Paris had said that our hotel was right across the street, but when we emerged into the cavernous main hall, glass doors stretched along both sides into what appeared like a yawning, black void, as if the station sat in the middle of an ocean. I looked around for the ladies from the train, but like the rest of the passengers, they seemed to have melted into the night.

As we stood scrutinizing the pamphlet from the hotel, a man in a leather jacket approached us and said "Taxi," and then, his voice low and insinuating, "Change money." His breath smelled like onions and cigarettes, and I tried not to wrinkle my nose. Lea, her eyes now desperate, showed him the pamphlet. He glanced at it and motioned for us to follow him. It seemed like a terrible idea, but we didn't have much choice, so we fell in behind him and made for one of the exits. Outside, the reason for our disorientation became apparent. The station did in fact sit in a sort of island, surrounded by wide, deserted boulevards and an open area that looked like a field. I could make out neon signs on surrounding buildings, their colors strangely etiolated, their design quaintly old-fashioned, like something out of an old movie. One of them said HOTEL POLONIA, and I wished we'd made a reservation there, as it seemed the only shelter at hand. Then our guide pointed to a taller shape in the distance, and the words HOTEL FORUM came fitfully to life atop it, before blinking out again as if exhausted by their brief illumination. Since there was no visible means of approach, we accepted his offer of a taxi, several of which stood nearby in line. As we got in, I saw Lea hand him a bill.

The brief ride to the Forum cost us twenty dollars, but it seemed worth every penny when we entered the lobby, which, though drab and ugly, bore generically familiar signs of hotels the world over. In the corner was a bar area with leather couches and ashtrays, where a group of Arab men sat with blond women in angora sweaters who eyed us disinterestedly as we went by. The wall near Reception held a display case full of dusty amber jewelry, and pictures of girls in flower headdresses and folkloric outfits that looked like they had been taken twenty years ago. Lea presented our passports to a woman with burgundy hair and penciled eyebrows who spoke precise, clipped English and made us fill out several forms before surrendering our room key. "Welcome to Warsaw," she said as she handed it over, and for a wild moment, I thought she might be joking, until I realized that she was just doing her job.

23

A GAIN, I SLEPT LIKE THE DEAD, but when I looked at Lea in the morning, the blue circles under her eyes betrayed that she had found no respite in slumber. While she took a shower, I pulled open the curtains, and found the same pewter sky lowering over a row of prefabricated buildings that reminded me of those that the government had thrown up in the Paris suburbs for immigrants. I had read somewhere that Warsaw had been destroyed during the war, bombed to rubble by the Germans, and the area around our hotel had clearly been rebuilt with an eye to expediency rather than beauty or grace. Below, a tram rumbled by, disgorging its passengers into the underground passage that seemed to be the only way of fording the boulevard which, I now saw, led to a vast, crenellated building of extraordinary ugliness that squatted in the center of the city—for I assumed that was where we were—like a brooding concrete octopus. It seemed unbelievable that this blighted landscape could contain my mother. It was all a terrible mistake, one that would be cleared up as soon as we got to the American embassy, which suddenly seemed to hold our salvation. We dressed quickly and, without stopping for breakfast, asked at reception for a taxi.

We drove along a road lined with black snowbanks, past massive column-fronted buildings that seemed disproportionate to their surroundings, as if the architects had mistaken Warsaw for ancient Rome. There were no stores or holiday lights, and the streets were deserted, though this might have had to do with the bitter cold that had gripped us as soon as we left the hotel. Some façades sported red banners emblazoned with slogans. Under different circumstances, I might have wondered where people bought bread or shoes, or whether it looked prettier in the spring, but as it was, I could only stare passively out the window, wishing the taxi would go faster. Presently we reached a wide road lined with official-looking buildings. The neighborhood looked older, as if it might have escaped the bombing, the houses set back in parks, some scattered with statues and fountains. The American embassy occupied a modern office block behind a tall black gate, next to a small palace with the Swiss flag fluttering on a pole in front of it. Once again, Lea handed the driver twenty dollars and he mimed that he would wait for us, but she refused, though I wondered how we would ever get back to the hotel. We got out and presented our passports, and when the Marine in the booth grinned and said, "Hi, girls," I thought I might burst into tears.

Inside, the same anodyne atmosphere reigned as at the American embassy in Paris, where I had been to renew my passport, though the functionaries in this far-flung outpost seemed a bit dowdier, untouched perhaps by the glamour of a large European city. All the same, the sight of resolutely cheerful Americans going about their business filled me with hope, as did the bulletin board in the lobby with its neatly xeroxed announcements, one of which advertised a weekend getaway to Paris. I had the sense of being everywhere and nowhere at once, and as a smiling lady with a pattern of snowmen on her sweater asked if she could help us, I took her so literally that I almost reached out to embrace her.

"We'd like to see Roger McCormick," my sister said stiffly after giving our names. "I believe he's expecting us." My heart sank when I saw the woman's eyes harden in response to Lea's cold formality.

"I'll see if he's in," she said, and I shot Lea a desperate glance, wondering if she intended to alienate every well-disposed soul who came our way. Comforting American food smells, of bacon and coffee and waffles, drifted out from what must have been the cafeteria, and I was seized by a hunger that shamed me. The woman in the snowman sweater returned and informed us that Mr. McCormick would see us. She led the way and I saw her suddenly through Lea's eyes, her broad haunches comical below the childish sweater and Dorothy Hamill haircut.

Roger McCormick was familiar, too, his navy blazer and horn-rimmed glasses the somewhat self-conscious uniform of the East Coast prep schools my father had attended; but on Roger McCormick, they didn't look quite right, as if he had borrowed someone else's clothes. Though the skin of his face, which I had first taken to be merely florid, was subtly incandescent about the nose with rosacea. A small American flag stood almost apologetically on his desk, next to a mug emblazoned with the crest of the University of Pennsylvania. From the wall behind him, Jimmy Carter smiled benevolently, and I remembered Frank saying, as everyone had when he was elected, that he seemed like a decent man.

"Have a seat," he said. "Coffee?" We shook our heads and he sat down, bringing his pink hands together on the desktop. The same affable smile with which he had greeted us hovered on his lips as he asked, "What can I do for you?"

I gaped at him. Did he have no idea why we were here?

"We rather thought it was you who could do something for *us*," Lea said.

I could tell that he was amused by her nerve. I was horrified. As if to further humiliate me, my stomach began to growl, tormented by the waffle smell that hung lasciviously in the air.

"Well, there's no point in beating about the bush: Your mother's gotten herself into a hell of a mess." Again Roger McCormick smiled his smooth smile, as if he were relating an entertaining anecdote that had nothing to do with us. His voice was ever so slightly nasal, the voice, I suddenly realized, that Astrid and Grace put on when they were describing a particularly buffoonish kind of American.

"We're aware of that," Lea said. "But surely you can help her." I noticed suddenly that she was wearing mascara, and the discovery made me feel sick. Lea only wore makeup to parties, and then sparingly.

Roger McCormick shrugged. "It's not so simple. She was arrested in an apartment that was a front for a clandestine printing press. She stands accused of aiding and abetting the activities of the proprietor, a certain Marek Pawlikowski, who happens to be a well-known opposition figure, by delivering a package of cash from supporters in the West. Do you have any idea how serious this is?" he asked mildly.

"There must have been some mistake," Lea said. "My mother has nothing to do with any of this. She was just visiting a friend."

In a way I had to admire Lea's sangfroid, even as I sensed its futility. Roger McCormick wasn't the one we would have to convince.

"A friend who just happens to be a well-known dissident. The Poles take this kind of thing seriously, you know. Not to mention their friends the Russians."

My heart stopped. Years ago, when everyone in Paris had been reading *The Gulag Archipelago*, I had filched Astrid's copy and devoured with fascinated horror Solzhenitsyn's account of life in a Soviet penal colony. Visions of barracks and watchtowers rose in my mind, black and stark against the frozen Siberian wasteland.

"Your mother says she had no idea what was in the package, but the Poles aren't buying it. It seems they've had their eye on her for a while."

"This is preposterous," Lea exclaimed.

But it wasn't. Astrid was capable of madness, of smuggling packages across borders and trying to save people—not people but a man, a man she couldn't live without—even if it might spell her own ruin. And ours. Was it really possible that my sister didn't know this about her?

"Does she know we're here?"

Roger McCormick regarded her blandly, and I suddenly understood my sister's predicament: He was untouched by her beauty. The mascara had been a waste, a pointless self-cheapening. I grew numb as the implications of this intuition unfurled in my mind: Not only was this man unmoved by Lea, he had not fallen under Astrid's spell. My mother was, in fact, distasteful to him. At this moment I realized that he knew everything: that Łukasz was her lover, that she had betrayed us, that she was not glamorous but pathetic.

"Yes. She's been told. I'm going to see her this afternoon—I assume you'll want to come along."

I looked at him helplessly. From the corner of my eye, I saw with horror that Lea's lip was quavering. She bit down on it.

"We've come to take her home."

Roger McCormick smiled. "I don't think you understand the gravity of the situation. Your mother, by accident or design, has done something incredibly stupid, and there's frankly not a whole lot we can do about it, except sit and wait and let the Poles have their fun with her. They won't keep her forever; they've got too many other fish to fry. They'll put the fear of God in her, and then let her go. It's a little game they like to play. We've hired her a lawyer who knows how to work the system, and now we just have to sit tight and let the matter play itself out. My advice to you is to go back to Paris. There's no point in hanging around Warsaw, which, as you probably noticed, has nothing to recommend it. I'm not even sure you should see her; you'll just get upset. If it'll make you feel any better, she's getting the royal treatment. She even has her own bathroom."

When he had finished this speech, he gazed at us benignly from behind his glasses and then said, "Look, girls, you're going to have to trust me."

"I don't believe you can't help her," Lea said in a level tone. "She hasn't done anything."

Roger McCormick shrugged again. "That's completely immaterial."

"I don't believe it is. My mother isn't just anybody; she knows many influential people. Adam Lubomirski happens to be a close personal friend; surely he can do something."

I gazed at her in wonder. Serge's father? What on earth did she think she was doing?

Roger McCormick smiled his thin smile again. "That's very nice, but I wouldn't count on the Knights of Malta to get you out of this pickle."

I was beginning to feel like Alice, spiraling helplessly down the rabbit's hole. Through the wall, I heard the monotonous clack of a typewriter, voices, purposeful steps that stopped at the door, which opened to reveal another caricatural American, his teeth perfect, his grin broad and empty.

"Oh, sorry, Roger, I didn't know you had company."

"That's all right, Bill, come on in. These are the Sanders girls."

The man's face first went blank and then, as understanding dawned, composed itself into a commiserative smirk. I saw my sister redden, and for a second, I, too, hated Astrid, for doing this to us, for bringing shame and dishonor on our family and grief into our hearts, and I thought savagely that maybe Roger McCormick was right, that we should go home and leave her, that it would be a good lesson.

24

But we insisted on seeing her nonetheless, and Roger McCormick promised to take us later on that afternoon. In the meantime he sent us back to the hotel in an embassy car, and Lea finally broke down and ate, in the hotel's hideous brown-and-orange dining room, where an obsequious waiter with shifty eyes served us something that was called *kotlet de volaille* on the menu, and turned out to be Chicken Kiev. I wolfed it down hungrily, along with the vinegary grated beets and carrots that came with it. Lea, to my surprise, ordered a glass of wine, and asked if I wanted one, too. I shook my head, but when hers came, I took a sip. It was sour and thin, not at all like the wine Astrid and Frank drank at dinner, and of which we were frequently given a taste to, as Frank joked, develop our palates. A wave of despair so acute swept over me at that moment that I thought I might burst into tears again, but it passed. I was beginning to understand that you can get used to anything.

The restaurant was nearly empty, but at a table nearby, the Arab men we had seen in the lobby were eating lunch, and drinking quite a bit as well, to judge by the thicket of bottles on their table. Lea's face had frozen into a moue of distaste, but I kept glancing at them with a sort of stealthy fascination. When our waiter appeared with two glasses of champagne on a tray, indicating their provenance with a smirk, I turned bright red, convinced it was I who had attracted their attention.

"Thank you," Lea said firmly, and got up. I followed her, acutely aware of the men's glances, and of the sudden spate of murmured commentary at our backs.

Roger McCormick pulled up punctually at two, in a black Chevrolet wagon with tinted windows that looked almost comical amid the small boxy cars in the hotel's parking lot. He was sitting in the front with the driver, and when we got in, he turned around and made a friendly face.

"Look, girls, I have to warn you: It's not the Ritz."

Did he think we were stupid as well? As we drove through gray streets, he kept up an amiable stream of chatter, to which we responded in monosyllables, until he remarked, out of the blue, "Paris, wish *I* were there right now. . . . There was a great bistro near the embassy, *Chez* something . . ."

"Half the restaurants in Paris are called *Chez* something," Lea said.

"*Chez Jacqueline*. Great steak frites—you girls go to the American School?"

"No," I said, as it was evidently my turn.

Again he twisted his neck around, affording me a view of his inflamed capillaries. "Gone native, huh?"

I took this as the barb it was surely meant to be. "We don't wear grass skirts and nose rings, if that's what you mean."

But he took no notice of my sarcasm. "Palace of Culture," he said, pointing to the sprawling building I had seen from our hotel room window. "Stalin's little gift to the Poles, and they're grateful as hell, right, Staś?" he said to the driver with a knowing smirk.

"Right, boss," the driver responded in kind, as if this were an old joke between them.

It seemed we hadn't driven very far when we stopped in front of a nondescript building on a side street that didn't, to my relief, look like a jail at all.

"Time to hit the slopes," Roger Mc McCormick remarked with a glance at the sky as he alighted, and I wondered if he really found himself amusing, or if it was just a pose he had adopted to mask the emptiness of his soul. We followed him up a set of concrete steps and waited silently while he rang the bell. After several seconds, a buzzer sounded, and we stepped into a dingy lobby that smelled of disinfectant and cheap coffee, its only furnishing a Formica-topped desk from behind which a man in a gray uniform regarded us with suspicion. Roger McCormick strode up to him and pulled out an ID, saying something in Polish, which I was surprised he spoke.

The policeman, for that was what I assumed he was, glanced at us and then got up and, indicating that we should wait, disappeared through a door behind him. Roger McCormick smiled reassuringly and adopted the patient posture of one who is used to waiting in hallways, one that I found impossible to imitate. My eyes skated along the walls, which were painted a sickly institutional green, and down to the scuffed linoleum floor before returning to the walls again. Lea looked like she had frozen in place.

The policeman returned with a woman with painted-on eyebrows like the hotel receptionist's. I took this as yet another reassuring sign even though she regarded us coldly. As we followed her down a hallway lined with closed doors, behind which could be heard voices and the clack of typewriters, my heart lifted. This wasn't a jail but an office, some sort of government building maybe. Clearly these people had taken one look at Astrid and realized the mistake they had made. Now that we were here, they would let her come home with us. By the time we had followed our guide up a flight of stairs and down another hallway, lined at intervals with hard chairs, I had buoyed myself into believing that this was all perfectly normal, or at least the kind of manageable scrape that Astrid was always getting herself into. Soon it would be another story to laugh over with Grace, like the time they'd almost gotten arrested in Afghanistan, its details burnished over time until it didn't matter anymore what had really happened.

The woman with the penciled-on eyebrows took us to a large, bare room with a table in the center, and indicated for us to wait there. It wasn't a pleasant room, but it still didn't look like a prison. We sat for what seemed like a half hour, in a silence unbroken even by Roger McCormick, who seemed to have retreated into his own thoughts, until the door opened and a man came in. He wore a leather coat and cap, and he handed them to the eyebrow woman with the air of one used to having people do things for him. Relieved of this apparel, he strode over to us with an apologetic smile. I had expected Roger McCormick to rise, but he didn't, and so I waited for the man to cross the room, which he did with a cordial expression that intensified when he reached Roger, who stood then and shook his extended hand. The man wore a suit and tie that I knew instinctively to be cheap, and a dark shirt that struck me as an odd, sinister touch. Having shaken hands with Roger, he turned to us, his expression shifting to one of slight puzzlement. Roger said something in Polish and the man raised his eyebrows a fraction.

"They were expecting your father," Roger said, his tone neutral.

I felt a wave of shame, but Lea said curtly, "He couldn't come."

Again the man raised his eyebrows, and when Roger didn't translate for him, I wondered if he understood English. He said something in Polish, with a smile this time.

"He says he sees the family resemblance," Roger said, his eyes on me.

I stared helplessly. Where was Astrid? Weren't they going to bring her?

"We'd like to see our mother," Lea said coldly.

The man looked amused. He sat down and steepled his fingers, and there was something curiously fastidious about this gesture, as if he had taken especial care in the alignment of the fleshy pads at their tips. When he fixed his gaze on me again, I realized what it was about him that I found so unnerving: His eyes were completely expressionless. For a few seconds he said nothing, then he smiled again, his blank eyes boring into mine. I felt myself flush, but it seemed suddenly a matter of honor to hold his gaze. When he finally turned back to Roger, I felt like I had won a small victory.

"She'll be here shortly," Roger translated. He, too, had turned expressionless, and I had a feeling that this was a game these two had played before, that they might even enjoy it, like chess or backgammon. I heard footsteps in the hall and the door opened, and Astrid came in with two men in leather jackets on either side of her. When she saw us, she made an awful whimpering sound, her arms reaching out in a parody of her familiar gesture, and I ran to her without thinking, shoving my way past Lea. I held her so hard that I could feel her heartbeat. Her guards must have stepped aside, because we stood there for what seemed like an eternity, rocking like slow dancers.

"Lea," she whispered imploringly after I had let go, and only then did my sister rise and move across the room, with the ponderous gait of a sleepwalker. When she came level with Astrid, she just stood, facing her, and I had a horrible feeling that she was going to refuse to touch her, but then I saw the tears welling in her eyes, and I understood that what had threatened to tear me apart had nearly rent my sister in half. I could handle aberration and disorder; Lea couldn't. Her composure was causing her such an effort of will that I feared she might crumple like a puppet released from its strings, and I had to repress the impulse to reach out and steady her.

Astrid looked tired and thin, her skin almost translucent. She was wearing her own clothes, but they must have taken away her makeup, because her face was bare, and I felt a stab of anguish, that she should have been so intimately revealed to strangers. Only when Lea finally pulled away did I realize that my mother wasn't crying. Her eyes were huge and dry, the pupils like wells. The man with the blank eyes pulled out a chair for her, and she sat, accepting this ironic mark of courtesy as she would that of a waiter in a restaurant. We returned to our seats as well and for several minutes we just sat, drinking each other in. Then her jailer cleared his throat and spoke, and I was amazed, and proud, to detect in my mother's eyes a queenly flash of annoyance.

"As you can see, your mother is in good health," Roger McCormick translated, "though the standard of the accommodations is perhaps not what she is accustomed to."

"I've stayed in worse," Astrid said.

I couldn't believe it: Was she making fun of them? But when I searched her face, I found only a blank expression that mirrored theirs. Once again a feeling of unreality gripped me, as if I had wandered into a play where everyone but me knew their parts. The man in the leather coat made another remark in Polish to Roger, who told us that Mr. Kasprzyk would be joining us shortly. "Your mother's lawyer," he explained, and the man in the leather coat nodded approvingly. The door opened again, and a short balding gentleman with a briefcase was ushered in by the eyebrow woman who must have been hovering the whole time in the hallway. Having, to my bemusement, kissed my mother's hand, the lawyer shook ours and sat down, too, removing from his case a bulging manila folder, which he placed on the table before him. He seemed pleasant enough, if a little resigned in his cheap suit, resolved to play his part as well in this curious little drama we seemed to be enacting. A conversation ensued in Polish between him and Roger and the man in the leather coat, with papers periodically emerging from the manila folder and being passed around and examined, and Roger looking in turn aggrieved, exasperated, or conciliatory, while the man in the leather coat alternated between smug and dolefully sympathetic.

I wanted desperately to smile at Astrid, but I was afraid to introduce what might be taken as an unseemly note of levity, so I contented myself with gazing at her while I sought her foot under the table. I had stopped caring what happened next: If we had to spend the rest of our life in this ugly, bare room, so be it, as long as we could stay together. Every now and then she would raise her eyebrows a fraction, and a faint tremor would animate her mouth in a way that only one who knew by heart every nuance of her expressions could possibly interpret as the hint of a smile. Then the man in the leather jacket stood up and left the room.

"How are they treating you?" Roger asked when he was gone.

"Fine," Astrid said, and then, turning to me and Lea, "Girls, I want you to go home."

"Not until they let you go," I said fiercely. She took my hand. Now that the man in the leather coat had gone, it must have seemed all right to do so, though it occurred to me that he was probably watching us from another room.

"My brave, foolish girl," she said, her voice catching. "There's absolutely no point in your staying. They'll let me go eventually; I haven't done anything."

Lea spoke then, for the first time. "No, you just destroyed our lives."

I looked at her, horrified. All of a sudden I understood why she had come all this way—not to comfort but to accuse. The lawyer looked exceedingly ill at ease, and even Roger McCormick seemed to wish that he were somewhere else.

"I'm sorry," Astrid said simply.

"No you're not. You've been doing this your whole life—it's just that this time you got caught, and now we have to suffer the consequences."

"I'm sorry," Astrid repeated. But Lea was right: She wasn't. She had done it for love, and if this was the price she had to pay, she was willing. I had never understood until that moment what people meant when they said that love can be terrible, that it can wound and destroy and leave mayhem in its wake.

The lawyer cleared his throat and said, in accented English, "I remain optimistic of a positive outcome: The case against Madame, your mother, is largely circumstantial." But he had no chance to explain the exact reasons for his optimism because Astrid let out a caw of laughter, which she only half-successfully suppressed by putting her hand to her mouth.

"I apologize," she said to the puzzled lawyer. "Nerves . . ." I could tell by the way Roger McCormick regarded her that he thought she was off her rocker. I, on the other hand, felt a rush of elation, for in that moment I understood that she was far from cowed. She had drawn strength from us, and now she was ready for anything. When the man in the leather coat returned a second later, she resumed her meek expression, and I could have sworn that for a second he looked suspicious. He said something to Roger and the men in the leather jackets reappeared. Astrid rose.

"I'll be fine," she said, "Go home," and before I could gather my wits she was gone.

As soon as we were outside, I approached the lawyer.

"What did you mean when you said the evidence was circumstantial?"

Roger McCormick laid an impatient hand on my arm. "I'll explain in the car. Can we drop you somewhere, Mr. Kasprzyk?"

The lawyer shook his head as if he had had quite enough already. "Thank you, I will walk," he said and having hastily shaken our hands, he made his way down the darkening street.

25

W HAT HE MEANS," Roger McCormick said when we were safely back behind the tinted glass of the embassy car, "is that they don't have a thing on her: She wasn't actually holding the money when they busted in. We know that, and they know that, and they couldn't care less, because they can do what they want, including throw her in jail for whatever trumped-up charges they care to fabricate. The good news is that they've got enough problems right now without stirring up a diplomatic incident over a broad. We're going to let them have their fun; we'll even play along with the fantasy that there's something like due process going on here, and eventually they'll get bored and let her go. If I were you, I would take her advice: Go home. She'll be fine."

"We're staying," I said.

"Whatever, kid, but you're wasting your time."

When we walked into the hotel, Maybelle was standing at the reception desk, evidently in the process of stirring up a diplomatic incident of her own.

"What do you mean, you don't know where they went? Ah'll have you know these are minors!"

With a cry, I ran toward her, practically swooning with relief as I was engulfed in the familiar scent of Emeraude.

"There, there," Maybelle clucked, holding me like a vise. Then she caught sight of Roger McCormick and, letting go, demanded, "Are you from the embassy?"

Roger admitted that he was, at which point Maybelle drew herself up to her full stature and said, "Well, then, maybe you can tell me what the *hell* is going on."

Soon we were all seated in the restaurant, Maybelle having declared that she wasn't taking her underage nieces into the bar, a remark that caused my worldly sister to cast her eyes ceilingward and light one of the cigarettes she had bought earlier, which Maybelle promptly snatched and put out. For a second I thought Lea might actually light another one, but she evidently thought better of it because she retreated into a contemptuous sulk. I felt happy for the first time in days: Maybelle was here, and everything was going to be all right. As for Roger McCormick, he had seemed relieved at first to be dealing with an adult, until Maybelle made it clear that she wasn't exactly impressed with his handling of the situation.

"You're telling me they haven't charged her with anything?" she uttered incredulously.

Roger McCormick adopted an expression of long-suffering patience. "Ma'am, they don't have to. This isn't America. It's not even France."

"Ah can see it's not France," Maybelle snapped, her eyes sweeping disdainfully around the seedy restaurant, which smelled of stale cigarette smoke and gravy. She ordered Cokes for us, and Roger ordered coffee, though I would have bet he would have liked a drink. I could tell that, for all the distressing circumstances, Maybelle was getting into the spirit of being in a foreign country, albeit one that seemed to have little to recommend it. When the Arabs from earlier walked in and threw admiring glances her way, she preened and batted her eyelashes, and I heard Lea mutter, "Oh Lord," under her breath.

"When can I see my sister?" Maybelle asked. With a sigh, Roger said he would try to arrange a meeting for the next afternoon.

It wasn't until we were back in our room that it occurred to me to wonder how Maybelle had found out we were here.

"That nitwit Grace called me. What *ah* want to know is why I wasn't told earlier, by *you*."

I lowered my eyes. "I thought you'd be mad," I mumbled.

"I'm mad all right, at Her Royal Highness, the Queen of Fools!"

I thought she meant Grace at first, until Lea acidly cut in, "That's exactly why we didn't tell you."

"Ah beg your pardon?"

"Because we knew you'd never let her hear the end of it."

I regarded Lea with renewed respect, until she added, "Still, it's just as well. Now that you're here, we can go home."

"You're darn straight you're goin' home, on the first flight I can find."

"No!" I cried. "I'm not going anywhere!"

"Oh yes you are! You've missed enough school already."

But Maybelle knew perfectly well that I wasn't going to budge, just as I knew that she wanted me to stay. We were in this together, Maybelle and I; we were a team again.

"Well," she relented. "Ah guess ah might need a translator," which was a joke of course, because I spoke as much Polish as she did.

"I've got a huge test coming up," Lea said, lighting another cigarette, which Maybelle ignored this time, "but Charlotte can miss a couple days of school." I knew she was thinking the same thing I was, that my meager diplomatic skills might be needed to sustain Roger McCormick's cooperation.

"We might as well have some dinner," Maybelle said, even though it was only five o'clock, but that was when people ate dinner in Kentucky.

Early the next morning we put Lea on a plane, which Maybelle paid for. Lea protested vehemently—she knew as well as I did that our aunt didn't have much money—until Maybelle told her, "Don't worry about it. There's not much you can be sure of in this life, but of one thing I'm certain: You'll be in a position one day to pay me back."

To me, Lea said, "For God's sake, don't let her make things worse."

"Don't worry," I said. "I can handle her."

"I'm sorry," Lea said.

"It's better this way; you need to take care of Dad." It was the first time it had occurred to me that Frank would need taking care of, and that I couldn't be the one to do it.

"I'll never forgive her," Lea said.

"Don't say that. You know it's not true." I knew I should also say, "Tell Dad I love him," but I didn't; it stuck in my throat, and before I could regret it, she was gone.

26

With Maybelle in charge, I became more aware of my surroundings. Except for the Arabs and a tour group from Chicago, who checked in the morning Lea left, we seemed to be the only guests in the hotel. The Americans, who all had Polish-sounding names like Makowski and Rybak, tried to chat us up at breakfast, but Maybelle put her natural gregariousness in check, undoubtedly having realized that it was going to be awkward to explain the reason for our presence in Warsaw. The Americans seemed particularly eager to talk, albeit in hushed tones, about the "political situation," but we made pleasantly neutral noises and, having loaded our plates with cold cuts and hard-boiled eggs, retreated to a corner table. Afterward, while we waited for Roger McCormick to call, Maybelle went to inspect the amber display in the lobby, and I went up to take a shower. I was wrapping a towel around my wet hair when I realized that today was Patrice's birthday. It hit me like a thud; my intended gift, now impossible. I had been gone for four days and, for all he knew, had dropped off the face of the earth. I didn't care what Lea said, I was going to tell him the truth. I had a right to comfort. Maybelle's arrival had made me realize that I didn't have to shoulder this burden alone. Patrice would understand. Did he not come from a broken family?

The words startled me as they formed themselves. Was that what we had become? It hadn't occurred to me until then to wonder what would happen next, even as I knew, instinctively, that there was no going back. What had Frank said? Some things are unforgivable. But just because I had taken my mother's side didn't mean that I had to share in her disgrace. Surely there was honor in loyalty. For the first time in days, I allowed myself to look beyond the next hour, to the possibility of returning to some kind of normalcy. Feeling suddenly buoyant with relief, I went over to the desk and asked if they could connect me to France, hoping that it wouldn't cost a fortune. I gave the receptionist Patrice's number, and she directed me to a row of booths in the corner.

Since it was Saturday morning, I had expected Patrice to be home, but I got his mother, who told me coldly that he was out. I hesitated, the bad connection crackling in my ear. She probably thought I was a spoiled rich girl—Patrice did—and though I had no proof of it, I took offense at a judgment that now seemed all the more unfair. In my most polite voice, I asked her when she expected him back—I didn't dare leave the hotel number, since I didn't want it to seem like I expected him to make an international call—but all she would say was that it would be sometime in the evening. I asked her to tell him that I had called, and would try again, wishing I could add something in code that would convey to him that I had remembered, and how sorry I was. Seconds after I hung up, the phone rang again. It was Roger McCormick, informing me that we wouldn't be able to see Astrid until Monday. I stared dumbly at the receiver: How could I have been worrying about whether Patrice's mother liked me when my own mother was going to spend the weekend alone in a jail cell?—though Roger had assured us that it wasn't really a cell, just a room in the upper story of the police building, and that she had books and a radio. I started to raise objections, but he said curtly that there was nothing more he could do about it, and that kicking up a fuss would only make matters worse. "Why don't you do some sightseeing?" he suggested. I couldn't tell if he was being sarcastic or just obtuse.

When I came back down, I found Maybelle leafing through the pamphlets that were displayed on a rack at Reception. She had bought an amber necklace from the hotel souvenir shop, for a price

that she assured me was a real bargain, and had put it right on over
one of the exuberantly colored drip-dry polyester blouses that were
the mainstay of her traveling wardrobe. I told her what Roger had
said, expecting her to have a fit, but to my surprise, she took the
news philosophically.

"Well, I guess a couple days won't make a difference at this
point. Why don't we go check out Chopin's birthplace?" she suggested, handing me one of the flyers she had been studying.

"I don't know," I said doubtfully. It didn't seem right to have
fun under the circumstances, not that visiting Chopin's birthplace
would have been my idea of fun. But I was tired of feeling awful
all the time. Maybe she was right: Why shouldn't we make the
best of it?

Maybelle smiled reassuringly. "We're here, and she's not going
anywhere; we might as well see the sights."

Under the present surreal circumstances, I had to admit that
there was a certain logic to her reasoning. Poland hadn't exactly
made a great impression so far, but I had seen it only through the
jaundiced eyes of Roger McCormick. Where, I couldn't help but
wonder, were the brave striking workers, the protest marches that
they were always showing on French TV? The few people I had seen
so far on the streets had only seemed eager to get off them. I was
going to suggest that maybe we just walk around when the receptionist beckoned to us.

"You have a phone call," she said, and she pointed to a booth in
the corner. I made my way over, thinking it would be Lea, who had
promised to call when she arrived, but instead, an unfamiliar voice
said, "Hello, Miss Sanders, I am confirming your reservation for two
tickets to the opera tonight."

"Ah—" I started to protest, but the woman, who spoke precise
British-inflected English, cut me off.

"You may pick up the tickets at six from the box office at the
Teatr Wielki," she said, sounding like someone reading from a phrase
book, and before I could reply, she hung up.

"Was that Lea?" Maybelle asked.

"No," I said. "Some woman about picking up opera tickets. She must have made a mistake."

"I wouldn't mind going to the opera," Maybelle said, admiring the huge amber ring she had purchased to go with her necklace. It had a dead bug embedded in it that was supposed to make it even more valuable. My aunt, whose musical tastes ran to Barry Manilow and Neil Diamond, couldn't set foot on European soil without feeling obligated to subject herself to high culture. Since Astrid refused to indulge her, I was invariably the one who ended up getting dragged through the Louvre or to the ballet, where Maybelle always fell asleep. I was going to remind her that she had barely made it through the first act of *Manon Lescaut*, when she narrowed her eyes and snapped, "What did she say?"

"Who?"

"The woman who called about the tickets."

I thought about it for a second. "She said, '*Hello, Miss Sanders,*' and that we should pick up the tickets at six from the box office."

"Are you sure she used your name?"

"Yes." I stopped and thought about it. "I guess that *is* kind of funny. . . ."

Maybelle's expression turned subtly cunning. She glanced over her shoulder, as if to make sure no one was listening, and then whispered, "That was no mistake, she was sending us a message."

I rolled my eyes. Maybelle had clearly been reading too many spy stories. She was currently on a Len Deighton kick, and had just finished *Berlin Game*, which I had started. It seemed appropriate to the circumstances to be reading a book about cold war spies.

"Who would want to send us a message?"

"Your mother's friends, that's who."

I frowned. As far as I knew, the only friend Astrid had in Warsaw was Łukasz, and I wasn't eager to be reminded of his role in our predicament. Maybelle must have sensed what was going through my mind because she put her hand on my arm and said, "Look, honey, I won't pretend to understand why my sister does the things she does, but we're all she's got now, and it sounds to me like someone is reaching out to us."

"What if it's a trap?"

"Don't worry; I have a sixth sense about these things."

I wasn't comforted. If Maybelle had a sixth sense, why hadn't it kicked in before now? All of a sudden, I remembered all the things that were ridiculous about her: her gaudy outfits, her mawkish sentimentality, her unshakable, not to mention completely unfounded belief that men found her irresistible. At moments like this, I was painfully reminded that I was only fifteen, dependent on the goodwill of adults who seemed determined to behave like children. With an air of elaborate casualness that struck me as suspect in the extreme, Maybelle approached the receptionist and asked her where the Opera was located. It was, the woman informed her, just a few blocks away. In dulcet tones, Maybelle thanked her and asked if she could be so kind as to draw us a map? The woman, who now *did* look suspicious, handed her a pamphlet entitled "Welcome to Warsaw" which, like all the other literature at the reception desk, looked like it had been printed in the fifties.

"There is a map inside," she said.

As we walked out, Maybelle whispered to me, "They all work for the KGB," to which, having finally had enough, I said, "We're in Poland, not Russia."

"It's the same thing," Maybelle imperturbably replied. "Why do you think they call it a satellite?"

Outside, the sky had turned the color of oatmeal. I wondered if it was going to snow—it seemed like it should snow in Poland in winter. Maybelle had put on an ankle-length purple parka with a fake-fur collar that made her look like she was wearing a sleeping bag, and I felt self-conscious stepping out into the street with her, especially as we were instantly besieged by a gaggle of men in sheepskin jackets who all offered to change money, and with whom Maybelle naturally felt obligated to flirt.

"No thank you," I snapped, and dragged her off. Since our mysterious caller had specified six o'clock, it didn't seem worth showing up at the Opera before then, and so we had the whole afternoon before us. We had decided to head for the Old Town, which had apparently been rebuilt after the Germans destroyed it. Our hotel stood at the corner of two boulevards. Following the receptionist's directions, we turned right on the one called Marszałkowska, which was described in the pamphlet as a main shopping street. On the other side of the boulevard was the Palace of Culture, the octopus-like concrete building Roger McCormick had called Stalin's present to the Poles. It didn't benefit from being viewed at closer range, nor did the shop windows we walked by, which contained a curious and dismal combination of utilitarian objects: plastic buckets and packs of powdered soup, clothes no one would want to wear, and shoes so hopelessly unfashionable, it wasn't surprising they seemed to have sat there for years.

Maybelle certainly wasn't impressed. "No wonder they want to get rid of those Communists," she remarked as she eyed a listless display of cosmetics. The few people we passed seemed no more eager than we to purchase these sad wares: Most of the stores were empty, with the exception of one establishment where a long line snaked out the door. As we tried to figure out what they were selling inside, a man emerged with several toilet-paper rolls slung from a string around his neck in the manner of a garland. Maybelle shook her head and muttered, "Pitiful . . ."

But once we had reached the Old Town, she perked up. My aunt had decided opinions about what constitutes European charm, and cobblestones and churches featured prominently among them. The drivers of the horse-drawn carriages that were parked in a circle on the Market Square must have seen us coming for miles, because as soon as we stepped onto its uneven pavement, we were surrounded by red-faced men in fur hats whose frosty breath hinted at the source of their good cheer. Amid a chorus of "*twenty dollars*" and "*change moneys*," blankets were proffered and seats invitingly patted, and, as Maybelle turned ominously coy and giggly, I braced myself for a madcap jaunt that I knew was more than likely to end with her embarrassing me. Before I could protest, we were bundled into the back of one of the cleaner-looking carriages, and with a jingle of bells, we clattered off, Maybelle whooping loudly, much to our driver's delight, when we lurched over a bump in the road.

As for me, although I would rather have died than confess to it, I was having fun for the first time in days. As we trotted through the empty streets, I sat back and closed my eyes, the better to succumb to the bliss of not caring. Our driver was called something unpronounceable that sounded like Shemik, and, having imparted the information that he used to drive a taxi in Chicago, undertook to show us the city, interspersing his descriptions of various landmarks with tirades against the government that Maybelle seemed to find enormously entertaining, and that I was sure were just the kind of thing that had gotten Łukasz thrown in jail. Since I had been trying very hard not to think about Łukasz for the past week, the intrusion was most unwelcome, and I focused my gaze on the spidery treetops overhead with the firm intention of banishing it. But rocked by the carriage's swaying motion and the hypnotic *clip-clop* of the horse's hooves on the pavement, I found myself returning, at first cautiously, and then with a sort of ghastly fascination, to the one subject I had so far not allowed myself to entertain: What was it about Łukasz that had made Astrid commit this folly?

Gingerly, I tried sophistication: People took lovers all the time. It was, in Paris, the frequent and amusing subject of dinner party conversations, something to be laughed about and even admired, the men in particular always coming off as rather dashing, unless they were cuckolded, a comical condition that every French schoolchild understood from Molière. In our home, Grace's hapless lovers were an endless source of entertainment, though it suddenly occurred to me, in the unbidden way of uncomfortable thoughts, that it had been Astrid more than Frank who had laughed at them. Besides, even I understood that what made Grace's lovers comical was that she took them for the wrong reason: to get back at her husband for not loving her.

Frank's love for Astrid, however, was the stuff of legend, the very fabric upon which our family reposed. We all knew the stories by heart: the time he sat on her hat; the time she went back to Kentucky for a week and he followed her after three days because he couldn't bear to be without her; the time Astrid found a kitten on the street and brought it home, and Frank had to take triple doses of antihistamines in secret because he didn't have the heart to tell her that he was deathly allergic to cats. No, the idea of my father not loving my mother was too laughable to be contemplated, which left only the other possibility: that it was Astrid who had fallen out of love with him.

In the abstracted state I found myself in, I actually felt able to contemplate this awful thought. There were women in Paris who had affairs for sport, but Astrid wasn't one of them. My mother was too romantic for the tawdry theater of casual infidelity. Only the most extraordinary of circumstances could have jolted her out of what I knew, or thought I knew, she regarded as a sacred vow, and, except for being a dissident, there hadn't been anything extraordinary about Łukasz. Feeling like a traitor, I placed him mentally by my father's side: Frank was not only better-looking and infinitely more distinguished both in manner and dress, he was—fat tears welled up in my eyes—he was my father, her husband. How *dare* she! Angrily, I wiped at my face with my sleeve, trying to quell the helpless rage that ripped through me. But no one was paying attention. Our carriage had just come to a halt and Maybelle let out a squeal of delight. At some point we had entered a park with wide, tree-bordered alleys. A wintry fog had risen, and as it wove its way through the treetops, the city around us seemed to dissolve into the mist. The carriage stood before a lake, and the source of Maybelle's delighted cry was visible ahead: In the middle of the lake, a small palace seemed to float on the water, its slender colonnades rising like ghosts from the frozen surface.

"It's like something out of a fairy tale," Maybelle sighed, and even I, in my misery, had to recognize that it was lovely, all the more so perhaps for being so unexpected in this ugly city. Maybelle had put on a preposterously silly pair of white earmuffs that made her look like she was twelve years old, and with her cheeks pink from the cold and her bright, blue eyes, she almost looked pretty. The driver certainly seemed to think so. He leaped down from his perch and offered her his hand and, giggling, she descended from the carriage, observing to me, "Boy, am I glad I brought this coat!"

I stayed behind. From under the blankets, I watched them make their way toward the edge of the water, the driver guiding Maybelle with exaggerated caution over the frozen ground. Daylight was already fading, and as they advanced through the mist, they could, though Maybelle stood a head taller, have been mistaken for a pair of Wagnerian lovers, an impression that was instantly dispelled when she slipped on a patch of ice and, hooting with laughter, was prevented from crashing to the ground only by the swift intervention of her escort. I was beginning to feel the cold. Maybelle had said something about a nice lunch, and all of a sudden, my stomach began to growl, as it always did when I felt wretched, unwilling, clearly, to bow to the dictates of my heart. When they finally returned, I reminded Maybelle that it was nearly three o'clock. She stretched her lips into a seductive smile and said, "Shemik, honey, the girls are getting hungry, and I'll bet you could use a hot meal yourself. . . ."

The driver responded by grabbing the reins and calling back to us, as we set off again, "I take you to wonderful place! Typical Polish!"

"See," Maybelle said comfortably to me, "you should always ask the locals," and before I could respond, we were off again.

The restaurant Shemik took us to, on a side street back in the Old Town, was located in a cellar that he said dated back to the fifteenth century. Boars' heads lowered over the long oak tables, and the waitresses wore folkloric costumes with beaded bibs and red orthopedic shoes. It was the kind of place that Astrid would have pronounced dreadful, and that Maybelle adored, and she insisted on ordering champagne, though I had a feeling Shemik would have preferred one of the big tankards of beer that he informed us twice were a specialty of the house. Maybelle was in such high spirits that she forgot her rule about underage drinking and offered me a glass. We had a gigantic meal during which Shemik, whose real name, as it turned out, was Przemek, short for Przemysław, told many funny stories about his adventures driving a taxi in Chicago, Maybelle, in truth, finding them a lot funnier than I did. I felt better for having eaten, but I kept glancing at my watch, worried that we would miss our rendezvous. Maybelle, however, seemed in no hurry to leave. After a dessert of cheesecake, we lingered over coffee and liqueurs, she and Przemek now engaged in a passionate discussion about whether Jimmy Carter had the backbone to stand up to the Russians. Maybelle's animation was baffling since I had never known her to take an interest in politics. As I sat and listened, boredom turned to anxiety: If Maybelle thought the hotel staff were KGB agents, what about the waiters in this cheesy tourist trap?

Przemek called for the bill, which he insisted on paying. He had refused to accept money for the ride, either, but Maybelle seemed not the least bit bothered by a largesse that struck me as problematic. The champagne and liqueur had clearly gone to her head, and when Przemek offered to drive us back to the hotel, I was afraid she would accept. I tugged hard at her sleeve. It was five thirty, and though the Opera hadn't seemed far on the map, we would have to find our way there. Finally, Maybelle came to her senses. She told Przemek firmly that we would walk, as we needed fresh air and had "girl stuff" to discuss. Reluctantly, he desisted, but only after she agreed to meet him the next day.

We hurried through dark streets, Maybelle glancing frequently and dramatically over her shoulder. By then I felt that the whole day had been one big betrayal of Astrid, and I was impatient to meet our mysterious caller and resume our mission. The Opera was located, as so many official buildings in Warsaw, in the middle of a vast, empty plaza with an ugly statue in the middle. As we traversed the plaza, I was beset by the conviction that it was all a cruel joke, or worse, a trap. All of a sudden I wanted desperately to turn back, but by then we were standing in front of the theater. Marble steps led up to the entrance, and we had just begun to ascend when a woman brushed past me on her way down and, without a word, thrust a piece of paper in my hand. I closed my fist around it and stuck my hand in my pocket.

I didn't say anything to Maybelle. We entered the theater lobby and made for the box office where, having given my name, we were handed an envelope marked "Charlotte Sanders." Inside the envelope were two tickets to *Don Giovanni*, one of Frank's favorite operas. Maybelle gazed at them bemusedly, and checked the envelope again.

"Come on," I said, indicating the exit. "It doesn't start till seven." Maybelle looked at me as if I were mad, but I wasn't about to tell her about the slip of paper in the middle of the lobby, where her coat and earmuffs were already attracting enough attention. On the way in, we had passed a taxi stand, and the back of a cab seemed safer than the street. "Just follow me," I muttered. "I'll explain."

We found a taxi immediately. Once we were inside, I pulled out the piece of paper. An address was written on it.

"Would you mind telling me what's going on?" Maybelle hissed. I handed her the note and she studied it. "Where did you get this?" she whispered.

I explained about the woman on the steps, and she looked impressed. "*Well*," she said, "I guess we're not going to the opera," and we spoke no more until we were back at the hotel, where we were informed at Reception that Lea had called three times.

27

WHEN WE WERE SAFELY BACK in our room, Maybelle put her finger to her lips and went over to the desk. She scribbled something on a piece of hotel stationery and handed it to me. *The room is probably bugged. I think we should go to that address.*

I nodded in agreement and, feeling rather foolish, wrote back that I wanted to try calling Lea first. When the receptionist put me through though, the phone rang and rang. I thought of trying Grace, but Maybelle was getting impatient.

"You can try again later," she hissed. I put down the receiver and grabbed my coat.

I handed the taxi driver the address and we set off into the night. I was getting used to the sensation of having no idea where we were going. We drove down the boulevard in front of the hotel, and pretty soon we had left the center, its big ugly buildings making way for smaller ugly buildings, the rumbling trams growing less frequent as we reached what looked like the outskirts of town. When it started to look as if we were leaving the city altogether, I became alarmed. The longer we drove, the fewer lights I saw out the window, until it seemed that we were driving through black fields. After a while, lights began to reappear, first sparsely and then in denser concentration, as thickets of high rises materialized like some fantastical city in the middle of a plain. I was reminded of the housing projects that stretched for miles outside Paris, and was comforted by the thought that, all around us, people were doing the things people do everywhere in the evening: eating dinner and watching TV, and nagging their children to do their homework.

At length, we left the road and entered a vast complex of tall buildings, stopping finally before one that stood at the far edge. Maybelle handed the driver the twenty dollars he requested, and he motioned that he would wait for us. I realized at that moment that, having no idea where we were going, I hadn't thought of how we would get back, and the same must have occurred to Maybelle because she nodded in agreement. We got out and stood at the entrance of the building. There was a bank of buzzers to the right of the door, and an intercom, and after some hesitation, I pressed number seventeen. A long silence ensued. I was beginning to think that we had the wrong address when the intercom crackled and a voice said, in English, "Yes?"

I gave my name and the door clicked open. Inside, a naked bulb illuminated a dingy lobby lined on both sides with banged-up metal mailboxes. At the end was an elevator. We headed toward it and I pressed the button, but when we opened the door, the narrow cubicle inside remained dark. Maybelle and I glanced apprehensively at each other. "She didn't say what floor," Maybelle finally said and, to my relief, led the way toward the stairs.

The stairwell was as cold and barren as the entrance, and smelled of something I couldn't pin down, but that Maybelle identified as boiled cabbage. The apartments were tightly packed along narrow hallways, and we found number seventeen on the third floor. Before we could ring the bell, the door was opened, by a woman in jeans and a blue turtleneck who had the anxious look of one who has been waiting.

"Come in," she said simply, stepping aside to let us pass, and then, to me, as we stood uncertainly in the foyer, "You must be Charlotte. My name is Ania."

I extended my hand, and though she looked a little surprised, she shook it. Then I introduced Maybelle.

Ania led us into a small, neat living room lined with books and records. It reminded me of Patrice's apartment. I felt a pang as I remembered that I hadn't tried to call him again.

"Please sit down," she said, motioning to a table in the corner. "Would you like some tea?"

We said we would and she went into an adjoining room, from where we heard the sound of water running. Maybelle and I sat in silence. My eyes roamed along the spines of the records lined up along a low shelf next to a stereo. Most of them were jazz, but there was some classical music as well, and several Beatles albums, including Sgt. Pepper's Lonely Hearts Club Band, Astrid's favorite. Frank hated rock, and used to retreat to his study when she played it.

Ania returned with a tray and three mugs, which she set on the table before us. She wore no makeup and, with her wire-rimmed glasses and straight, shoulder-length blond hair, looked both youthful and weary, though I guessed her to be around forty. She had a round face, and deep-set eyes, the skin around them webbed with fine wrinkles. She offered us sugar and then sat down herself, taking from her pocket a pack of unfamiliar-looking cigarettes that she held out to Maybelle.

"I hope you don't mind if I smoke," she said when Maybelle shook her head, pulling one out and lighting it with a thoughtful expression. It smelled very strong, like a Gauloise or a Gitane, but harsher, and I wished suddenly that I had thought to bring Astrid cigarettes, because she hated black tobacco.

"Your English is amazingly good," Maybelle said. With a brief smile, Ania replied that she had studied in London. Then we all sat looking at each other, until Ania said, "You must wonder why I asked you to come."

We both nodded, and again a silence fell. It was broken by Maybelle, who blurted out, "Excuse me, but who are you?"

Ania smiled again in the same way, as if she couldn't quite pull it off. "I am Łukasz Baran's wife."

I used to wonder what people meant when they said someone's

jaw dropped, until Maybelle's actually did. She gazed blankly at
Ania until, realizing perhaps that her mouth was open, she shut it
and made a sound like "oh." I remained frozen in the same polite
expression that I had been taught to assume around adults. Ania
crushed out her cigarette.

"I'm sorry, it's actually quite irrelevant."

"I wouldn't say so!" Maybelle exclaimed.

Ania observed her dryly. "Well, let us say, then, that it is not in
that capacity that I summoned you here."

"Then why did you?" Maybelle asked suspiciously. I could tell
that she was having trouble getting a grip on the situation, and, until
she could figure it out, was going to take refuge in being defensive.

Ania, however, seemed unperturbed, her cool tone at odds with
her words. "There are larger issues at stake. Because of your sister's
impulsive behavior, three people are now in jail, and a vital commu-
nications network has been severed."

I gazed at her in horror. Didn't she understand that my mother
had been trying to help?

"It will take months to repair the damage," Ania continued, evidently not noticing, or not wanting to see my distress. "Valuable
time that ought to have been spent on other, more important objec-
tives. You are perhaps not aware of this, but Poland is on the verge
of a revolution."

"Could've fooled me," Maybelle muttered.

Again the dry smile. "To you perhaps it does not seem like much,
but to us, it is everything."

I could tell that Maybelle was ashamed because she dropped her
eyes. Shame rose in me, too, hot and ugly. My eyes flew to the wall
opposite, where they fell upon one of those corny pictures of huge-
eyed waifs that are sold in every souvenir shop in Paris. The girl wore
a beret and had a red scarf around her neck, and the Eiffel Tower
loomed like some hokey prop in the distance. Had Łukasz brought
it back from one of his trips to Paris? I felt nauseous.

"She brought you money!" I cried.

"We did not ask for it. She led the police to one of our main presses. A vital operation has been jeopardized. Innocent people have suffered."

"Why are you telling us this?" Maybelle said.

Ania lit another of her foul-smelling cigarettes. "Because we are afraid that she will try to remain in the country. We are asking you to take her home with you when she is released."

"And what makes you so sure she will be?"

Ania made a wry grimace. "They always let the foreigners go."

"Well, I'm sure glad to hear that, I'm sure glad you're so confident. You see, in our country, people don't get thrown in jail for no reason, so we don't have a whole lot of experience dealing with this kind of thing."

I stared at Maybelle, aghast. Couldn't she see that she was only making things worse?

Ania, though, just sounded tired. "Your sister was arrested through her own foolish actions. The stakes, however, have become too high: Things that I am not at liberty to discuss are happening; the future of our country lies in the balance. We cannot have an entire movement jeopardized by the caprices of a bored society woman."

My eyes had grown so huge, I thought they might pop out of my head. Ania must have noticed, because she turned to me, and I thought I discerned pity in her calm blue gaze. "I am sorry," she said. "I should not have said that. Please, it is imperative that you take your mother home."

Maybelle rose abruptly. "I think we understand. Come on, Charlotte." And she scooped up both our coats from the couch.

"Let me call you a taxi," Ania said.

"We've got one waiting."

As Maybelle hustled me out, I glanced back helplessly at Ania, who had remained standing by the table. She looked sad and dignified, and in that terrible moment, I wished that I were dead. But Maybelle was beside herself. She tore down the stairs so fast that I had a hard time keeping up with her, and once we were outside, she practically shoved me into the taxi.

"*It's not as his wife that I summoned you!*" she mimicked, her rendering of Ania's accent not exactly successful.

"Stop it!" I pleaded.

"Not till I'm done. Let me tell you something about big ideas: They're real convenient to hide behind, especially when your husband's dumped you for a better-looking woman."

"No, Maybelle—"

"I know that half-wit sister of mine is no angel, but I'll tell you one thing: She's no home wrecker, either. She didn't know he was married."

"What's the difference?" I said numbly, my eyes fixed on the black window.

"You're too young to be world-wise, Miss. I've been around longer than you, and I can tell you there's plenty."

But I didn't care anymore. I just wanted to go back to the hotel and hide. I hated Maybelle. I hated my mother. I hated Łukasz. I even hated Lea, for abandoning me, but most of all I hated Ania, because I knew that she was right, and I hated myself, for knowing it.

28

WHEN WE GOT BACK to our room, the phone was ringing. I ran to pick it up. It was a bad connection and, at the other end of the line, Lea's voice sounded hollow and disembodied.

"Where have you been?!"

I started to tell her, but she cut me off. "Dad's gone."

"What?"

"Dad's gone. The apartment's empty. He left a letter."

I opened my mouth to speak, but nothing came out. Finally, I croaked, "Where are you?"

"I'm staying with Nahid." Lea's voice sounded robotic. I tried to picture our apartment empty: the pictures, the lamps and statues and vases and variegated objects that made shadows on the walls, the voluptuous drapes, the velvet couch that received you with a sigh; all gone. The image wouldn't coalesce. Stubbornly, my mind's eye clung to the trappings of our life.

"Are you still there?"

"Yes," I whispered. Maybelle had come out of the bathroom now, and was shooting me questioning glances.

"The letter says that we have to choose, him or Mom. He's seen a solicitor about a divorce. He's rented a new apartment, in the Eighth."

"Oh," I said. Frank had always wanted to live in the Eighth. It was Astrid, obsessed with Paris's bohemian ghosts, who had insisted on Saint-Germain.

"He says that, whatever we decide, he'll respect it."

At the other end of the room, Maybelle was gesticulating, her eyebrows dancing up and down. I fixed my eyes on the wall.

"I've made my choice. I'm going over there tomorrow."

"I understand," I said.

"Good, because you should do the same. Charlotte, are you listening to me? You need to come home now. Maybelle can stay there."

The hardest decisions are always the easiest to make. I only hesitated for a moment, and even that was just for form.

"I'm staying with Mom," I said.

"Don't be a fool, Charlotte."

"It's what I want."

"What about exams? If you don't come back to school soon, you'll have to repeat the year."

"I don't care."

Lea made a strangled sound. Her voice turned frantic, and I realized that she was crying. "I've never seen him like this. He's going to completely cut her off."

"That's why I'm staying," I said. "It's all right."

"Please, Charlotte."

It was Lea begging that was unbearable. I was afraid I would start crying, too, and I didn't want to in front of Maybelle.

"I have to go," I said, and then, idiotically, "Everything's going to be all right."

When I hung up, Maybelle was instantly upon me. I related the bare bones of what Lea had said. I didn't tell her that Frank was making us choose. She sat heavily on the bed.

"I always warned her," she said.

I went into the bathroom and splashed cold water on my face. Then I studied myself in the mirror, surprised to find a child staring back. I read in her huge eyes the terror that I fought to repress. What was to become of me? Outside, the phone rang again. When I came back out, Maybelle was putting down the receiver.

"That was Shemik. He wants to take us to see a palace tomorrow. I said yes."

I must have looked at her as if she were mad because she blushed and averted my gaze. "It's Sunday. They're not gonna let us see her anyway."

"You go," I said coldly.

She met my eyes. "I'm not going to let her ruin my life."

"Nobody asked you to."

"I'm putting you on a plane to your father. What he's doing is for show, you have to understand that. He's drawing the line, something he should've done a long time ago."

I ignored the cheap stab. "I'm staying right here."

Her expression softened. "She would want you to go back to Paris," she said, and I felt a surge of disgust, because Maybelle knew perfectly well that that wasn't true. Hadn't Astrid given us ample proof of her selfishness?

"You run off with your boyfriend," I said, my tone icy. "I can take care of myself."

But now she just looked sad. "One day you'll understand."

"No I won't," I said, though I knew I was being unfair, but it was easier to blame Maybelle for poor taste than my mother for something far worse.

When Maybelle came back from visiting the palace the next day, I knew she had fallen in love. Maybelle fell in love at the drop of a hat, usually with unsuitable men who didn't return her feelings, and, more often than not, took advantage of her. Astrid said it was because her heart was too big, but I knew the truth: She was just too dumb to know better. While she was off with Przemek, I had finally managed to get through to Patrice. He had been strange and distant, responding in monosyllables. Because I was worried about the phone call being expensive—Maybelle had remarked at some point on the outrageous price the hotel charged for international calls—I had tried to be as brief as possible. I don't remember anymore what

I said, some half-baked story about my mother being in trouble, and needing me. He said I'd told him I was going to London. I know, I said, I would explain. I would make it up to him about his birthday. I would explain when I got back. He asked when that would be, but he didn't seem all that interested, and when I told him in a few days, he just said okay. Before I could repeat that I would explain, he said that he was late for the movies.

"You should have come, honey, it was lovely, so elegant," Maybelle was babbling as she removed her ludicrous coat. "Just lahk one of those French shah-toes. . . . Then we went to the most charming little restaurant—" The peal of the phone interrupted her. I picked it up, not even caring who it was.

"They're letting her go," Roger McCormick said. "Tomorrow morning at seven. She's got twenty-four hours to leave the country. I'm counting on you to make sure that she does."

I didn't say anything. I felt completely empty.

"Did you hear me?" Roger McCormick snapped.

"Thank you," I said. "We'll be there."

29

FOR SOMEONE WHO HAD CAUSED so much grief and trouble, Astrid, when we picked her up from the police station, looked remarkably serene. The same couldn't be said for Maybelle, who carried on as if her sister had just been released from one of Solzhenitsyn's gulags, clutching her and sobbing and generally making a spectacle of herself. I hung back, not wanting to give her jailers the satisfaction of my relief. As Maybelle clung to her, Astrid shot me a secret look over her head, and I returned it, conscious of the man in the leather jacket's smug gaze. I didn't hate him. He had, after all, taught me a valuable lesson, that you are only as weak as you show. As we all played our part in the charade of my mother's release, one whose rules I instinctively sensed, I was conscious, for the first time in my life, of being the mistress of my own fate. It was an exhilarating sensation, one of those pure moments where you don't care what's come before or what's next. Astrid was made to sign a form in triplicate, presumably a promise to leave the country, and then we piled into the embassy car with Roger McCormick, who acted as if he had engineered the whole thing. Having delivered a stern lecture on the imperative of our making the evening flight, he told us that he would pick us up at six, and I could have sworn that I discerned a sarcastic smile on Astrid's face.

At the hotel, Astrid said all she wanted was a bath. There was a store in the lobby that sold Western cosmetics for dollars. They stocked none of my mother's favorite brands, but I had bought whatever looked most luxurious, including a bottle of Yardley's lavender-scented bubble bath and a big pot of Pond's cold cream. None of us really said anything. In the back of the car, I had finally allowed myself to touch her and now that I was reassured of her presence, I no longer felt the need for words. Even Maybelle was quiet, though her expression suggested that she had merely put herself on hold. I was right to worry: Astrid hadn't been in the bath a half hour before Maybelle, under pretext of needing to floss her teeth, bustled into the bathroom and closed the door. At first only a low buzz of conversation came through, but the walls were thin, and though I couldn't hear Astrid's responses, Maybelle's rising voice soon transcended the flimsy barrier.

"Do you realize that everything's in his name! You don't even own your home!"

I felt sick. Had she not earned the right to a few hours of respite? I knew I would have to tell her eventually about the apartment, and the rest, but it could wait until we got to Paris. I wanted to tear into the bathroom and scream at Maybelle to shut up, but I was beginning to feel again as if I were lying under snow. Through the door, I heard water sloshing, then Astrid's weary voice.

"Leave me alone, Maybelle."

"It's not just about you! You have your daughters to consider!"

"Leave me alone."

Maybelle came storming out. She looked like she would have slammed the door if she hadn't caught sight of me. "Oh, honey, I'm sorry," she murmured. She was wearing a perfectly ridiculous outfit: a flowered blouse in screaming colors with a hideous brooch in the shape of a parrot pinned to it, and the stretchy polyester pants that she called "slacks," though there was nothing slack about them as they strained across her big butt. For a second, I entertained the thought of telling her that she looked grotesque, that everyone knew fat women shouldn't wear big prints, but again the phone rang. Maybelle dove for it. She couldn't even keep the dumb smile off her face.

"I can't talk right now, Shemmy. I'm gonna have to call you back.... No, I *promise* I'll call you back, honey...."

"Lover boy?" I enquired with a smirk when she'd hung up. I might as well have stabbed her in the heart.

She gave me a long look, her eyes blurring with tears. "That's not like you, Charlotte."

I tried to smirk again, but it froze halfway, and I ended up dropping my eyes in shame. From the bathroom came the sound of the hair dryer that Astrid had asked me to get from housekeeping. In wounded silence, Maybelle made her way to the vanity, where she proceeded to powder her face. Then she painted her nails. She was fanning them out to dry when Astrid came out of the bathroom and, catching sight of her, asked, "Do mine?" She had put on the Guerlain lipstick I'd bought her, and mascara, and, though her face still looked drawn, her hair once again fell in soft waves to her shoulders.

"Sure," Maybelle said without looking up.

Astrid pulled over the other chair from the desk.

"Your cuticles are a mess," Maybelle observed, and she started to apply the polish.

30

M Y PARENTS' DIVORCE kept dinner parties from Saint-Germain to Neuilly humming for weeks. Possessing elements of both Balzac and Danielle Steele, it reached across cultural lines, the French deploring the sundering of our family and the Americans pondering its financial implications. The fact that Astrid had left Frank for a Polish dissident was viewed by one side as rather grand, and by the other as rather stupid. It was apparently well known, in the mysterious way that these things are, that the money was all on Frank's side. Maybelle had been right: Everything was in my father's name. His wealth was locked up in family trusts, which had been set up expressly to shield it from just this type of situation. The Paris apartment had been rented by Frank's law firm, and his New York place, the whole building, belonged to his mother. Astrid, of course, might have fought him—in fact was urged to do so by both Maybelle and Grace, but as she told me, almost apologetically, she didn't have it in her. "In order to fight, you have to believe," she said sadly, "and your father is in the right." We didn't talk about Lea, who refused to see Astrid. There was really nothing to say.

Not only was Frank in the right, Astrid was no one in Paris without him. She couldn't even get a *permis de séjour*, let alone working papers. Her identity was tied to Frank's and, from the point of view of the French bureaucracy, once unmoored from him, she ceased to exist. We moved in with Grace, who tried hard to be helpful, conjuring up one impossible scheme after another—perhaps Astrid could become an interior decorator, she had such an eye, or open a boutique—but you needed money to start a business, and Astrid's was running out. She tried all the people she knew, but without papers, no one would hire her, and anyway, in Paris, women like my mother didn't work. She still, however, had friends in New York, as did Grace, who was from there. Maybe, Grace suggested, it was time for a new start: Why stay in a city that could only be a source of painful memories? America was the land of second chances. Grace made more phone calls; a plan began to take shape. Astrid pulled me aside.

"I don't expect you to go with me. I want you to go to your father's."

"No."

"Baby, I don't even know where we'll live, not to mention what we'll live *on*. And you have to go back to school." I hadn't been for three weeks, though we were now in the middle of February break, and everyone had gone skiing. Still, once the new term began, a decision would have to be made. You couldn't legally not go to school; not in France, not anywhere.

"I'll go to school in New York," I said. Astrid wasn't the only one for whom Paris was full of painful reminders. Right after we got back, Lea had told me, with characteristic bluntness, that Patrice was going out with Delphine. It seemed to have happened overnight. That was the real reason I hadn't gone back; I couldn't bear to see him, though I saw him everywhere; in every tall, gangly boy on the metro, in every Ciné-Club line, in every nuzzling couple on the street. I, too, yearned for a fresh start. I had only been to New York twice, but there was something pure and intransigent about its skyline that reflected the new resolve in my heart: Like Scarlett vowing never to be hungry again, I would never again allow myself to be hurt.

Having made my decision, I could no longer put off seeing my father. Frank had written, asking me to come, and he said he would respect whatever decision I made, but that we had to regularize my situation. It seemed like a weirdly French thing to say. I hadn't gone,

because I was afraid I would cry, and because I had overheard Grace
telling Astrid that he would have to support me; there were laws,
even in the States. Even more unbearable than the prospect of
breaking down before him was that of his thinking that I had come
for money. Because money, something I had never thought about,
now came up all the time. Everything, it seemed, cost money,
including going to school, though Frank had made it clear that he
would go on paying my tuition at the École Colbert. In the end I
went, because it felt cowardly not to, and even worse than humiliation was the prospect of not seeing my father before I left.

Frank had moved to a street off the Avenue Montaigne, right
around the corner from his office, a neighborhood that Astrid had
always hated because it was full of rich Arabs and Americans. Maria
opened the door. When she saw me, she shook her head, as if to
bemoan the madness of this world. She had never made an effort to
be part of the family, and at that moment I appreciated her reticence.

The apartment, in a grand corner building in the Haussmann
style, was brighter and more spacious than our Saint-Germain
home, its wide hallways painted a pastel gray that Astrid would have
derided as *bo*ring. Frank's study looked the same, lined with his
leather-bound volumes, his desk set back at an angle so that the
chair faced the door. He was sitting in it when I came in, a pained
expression on his face. To my relief, he rose and came to me, meeting me halfway across an Aubusson carpet that I didn't recognize.
He held me and kissed the top of my head, and when he let go, his
eyes were moist behind his glasses.

"Your room is down the hall," he said. "Everything the way you
left it. You can still change your mind."

My throat felt like it was full of sawdust. "I can't, Dad."

"Have you really thought about this?"

"Yes," I whispered. We gazed at each other like trapped animals,
and at that moment I realized that, although my father had never
told me he loved me, I had always known that he did, with the calm

assurance of a plant in the sun. Now it would have to be said, by me, to mark a new beginning, but the words wouldn't reach my lips. I wanted, desperately needed for him to reach across the line that he had drawn, and so it was with dumb horror that I watched him retreat, his expression turning lawyerly even as I read the helplessness in his eyes. Suddenly I saw him as my mother must have: a mild man, a man of few words, a man of careful passions who had seduced her years ago by briefly assuming, as certain birds do for mating, the riotous plumage of a lover.

"I'm setting up an account for you in New York," he said. "Whatever happens to your mother, I don't want you to be penalized."

So he wouldn't name her. She would exist, from now on, only in relation to me.

"I've also arranged for an interview for you at Briarwood. Your grandmother went there. She'll be expecting a call when you arrive in New York."

He went to his desk and returned with an envelope, which he pressed into my hand. I knew there was money in it. "Let me know if you need more," he said, and I nodded, trying to look dignified. When he embraced me, to signal, I assumed, the end of our interview, I stiffened in his arms, but, having always been awkward in touching, I don't think he noticed.

Lea was lying in wait when I came out. The Aubusson carpet, she informed me, was the work of Frank's secretary, Inge the Swedish Sex Bomb, who had taken him in hand when it became known— and in the expatriate demimonde that we inhabited, such news traveled at the speed of light—that his wife had deserted him. "Wait till you see how she did up his bedroom," she sniggered as she led me down a corridor lined with botanical prints, one end of which was occupied by an extravagantly gilded console. "She told him he should get rid of all of Mom's stuff. Too painful, you know . . . ," and she opened the door to an elegantly proportioned room with molded ceilings and a gray marble fireplace, its sole furnishings a dresser and a vast bed that sat atop a pale pink-and-gray carpet.

It didn't reflect my father any more than my parents' bedroom in Saint-Germain had, and I wondered if, like a foreign visitor, he had spent his whole life in interiors arranged by others.

"Think he'll get lonely?" my sister sweetly enquired, and then, as she closed the door softly behind her, "Poor Dad, he'll be lucky if he gets out alive."

I tried to smile but I couldn't. I knew that Lea was doing what came naturally to her: making the best of things. The breakup of our family had already taken its place in her bestiary of human folly, a lamentable breach of decorum that, as most disasters, would in time reveal its humorous side. All I could see, though, was Lea's monumental callousness, and it appalled me.

"I'm supposed to show you your room," she said.

I didn't want to see my room. I was afraid it would look like a museum, or the room of a dead child, in which everything has been left intact. We went to Lea's instead. It looked the same as it had in our old apartment, the walls decorated with horse posters and ribbons, a depression on the bed where she had been lying, reading *Les Malheurs de Sophie*. Lea always retreated in times of unrest to the untroubled world of the Comtesse de Ségur. There was a picture of her and Serge on the dresser—a marker, no doubt, of a new stage in their relationship—and, surrounded by the seamlessly transposed accoutrements of my sister's life, I saw her as if for the first time, in all her obtuse grace, her eyes resolutely fixed on a horizon that was perfectly clear to her, and that would only reveal itself to me swathed in shadows. We sat on the floor with our backs against the box spring, our legs touching.

"What now?" Lea said.

"We're leaving Monday. Mom booked the tickets."

Lea leaned her head back against the mattress. "Lucky you: New York!"

I gazed at her in bewilderment. "Do you really think I'm lucky, Lea?" I asked. She averted her eyes and picked at an invisible thread on her sweater.

"Because I don't think I'm lucky at all," I continued flatly, "and neither are you, whatever you may pretend to believe. And I think it's odious of you to refuse to see Mom."

"I can't."

"I see. You're just going to go on with your life and pretend nothing happened. I think you're either insane, or completely devoid of normal human feeling." I knew this wasn't true, or at least I hoped so, but in the new world I inhabited, nothing could be taken for granted.

Lea looked at me now. "You were always their favorite, you know," she said.

"Stop it, Lea—"

"No, it's true. You always needed them more. If the choice had been up to Dad, he would've kept you."

"It's not true, Lea. You're the perfect one."

"That's exactly why. Do you know why I like Serge? It's because he expects people to be like me. His whole family's like that. In a way I feel more at home with them than with you."

"Is that why you're staying?" I said, because I didn't feel up to addressing the other part.

"Partly. I spend more time with them than here. Inge's always popping in, and I can't bear her, and Dad has gone completely weird. He spends most of his time shut up in his study listening to opera."

"He always did that."

"No, it's different. I hardly ever see him, and when I do, he doesn't seem to notice I'm there. Anyway, I'm staying. This is my home; I don't want to go to the States. You've always been more of an American; I'd feel like a fish out of water there. And I start university next year."

I thought she was right. I could see myself in America. It was a big place you could disappear in.

"Will you come visit?"

"Yes."

We sat in a silence that I knew Lea would be the one to break. She could only take so much of this stuff.

"D'you think they'll get married again?"

"People usually do," I said, though the idea was horrific.

"God, I hope Dad doesn't marry Inge."

"You'd have to call her Mom."

We both made a great show of finding this hilariously funny. It wasn't very convincing.

"I wish none of this had ever happened," Lea said.

In the end, she came to the airport, as I knew she would. We all cried hysterically, Grace the loudest, and people stared. It was the last time for many years that we all acted the way we felt.

31

ASTRID HAD WANTED TO LIVE in Greenwich Village, her old haunt, but it wasn't cheap and bohemian anymore, so we had to settle for Yorkville. When we went to look at the local high school, she burst into tears. I would never have admitted it, but the fortresslike building terrified me, too. There was a security guard at the entrance, and as we walked in, a group of black girls sized us up—not the chic African diplomats' daughters familiar to me from the École Colbert, but tough urban girls with knowing eyes. That was when I told Astrid about Briarwood, though I hadn't called Frank's mother, who I understood was instrumental to my getting in.

"Call her," Astrid said, her eyes hard. "I'm not putting you in a school for teenage mothers and drug addicts."

Briarwood was arranged, the price Sunday lunch in Greenwich. I took the train from Grand Central and was met at the station by a driver. The car was an old Volvo, and it wove its way through the winding lanes that led to Frank's childhood home, which, I now recalled from my two prior visits, was a white house with columns, like a Greek temple, that stood at the top of a hill. They didn't have houses like that in France, and at the time it had seemed exotically grand, like something out of *Gone With the Wind*. Now it just looked forbidding. My grandmother was waiting at the door when we drove up. She presented a talcum-scented cheek, and stepped back to inspect me.

"You look just like your mother," she said, her tone so dispassionate that I couldn't tell if it was an observation or a judgment. I remembered Astrid calling her cold and cheap, but my mother had always found formality suspect. I wondered suddenly if I would be expected to be disloyal. Would that be the price of the extended hand? But my grandmother only smiled, and said that I must be hungry, and that lunch was waiting in the dining room. As we crossed the vast living room, its windows looking out on Connecticut's preternaturally blue winter sky, I searched for signs of habitation; but the pale carpets that muffled our steps, the pristine chintz-covered sofas and armchairs seemed unacquainted with human traffic. Where were the marks and mess of life? The stacks of books and magazines, the wine stains, the half-eaten chocolate bar accidentally sat on? I shivered in my thin sweater, a reaction that I first attributed to nerves, until I realized I was just cold.

In the dining room, a maid served us Campbell's tomato soup in china dishes. I knew it was Campbell's tomato soup, because Maybelle used to bring cans over for Astrid, who had a secret fondness for it that I shared. With the soup came a basket of little plastic packets of oyster crackers, bearing the name, I noticed, of various establishments, such as Captain Sam's or The Chowder Hut. I could hear myself reporting to Astrid, that Grandma stole crackers from restaurants, though even as the thought formed in my mind, I quashed it, for I was here as a petitioner, not a critic. And so I dutifully responded to my grandmother's questions, about whether I shared Lea's passion for riding, and how I thought I would cope in an American school, a question that bemused me, since Lea had assured me that I would be way ahead in math and science. My grandmother, however, clearly regarded French education as inferior, if not downright frivolous, and expressed the view that it was probably for the best that I had come back to America, where I would at least get proper preparation for college.

As we concluded our meal, with a slice of pound cake and ice cream that I assumed had been provided for my benefit, since my grandmother barely touched hers, she assumed a stern expression and said, "Divorce is never pleasant, but you're a smart girl. I would advise you to regard this misfortune as an opportunity. Frankly, it has always been a disappointment to me that your father chose to bring you up in Europe, not that I was ever consulted on the matter. Sanders women have attended Briarwood for generations. I have spoken to the headmistress, and she has agreed to make an exception in your case: New students are normally only admitted in the fall. It goes without saying that I expect you to acquit yourself with distinction."

As she spoke, I was acutely aware of her pale blue eyes on me, the same color as Frank's and Lea's. Mine, like my mother's, were flecked with gold and changed with the weather. I searched them for signs, of sympathy, or regret, or even distaste, but they remained expressionless, and I understood at that moment that, although she was undoubtedly an honorable and upright woman, my grandmother's heart was unavailable. Try as I might, I simply could not imagine her as a mother, and a bleak sadness took hold of me as I realized that Frank might have felt the same.

When it was time for me to leave, I sensed that a display of gratitude was expected. I had no idea what form it should take, other than being quite sure that my grandmother would be dismayed if I threw my arms around her. In the end she offered her cheek again, and, having grazed it with my lips, I said, humbly, "Thank you, Grandma."

"You have nothing to thank me for, child. I only ask that you not disappoint me."

It seemed a small thing, and I promised that I wouldn't. It was only then that a crack appeared in the armor, though so briefly that I may well have imagined it. As she took me in one last time, an expression of faint bewilderment passed over her face, and I actually felt sorry for her, because while I had lost my father, she had lost her son, and I, the poor substitute presented in his place, was the living image of the woman who had led him astray.

When I got home, Astrid was unpacking a box. It was a task she had only attended to fitfully since we'd moved in, and there were still stacks of them in the narrow hallway. It seemed strange that there should be so many, when we'd come with nothing. Later I discovered that Lea had gone through the contents of our apartment, which Frank had put in storage, selecting things she thought we might want. They never did all get unpacked; they just sat in the hallway, and one day, they disappeared.

The carton Astrid was working on was full of clothes, and when I came in, she was holding up her Fortuny dress with a bemused expression, as if it were an archaeological artifact resurrected from Atlantis. When she saw me, she dropped it back in the box. We'd both become secretive, hoarding our thoughts. It seemed a necessary act of self-preservation.

"Well?" she said.

"It was all right. I have to go to the school tomorrow." I didn't say the other part, which was that I'd understood that Astrid was not to accompany me.

"Do you want some dinner?"

"No thanks, I had a big lunch." This was when, in our former existence, I would have made the joke about the oyster crackers, but we didn't joke around that way anymore. I often got the sense that we were both grappling for a form of communication that would suit our new circumstances.

"You should eat something," Astrid said, though I knew the fridge was empty. We'd been living on Chinese food that we picked at and then threw out. We didn't know about leftovers. We didn't know about cleaning the toilet, or sponging down the tub after a bath. We would learn eventually, but at that time, it had a scummy ring that we ignored by taking showers instead. When the electricity bill came, Astrid looked at it with perplexity, and then never paid it. I found it three weeks later on her dresser, under a pile of other bills, and from then on, I started opening the mail myself.

32

IT WAS A GOOD THING we had Frank's account to fall back on, even if I had to dissemble about it. Thankfully, Astrid was so used to having money that she never questioned the appearance of three hundred dollars in her underwear drawer, or in the jar by the coffee machine. I had never had any idea how much life cost, especially the kind of life we had led, with fine restaurants and ski vacations, summers in Cap Ferrat and winters at Val d'Isère. Patrice had been the first person I had known who wasn't rich, and like ours now, his poverty had been relative, attenuated by a monthly remittance by his father. Still, we couldn't eat out every night, and Astrid had to find work, a prospect that didn't daunt her because, as she reminded me, she wasn't born with a silver spoon in her mouth. *Right*, I thought, *that's why you don't know about paying the electric bill.* This, too, joined the ranks of my secrets, that her cluelessness dismayed me.

The old friends who had promised help rapidly vanished. Some of them had husbands who found Astrid a bit too attractive, and others had made the offer in haste. My mother hadn't lived in New York for ages: Things had changed, people had hardened. In the end it was Grace, once again, who came through. Through a connection in Paris, she found Astrid a job as a personal shopper at Bergdorf Goodman, where my mother's sense of style, and the European lilt her voice had acquired during her years abroad, were deemed alluring enough to give her a chance. I worried that it wouldn't last, but I had underestimated her. Having a job focused her, the same way school did with me. She began to acquire confidence, and came home with stories about impossible clients whom I unkindly thought she might have once resembled. Still, we never had quite enough money, and I found myself in the curious position of being one of the few poor girls at Briarwood.

Briarwood bore some resemblance to my old school in Paris: It was private and expensive, and full of wealthy girls who didn't worry about things. But the shadow of its Protestant founders loomed large: Unlike the indolent denizens of the École Colbert, Briarwood girls approached their studies with the same competitive zeal that they brought to sports, an area in which I was conspicuously inept. Lea, for all her assertions to the contrary, would have been right at home among the Upper East Side princesses who made up the majority of my classmates, and it seemed yet another of life's many ironies that it was I who had washed up on these gilded shores. I could have sought refuge among the rebels, but even they had an assurance I lacked, their punk-inspired look a conscious mockery of the Park Avenue aesthetic. I became an oddball instead, my nose constantly in a book, beloved by teachers and vaguely mistrusted by my peers, who concluded that I was angling for an early spot at Yale. The absence of boys made it easier. If friends and lovers could both betray you, it was best to remain alone. I turned to novels for company, finding solace in George Eliot's astringent wit, and in Jane Austen's brisk ironies.

Things improved between me and Astrid. I learned to do housework; it really wasn't that hard to wipe a sink, and as our surroundings became less chaotic, we relaxed into a sort of ersatz closeness. We started to chat again: about Astrid's job and the girls at my school, and Grace's news bulletins from Paris, carefully purged of all reference to Frank, and delivered weekly by phone. Her husband had a new mistress—not in itself a matter for concern, except that this one was unmarried, and of childbearing age, and Grace was beginning to think that he might actually leave her. Lea called weekly, too, and Astrid always concluded with a breezy "I love you," though their exchanges were brief. I would then take the phone into my room, and assure her that we were really getting along fine, that

I was making friends (a lie), and that she would love New York, where she promised to come for at least part of the summer. Lea was preparing for the *bac*. She was still going out with Serge and spent most of her free time with him at the riding club. Delphine and Patrice had broken up, and Delphine asked about me all the time. Since I never heard from her, I assumed she had the decency to be ashamed. Inge the Swedish Sex Bomb still found various and sundry reasons to stop by, but Lea was hardly ever home, and anyway, one could only be embarrassed for her. Frank's desk was littered with cocktail party invitations, not that he ever went, and he was bound to be snapped up sooner or later by some divorcée. I laughed dutifully. I had received a few letters from my father by then, and they were anodyne and terse, though he always ended by expressing the hope that I would come to Paris on one of my vacations. He didn't call it home anymore.

Maybelle called, too, and promised to visit soon. To me she confided that she and Przemek had kept in touch, and that he might come to the States. I didn't think she had told Astrid. We'd both discovered that my mother could be biting, and Maybelle probably didn't want to expose herself to ridicule. The only person who didn't call was Łukasz. I assumed Astrid had written to him, but this, in our newly selective intimacy, was an off-limit topic. All the same, I knew she was waiting, because every time the phone rang, she picked it up a little too eagerly. I had given up hoping that she might ever explain what had happened between them. Though she was scrupulously affectionate, and as attentive as she could be now that she worked long hours, my mother had closed off a part of herself. I began to understand that she had always had a secret life, that under her seeming artlessness lay a discretion that precluded soul-baring. As far as I was concerned, it was just as well. I didn't want to bare my soul, either, and so we became more like roommates, considerate of each other but fundamentally distant.

And then, that June, Lea came. She flew over with Grace, and within days, the precarious balance of our household was shattered.

33

I HADN'T REALIZED how much I had missed Lea. We had been close without knowing we were, but I had lost the habit of our intimacy and I circled her warily at first, like a cat sniffing for familiar scents. From the moment my sister arrived, though, it was clear that she had put the past behind her. This didn't trouble me, since it was exactly what I'd expected. What did trouble, and wound me, was Astrid's willingness to play along. Before my bewildered eyes, she and Lea slipped right back into their old bantering rapport, which had always had the ease of a certain superficiality. I looked on in helpless envy as my mother smiled when Lea related an idiotic anecdote involving Candy de Bethune and her tennis instructor, or reported with malicious glee that Chiara Grzebine had appeared naked in one of her father's movies.

Astrid and I had lived for the past few months in a fragile symbiosis that relied more on instinct than conversation, and that she and Lea could slip right in to their former selves felt like an assault. Could she really be that cheaply bought, I wondered bitterly, or had I, the loyal daughter, been tarnished by the very virtues that had once ennobled me? I was mulling miserably over what was beginning to appear like outright treason when, Lea and I having retreated to my room for the night, she exclaimed, "You live like paupers!"

I was stunned by the fury that rose within me. It was true that our apartment was small—there was only one bedroom, which Astrid had insisted I take, screening off for herself an alcove in the living room—and that it lacked the luxurious appointments of our

Paris home, but that had nothing to do with money. Our mother could have re-created Marie Antoinette's boudoir out of thrift shop finds and fabric ends, but the impulse to decorate had left her, and the asceticism of our interior seemed like an unspoken understanding between us. I could, and would have slapped Lea across her blank, perfect face, had her eyes not suddenly filled with tears.

"Oh, Charlotte, I've missed you so," she blurted out, and as I allowed her to reach for me, my anger shifted to a numb awe. It seemed impossible at that moment that we could be related. My sister towered over me like a Greek goddess, blithely sure of her powers: essentially benevolent, but mindful of her place in the natural order of things. And my place was equally clear: I would have to dwell in shadows so that she could remain in the light.

The balance restored, Lea soon recovered. She was eager to fill me in on the latest in Paris, where life had resumed its course, with some minor alterations. Inge was trying hard to make herself indispensable: dropping off Frank's shirts at the laundry, finding fault with Maria's cooking, and supervising the renovation of the *mahster bahth*room. Frank bore it all with distracted resignation, not particularly noticing her, but not minding her presence, either. One almost felt sorry for the poor girl. Anyway, Lea was never home. The Lubomirskis seemed to have practically adopted her, and life was a lot more exciting at their place than at the gloomy apartment on Rue du Boccador. Things were heating up in Poland, and Serge's father had assumed a discreet advisory role in the reinvigorated uprising, traveling frequently between Warsaw and Rome and the Vatican, where he was apparently quite chummy with the pope. I couldn't see what the pope had to do with any of this, but Lea, regarding me as if I were slightly dim, said that he was dying to get rid of the Communists. The Lubomirskis' apartment was constantly full of priests and bishops. People came and went at odd hours, and there was lots of whispering behind closed doors.

I was more than a little puzzled by Lea's interest in these events.

I could understand that they might resonate with Serge, whose ancestors had once ruled half the country, but as far as I knew, Poland was a place that Lea firmly intended to forget. I certainly did.

"Did you ever tell him we were there?" I asked curiously.

"Of course I did," Lea said lightly, as if there had never been any question that she would.

"And?"

"And nothing. His parents are really religious; it's not exactly the kind of thing they discuss at the dinner table."

"What does it have to do with his parents?"

"Quite a bit if we get married. It's bad enough that I'm not Catholic, or Polish. They don't need to be reminded that Mom is a fallen woman."

I ignored the barb. Lea's insults were so thoughtless as to carry no weight. "You're going to *marry* Serge?"

"Not until he asks me, but it's bound to happen sooner or later," my sister said with calm assurance.

"A regular fairy tale," I sourly remarked.

"Charlotte, don't be small."

"Hey, if you want to marry the former Casanova of the Eighth— which reminds me, I wonder what his religious parents would make of a certain bet involving Delphine?"

"I don't expect you to understand," Lea said.

"I guess they'd chalk it down to youthful high spirits," I persisted.

"Honestly, Charlotte, people do make mistakes."

"When did you become so magnanimous?"

"It doesn't suit you to be bitter," Lea said.

"I'm not bitter," I snapped. But I was. Why did all good things come so effortlessly to Lea, who struck me suddenly as monumentally undeserving? Where was *my* knight in shining armor? Not that I would have wanted Serge, but why did no one fall in love with me? I could answer that one: because I was stunted and bleak and, yes, bitter.

"You're barely eighteen. What about college?"

"I didn't say it was going to happen immediately. It's just that, you know, some things are inevitable."

I wondered if she knew that she sounded like one of the silly characters in the Regency romances that I devoured secretly at night. Intellect, like everything else about me, had become a pose. I didn't understand why my teachers thought I was so smart. I didn't feel smart, and if they'd known about the effort that went in to seeming so, they might have guessed the truth. Maybelle was right: I was a worker bee.

"Well," I said, "Mom will be delighted."

"I wish you wouldn't tell her."

Aha, I thought, so she's not so sure of herself after all. The discovery, if it didn't exactly make me feel kinder, comforted me in a bleak sort of way.

"I think you're out of your mind, but it's your life," I said dismissively, and that was the last we spoke of it.

Grace was a welcome distraction. Because we had no room for her, she was staying in a hotel, but she was over constantly. Unlike my sister, she found our reduced circumstances romantic. "Isn't this fun, just us girls!" she kept exclaiming. I suspected that Grace admired my mother for having the courage to start over, and would have followed her to New York had she had the nerve. What, after all, kept her in Paris? Astrid had been her only friend, and Grace was the kind of woman who perpetually needed reassurance. New York brought a spring to her step; she livened and brightened, as if shaking herself from a long winter, and Astrid brightened, too. All of a sudden it was okay to be silly again, and even I fell under her sway, though I tried to cling to my festering resentments.

With Grace in charge, the first order of business was, naturally, shopping. She dragged us at a relentless pace through every fashion emporium on West Broadway, where she filled huge bags with slithery knits and angular jewelry, their sometimes questionable appeal mitigated by the SALE signs that loomed large in every store we entered. The eighties had begun and everything was big and bright.

As we made our way through blinding white hangars staffed by black-clad salesgirls who, Grace kept exclaiming, were *so* much more helpful than their Parisian counterparts, it almost felt like old times, and I didn't even mind being entrusted, sherpalike, with two Armani garment bags, whose plastic casing stuck moistly to my bare arms.

Grace had discovered sushi, and we had dinner at a Japanese restaurant she had read about in *Vogue*. As I picked at the raw fish slivers on my plate, and sipped the warm sake that Grace had insisted on ordering, I surrendered to the forgotten pleasure of being part of the crowd. We all got a little drunk that night, and, still giddy from her new acquisitions, and the opportunity, of which she had amply availed herself at dinner, of relating her husband's latest assaults on her dignity, Grace insisted that we go back to our apartment for a nightcap.

Since we never watched TV, it must have been Grace who turned it on. She was in that early stage of expatriate infatuation, where everything about America seemed new and better, and she wanted to watch the David Letterman show. Nobody knew what channel it was on, though, or how to work the remote control, and as we clicked haplessly about, we landed on the BBC international news. Grace had just poured everyone champagne (she'd brought six bottles from the duty-free) and, flutes in hand, we watched as thousands of strikers streamed through the streets of Warsaw, at one point going right past the hotel we had stayed in. The marchers looked giddy and elated, waving huge banners emblazoned with the slogan *Solidarność*. Then the camera cut to a meeting, some kind of strike committee, and there was Łukasz, sitting right next to Lech Wałęsa with his walrus mustache. Grace gasped, and when I glanced over at Astrid, I saw that she had gone quite still. The British commentator was going on about how the strikers were trying to force the government to legalize their trade union. Łukasz looked the same, maybe a little thinner. He had clearly become an important personage: You could tell by his ease, and the steady way he looked into the camera. I wondered if he had gone back to his wife, if that was why he hadn't contacted Astrid, but the truth was right there on the television screen: My mother couldn't compete with history.

Deflated, Grace left shortly afterward, a stricken look in her eye, and in the silence that hung in her wake, we retired for the night. I had unrolled the futon on the floor but Lea climbed into bed with me. I must have been five years old the last time I had shared a bed with my sister. I had woken, terrified, from a nightmare, and had sought refuge in her room where, in an uncharacteristic moment of mercy—for we were more apt at the time to pull each other's hair, or get into a pinching contest—she had wrapped her thin arms around me. Now she did the same. She smelled like Monsavon, and of something more intimate, some womanly body exudation. I wondered if she'd slept with Serge, and if it had changed things between them. But sex seemed a very small thing suddenly, compared to what had ripped through our family. It was the other part, love, that I was convinced would mark for me the beginning of losing myself. It was this that made me cling to Lea, who would always find her way home.

"Shhhhhhh," she soughed, but I hadn't said a word.

34

MAYBELLE INVITED PRZEMEK to visit her in Louisville that fall, a laborious process that had involved sending him an official invitation, and traveling to the Polish consulate in Chicago, where reams of forms had to be filled out in triplicate. Astrid had rolled her eyes at the news, but I had assured her that Przemek was all right, though I barely remembered him. When Maybelle broached the subject of a visit to New York, which it would be a shame for him not to see, I responded with an enthusiasm that I hoped would mitigate Astrid's disinterest.

We hadn't seen Maybelle since Warsaw, and both she and Astrid assiduously maintained the fiction that circumstances prevented a reunion. Maybelle had used up all her vacation time (that this was because she had had to go to Poland was not mentioned) and Astrid was busy at work. But the truth was that it was Astrid who kept Maybelle at arm's length. She talked about men taking advantage of her sister, but she had been the greatest beneficiary of Maybelle's kind heart, and I guessed it was this knowledge that shamed her—this and the fact that Maybelle, even as she forgave her, would never quite be able to conceal her belief that Astrid had behaved badly.

Przemek arrived in Louisville that November, and Maybelle lost no time in forming a plan to come east. Astrid resignedly agreed, though, with the holidays upon us, she was busier than usual at work, and it was left to me to worry about the details of welcoming them. I had expected this, for the running of our household had by then pretty much fallen entirely on my shoulders, Astrid having neither the aptitude nor the inclination for housework. I didn't mind. It turned out that I had a knack for order, or at least the appearance of it; and watching my mother jam unrinsed plates into the dishwasher was ten times more aggravating than doing the job properly myself. Had it not been for Maybelle's existence, I would have started to believe that her impoverished childhood was a fabrication. Now I understood what had probably happened: Maybelle had done all the work.

What I did mind, very much, was Astrid's refusal to get involved. It was clear, for instance, that we would have to find them a hotel, but how to do this without hurting Maybelle's feelings?

"We'll pay for it," Astrid said blithely. Although she was making more money by then, I don't think she had any idea how much five nights in a hotel would cost. Of course I could always dip into Frank's account, and intended to, but none of this addressed the problem that Maybelle would be expecting to stay with us.

"Oh God," Astrid snapped when I voiced this thought, "tell her we don't have the room!"

"Why don't you tell her?" I said challengingly.

"None of this was my idea" was her response. More and more, that was how things were between us: my ideas, her ideas; my tastes, her tastes; my neatness, her slovenliness, all unspoken but hanging in the air. She had closed another door after we saw Łukasz on TV. You might have thought the loss of hope would dim her, but her luster returned; she threw herself into work and started using her discount to buy clothes. I wore black, the color of dull defiance.

I called Maybelle. To my surprise, she didn't mind at all: Now that she was in love, everything was exciting to her, and so I relaxed and made a hotel reservation, which I prepaid, both as a surprise, and because then she wouldn't be able to fight it.

On the day they arrived, I skipped school and spent all morning cleaning the apartment. I liked the mindlessness of housework. Astrid had remarked several times on this unsuspected facet of me, and I couldn't help but detect a slight mockery in her tone, and in what seemed like her growing determination to not replace the cap on the toothpaste, or hang up her towel after a shower. I took up cooking, too, and turned out to have a knack for it. I told myself that I was sick of Chinese food and deli salads, which Astrid would happily have lived on, but in fact I had little appetite for the elaborate dishes I prepared, and often ended up throwing out the soup and stews that lingered for days in the fridge. My childhood gluttony had deserted me and Astrid, alarmed at how thin I had become, would occasionally remember her maternal duties, and press me to eat breakfast, or have at least a few more forkfuls of potatoes. My mother, however, inhabited a world where there was no such thing as too thin, and her attempts to feed me lacked the force of conviction, as did her disapproval of my smoking, for I was now searing my lungs with the greed I had once sated with macaroons and chocolate éclairs. On the days when I didn't have time to cook dinner, we both often made do with popcorn or carrot sticks, and the pink cans of Tab that we ordered by the case. Still, I loved the rituals and sensations of preparing a meal: the smell of frying onions, the rich aroma of braising meat. In Maybelle's honor, I had made Julia Child's Boeuf Bourguignon, my gala dish, which was simmering on the stove when she and Przemek arrived.

I had forgotten what a funny-looking couple they made. My first thought when I opened the door was of Jack Spratt and his wife. Przemek stood a full head shorter than Maybelle, and had the bandy gait of a pugilist. He handed me a bunch of roses and kissed my hand, and looked like he might have launched into a speech as well, had Maybelle not hustled him aside and grabbed me.

"Honey, you're skin and bones!" she exclaimed when she released me. I placated her with the assurance that I had just been through a growth spurt. It was true, I had shot up again in the past few months, was in fact now as tall as Astrid, who lamented that I would never get a date till college. It was the only time she ever alluded to the fact that, at an age when most girls were lost in dreams of love, I remained resolutely celibate; and I didn't encourage her to press the issue. I wanted to be alone. Solitude conferred

on me an austere aura that I felt lent me dignity, and seemed, further, like one of the few bonds left between us. Maybelle, however,
had not seen me for months and, once over her initial shock, eyed
me critically.

"You smell like cigarettes. You're not smoking, are you?"

"Only occasionally," I lied.

I could tell by her expression that this would be taken up with
Astrid. My heart sank.

"Shemmy, look at her, she's gorgeous!"

Przemek politely agreed, though he clearly only had eyes for my
aunt. I had never seen Maybelle like this. She exuded a feline sense
of complacence, a lazy well-being that I could only ascribe to her
companion's besotted attentions. As he hovered and danced about
her, helping her out of her coat and making sure that she got the
best chair, I watched in amazement, part of me wanting to laugh,
and the other part in awe at the imponderable chemistry of attraction. Przemek's English, albeit heavily accented and more than a
little idiosyncratic, was better than I remembered, and he was entertaining us with the latest details of the situation in Poland, when the
click of the front door heralded Astrid's arrival. She came in with
her coat still on, and as Maybelle leaped up to embrace her, Przemek
rose, too, waiting politely until they had finished. Maybelle introduced him. As he bowed to kiss my mother's hand, a look of distaste
passed over her face, one that she tried to mask with a smile, but
that lingered nonetheless in her eyes. Przemek seemed oblivious to
her reaction, but I looked on, mortified, as my normally gracious
mother withheld her charms from the first man who had ever made
Maybelle happy.

During dinner, Astrid made no effort to include him in the conversation, and I could tell that he felt awkward. Maybelle, uncharacteristically, had several glasses of wine. I had bought only three
bottles, one of which had gone into the Boeuf Bourguignon, and I
was worried that we would run out, especially since Astrid was
keeping up with her. Przemek stuck to mineral water. I tried

valiantly to keep the conversation going, but he was better at exposition than small talk, at least in English, and we lapsed into several silences. By dessert—chocolate mousse, my other specialty—he seemed desperate to leave. Astrid was no longer bothering to hide her boredom and there was a truculent gleam in Maybelle's eye. *Now she's going to bring up the smoking,* I thought, for Astrid and I were both puffing away like dragons, but suddenly, Maybelle seemed to deflate, and a wrenching look of sadness came over her. *We have ruined this for her,* I thought, and stole an appealing glance at Astrid, but when I saw the indifference in her eyes, I went cold. They left quickly after that. Maybelle didn't kiss Astrid, and her look said, I will never forgive you for this, but she gave me a tight, exonerating hug. I knew she appreciated the effort I had put into the dinner. I knew she understood that I was not responsible for my mother, that we were not the same person, and the bleak anguish I had once felt at this realization transformed itself into defiant pride.

I wordlessly cleared the table. With a brooding look, Astrid poured herself another glass of wine. I was going to point out to her that she had had quite enough, but that would have meant speaking to her. I went into the kitchen instead and started doing the dishes. Presently she appeared in the doorway. I couldn't take it any longer.

"Why were you so rude to him?" I snapped.

She regarded me blankly. "Who? That dreadful little man?"

I wondered if she was drunk. She wasn't stumbling around, though, and her voice was clear. "He's not dreadful, Mom, he's nice, and he's in love with Maybelle." I was so stunned at the dislike I felt for her at that moment, however, that I found myself unable to elaborate on the thoughts that had been going through my head all evening. I knew what Maybelle saw in Przemek: a fellow survivor, a real person, a man who made the best of things—the very qualities Astrid herself would have appreciated, had she not been soured by prejudice and disappointment and, yes, lost love. That Przemek returned Maybelle's feelings seemed nothing less than a miraculous blessing.

Astrid's expression turned disdainful. I had never seen her like this. "He probably just wants a green card," she said in a bored voice, and then added, "Oh well, it was bound to happen one of these days—at least he's not an Arab."

My eyes grew huge. I had never heard my mother make a racist comment. Racists were boors, small people who yelled at soccer games and beat their wives. Half the students at our Paris school had been Arabs, and Astrid hadn't thought any the worse of them; had in fact admired their panache and style. Of course I knew everything that was wrong with Przemek in her eyes: He was lower class and strange-looking and had worn a cheap suit and ugly tie, but Maybelle didn't care about these things, and neither did I. "You're wrong," I said stonily. "He's kind and thoughtful, and he's obviously crazy about her."

At that moment, Astrid did something awful: She started to laugh, as if the mere idea of anyone being crazy about Maybelle were so preposterous as to invite only derision. I saw red.

"Frankly," I said. "I like him a lot better than Łukasz."

Astrid's eyes went wide now. "How dare you say that! Łukasz is an intellectual, a dissident—"

"Is that why he doesn't call?"

Astrid was silent for a second. "That was unworthy of you," she finally said.

But I wasn't going to bow down. "So was your behavior toward Przemek."

It was the first time that we had overtly disagreed about anything, and we moved through the next few days in a fog of shocked resentment, Astrid invoking spurious work obligations as I showed Maybelle and Przemek all the tourist sights that I knew they would enjoy: Times Square, South Street Seaport, and Ellis Island, where Przemek was thrilled to find his family's name, Kozłowski, on a list in the museum. Ferrying them about town, I discovered that I felt at home in New York. Though the geography of Paris was etched in my bones, I had entered a new space that, all of a sudden, seemed alive with possibilities. Standing with Maybelle and Przemek at the top of the Empire State Building, looking down on the forgiving city below, where you could stand, ranting, on a street corner, with a paper bag on your head, without anyone batting an eyelid, I was seized with the exhilarating certainty of being part of a larger landscape; and as I explained the intricacies of the subway, or humored a surly waiter in the steak house where Maybelle had insisted on dining at the unfashionable hour of five in the afternoon, it was suddenly clear to me why I had come to America. I belonged here.

But I couldn't share my new ease with Astrid. After Maybelle and Przemek left, a divide remained between us, one that the memory of my mother's smallness made it impossible for me to bridge. We lived in the same apartment, and were polite to each other, but we might as well have inhabited separate continents and, for once, I thought that maybe that wasn't a bad thing.

35

I HADN'T SPOKEN TO FRANK since we left Paris. We wrote each other awkward, stilted letters about school and my plans for college. This topic he entered eagerly, for it was a neutral plane of concrete discussion. I was in my junior year, and at Briarwood, that was when you started preparing for the all-consuming competition of college acceptance. Even the girls who would become society hostesses like their mothers got swept up in the fever, and I imagined that, years later, their faded diplomas from Princeton and Stanford would gather dust in the storage closets of their Park Avenue apartments. Frank hoped I would apply to Yale, even as he encouraged me to keep my options open. He was glad I was doing well. His mother apparently was, too, for I was invited to Greenwich again for lunch, and she counseled me with great seriousness on the opportunities and responsibilities ahead. It made for easy conversation. I don't think she and Frank spoke any more than they ever had, because he was rarely mentioned. It appeared that we were to have our own, separate relationship. It was a little weird, but it was better than having to pretend that we were bound by normal family ties. In truth, I found the formality of our rapport curiously restful.

The divorce went through. I wasn't privy to the details. Papers were signed, the matter settled. Astrid never mentioned it, and I didn't ask. I was drawing less and less on the account Frank had set up for me, a restraint that proved all the easier as Astrid's star began to rise. She had developed a loyal following at Bergdorf's, where she had been promoted to buyer, and was now making enough that little luxuries were beginning to reappear in our lives: a new sofa, fine linens that, to my annoyance, needed to be ironed. Several of her clients were encouraging her to open her own boutique, and though she lacked the financing, she was beginning to believe that it might be possible.

Inge was finally making headway in what was now quite nakedly her plan to marry my father, and Lea went as far as to say that, although our mother's conduct had been deplorable, Frank was catching up to her in leaps and bounds, and I was lucky I didn't have to be around to watch him making an ass of himself over a two-bit adventuress. I couldn't imagine Frank making an ass of himself. I suspected, rather, that he was just capitulating to the inevitable. All the same, I was surprised at how dispassionately I took the news. I had long surpassed Lea in cynicism. Half the girls at my school had fathers who had married women twenty years younger. It was so banal as to not warrant comment. I knew that Grace had mentioned it to Astrid, because I heard her say on the phone, "Frankly, I'm surprised it took so long." For all our estrangement, I had retained the ability to divine the subject of their conversations.

It was around this time that Astrid started dating Harold. He had come in to Bergdorf's to buy a scarf for his mother, and Astrid had been so helpful that he had ended up asking her to dinner. I had only met him twice, when he came to pick her up, and he seemed nice enough, if a bit bland, but then most people seemed bland around my mother, one of whose singular gifts was making the dull feel scintillating. While I wondered what Astrid saw in this staid and courtly banker, who reminded me in a rather unsettling way of my father, I had lost the inclination to ask. She, however, became more chatty. As she grew busier with work and social obligations—for, as her reputation grew, she began to be invited places—she started coming home late at night again, and would comment the next morning on the party she had just attended, the ballet ("It's as boring here as it was in Paris") or some new restaurant where they served teeny portions on huge plates. I reciprocated with funny stories about the girls at school, some of whose mothers were well

known to her. Since I knew so much about them, I think Astrid
assumed I had friends, mistaking observation for participation. I was
home as little as she was, and she probably thought I had a social life.
In a way, I did.

I was seventeen by then, cramming for the SATs, taking
advanced courses, and studying late into the night, for academic distinction didn't come to me quite as easily as was generally assumed.
Unlike Lea, I had never possessed a quick mind. Mine was of the
ponderous sort that shines in ruminative essays and panics during
tests, and I was especially worried about the SATs, which seemed to
measure precisely the celerity I lacked. As a part of my program of
sedulous application, I began to haunt the Columbia University
library, where I had been sent by a teacher to research an art history
project. It was there I discovered that my mother's seductive wiles
hadn't entirely passed me over. I was poring over *Vasari's Lives* at
one of the reading tables when I felt a man's eyes on me. As a social
nonentity, I had long passed under the radar of the Buckley and
Collegiate boys who buzzed around Briarwood's queen bees, my
invisibility only accentuated by the baggy jeans and T-shirts that
were my standard attire. And yet, when I felt this man's desiring
gaze, I knew instinctively how to respond.

He was a graduate student named Massimo, and under the
impression that I was a Columbia girl, he took me back to his apartment, where my virginity was speedily dispatched, along with my
belief that my scrawny loins would never please. It appeared,
indeed, that I had pretensions to beauty—not of the fresh-faced
kind prized at Briarwood, but of the troubling sort that appealed to
the more sophisticated urban Lothario, and that Massimo obligingly
expounded on, convincing me that there was a place in the annals
of female beauty for skinny redheads with big hips and breasts.

After Massimo came Wolfgang, who was in turn followed by
Hugh, a forty-year-old associate professor of anthropology who
introduced me to Malinowski and analingus. They were all nice, or at
least eager to please me, but I treated them only as an apprenticeship,

my heart shielded by my assumed persona. I enjoyed being made love to by men who thought I was someone else. I enjoyed being fucked like an adult because I had been one for so long that I felt entitled to the privilege. At seventeen, I had figured out something that young girls aren't told: that desire has little to do with love, and more with the kind of impulse that I imagined had led Harold to finance a SoHo boutique for my mother that year. But I had no interest in such coarse traffic—what enthralled me was the power I wielded when grown men discharged themselves into me with a shudder, whimpering like little boys.

By the time news arrived of my father's impending marriage, I had long ceased to wonder at the means that Inge had used to ensnare him. Like legions before her, she had worked out that she could have a comfortable life for the small price of her body, an offering that must at first have left my father indifferent—she was, after all, hardly his type—but that she had slowly and laboriously convinced him held the key, if not to his happiness, then to a lasting reprieve from her efforts. To my jaded eye, the whole business of mating was beginning to appear as sordid as the debacle of my parents' marriage, and the only thing that surprised me was that Frank would be willing to make the same mistake twice.

36

THE WEDDING WAS to take place in June. My father hoped I would be able to come. It would mean very much to him. I read between the lines that he was mortified by the whole business. There was something about the letter, however, a certain maudlin quality, that made me think Inge might have dictated it. Astrid's only comment was that she had always thought he would remarry. I eyed her for signs of rancor or spite, but she seemed genuinely relieved, and urged me to go. Not only was it the right thing to do, it would be fun; I must miss my friends. But the truth was that, except for responding to a letter from Delphine, its anguished self-reproach eclipsed only by its bad spelling, I hadn't kept in touch with anyone, relying instead on Lea to update me on Nahid's most recent extravagance, or the latest twist in Chiara Grzebine's scandal-prone love life. In the end, I wrote Frank that I would attend, hoping that he wouldn't mistake magnanimity for approbation. According to Lea, although how she came about this information was a mystery, his mother was appalled, Inge being not only practically a minor—she was twenty-three—but a secretary to boot, which was just as bad as an actress. It was thus left to me to represent the American branch of the family, and I began to pack my bags, surprised at how much I was looking forward to the trip.

I had ample warning from Lea as to what to expect of my father's new domestic arrangements. Now that Inge was safely ensconced, she had taken on the manners of the *grande bourgeoise* she yearned to become, ordering two more Aubusson carpets and a set of Louis XV chairs upholstered in pale blue silk. "I'm sure she's hoping I'll move out for good," Lea sniggered, "but I think I'll hang around just to annoy her . . . God, the thought of the two of them in bed is simply too grisly to contemplate!" More alarmingly—or hilariously, in Lea's opinion—Inge had lately betrayed her ambitions of playing a starring role in our family reconciliation, holding forth at every opportunity, and at suspicious length, on how she looked forward to meeting me, and baking, in honor of my arrival, a special Swedish cake.

In the face of this barrage, I had set my expectations low, and by the time the airplane began its descent toward Paris, had winnowed my hopes to the single one that my father would come to the airport alone. I need not have worried. When I emerged, he was waiting at the front of the crowd, an anxious expression on his face that must have mirrored mine, because all my fears suddenly evaporated. He was wearing one of his summer suits from Brooks Brothers, and a light gray fedora, and as I went to him, he blinked as if in panic, and I felt a rush of helpless, forgiving love.

"Hi, Dad," I said, embracing him, and that he didn't flinch or hesitate, but held me as tight as he knew how, was all the affirmation I needed. When he pulled back, suddenly self-conscious, our eyes were nearly level.

"Look at you, all grown up!"

I was going to say something about the wedding, get it out of the way; wish him well, tell him I understood and forgave him, but he had the stunned look of a man overtaken by events, one that would last through the next few days as hordes of energetic Scandinavians descended upon us with maps of Paris and duty-free bottles of aquavit. Instead, we just stood with awkward smiles on our faces, until Frank remembered where we were and, determinedly, picked up my bag and led the way to the exit.

I would come to wonder if Inge was really the monster that we made her out to be, but at that point, Lea had so thoroughly poisoned me against her that civility was the best I could manage. My distaste, however, was not perceived by Inge, who greeted me with sisterly affection. Still, while she may have settled on an attitude of noblesse oblige, she was clearly determined to mark her territory. As I tried to look inconspicuous, she wrapped her arm around Frank's waist and planted a lingering kiss on his lips, during the course of which I could have sworn I saw dismay in his eyes. Then she observed, in a maternal tone, "Charlotte has become so stunning." She was quite pretty herself, in a stolid Nordic way that was the antithesis of my mother's equivocal charms, and one could just as easily have pictured her herding geese as leading a charge of Valkyries into battle.

Whatever awkwardness hung in the air was subsumed by the exigencies of making me feel welcome, and Frank retreated gratefully to his study while Inge bustled about, showing me to my room, which no longer bore any resemblance to me, and bringing out, with much ceremony, the Swedish cake, though none of us were the least bit hungry. Sadly, she and Frank ("How funny that you call him by his Christian name . . .") were dining out that evening with her parents, at La Coupole, but as she understood that my friends had organized a party, she didn't feel so bad. Besides, we would have "many opportunities to get acquainted in the coming days."

"*Many opportunities to get acquainted in the coming days . . .*" Lea mimicked when we were safely behind the closed door of her room. She was applying lipstick in preparation for my welcome dinner at Café Costes, the trendy restaurant where Nahid had reserved a table that evening. Nahid had by now had her hymen restored so many times that they were running out of bits to patch up, and would be attending a small college in California to which her father had made a substantial donation. The big news was that she and Delphine were having a fling.

"No way."

"Nahid's just amusing herself. Delphine follows her around like a puppy; it's a bit pathetic. Maybe you should talk to her before she embarrasses herself again."

"Right," I said. "She always listened to me."

"Oh, guess what: Grace's husband is divorcing her. Says it's because she's barren, the nasty old goat, after making her have all those abortions. . . . He's marrying a Belgian girl."

"Yeah, Astrid mentioned something about that. Poor Grace."

"She'll be all right. She swears she's going to take him to the cleaners, and she has a new boyfriend, an Albanian painter. God, the sordid drama of it all. . . ."

When Lea and I got to the restaurant, Nahid and Delphine were already there. Chiara would be joining us later. Now that she was a hot young actress (comparisons had been made to Sophie Marceau and, rather less flatteringly, when she released a pop single, to Stephanie of Monaco), she had to worry about stalking paparazzi. Delphine leaped up when she saw me. She had grown even blonder (Nahid's hair stylist, she confided) and had lost weight on a diet of sushi and grapefruit, so that she now looked like a younger version of half the starving women in the room. I wondered how whatever it was that was going on between her and Nahid sat with her parents, who would surely take a dim view of Sapphic dalliances; but she told me that her father had been in and out of the hospital all winter, and that Sylvia now spent all her time nursing him. "If he dies," she said brightly, "Grandma wants us to move to New York!" I was a little taken aback at her cold-bloodedness: Was this the same girl who had wept over the death of a hamster?

But then I, too, had toughened. I had begun paying more attention to my appearance, my growing, if still hesitant assurance demanding commensurate trappings. I shopped at Reminiscence and Trash and Vaudeville, and, with a sure instinct that I must have inherited from my mother, had cultivated a Patti Smith–inspired look that was approved as *très New York*. Astrid, of course, found my leather jackets and scuffed boots distressingly punk, but she was far away, and I basked in the novel sensation of being admired, even a little envied, by these sleek, and rather silly *Parisiennes*. Most insidiously seductive, however, was the faint superiority I felt in their company. It wasn't long before Chiara joined us, along with two other girls from school, and the conversation turned to the reason for my being there in the first place.

"At least he's not marrying the au pair," Nahid volunteered.

"Or a former stripper," Chiara drawled, for Candy de Bethune just then came tripping toward us on her stick legs, crying in her Texas accent, "Whah, if it isn't Astrid's girls! Is it true what ah hear, that you're going to be brahdesmaids at your daddy's wedding?"

"No," Lea said with a seraphic smile. "The brahde's barely older than we are, and we'd hate to upstage her."

Candy's bird eyes narrowed in suspicion, but she couldn't make up her mind whether Lea was being complicit or insulting.

"Ah, for one, do not plan to attend" was the rejoinder she finally settled on, adding in parting, "Y'all tell your mama ah said hi."

"Funny," Lea remarked as Candy walked away. "I don't believe she was invited."

"My aunt saw her coming out of Dr. Villier's office," Nahid gleefully whispered when she was gone. "Eye job *and* tummy tuck."

"I don't know why she bothers," Delphine waspishly put in. "Everyone knows her husband's cheating on her with Laure de Savigny."

I let the chatter roll over me, amazed that this could once have been my world. Delphine kept disappearing with Nahid to the bathroom, whence they returned giddy and alert, their nostrils flaring nervously, and I wondered at their ability to make even vice look childish. I was invited repeatedly to join them, but I stuck to champagne. We drank several bottles, and smoked much more than we ate, and by the time Chiara's boyfriend showed up with three friends, it was decided that the Bains Douches was the only natural venue for the conclusion of the evening. The jet lag was catching up on me, however, the champagne taking its toll, and the gossipy malice beginning to wear thin. My thoughts kept returning to Frank's haunted look at the airport. But there would be no mercy in this crowd. Chiara's father had been married three times, to successively younger women, and Nahid's would probably be at the Bains

Douches himself, his shirt open to his navel, cruising the room for prey. I longed for bed and peace, and so apparently did Lea, for she turned down the invitation as well, claiming, to general derision, that she didn't like to go to clubs without Serge. She held her ground, though, and we dispersed into separate taxis, Lea confiding to me in the back of ours that, frankly, Chiara and Nahid were beginning to get on her nerves. By the time we got home, sometime after one in the morning, we were sunk in gloomy silence. As we passed our father's bedroom, muffled sighs issued from behind the door. I queasily banished a picture of a white, naked Inge, laboring to please like an ox in a field. "Poor Dad," Lea said grimly, and with a quick peck on my cheek, she disappeared into her bedroom.

Inge had wanted a church wedding—*Notre Dame, can you imagine!*—but, in the face of Frank's opposition, had settled for the Mairie of the Eighth, which Lea assured her was where *everyone* got married (the second or third time, anyway). And sure enough, Inge's relatives oohed and aahed most gratifyingly at the salle des mariages's bombastic Second Empire *luxe*, with its rococo moldings and sultry statuary and the cherubs on the ceiling sticking out their rosy pink bottoms. It was a good thing they descended en masse, for Frank's circle was conspicuously underrepresented by Candy de Bethune, who gate-crashed. Later I would find out that he hadn't even wanted *us* there, had invited us only in the face of Inge's entreaties. It was Candy who threw light on the cause of his reticence. She had positioned herself behind me during the ceremony, so that we both had the same view of Inge in profile as she rose for the deputy mayor. Her cream satin gown was snugger than the casual outfits she'd worn up to then, and there was no mistaking, to Candy's eagle eye, the slight swell at the waist. "Well," she whispered, loudly enough for the whole row to hear, "*that* explains it!" And, for once, I had to agree with her.

The reception was held at Taillevent—Inge's recompense for the civil ceremony—and I found myself seated next to her uncle Olaf, a red-faced osteopath with an interest, betrayed between the *amuse-*

gueules and the langouste, in erotic art. Not realizing who I was, he made no bones of his surprise at his dull-witted niece's having done so well for herself. I not only did not rebuff his advances, but positively encouraged them and, as his foot sought mine under the table, positioned myself to give him an unimpeded view of my cleavage. To Lea's disgusted glances, I replied with the mutinous look of one determined to sink as low as the occasion demanded. I avoided my father's eye, but he could not have failed to see me leave with my by-then boozily emboldened swain. We repaired to his room at the Lutétia where, dispensing with further niceties, we fell into bed. As he chuffed noisily over me, his stomach slapping against mine, I thought of the sea lions at Central Park Zoo. I decided then that I would never marry. I would be the mistress, the harlot, the red-headed temptress who stole away in the night, which was what I presently did, sneaking off as he lay snoring to the peace of my maidenly bower.

Delphine and I got together the next afternoon. "I missed you so much," she said, grasping my hand, and in that moment, I was seduced into believing that I had missed her, too, though in fact I had neither yearned for her nor felt her absence. We were sitting in the same touristy café on the Madeleine where she had convinced me to lie for her years ago, and it seemed like such a small thing now. I'd forgotten how sentimental she was; it couldn't have been an accident that she guided us to the same table where we had sat then.

"I was always half in love with you," she confided.

Had I been in love with Delphine, or had I always felt this slight condescension? I felt awkward, and embarrassed by her effusion.

"That was just kid stuff," I said.

Delphine looked at me dolefully. "Don't you remember our secret garden?"

"Of course I do," I said. "Are the hamster graves still there?"

"No, they're all overgrown now. Poor little hamsters. You've changed."

I laughed. "So have you."

"Not really." An earnest look came over her. "Do you know why I slept with Patrice? I wanted to be like you."

"Oh, come on. . . ."

"No, I mean it. He wasn't very nice to me—I think he wanted me to be you, too. Nobody ever wants me to be me, beginning with my mother."

"Delphine, it was a long time ago."

"I used to want to kiss you, did you know that?"

"It's called a schoolgirl crush," I said lightly, though in fact I felt bad, because I had never wanted to kiss Delphine. Own her, yes, in that ruthless child way, control her, sometimes even smack her, but never kiss her.

"I'm a lesbian," she said.

"Well, I kind of figured that you and Nahid . . ."

Delphine sighed wearily. "She'll break my heart."

This, I thought, would most certainly be the case, but I was humbled by her guileless candor. How could we ever have been friends, when she was so open, and I was so closed? Delphine was wrong: I hadn't changed. I had always held back a part of myself, the not-so-nice part.

"You're not a lesbian; you're in love with Nahid. Anyone would be in love with Nahid."

"Even she admires you," Delphine said petulantly. "She was going on about how hot you look."

I tried not to be as pleased as I was by this revelation. I was vain enough to like the idea of anyone finding me hot.

"How's your mom?" I asked, for it struck me then that my real romance had been with Sylvia, who had possessed the mystery that her daughter so conspicuously lacked.

"She takes care of my father. Everyone thinks she's a saint," Delphine said disgustedly.

"I always thought she was kind of saintly," I said. I didn't add, *for putting up with you.*

"Yeah, well, she always liked you, too."

"Delphine," I said, "don't be a boob."

The day before I went back to New York, I saw Patrice on the Rue de Rennes. He was coming out of the FNAC with a bag of books, and I remembered how he had entranced me with his moody French-boy intellect. Now, the only emotion his stooped figure evoked was a melancholy that gave way to the suddenly intense desire for him to see me. Men had been glancing at me all day, and I felt their longing, clinging to me like a honeyed sheen. If he wanted me, would I wake up and magically recover my girlhood? I was about to cross over, my hand half-raised, when a girl ran up behind him and linked her arm around his waist. As they embraced, something tightened in my chest. I stood and watched them, a little envious, a little sad, the way I often felt watching old movies, knowing that the boy running across the plaza was now an old man, the café long shuttered, the waiter dead, the girl's black hair, which the boy brushes aside to kiss her, as gray and brittle as the celluloid on which it is fixed forever.

37

STRID'S SHOP WAS A BIG SUCCESS. All her clients followed her to SoHo, and brought their friends with them, and before long, she was being written up in *Vogue* and *Glamour*. To crown her triumph, we moved to a bigger apartment, in Greenwich Village, which she had always felt was her rightful home. She painted the living room a smoldering red and strewed it with poufs and Berber rugs. She started traveling to Europe again, for the trade shows. Sometimes Harold went with her. Their formal relationship seemed to suit them both. They dined together, and went to the theater, and when he came over, he always brought flowers. If he ever spent the night, he was gone by the time I got up. It neither surprised nor dismayed me that my mother should have, as I imagined, chosen convenience over passion. In my more generous moments, I even perceived a certain dignity to the arrangement, especially when contrasted with the fiasco of my father's second marriage, or the ongoing melodrama of Grace's divorce.

Still, while I appreciated the material benefits of Astrid's rise, most notably the new apartment where we had our own bedrooms at opposite ends, I had become rather full of myself, and increasingly regarded her pursuits as frivolous and laughable. I rarely went to her shop, and when I did, could barely keep a derisory smirk off my face as I watched her cater to women who, in my pitiless eyes, were obsessed with their appearance. Sometimes, when we collided in the morning, I saw her wince at my studied slovenliness, but she was too smart to say anything. Now that the lines were drawn, we were easier with each other. I would pick up the chocolates she liked and, with her unerring instinct, she gave me for my birthday the perfect vintage leather jacket. The news of Inge's pregnancy she greeted only with a sad smile and a shake of her head, though she did laugh at Candy's role in its unveiling.

I threw myself into college applications, writing and rewriting my essays, and hoping that my grades and fluent French would distract from a glaring lack of the elusive quality prized at Briarwood as "leadership," my only extracurricular activities being my library conquests, for which, truth be told, I had of late lost the appetite. I had acquired by then, if not actual self-confidence, the ability to fake it, and was able to portray myself convincingly as a serious scholar with a passion for nineteenth-century French literature. It was around this time that Maybelle and Przemek got married, in a quiet civil ceremony. Przemek had started a construction business in Louisville, the manpower supplied by Poles desperate to escape the deteriorating situation in their country, and he was doing so well that Maybelle now only worked part-time at the hospital, and was thinking of quitting altogether in the spring. Though Astrid had perforce come around to the view that Przemek was the best thing that had ever happened to Maybelle, they had never really made up. Astrid would have had to take the first step but, either because she was ashamed of herself, or because, as I meanly suspected, there was no room in her new life for a fat, loud sister with a predilection for polyester pantsuits, she had never formally apologized for her behavior. The truth was that there was no room in my life for Maybelle, either: She didn't fit the hard new me.

And so we had little contact, but in December, Maybelle called in the middle of the night to tell us that martial law had been declared in Poland. All the phone lines were down, and Przemek, whose whole family was over there, was threatening to get on a plane. Astrid soothed and humored her—even if he was serious, all the flights had probably been canceled—and, after she had hung up, she turned on the news. The crowds and banners had vanished, replaced by a general in dark glasses, a puppet installed by Moscow to quash the insurrection once and for all. There were mentions of mass arrests, of dissidents escaping to the West, and I glanced anxiously at Astrid, but she seemed unperturbed, as if none of this had anything to do with her. She switched off the TV before the newscast was over, and, one by one, turned off the lamps, and the lights on the Christmas tree that stood in a corner of the living room.

"Bed?" she said, and for a crazy moment I thought she might be inviting me to join her, as she used to do when I was little.

"Math test tomorrow. I have to study."

She put her hand lightly on my head. "Don't wear yourself out, honey."

"Just another half hour."

She kissed me. We'd never stopped kissing good night, even when we didn't mean it. She smelled of her old self, perfume and cigarettes and other mysterious female essences.

"I love you," she said. It was the reinstatement of the *I*. For a long time, we had truncated the phrase, and the words had floated meaninglessly. I thought, *we have landed*.

"I love you, too," I said.

I got into Yale. I found out afterward that Frank had written to a couple of old connections in New Haven, but I still believed they took me on my own merit, since Princeton and Columbia accepted me, too. I was wanted. I had a place, and I couldn't wait to leave. Yale beckoned as the polar opposite of everything I had come to reject in the New York of the early eighties: the shallowness, the vulgarity and crass ostentation, the torrents of money, the whole tawdry spectacle that people would soon be writing books about, as if they'd woken up with a hangover and a bad taste in their mouths. Released from this three-ring circus, I imagined myself taking my place in a coterie of like minds, whence I might look down undisturbed at the inane pursuits of my lessers; for that was what they seemed now that I had received confirmation of my gifts. When the letter came, Astrid insisted on celebrating. Her pride—she had never gone to college—moved me to generosity, and I traded my punk rags for a dress by a Japanese designer selected from her store, surprised, and a little disconcerted, by how good it looked on me. Thus attired, I graciously submitted to dinner in an expensive restaurant full of fashion plates, buoyed by the thought that I would soon be miles above all this nonsense. That evening, after she had kissed me good night, Astrid stepped back to have one last look at me and, the old mischievous glimmer in her eye, said, "You know, it's possible to be both smart *and* chic."

"I know," I said, though I very much doubted it, even as I had to recognize that the idea possessed a certain allure.

"I'm so proud of you," she said. "My brilliant daughter."

"Better you than me," said Lea upon hearing the news, which only confirmed her belief that I was well on my way to becoming a bluestocking. My sister made no bones about her lack of interest in her studies: In the time-honored manner of upper-class Parisian girls, she had taken up the law with no intention of ever practicing it. Serge, who hadn't made it in, had at least bowed to practicality, and had enrolled in an animal-husbandry program near Tours to study horse breeding.

"What's the point?" I asked. "You're taking up the space of somebody who might actually be serious about law."

"That I very much doubt. Pascaline de Sauveterre is there," she said, mentioning a girl from her riding club, "and everyone knows she's going to marry Godefroy and have zillions of babies. Anyway, I exhausted my last remaining brain cells on the *bac;* I deserve a rest."

Lea had come for her summer visit. She was very much impressed with the new apartment ("Finally, an end to squalor!"), and spent hours at Astrid's shop in SoHo, where she chattered happily with the clients, and was discovered to have a knack for sales. She took immediately to Harold, whom she declared to be charming.

"Think how much worse it could have been: Grace is making a spectacle of herself around town with an Italian waiter she picked up in Capri. And I won't even mention Dad. . . ."

The big news was that Inge had given birth to Marguerite, a strapping Viking baby who weighed in at nearly ten pounds, setting a record at the Salpêtrière where she came into the world after a brief and efficient labor that Frank was forced to attend. There being no other suitable room, she had turned mine into a nursery, painting it pink with a border of frolicking lambs and bunnies. When Lea asked where *I* was meant to stay when I visited, Inge had retorted that there were two maids' rooms upstairs.

"Still, there's a bright side: Now that she's got what she wanted, maybe she'll lay off poor old Dad."

As to the baby's nature, Lea had little to offer, other than it shrieked and was quite bald, poor thing.

"You were bald, too," Astrid reminded her.

"I know, but I was a lovely baby, you always said so."

"Pity it didn't last," I remarked.

Harold had a house in Maine and we were invited for a week in August, the first time Astrid took him up on an oft-repeated invitation. I had intended to stay behind, but Astrid wouldn't hear of it. When was the last time we had taken a proper family holiday? I wondered if by "family," she also meant Harold, who had so far made himself very easy to ignore. I wasn't at all sure I wanted to get to know him better and, as far as I could tell, he was equally disinterested in me. Lea, however, took me aside and severely informed me that I was being a pill. That she still had the power to shame me when I felt superior to her in every way both maddened and cowed me, and in the end I caved in. As we drove north in Harold's Volvo, the talk was of lobsters and corn and the proximity of the Bush family compound in Kennebunkport. Grim visions assailed me, of red-kneed men in pastel shirts and half-witted Labradors. I shrank back in my seat, my eyes fixed on the bleak Maine coast.

"Heavens," Lea exclaimed when the huge house on its rocky promontory came into view. "How grand!"

I was surprised, too, though it had more than once crossed my mind that Harold's appeal might have resided at least in part in his willingness to finance Astrid's store. I had to concede, however, that they seemed genuinely fond of each other, and Harold's quaintly old-fashioned gesture in giving Astrid her own room was clearly made out of regard for us. This completely unnecessary courtesy couldn't help but touch me, as did his concern for our comfort, evident in small touches like the fresh flowers in our bedrooms. Still, I bristled at these kind civilities, for they lacked the raw edge of the only thing I understood as true feeling. Astrid appeared unaware of my moodiness. When Harold challenged Lea to a tennis game—a passion they shared—she and I stayed behind on the shaded porch, and I waited for her to make a disparaging remark, for she felt about tennis as I did, but none came. Instead she rose and, claiming sudden exhaustion, went inside to take a nap.

I was still sunk in self-pity when I took my seat at dinner that night, in a ripped Sex Pistols T-shirt that I had slipped in my bag in a moment of defiance. I noted Lea's disapproval with satisfaction, but lost my composure when I glimpsed a pained flash in Astrid's eyes. If Harold had any thoughts on the matter, he gave no sign of them, and I was left to feel foolish and ashamed, my discomfiture turning to truculence as the conversation proceeded from that afternoon's tennis match, which Lea had won, to the sailing excursion planned for the morrow. Sailing! What next? Croquet? I had found out recently that Harold, whose occupation had long been a mystery, was a political analyst for one of the big Wall Street firms. He was also, I guessed, a Republican, though he had never said anything to support this assumption. As it happened, my latest library fling had been a left-wing German political scientist who had made much of Reagan's recent overtures to the Iraqi regime. It was a topic about which I knew little and cared even less, save for an instinctive distaste—shared by Astrid—of anything to do with the Reagan administration, but as we fell upon our lobsters, some inner demon goaded me to introduce it. As I put forth Dieter's views as my own, I waited for Astrid to jump into the fray, but she only averted her eyes, leaving me at the mercy of Harold who not only did not take the bait, save for remarking that it was a sorry business indeed, but actually cut me off and, with a twinkle in his eye, observed that I would feel right at home at Yale.

Afterward, Lea exclaimed, "Really, Charlotte, what got into you?"

"Ever heard of political awareness?"

"Political awareness, my foot," my sister imperturbably replied. "You were just being rude—and after being served lobster, too!"

"It's not like France—it's cheap here" was the lame retort that rose to my lips, for I knew perfectly well that she was right.

"Why are you trying to ruin things? Can't you see that Mom is happy with him?"

It was my turn to be disdainful. "Happy?" I sneered. "He's just like Dad: the Yale thing, the sailing, the stupid cocktails on the porch . . ."

A pitying look came into Lea's eyes. "Harold isn't at all like Dad. Dad neither plays tennis nor sails, and he's moody. Harold is not moody, and Mom isn't constantly trying to shock him. They just enjoy each other's company."

Of course I knew Harold wasn't like Frank. That was the problem. "Well, isn't that lovely and civilized?"

"As a matter of fact, it is. I really don't know what's come over you. You've been a different person since you came to New York."

I glared at her. "Get used to it. This is the real me."

"I find that hard to believe," my sister said, before turning on her heel and leaving the room.

But I behaved after that. I still knew how to be a good girl. I went sailing, where it turned out I had nothing to do, since Lea and Harold manned the boat; I sat on the porch and read; I helped out with the clambake. I hoped Astrid was grateful. The truth was that none of it meant anything. I was just marking time.

38

HAROLD WAS RIGHT: I did feel at home at Yale. Having impersonated an undergraduate for so long, I was finally legitimate. Most of the girls in my college, however, were on their own for the first time, and I observed with amusement the dormwide bacchanal that led to more than one of them sobbing in the bathroom at three in the morning, or standing nervously in line at Health Services, where birth control pills could be had after watching a movie that would turn even the most rugged enthusiast off sex forever. My roommate, Meredith Traubman, hailed from New Mexico, whence her mother sent care packages full of sweets that were responsible for Meredith gaining fifteen pounds in the first semester, a course that she subsequently reversed by embracing bulimia. We had little in common, and even less to say to each other, but were saved from the acrimonious disputes that erupted between similarly mismatched pairs by her good nature and my indifference. She found friends soon enough, and I was there to study, not socialize. The things the other freshmen aspired to: sex, independence, unsupervised drinking were all old hat to me. What I yearned for was austerity and unique experience.

Because of my French, and the two classes I had taken at Columbia via an arrangement with Briarwood, I was allowed to enroll in a graduate seminar on Rabelais. It seemed just the place where I might bump into like minds, even though I had only the sketchiest notion of Renaissance literature. As I paid for my books at the Co-op, I experienced a gratifying swell of self-importance, which was instantly crushed when I showed up for the first class, in a small seminar room in the French Department. One look around the table was enough to determine that my classmates were not only older, as I might have expected, but undoubtedly smarter and better read. In physical appearance, they were all familiar types from Columbia, with the exception of one man, whose chiseled features and air of indolent hauteur set him apart. As I took my place at the table, he glanced at me indifferently. He looked to be from India or Iran, and had the unsettling green eyes one sometimes finds in that part of the world. He was dressed fastidiously, in a blue checked shirt and V-neck sweater, and his shoes were not only leather, but polished. He sat slightly apart from the others, and I wondered if they disliked him, or were put off by his formality. The professor seemed delighted to see him. "Ah, Azher," he exclaimed when he came in, "I was afraid we'd lost you to the Bard!" The haughty Indian, as I had already begun to think of him, got up and shook his hand, and I noticed a couple of the others exchanging snide glances.

All of my other courses were lectures, and, once my initial trepidation subsided, I came to look forward to the intimate Rabelais seminar, which met on Wednesday afternoon. The professor took a liking to me: My French was the most fluent in the class, and though I struggled with the Renaissance syntax, he often asked me to read. I submitted gratefully, happy that I could contribute something. My fellow students were so much more erudite than me as to make my presence seem an act of mercy on their part, and they treated me with a benevolent condescension that verged on protectiveness—all, that is, but Azher, who ignored me. It soon became clear why the professor had wanted him in the class: Azher was a true Renaissance scholar. He was a recent holder of one of the more eminent fellowships in the field, and had just spent a year in France, part of it at Chinon, doing research. I assumed from his accent, and his pompous manner, that he had been raised in England, and was surprised to find out, from the Graduate Directory, that he was from New Jersey. He had done his undergraduate work at Rutgers.

He seemed to have no friends. I saw him sometimes at Sterling Library, and in a coffee shop on Chapel Street, where he always sat alone, reading and smoking Dunhills, his long legs crossed under the table. Since I often sat in the same coffee shop myself, I wondered if he would ever approach me, perhaps to ask me how I liked the class, as Harvey, a genial midwesterner, was always doing, or to suggest we have a drink sometime, as Harvey had also suggested. Once I went over to his table, and asked if he happened to have the syllabus on him. He said that he didn't, and then made it quite clear, by tapping his pen impatiently against his notebook, that he was disinclined to conversation. I wrote him off as a churl and thenceforth ignored him, except for class, where his iconoclastic remarks often brought discussions to a halt.

And then, one day toward the end of the semester, he spoke to me. I was in the coffee shop, studying for my European History final, when he came over to my table. Though I was nearly as tall as he, I found myself in the disconcerting position of having to look up at him. He grimaced in what I took to be an attempt at an artless American smile. "May I sit down?"

"Sure," I said.

"I don't think we've ever properly been introduced, not that it seems to matter in this country."

"What country are you from?" I coolly asked, wondering why he'd decided all of a sudden that I was worth the time of day.

"Pakistan."

So I had been close. "But you were brought up in the States?"

"That's somewhat overstating the case. I survived, shall we say, a miserable childhood in New Jersey."

"I've never been to New Jersey."

"Then you must count your blessings. Would you like a coffee?"

I had just finished one, but I said yes. He ordered mint tea for himself, and biscuits. He called them biscuits. Emily, the waitress, reappeared with four digestives on a plate, and I wondered if they kept them especially for him. She was a local girl who didn't have much patience for snotty Yalies, but she smiled at Azher as if she knew and liked him.

"Why do you always sit alone?" he asked.

"Because I like to," I said. It wasn't altogether true, but it sounded better than "because I have no one to talk to," which was the insight that came to me at that moment.

He considered this seriously. "Girls your age usually hang around in packs."

I thought at first that he was being funny, but he said it more the way an anthropologist might remark on the habits of an unfamiliar tribe. It dawned on me that he might be not so much rude as awkward.

"I'm not much for packs."

"Why not? You're young and beautiful; people must seek your company."

This remark was delivered so dryly that it would have taken considerable poetic license to interpret it as a compliment. And I didn't feel beautiful. I knew how to arouse men, lure them, but it had come to seem a bleak business, a series of learned moves that had little to do with me, and which I no longer practiced, because it was one thing to be bold at Columbia, and quite another at Yale, from which I couldn't disappear.

"Not really," I said, meaning that no, people didn't particularly seek my company, although my concerned roommate, I remembered with a smile, noting my absence from the mixers that were constantly held for our benefit, *had* left on my bed a flyer from the campus gay and lesbian organization.

My private mirth seemed to offend him. "Your French is awfully good," he said abruptly, making me wonder if he *had* meant to compliment me after all.

Clearly, I would have to smooth the way. I summoned an image of Astrid and, with my most charming smile, said, "I grew up in Paris." This proved an open field. We talked about Paris, which he loved with the reverence of those who have only spent a year there, about the cafés and bookshops he had frequented, the women in African dress, the stink of the metro. In Pakistan, he said, odors were a whole dimension unto themselves, the foul and the aromatic inextricably entwined. His parents had moved to the States from Lahore when he was six, and for the first year, his mother had sunk into a kind of sensory deprivation, wailing that nothing tasted right, and that the roses in the garden withheld their perfume. They had wanted him to be an engineer—like all the other good Paki boys, he smirked—and he had had to placate them with a double major. They had only caved in when he got into graduate school with a full scholarship, "Because now they can tell people back home that I'm at Yale, which is almost as good as Harvard, and *Professor* still carries some cachet in our benighted country." He had two sisters, the younger of whom, Zakia, was applying to next year's freshman class.

He had a sense of humor, though I had suspected as much from his comments in class. More disconcerting was the abrupt transition from ignoring me to suddenly looking very much as if he wanted to take me to bed. I hadn't been taken to bed since I had left New York. I had thought I hadn't missed it, but the anticipatory thrum in my loins suggested otherwise.

"What about you?" he said, taking me aback because, in my surprise at his being so forthcoming about himself, it hadn't occurred to me that I might be expected to reciprocate.

I smiled self-deprecatingly. "Nerdy freshman."

"Come now."

"I'm from New York. I have a glamorous mother and a father who likes opera."

"I like opera," he said, giving me no time to wonder at how easily I had, for the first time in years, put both my parents in one sentence, and whether I had invoked Astrid's glamour in the hope of shining in its refracted light.

"I don't, but I used to go with my dad." I wanted him to think I was nice, and serious, and alluring, and possibly a little dangerous, and possibly really not so nice after all. I wanted him to think that I could be whatever he wanted. I also thought it was time to take the reins of a conversation that might stray into less comfortable territory.

"Why Rabelais?" I asked, for I knew from class that he was writing his thesis on him.

"Harvey had already set his cap at Montaigne, and the conferences are more fun."

"I don't know," I said. "You don't exactly strike me as the Rabelaisian type."

He assumed the expression he wore in class when correcting Harvey. "That's because you're viewing him like everyone else, through the prism of Bakhtin."

"I haven't even read Bakhtin," I protested, though Harvey had many times offered to lend me his copy.

"I'm delighted to hear so. I hold him personally responsible for misrepresenting to millions one of the most lucid minds in history—but then, what can you expect of a Marxist. . . ."

"You mean it's not all about fucking and farting?"

He smiled a little tightly, and I wondered if he was a prude as well, though it seemed unlikely considering his chosen field of study. "No, it isn't." His expression relaxed. "I'd be delighted to tell you sometime what it *is* about, but I suspect your interest in the subject is merely passing."

I was stung, but there was clearly no point in trying to match wits with him. "I don't know," I said. "I'm surprised at how much I like him. To tell you the truth, I *did* think it was going to be about sex and farting, but"—I hesitated, afraid I would sound stupid—"it seems that he was more concerned with unmasking hypocrisy."

"Good girl," he said as if speaking to a dog. "Keep on reading."

He finished his tea, and I wondered if he was going to invite me back to his apartment—Harvey had, several times—but instead he said rather formally that it had been a pleasure talking to me, one that he hoped I would be amenable to renewing, and he reached for his coat and scarf. I regarded him quizzically. Didn't he know that he could have me if he wanted? But then maybe he didn't want me. I found the thought curiously tantalizing.

39

LEA AND SERGE were coming that year for Christmas. I took
the train down after my last exam, my holiday spirits com-
pounded by a chance meeting with Azher at the New
Haven station. I had given him my Rabelais paper to review before
I handed it in, and he had made many helpful—and a few nit-
picky—suggestions that resulted in my receiving an A with honors.
Since I had given him my number, I had hoped that he would take
it as a general invitation to call, but he had remained punctiliously
proper in his dealings with me, my attempts at conveying that I
wasn't *only* interested in French Renaissance thought falling quite
flat. By the time I bumped into him at the ticket counter, I was
resigned to what was clearly going to remain a scholarly friendship.

I was wearing lip gloss and mascara, and when he remarked
approvingly on the effect, I was first caught off guard, and then foolishly pleased. When I explained that my mother made such a big
deal about the holidays that it felt churlish not to get into the spirit,
he seemed to appreciate the sentiment. He himself was going as far
as New York, where he would catch another train to New Jersey,
and we sat together all the way to Grand Central, chatting without
a trace of the awkwardness that had sometimes hobbled our previ-
ous conversations.

Azher's family didn't celebrate Christmas, but the holiday
coincided this year with an equally festive event: the engagement
of his older sister Safiyah, who had just begun a residency in pedi-
atrics at Mount Sinai. I listened eagerly, thrilled to be included in
something private. In his expansive mood, he spoke of his older

sister unaffectedly—he was obviously fond and proud of her—and a picture formed in my mind of a tall, graceful girl with thick black hair and the same green eyes, dressed for the occasion, I imagined, in one of those lovely flowing garments that Asian graduate students sometimes wore around campus. Her fiancé was from Pakistan as well, and it was some time before I registered that she had never met him. My dismay must have been evident, because Azher suddenly grew guarded.

"Why are you surprised?" he said testily.

I scrambled for an answer. After a moment's hesitation, I blurted out, "I'm not. It's just, well—I mean, she's a doctor. Well, yes, it *is* a little surprising," I finally had to admit.

"I would have expected you to be more sophisticated," he said coldly, and again I was taken aback, because surely he could see the incongruity of this remark.

"I'm sorry," I said, trying to make my voice soothing. "I didn't mean to sound critical. I have Muslim friends in Paris," I added desperately, though the only person who came to mind was Nahid, not exactly the poster girl for Muslim propriety.

Finally, he took pity on me. "I don't expect you to understand," he said with a tight smile, "but it was her decision. She wanted a traditional marriage. Incidentally," he added, his voice mocking, "her fiancé is a doctor, too."

I took this as a peace offering, though I wasn't at all sure it was meant as one. I started to ask if there would be some sort of traditional betrothal ceremony, but his expression made it clear that I had been shut out. We moved instead to my plans. Serge had never been to America, and we would be doing the usual things; dragging him through museums he had no interest in; shopping, which interested him more; and possibly visiting Maybelle and Przemek in Louisville. I hoped Azher might perceive that we were both, in a way, tourists, visitors in a strange land, but he seemed for now unwilling to further the connection between us. When we parted at

Grand Central, the spark had died, and I was left with the gnawing impression that I had disappointed him.

Astrid was taking a nap when I got home. I didn't wake her. Despite the recession, the holiday season had been busy, and I knew she had been working long hours to satisfy the whims of her clients, who counted on her to infuse them with the illusion of originality. Since we had only two bedrooms, Lea and Serge were staying upstairs, in the apartment of Astrid's friends Claude and Jasper, who had gone to Palm Beach for the holidays. After dropping my bag in my room, I went up to find them, but there was no answer to my knock. I was about to go back down when I heard them come in. Serge appeared in the stairwell, weighed down with shopping bags. Lea followed, a cake box in her hand.

"Oh, there you are—I hope you didn't wake Mom; she's a bit under the weather."

"What's wrong?"

"*Crise de foie*—we've been living it up in your absence; Harold took us to Bouley."

Inside the apartment, Serge kissed me on both cheeks, and Lea gave me a hug, mindful of the cake box that she was still holding.

"There's some champagne in the fridge," Lea said to Serge. "Why don't you open it, so we can celebrate properly?"

Serge went into the kitchen, whence the pop of a cork was shortly heard. Lea said she'd be right back, and disappeared down the hall. When she returned, a malicious smile on her face, she handed me a small white satin photo album. "Want to see the Little Viking? Inge made it just for you."

I opened the book. The baby looked like any baby, chubby and bald and vaguely offended.

"She's cute," I said.

"Don't be fooled: She howls day and night, and won't keep her food down, not even the nice *Bio* carrots that Inge purées for her. Poor old Dad has circles under his eyes like saucers. He suggested they hire a night nurse, but Inge says—here she affected a Swedish accent—"Oh no no no, dahling, ve must *bond*."

I smiled. The picture of Frank trying to bond with a newborn was as felicitously preposterous as the notion of his having had a hand in its conception. "Poor Dad; is he completely miserable?"

"If he is, you'll have to pry it out of him through torture. Let's just say he takes many of his meals out. God, the things men will do for sex. . . ." Lea sighed and gazed complacently at Serge, who had joined us with the champagne. By then, it required an effort of imagination to discern in this placid product of Paris's bon chic bon genre set the despoiler of Delphine's virtue. Indeed, I had come to believe Lea's explanation of what she assured me was a most uncharacteristic instance of debauchery: Serge had needed the money to pay a poker debt. I doubted he had played poker since, or engaged in any of the high jinks that had earned him a clearly undeserved reputation. Barely into his twenties, Serge already seemed to be anticipating middle age. He had even, I was amused to notice, adopted Frank's practice of affecting great interest in female banter while his mind sought refuge elsewhere. "Dad sends his love by the way," Lea happily continued. "He says he's going to come and visit you, take you on a tour of the old haunts. Clearly, any excuse will do."

I smirked in acknowledgment and accepted a glass from Serge. He handed one to Lea next and joined her on the sofa, where she stretched out to put her feet in his lap. I felt a pang of jealousy at their easy intimacy. Was it chemical? What did they talk about when they were alone? Was it enough that they shared the same interests, and were more or less of the same caste? I didn't fit anywhere. At Yale, there was a New York crowd, an arty crowd, a black crowd, the athletes, who formed their own subculture, even a sizeable European set that was dismissed by anyone outside it as Eurotrash, but I belonged to none of them. I wasn't even strange enough to be considered a genuine oddball. I was just me, waiting for someone to find me intriguing. Serge and Lea, I was sure, had never found each other intriguing. They had just fallen together like two pieces of a puzzle.

Even Serge's staunchly Catholic family had finally had to accept the inevitable that Lea had once so blithely invoked, and his mother had started dropping hints as to the advantages of conversion. I didn't doubt that Lea would oblige her when the time came. My sister was a lifelong adept at accommodation. She also hadn't lit up since arriving, and neither had Serge. I eyed them suspiciously.

"Why aren't you smoking?"

"Mmmmmmmmm?" Lea affected incomprehension. Serge's hand had come to rest on her ankle and, as she lay there like a contented odalisque, her eyes filled with a secret and rather bovine satisfaction.

"You're not!" I exclaimed.

Her lips stretched into a wicked smile. "I am."

"Since when?"

"We just found out. I did one of those home tests before leaving, but actually I've known for ages. I have to pee every five minutes; it was a real drag on the airplane," she added with a complicit look at Serge, who already had the air of a man resigned to learning much more about female body functions than he'd ever wanted to.

I jumped up. "We have to tell Mom!"

"I was waiting till you got here—poor Astrid, a grandmother at fifty . . ."

"Are you kidding; she'll be thrilled."

"Dad was thunderstruck—though he tried hard not to show it. I hope it's a boy, for his sake."

"What are you going to do about school?" I asked.

"I'll have to drop out."

I stared at her. "Are you crazy?"

"I'm not going to be one of those pregnant students."

I shook my head, but only for form. As usual, Lea was doing exactly what she wanted. As if to emphasize this, she smiled happily.

"I'm afraid that, in my condition, the only recourse is a shotgun wedding, and Serge's parents will see to that, won't they, darling?"

Serge smiled and made a sort of philosophical half shrug, as if to say, it's all out of my hands now. I guessed that he was pleased, since he didn't have the look of a man trapped. The look I'd seen on my father.

Astrid was indeed thrilled. We told her that night at dinner, at her favorite neighborhood restaurant, and she burst into tears and called all the waiters over. The waiters were all gay and made much of Serge being so handsome, and he took it all with good grace. Astrid couldn't have cared less about being a grandmother at fifty; she wasn't vain in that way, and, unlike me, she didn't ask about the practical details. Marriage never came up. Astrid never had much of a romantic notion of marriage, and I doubted Lea did, either. She really was French in that way: To her it was the formalization of an obvious state, a change in her *état civil*. It was one of the things that made sense, as opposed to the many that didn't, such as my parents' marriage, though I thought it had made a kind of sense to Astrid. It was my father who had taken a blind leap of faith in marrying, and I wondered if that was how Azher's sister saw it.

We had a lovely, quiet Christmas and spent New Year's Eve playing Scrabble at home. The only disappointment was that we never made it to Kentucky to visit Maybelle. Astrid had come down with a bug, and, although I suspected that it was a convenient excuse, I didn't press her. The truth was that I had no great desire to go, either. I, too, had grown distant from Maybelle; found her a little ridiculous, a little embarrassing, like a childhood toy I had outgrown. It seemed to me that my affection for her had always been tainted by pity, and now that she had found Przemek, I was let off the hook. And I was eager to get back to New Haven. I knew that Azher would be back early, too, to prepare for a course he would be assistant-teaching the following semester, and it seemed only natural that I might bump into him.

40

I DIDN'T HAVE TO. When I got back to New Haven, there was a message from Azher on my answering machine. I called him immediately.

"Hello," he said. "I've been thinking about you."

We became lovers with an expediency that betrayed us both. After an indifferent meal in an Italian restaurant, we went back to his apartment in the graduate student towers. We were barely in the door before he grabbed me and ground his mouth into mine, backing me up against the wall as he pressed hungrily against me. I was thrown off, at first, by his intensity, until it dawned on me that it might arise from inexperience. There was a fumbling awkwardness to his touch, which suggested that he hadn't had many lovers, and the idea that I, after all, might be the more sophisticated one affected me in the most unexpected of ways. Even as he tore at my clothes, and tried almost brutally to enter me, I was overwhelmed by a need to protect him, for it seemed clear, all of a sudden, that I had been the seductress, and his anguished cry as he came only confirmed my guilt.

He gave me no pleasure that time, but I didn't require it. Indeed, there was something strangely moving about his ineptitude. I was used to men roving my body with encyclopedic skill, their touch cheapened by its assurance. Now their solicitude seemed almost cynical. When we were finished, he helped me up from the floor, in a courtly gesture that brought a smile to my lips. Azher, however, wasn't smiling. He looked profoundly shaken, and I hoped he wasn't already regretting his fall from grace. "Would you like to shower?" he asked, avoiding my eyes. I said I would and he got me a big white towel from the linen cupboard, and showed me into the bathroom. As the hot water streamed over me, I leaned my head against the tiles and tried to compose my thoughts, sensing that the way I behaved when I emerged would determine the future course of our relationship. To buy time, I soaped myself, and washed my hair twice, though it didn't need it.

When I came out, he had regained his composure. He offered me a drink, and I asked for a glass of wine, which he poured for me, before putting on water for himself for tea. With dinner he'd had juice, a choice that had struck me as affectingly childish. I wondered if he had bought the wine for me.

"You don't drink alcohol," I said.

"I'm a Muslim."

I kept my next thought to myself, an image of Nahid, sitting at the bar in the Bains Douches with a tequila sunrise.

"Why are you smiling?" he asked.

"Nothing, I was just thinking of a friend of mine who takes a somewhat laxer view of the strictures of Islam."

"Then she can't be much of a Muslim," he said, and I was afraid I might have offended him, until I realized that he was just indifferent, that persons who took a lax view of Islam held no interest for him.

As we sat in the small living room, me with wet hair in a terry-cloth bathrobe that I had found on the back of the bathroom door, and Azher fully clothed, the fact that we had just made love receded into a sort of surreal implausibility; and when he asked what I had done over the break, I began to wonder if it had even happened. All of a sudden, I wished I had my clothes on, but they were scattered all over the hallway floor, and there seemed no way to retrieve them without invoking an intimacy whose moment had clearly passed. Gathering the robe more snugly about me, I told Azher about our family reunion, realizing as I did that I had never elaborated on the reason we required reuniting in the first place.

"Your parents are divorced?"

"Yes," I said, a little self-consciously, for there was something in his expression that suggested that he disapproved.

"And your father married his secretary?"

"Well, she was more of an administrative assistant. She's actually quite well educated," I added, though in fact I knew nothing of Inge's education, save to assume that it had been minimal.

Azher smiled. "Interesting," he said, and took another sip of his tea.

"Actually it's quite banal," I retorted, piqued.

He raised an eyebrow. "For men to divorce their wives and marry an office girl?"

"She wasn't an office girl," I said, apprehending as I spoke the reason for my embarrassment: I had left out, in my abbreviated retelling, Astrid's affair and her flight to Poland, casting Frank, I suddenly realized, in the role of a bounder.

"I don't know why people bother with divorce—the rewards seem incommensurate with the fuss."

I shrugged and assumed an air of world-weary boredom. "You could say the same about marriage." Who was he to pass judgment on us? Had he not just stood by as his sister was sold off as chattel?

Azher smiled again in his slightly superior way. He had very white teeth. Despite myself, I felt a pang of longing.

"I disagree," he said. "I think marriage is a very good thing indeed. In fact I quite look forward to it," he mused, affecting a distant air that made it clear that I wasn't the object of this pleasant anticipation.

I wished I could smoke, wreathe myself in alluring veils, but he evidently did not indulge in this weakness at home. I felt slack and desperate. More than anything, I wanted him to touch me, but the gulf between us seemed only to be growing wider. Maybe he perceived my anguish, for his expression suddenly softened.

"Come here," he said, and as I crossed the room, I could have whimpered with relief. We made love more slowly the second time, and fell asleep on his narrow bed, and the sound of his breathing when I woke up in the night lulled me back to sleep. In the morning, I watched him boil water for tea. He set a cup before me, along with a plate of biscuits, and joined me at the table. As I lifted the cup to my lips, he did the same. It was the most intimate thing that had ever happened between us.

41

BY THE TIME FRANK came to visit me, Azher and I had settled into a routine. I went to his apartment on Monday, Wednesday, and Thursday evenings, and he made dinner; rice and okra, or a curry he'd brought back from his parents' house, where he often spent the weekend. After dinner, we went to bed, where he proved, in time, to be a curious, even attentive lover. I never asked if there had been others, because I didn't care. I felt unique to him. I began to tell him things about myself; that I was slow, and often had to fumble for words; that my estrangement from my parents had caused me pain, even as I felt it to be necessary. He didn't understand. Family, to him, was a given, the immutable underpinning of his being. He rarely discussed his and, though his reticence frustrated me, I learned to accept it as discretion. His frustrations were intellectual: He was teaching a course on Zola that semester, and it drove him mad that the only book that his students had read was *Nana*. He abhorred the cheap sensationalism that had overtaken literary criticism. His dandyish exterior was a front. He was an ardent academic and devoted son, and probably the only person at the yearly Rabelais conference at Chinon who drank only mineral water. He loved the sixteenth century for its hard brilliance, and scorned the nineteenth, the one I liked, for its slackness. He admired the French even as he faintly despised them. He didn't like to kiss.

Frank was due shortly, and I awaited his arrival with anxious eagerness. I wanted to please; it was a once familiar state that now beguiled me with its novelty. To please: such an easy thing. The mere idea made me feel womanly. We would visit the Beinecke library, Frank would like that, and the British Museum, and there was always some concert being held; I would have to check into that. We would dine at Mory's. We would be like any of the other families I saw touring the campus, the parents eager and proud, the kids a little bored but putting a good face on it.

"Come have dinner with us one night," I suggested to Azher the day before Frank arrived, for this thought had been at the forefront of my mind all along. I pictured them in conversation, Azher impressed by my father's casual erudition, Frank enjoying a worthy opponent, me basking in the refracted brilliance of the meeting of these two like minds. I was so taken by this vision that it took me a few seconds to recognize the look in Azher's eyes as one of discomfort.

"I don't think that would be appropriate."

"Don't be silly," I said lightly, trying to mask my disappointment.

"Believe me, it's for your sake."

Had it not been for the seriousness of his expression, I would have burst out laughing. Did he think Frank was going to thrash him for dishonoring me?

"If you're worried about what he's going to think, let me ease your mind. As you pointed out yourself, his own situation wouldn't exactly stand up to moral scrutiny."

That I had said exactly the wrong thing was clear before it was halfway out. Azher now looked not only uncomfortable, but angry as well.

"It has nothing to do with you, or your father," he said, his voice tight. "It has to do with me."

I felt an angry flush rise to my cheeks. Since Azher and I had never fought, it was a little disconcerting. But then what would we have fought about, and what were we fighting about now? That he didn't want to meet my father, whom most people would be honored to know? That there was a me, and a him, and they had nothing to do with each other? How do you fight over intimations? You don't, unless you're the kind of hysterical woman that I was determined not to be. I unruffled my feathers: He had his reasons, undoubtedly honorable ones, and who was I to make demands, with my messily divorced parents and my dissipated past, of which Azher naturally knew nothing. Shutting up, I told myself, was the price of, well, of what? I wasn't sure, but it seemed worth it.

"It's all right," I said soothingly. "You'd probably be bored."

I couldn't remember the last time I had had Frank to myself. We hovered nervously about each other at first, but soon grew easier. He had stopped off in Greenwich, and I could tell that the meeting with my grandmother hadn't gone well. He mentioned it only once, and I didn't enquire further. We embarked on a visit of his old haunts, which were pretty much what you would have expected for a man of his generation, though when I teased him, as we passed its headquarters, about whether he had belonged to the Skull and Bones Society, he only smiled mysteriously and said that if he told me, he'd have to kill me. To my relief, he had no interest in attending a football game. We did, however go to Mory's, where the food was as bad as everyone said it was. It didn't matter. I ate my clam chowder with an oar hanging over my head and felt happy to be with my father. He asked me if I liked Yale, and I realized that I'd never asked myself. I did like Yale; I felt at home there. I felt inconspicuous, and that, to me, was the mark of belonging. That I was not inconspicuous to Azher was another reason I felt at home, though more uneasily. We talked about how much I'd enjoyed my Rabelais seminar, and about my major, probably Comparative Literature. It was just the kind of stuff we used to talk about, and I relaxed gratefully into our old camaraderie. All of a sudden it didn't seem so aberrant that we should have a separate relationship. In a way, we always had, and I was glad after all that Azher had turned down my invitation, because it would indeed have made things more awkward. He had shown delicacy.

I waited for Frank to say something about my new half sister. It was one thing not to mention Inge, but this child was related to me; to us. Finally, I took the plunge.

"How's Marguerite? I can't wait to meet her." This was a complete lie, but I was on my best behavior.

Frank shifted his gaze to a spot on the table. With an air of acute self-consciousness, he pulled a clip of photographs from his pocket and passed them to me.

"She's sweet," I said, and then, inanely, "She looks like Inge," which wasn't at all true since, like most newborns, if Marguerite bore a resemblance to anyone, it was to Uncle Fester in *The Addams Family.*

"You mustn't hate Inge," Frank said, looking so exceedingly uncomfortable that I had to deduce that she'd put him up to it.

Oh God, I thought. "I don't hate her, Dad. I'm glad you got married again. There's no reason you should be alone," I dutifully added, though I suspected that that was very much the state he would prefer. I didn't add that Astrid was no longer alone, either. The list of unmentionable topics was getting longer and longer.

Frank cleared his throat and looked desperately about before fixing his eyes on mine with visible reluctance. "She thinks you do. She—ah, I believe she's upset that you didn't send a present for the baby. I tried to explain to her that, well, that we're not that kind of family—" he stopped, defeated.

Little bitch, I thought, because in fact Lea had gone to Bonpoint and purchased, in both our names, an extravagant layette. Suddenly I saw us through Azher's eyes: spastic, undignified, caving in to every puerile transport. No wonder he hadn't wanted to join us. Something rebelled in me at that moment, and I saw my parents' marriage in all its tawdriness. I saw that what I had always thought of as Frank's reserve was in fact a helpless muteness, a form of emotional autism that must have practically driven Astrid into other men's arms. I saw her carelessness, her barely concealed deceits, and the willful denial that had made Frank look the other way. I saw the whole carefully constructed edifice of their love as the fiction that it was, and I despised them both. As if he could read my thoughts, Frank winced.

"You are so much like her," he said, and he shook his head, as if in wonder, or to clear it of a painful memory.

But I wasn't. We both knew that. I lacked the unflinching will that would always make her prevail. For it had never occurred to me until that moment that she had won, that he was the one diminished. My father sat before me, crushed by life's unfairness, and I was seized with a terrible pity. I reached out my hand to hold his across the table, a gesture that he yielded to with a kind of relief.

We spent his last afternoon at the British Museum, where the Turners and Constables seemed to restore him to tranquility. It wasn't my kind of art—the Blake prints spoke more to me—but I could appreciate the sure and steady hand behind the lines. When he left the next day, he asked if I would spend the summer in Paris, and I said I couldn't, I already had an internship lined up in New York, but I would try to come for a visit. It was only afterward that I realized that it was the closest he had ever come to saying that he needed me.

42

I WENT HOME THE FOLLOWING WEEKEND. I hadn't seen Astrid since Christmas break, and I suddenly missed her desperately. I made plans. We would see an old French movie at Film Forum and then have dinner at one of her favorite places in the Village, or just laze around the apartment reading and playing Scrabble. She was always trying to get me to go shopping, and maybe I would let her—Azher had remarked more than once on the way I dressed, little realizing that I had sprung from the loins of one of the most elegant women on earth. Feeling very much like the prodigal daughter, I took a cab from Grand Central to Jane Street, and was getting out in front of our building when I spied Harold turning the corner, a folded *New York Times* tucked under his arm.

"Ah, Charlotte," he hailed me, pecking me on the cheek. "I didn't know you were coming down."

I tried to suppress my irritation. Harold hadn't figured in my vision of the weekend, nor had it occurred to me that he and Astrid might have made plans of their own. "I thought I'd surprise my mom," I said, scrabbling around in my backpack for my key.

Harold seemed ill at ease. He cleared his throat. "Ah, Charlotte, may I speak with you?"

I lifted my eyes, puzzled. Surely this could wait?

Apparently it couldn't. "It's a rather delicate matter. May I offer you a cup of coffee?" And he motioned to the French bakery on the corner, which, most unFrenchly, served cappuccino and low-fat muffins to the yuppies who were taking over the neighborhood.

Mystified, I followed him in, and waited at one of the small tables while he ordered. When he came back with our coffees in paper cups, he put them down carefully, then he folded his overcoat over the back of the chair. I was reminded of the way Azher always neatly folded his pants on a chair. Azher was spending the weekend at home with his family, and I would be, too, shortly, as soon as Harold got done with whatever he had to say to me. Suddenly I knew: He and Astrid were getting married. He wanted to break it to me gently. He probably figured I'd have objections, after the way I'd carried on at his summer house. Poor Harold; he didn't know about the new, accommodating me.

"I have misgivings about telling you this," he said when he was finally seated, "But I see no other solution. Your mother has been diagnosed with leukemia. It is treatable; she begins chemotherapy Monday at Saint Vincent's." He frowned.

I gaped at him as if he were speaking a foreign language. Then the words began to arrange themselves in order, but they remained afloat, suspended. I observed them with scientific disinterest, a curious phenomenon that had nothing to do with me.

"Charlotte?"

I had been reading one of the poststructuralist critics for a class. The idea was that text—they always called it text, as if it were written in hieroglyphs—was separate from meaning. It hadn't made much sense at the time, in fact had sounded kind of dumb and contrived. But at this moment, it seemed not only plausible but necessary that signifier and signified should have nothing to do with each other. Words. Harmless. Ineffectual. Meaningless.

"Why didn't she tell me?"

Harold creased his brow into that concentrated little frown again. "She didn't want to upset you." He must have realized how ludicrous this sounded, because he evaded my gaze again. "I—I am terribly concerned about her. I wanted her to go to Sloan-Kettering, but she insisted on Saint Vincent's. She says she wants to stay in the Village," he added, shaking his head in wonder.

I looked down at the scummy foam on my coffee, which I

hadn't touched yet. They'd sprinkled cinnamon on it. I hated cinnamon; it reminded me of airport lounges. I felt the queasy buoyancy of impending nausea. A thought came into my head that we needed to rewind this tape and start over. None of this had happened. It was like the tree falling in the forest. But Harold was speaking again.

"I'm sorry?" I said.

"Perhaps it was wrong to tell you. I—I'm afraid it's quite serious. Of course, I only know what she has chosen to tell me."

The tree fell. "She's going to die," I said.

Harold awkwardly placed his hand on my forearm, and I had to restrain myself from not shaking it off. "It's not what it used to be; there are new treatments. I understand the doctor is quite hopeful."

Was he completely stupid? I knew all about leukemia. I'd read a book years ago called *Death Be Not Proud*, about a boy who died from it. Delphine had given it to me; we'd both wept ourselves sick over it.

"I'm going up to see her," I said, rising.

Harold followed suit. "Of course." He looked crestfallen. "I apologize. I have committed a breach of trust. But I believe that your mother would have been fully capable of hiding this from you. She's a very stubborn woman," he added, in the voice of one who admires stubborn women, but also fears them.

Outside he said, "I'll leave you now," but I had already turned away. I walked the few steps to our building and let myself in. I went up the stairs. We lived on the second floor, but it felt like I climbed forever. From behind our door, I heard music. "Lucy in the Sky with Diamonds." Forgetting that I had a key, I pushed the buzzer. Astrid opened the door. She was wearing red harem pants and a long shirt the color of fresh lettuce, and I thought, this is not what a woman with leukemia looks like. Then I saw that she was pale, and the little furrow on her brow. I started to wail.

"How?" she cried, but I was clinging to her like a lifeboat, and the rest got muffled by my sobs.

Eventually we went into the kitchen. "Let's have a glass of wine," she said. And then, "How did you find out?"

I told her.

She smiled sadly. "Poor Harold; I knew he couldn't keep it to himself. He's taking it harder than I am."

I searched her face for some terrible mark, but she looked the same, just tired and worried. "How did you think you could keep this from us?" I blurted out.

"I've kept all sorts of things from you," she said with a flash of her old slyness. "Why not this?"

"Mom!" I cried.

"I'm sorry, baby. One of the dreary little pamphlets I got at the doctor's said that other people always take it harder. That's as far as I got, to tell you the truth, before tossing them all in the garbage."

Compassion isn't the only emotion that the sick elicit in the healthy. The other is annoyance, at their refusal to bow to our suddenly immense expertise. In my most sanctimonious voice, I scolded, "You can't do this, Mom. You have to educate yourself, get a second opinion—there are all sorts of new therapies; you have to take control, you—" I stopped. I had no idea what I was talking about. I didn't know anything about leukemia except that it killed you.

Astrid smiled. Crazily, this conversation seemed to be cheering her up. "Honey, I've educated myself as much as I care to. Either this treatment will work, or I'll die, and my doctor, who is perfectly good, if a bit humorless, seems to think the former. It appears that otherwise I am in excellent health. Fancy that, after all those cigarettes. . . ."

I almost felt sorry for her doctor, whoever he was. There was clearly no reasoning with her. Still, I tried. For lack of anything else, I summoned Harold's words. "Why won't you go to Sloan-Kettering? "

"Sweetie, *everyone* has cancer there. I want to be somewhere with babies."

I could feel the scowl etching itself into my face. A mad thought ran through my mind, that this time, she wasn't going to get away with it. "I'm taking a leave from school."

She turned dead serious. "You will do no such thing. I've caused enough trouble." I was preparing myself for a glaring contest when she broke into a mischievous smile. "Besides, Grace is coming over. You know Grace, she loves a project. . . . She's threatening to put me on a macrobiotic diet, which is incentive enough to get well."

This would all have been very convincing, had I not seen the fear in her eyes.

"The semester just started. It's no big deal."

"You are not leaving school, Charlotte."

"You can't stop me."

We eyed each other mutinously, then something seemed to falter within her. "I know I can't. I am asking you not to quit school. One in the family is enough."

Damn you, Lea, I thought. "How long does the chemotherapy take?"

"Five days," Astrid said resignedly. "I'll be in the hospital, and Grace will be with me. She's flying in tomorrow."

Grace? Why Grace? Why not me?

"Fine. I'll take next week off. People do it all the time; it's called family reasons. I have all my reading—I can work in the hospital."

"Baby, I wish you wouldn't."

"And you have to tell Lea, and Maybelle."

"No!"

"Mom, you cannot keep this from them."

She closed her eyes wearily. *Oh God,* I thought, *I've defeated her.*

"Maybelle will take over. I can't bear it. That's why Grace is coming: She'll be silly and useless and get in the way; it'll cheer me up."

"They have a right to know, Mom," I said.

Anger flashed through her eyes. "No they don't! It's my illness and I will tell whomever I please. I will not have this whole thing turned into a three-ring circus. Tell them if you must, but for God's sake, keep them away."

"I'm sorry," I said.

"Do you know what I'd like? A normal evening out, with my daughter."

"That's why I'm here."

"And I wasn't even expecting you. Let's get dressed up and go out to dinner. Let's live it up."

"Okay," I said. "Can I borrow something to wear?"

"Can I choose?"

"Yes," I said. "You can choose."

It seemed like such a big gesture, and now I don't even remember what I wore that night. Something gorgeous, I'm sure. People looked at us. We went to Max's, a little place around the corner where the waiters loved her and they had a piano. Waiters always loved Astrid. Waiters, busboys, hotel clerks, the mailman, the guy with the mole in the stationery store. I loved Astrid; the loss of her was unthinkable. In fact, I had already unthought it. My mother had leukemia, but here we were at Max's, just as if nothing had happened. "Might as well live it up," she said gaily, and I tried not to notice that she was out of breath from the short walk. I didn't know yet about white blood cells, about how they pullulate and crowd out the red ones out, the ones that carry oxygen. I didn't know anything. We had duck and fried potatoes, which she picked at, and a bottle of wine, of which she only had one glass, though she said she wanted to get drunk. I drank the rest. I told her about Frank's visit and she sighed commiseratively. "To think of all the women who would have snapped him up in two seconds. . . . Is the baby sweet?"

"I think he feels terrible because he doesn't love it."

"How sad," Astrid said with feeling.

"Yes," I lied, because I happily would have traded Marguerite's, anyone's life for hers. I glanced around the room, which appeared to me to be full of infinitely more suitable candidates: The seedy-looking guy at the bar; no one would miss him, or—I stopped myself. We were living it up. I told the story of how Frank had been forced to assist at the birth.

"Your poor father; he never could stand the sight of blood. Honestly, I don't know who came up with the idea that men should watch us have babies—next thing you know, they'll be following us into the loo."

"Lea says she's throwing Serge out as soon as the contractions begin—much to his relief, apparently."

"I'm glad Lea's pregnant," Astrid said. "She's going to be one of those wonderful, no-nonsense mothers. And Serge is just dull enough to be thrilled."

I smiled. Partners in crime again.

"I'm not the least bit worried about Lea," Astrid continued. "She's exactly where she wants to be. I plan to wear red to the wedding—are they really having it in April?"

I assured her that they were, at the Polish Church. One simply did not get married in winter, and even April was stretching the limits, but Lea had found a brilliant *couturière* who specialized in *enceinte* brides, and just in case, Serge's father had applied for some kind of papal dispensation.

"Just as well, I should be in tip-top shape by then. Must we really tell her?"

I eyed her severely. "Mom . . ."

"Don't be so sanctimonious, darling; it doesn't suit you," Astrid said flippantly.

"Her doctor probably won't let her travel. You know French doctors . . ."

"Yes, but nothing will keep Maybelle away. I'm so tired of owing things to Maybelle. . . . Why can't *she* ever get in trouble?"

"You're not in trouble, Mom."

"You don't call this trouble?"

I didn't say anything.

"I'm scared."

I grabbed her hand. "We'll get through this," I said. "We've gotten through everything else, and we'll get through this, too."

43

ASTRID HAD SOMETHING CALLED acute myelogenous leukemia, AML for short. I went to the library and looked it up. The survival rate was 19.8 percent. By survival rate, they meant five years. I threw up in the library bathroom, went home via Astrid's favorite bakery, where I picked up brownies, and took out *Shanghai Express* from the video rental.

"*It took more than one man to change my name to Shanghai Lily . . .*" Angus, the nice gay man behind the counter, hammed it up. Why couldn't Angus get leukemia? Surely the Village could do without another silly queen. "How's your mom?" he asked with concern, and I was instantly consumed with shame.

"Fine." My mom had a 19.8 percent chance of surviving for five years. Which meant that she had an 80.2 percent chance of dying.

"Give her my love," Angus said, and I promised I would, though I wouldn't, because Astrid and I both knew that Angus's love wouldn't make any difference.

While Astrid was napping—that was how she had known something was wrong, she had started taking naps all the time—I called Lea.

"I'm coming over."

"Don't, not yet. If we all rush to her bedside, she'll think we think she's going to die."

"I *do not* think she's going to die; how can you say that!"

"Let her get through the treatment—you can come when she's home. It'll only be a few days."

"I don't know . . ." Lea hesitated.

"She's not going to die, Lea." I didn't add *"immediately."*

"What about Dad?"

"Don't tell him," I said. "There's nothing he can do." *And I can't deal with it.*

"I'll come next week."

"Fine," I said.

"But if you need me, I'll get on the next flight."

Maybelle took the news with astounding composure. She was, of course, a nurse, though I wasn't even sure what kind. She'd never told us much about her job, and we'd never asked; maybe she thought it would bore us, her unglamorous occupation. Whatever the reason, I was grateful for her calm. She asked about what kind of leukemia, and the treatment, and I told her what little I knew; then she said to make sure I spoke with the doctor, which I had in fact planned to do, in the hospital, if I could get him aside without Astrid noticing.

"I want you to call me after you talk to the doctor. I'm here if you need me, honey. Just call and I'll get on a plane."

"I think we're okay for now," I said. "Grace is on her way."

"Then I'm definitely not needed." She didn't sound bitter, just matter-of-fact.

I laughed. "Believe me, I'd rather have you."

"It's not a popularity contest. You let her have her way now, while she can."

I started to cry.

"And you can't cry around her. If you need to cry, call me."

"Okay," I whispered.

"You hang in there."

We watched *Shanghai Express,* Astrid's favorite movie in the world. She fell asleep halfway through. When she woke up, she said, "Oh no, I missed the best part."

"It's okay, Mom," I said. "You've seen it thousands of times."

Astrid had been right about Grace. She was a welcome distraction. When we arrived at the hospital, she pronounced Astrid's room uninhabitable and immediately ran off to remedy the situation. "It's a good thing we're not at Mount Sinai; SoHo is just around the corner. . . ."

I sat with my mother while they dripped poison into her veins. I'd read enough by then to know how toxic the drugs were. She would lose her hair, of course, but Grace had brought three fabulous wigs from Paris, though Astrid insisted she would just walk around bald. "Bald I came into the world, and bald I will walk around the cancer ward." The nurses were all brisk and cheerful, as if getting shot up with toxic chemicals was just a routine matter. In that place, I supposed it was. They took great pains to explain what they were doing, and how Astrid would feel afterward (tired, achey, possibly nauseous). They made it all sound very manageable. "I don't have to wear one of those awful gowns, do I?" They didn't mind Astrid keeping her own clothes on—I'd seen two women in hospital garb in the hallway on the way in. They looked like convicts. They were obviously much sicker.

"I don't know why they make the poor nurses wear those unflattering outfits," Astrid said.

"I can't feel anything," Astrid said, as the red drug—they were all different colors, snaked its way down the IV tube.

"Such a pretty color," Astrid said. "Will it make me feel dreadful?"

"It depends on the individual," the nurse said cheerfully. "Some people don't get nauseous at all."

"But everyone loses their hair."

"Well . . ."

"Baby, do me a favor—I should've thought of this earlier. Call Jason and ask him if he'd come in and cut it."

"In the hospital?"

"It's all right with us," the nurse said cheerfully. All these cheerful nurses were beginning to grate on me.

"Don't you want to wait—"

"No," my mother said sharply, and when I told Maybelle that night, she said it was actually a good idea, because otherwise it would come out in clumps, and Astrid would *hate* that. When I told Harold, he said, awkwardly, "Give her my love." She wouldn't let him come to the hospital. "Men are useless in hospitals," she said.

Grace returned, loaded down with shopping bags and flowers, just as Doctor Rosen arrived. He looked to be around sixty, which reassured me, and had a terse manner that managed somehow not to be unfriendly. He seemed to like Astrid. She had charmed him, won him over. He would go the extra mile for her. She was going to be a special patient.

"How are you feeling?" he asked.

Astrid smiled. "Fine." She did look fine so far. She had refused to lie on the bed, and was sitting in the ugly vinyl armchair. She was wearing caramel-colored cashmere pants. I had called Jason and he'd cried on the phone and promised he'd come tomorrow.

"You can't cry around her," I said.

The doctor looked at some charts and left after patting Astrid on the arm. While Grace was arranging flowers, I ducked out behind him.

"Excuse me."

"Yes?"

"I'm her daughter. Could I ask you a few questions?"

"Let's step into the waiting room," he said.

In the waiting room, which was painted mint green and, like the rest of the hematology/oncology ward, hung with framed impressionist prints from the Metropolitan, we sat down and Doctor Rosen said, "I'm sure you have questions. I'm afraid I only have a few minutes, but I'll try to answer them."

I had made a list of intelligent, educated questions, but at that moment they evaporated. "How bad is it?"

He regarded me appraisingly. He must have decided that I could take it. "It doesn't get much worse."

"Oh," I said.

"You're an intelligent young woman. I understand you go to Yale. I'm sure you've read some of the literature."

"Yes," I admitted, as if I'd done something sneaky.

"I can give you more if you'd like, but I suggest you focus on taking care of her. We take this one day at a time. I understand that your mother has a sister?"

"Yes."

"She needs to get typed."

"I beg your pardon?"

"In the event that your mother should require a bone-marrow transplant."

"But what about me, and my sister?"

"Siblings are usually a better fit. I'm sorry, I have other patients waiting. Go be with your mother; this is going to be a rough week," he said, more gently.

"I'm sorry—" I was, I didn't want to keep him from his patients. I didn't want to be pushy. I understood that we were only one of many. Or rather, I didn't, but it seemed best to stay on his good side. "It's just—about the transplant."

"We're not there yet. It may not be necessary, and it may not be an option. She has to achieve a meaningful remission first."

What was an unmeaningful remission?

Back in the room, Grace had flung a brightly colored throw on the bed, and lit scented candles.

"I doubt that's allowed," I said.

"We won't know until someone says so," Grace said blithely. "Who wants a brownie? I went to Dean & DeLuca."

"Ugh," Astrid said.

Grace rushed to her side. "Are you getting nauseous?"

"No, I just don't want a brownie."

"How about a milk shake?"

"Grace, why don't *you* have a brownie? You look like you're about to dwindle away. . . ."

"Colonic irrigation! Everyone's doing it; there's this fabulous new man who—"

"Now I *will* throw up."

"Oh, sorry."

The chemo nurse came back. She wasn't so cheerful when she saw the candles.

"That's against the rules," she said. I looked meaningfully at Grace.

"*Sorry* . . ." Grace gave the nurse's retreating back a petulant look and snuffed the candles out, then she collapsed into the other chair. "I guess smoking isn't allowed, either. How are you feeling *now?*"

"The same," Astrid said wearily.

"Laure de Savigny threw up the whole time, but then she *is* bulimic."

"How on earth would you know?"

"About the bulimia?"

"No, about the throwing up."

"Candy visited her in the hospital. She held the basin."

"Please make sure you keep Candy away," Astrid said. "I didn't know Laure had cancer."

"Breast, much worse. Double mastectomy."

They hooked her up to another drug. Green this time. We watched her. She said, "Stop watching me. Why don't you go for a walk?"

Grace went down for a cigarette, and I walked around the ward. The patients were mostly old, but there was a young man, in his twenties, tethered to an IV on a wheeled stand and walking around with his father. Except for being bald, he looked to be in pretty good shape. The younger you were, I had read, the better your chances. I wondered if everyone had leukemia, or if there were other cancers, too. I went back to the room, where Grace was lining up bottles on the bedside table.

"Aromatherapy, for the nausea."

"I'm not nauseous; I'm bored."

They brought dinner on a plastic tray, but Astrid made a face. "I know!" Grace said. "We'll order in."

"I'm not hungry."

"Can you feel anything?"

"Why don't you both go out for dinner and come back? You're going to drive me crazy."

I took Grace's arm. "Come on."

"Maybe she won't lose her hair," Grace said in the elevator. "Some people don't."

That was the first day. Astrid refused to let us spend the night so we went home. "*Shanghai Express!*" Grace exclaimed, picking up the tape. She slid it into the VCR and sat on the couch. We hadn't talked much on the way home. The movie came on.

"I'm going to bed," I said, but I lingered for a few minutes. It was my favorite movie, too, just as coffee, like Astrid's was my favorite ice-cream flavor. I realized suddenly that Grace looked exhausted.

"I always thought that could've been me and Astrid," she said wistfully.

I wasn't feeling kind. "Grace, they're prostitutes."

"Oh, darling, in a way we all are. . . ."

On the second day, Astrid lay on the bed, covered in one of the shawls Grace had brought. "See, I knew they'd come in handy." Jason came and cut her hair. "Gorgeous," Grace said. "Very gamine."

She didn't look like a gamine. She looked like someone in a concentration camp.

"Do you want me to save it?" Jason asked.

"Oh God, don't be morbid."

"You look fabulous—we should've done this ages ago!"

I found Jason crying in the waiting room. "Her beautiful hair . . ."

"Jason, get a grip on yourself."

He hugged me. It was the first of many hugs I would receive, sometimes from strangers.

By the end of the week, Astrid was in bed in a hospital gown, though she still wore her cashmere pants. The gown was more practical. They had to poke holes in her for tests, and blood transfusions, and platelets that came in plastic pouches like astronaut food. She didn't feel fine anymore. I held the basin while she retched. She got cold; we piled blankets on her and she still shivered. Then she got very hot. They brought in a machine that evening that I heard the nurses call the "shake 'n' bake." They didn't have to use it in the end, but I was constantly aware of its presence. I found myself dressing with great care. I wanted to be popular with those nurses. I wanted Doctor Rosen to find me appealing, more appealing than Grace, who kept bugging him about homeopathy and vitamin supplements. He quickened his step when he saw her.

"It's all perfectly normal," he said to me. "Not pleasant, but normal. Hang in there."

I fell asleep in the vinyl chair and dreamt that I was hanging from a pole across a ravine.

"I feel awful," Astrid said on the third day. And then, "Leave me alone."

Now it was Grace crying in the waiting room, and one of the nurses scolded her, said that Astrid had a right to feel lousy, that she shouldn't expect her to be charming and entertaining; it wasn't a cocktail party.

"What a bitch," Grace said, and I redoubled my efforts to be pleasant, especially with the nursing aides, who knew the mysterious location of basins and blankets and clean sheets, and moved with the regal languor of African queens. If they liked you, they came faster. They all seemed to be from the West Indies, and they took the meals Astrid wouldn't eat, the tuna salad and the rubbery chicken. They always asked first. I thought they probably didn't get paid enough, even though they did the worst jobs.

On the phone, I repeated to Lea and Maybelle the doctor's words. Everything going as planned. As well as can be expected. Astrid talked to them, too.

"Please don't make a fuss. I'm fine. You can come when I'm home."

We were there for two weeks. She began to feel better. After her hair started falling out, she'd wrapped her head in a scarf, but now she tried on Grace's wigs.

"Real hair!" Grace said.

"I guess I'll go for the red one."

"You can be a different color every day."

Doctor Rosen drew her bone marrow and came in smiling the next day.

"You're in remission," he said.

We all beamed.

"What next?"

"You go home and recover."

"You beat it!" Grace said.

Now I was the one crying in the waiting room.

She didn't like having to leave in a wheelchair. "I am perfectly capable of walking." She was, slowly. To be expected, the doctor had said. She'll regain her strength.

"Hospital policy," the cheerful nurse said.

"Oh God, just get me out of here."

44

LEA AND MAYBELLE CAME, and Astrid made me go back to New Haven. She also made Grace go back to Paris.

"Honey, I can stay as long as you need me. . . ."

"I don't. I have enough nurses; and Harold is starting to flirt with you."

"Don't be ridiculous."

She was trying to be nice. She hadn't been, in the hospital, and now that she was better, she felt bad. For once, Grace seemed to understand.

"Oh, well, I guess I might as well go back and deal with my divorce."

"Honey," my mother said, "it was a lousy marriage."

"Yes, but it was *my* lousy marriage."

To me she said, "Poor Grace, I haven't been very supportive."

"Mom, you were sick."

"I know, but she's been a good friend. I do think it's for the best. Hubert was a shit. Now who is this boyfriend of yours? Why didn't you tell me earlier?"

Azher had called. He was worried about me. I was elated.

"I'm not sure he's my boyfriend."

"Well then, get back there and make sure. I must say he has a very sexy voice. Is he English?"

"He's from Pakistan."

"Ooh," Maybelle said.

"Does he make you shave your pubic hair?" Lea asked.

"Why on earth would he do that?"

"That's what they do; Nahid told me."

"Nahid: world authority on personal grooming."

"She shaves hers."

"He's from Pakistan, not Iran."

"It's a religious thing."

I stayed for the weekend. We all ate a lot of ice cream, except for Maybelle, who was pretending to be on a diet. We watched *Shanghai Express*.

"Before I die," Astrid said, "I want a peignoir like that." She was still weak but she was cheerful. She slept a lot.

"Bitch to launder, I bet," Maybelle observed.

"She looks okay," Lea said to me. Astrid had showed her her bald head, now covered in a fuzzy down.

"You should have seen her two weeks ago."

"Was it awful?"

"Yes, but it's over now. She's in remission." The word rolled deliciously off my tongue. Remission, with its vistas of that other 19.8 percent stretching into dizzying infinity. We'd picked the lucky number. We'd won.

"How long will it last?"

"Hopefully forever," I said.

"I should have been there."

"She was really cranky. You get the good part."

"I always knew Astrid would make a terrible patient," said Maybelle, who had overheard this last remark.

I got on the train to New Haven. Azher was going to meet me— his offer. I sensed a new respect in his voice, the respect one would accord a dutiful daughter.

He brought flowers. He kissed me lightly on the cheek.

"How is your mother?"

"Great!" I said.

"You must thank God."

"Thank him for me," I quipped. "You're probably on better terms."

He didn't seem to find that very funny, but he didn't make an issue out of it. We went back to his apartment and made love very slowly. At some point I burst into tears.

"It's okay," I said. "I'm happy."

"I missed you."

45

ZHER WAS KIND AND ATTENTIVE. I was behind in all my courses and he helped me organize myself, getting books from the library and editing my papers. He made time for me. We saw each other every day. I flowered. I was taking a course that semester called, rather clunkily, Poststructuralist Feminist Literary Theory, a title that drove him to dizzying heights of irony. As he labored on his thesis, which argued that the ribald physicality of Rabelais had detracted modern readers from its philosophical message, I immersed myself in Hélène Cixous and Julia Kristeva, for whom the body was just a metaphor. They couldn't have asked for a better audience: I was both insecure enough to relish their abstruse jargon, and sufficiently cocky to pretend that I understood it. And I had the right look; for the new amazons were no longer hirsute and shrill, but edgy and dangerous and French. Astrid had been right: You *could* be both chic and scholarly. She had made me go through her closet before I left (*"Honey, you can't seduce a man in rags"*) and I went about now caparisoned in my mother's brilliant armor. Azher approved of the chic, though he dismissed my new intellectual interests as a load of hilarious rubbish.

I didn't care. I read Derrida by day and made love to Azher by night, and traveled to New York on the weekends to check on Astrid, whom Maybelle was nursing back to health with scalloped potatoes and meatloaf. Lea had gone back to Paris, to prepare for her conversion and wedding. The doctor pronounced Astrid's remission meaningful, and we celebrated with big steaks and a bottle of Pomerol. At his insistence, Astrid had even quit smoking (*"Honestly, it's not as if I had lung cancer"*), though she said that the truth was, she'd felt so lousy in the hospital that she'd forgotten all about cigarettes. I quit, too, because Azher did. Harold had resumed his courtly attendance, and when I asked Astrid if she was thinking of marrying him, she said, "Sweetie, I was married longer than Mandela was in jail."

Winter was coming to an end and timid buds appeared on the trees. We started to make plans for Lea's wedding, Astrid professing herself wounded that she hadn't been consulted about the dress.

"She has to hide her belly, Mom."

"Nonsense, I would've put her in something fabulously sexy that would've showed it off."

"Exactly."

"Girls today have no *fantaisie*," opined Grace who, now that her divorce was finalized, had come back to visit. "Candy was at Hubert's wedding to that little slut, who was six months' pregnant by then, and she said you couldn't tell the bride from the wedding cake."

Azher's younger sister, Zakia, was accepted by Yale, and she arranged to visit the campus. I proposed that she stay with me at Silliman College. Azher looked uncomfortable.

"She'll be staying with me."

"But that doesn't make any sense; you're miles away from campus. The whole point is to get an idea of undergraduate life."

"I very much doubt that Zakia will be interested in undergraduate life," he said primly.

"That's ridiculous. Of course she'll want to see how freshmen live," I insisted, even though I had had no such interest. I bet Zakia and I had a lot in common. I wanted to meet her.

"Zakia isn't coming here to socialize; her primary concern is to get an education."

"Why don't you send her to a convent then?" It was out before I could regret it.

Azher's eyes grew cold. "We don't have convents."

"Whatever. If you think you can keep her in isolation, you're deluding yourself."

I knew that I had gone too far, but my old perversity came flaring back. Why did I always have to respect his limits, when I shared everything—well, almost everything—with him? I knew what it was really about: He didn't want me to meet Zakia. He did not consider me proper company for his sister. He was probably afraid, I told myself bitterly, that she would fall in with girls like me; girls who read Derrida and fucked her brother.

But I swallowed my frustration. I needed him too much to alienate him. Astrid's illness, the relief that had swept through me when she was cured, had unhinged me. An abyss had opened up inside me: As if in tandem with her, I had started lusting after foods I hadn't had in years—pizza and sausage and marzipan, sugar and fat. I, too, gained weight. My flesh thickened, grew slack with desire, and Azher, who had always found me too thin, reveled in my womanly curves. This was what he didn't want his sister to see: the giddy delirium of satiety; not just mine, but his, too. By then everyone in his department knew we were lovers. You could practically smell it on us.

"Do as you like," I said, "but it won't be much fun for her."

"She isn't here to have fun."

And so Zakia came to New Haven, and we were not introduced. In the end, she stayed with some family friends in Camden. I told myself it was either Azher's way of ensuring that we didn't meet or, in the version I preferred, the compromise he had arrived at out of regard for my feelings. I didn't care. Much to my surprise, he had accepted my invitation to accompany me to Paris for Lea's wedding. He had some research to do, so it made sense. That he refused to stay with my father, I put down to male pride, and the disparity in our economic circumstances. He would, he insisted, stay in a hotel. It was unclear whether I would be allowed to stay there with him, but even this uncertainty couldn't tamp the thrill I felt at the prospect of showing up at my sister's wedding with my lover on my arm.

46

SPRING CAME TO PARIS EARLY THAT YEAR. The horse chestnuts unfurled their floppy leaves and the scent of their sticky blossoms hung in the air. An unusually affable Azher at my side, I abandoned myself to the forgotten pleasure of sitting on a café terrace with a sunbeam tickling my nose, watching the pretty girls go by. Paris seemed to liberate him. He held my hand and kissed me in the Luxembourg Gardens. He teased me. The hotel he found was in the far reaches of the Eighteenth, a fleabag with stained mattresses and a toilet down the hall. I didn't care. I had been so afraid he would insist I stay with my father that its discomforts felt like privileges. I barely knew that part of Paris and, as we strolled along the Boulevard Poissonnière, I felt like a tourist in my own city, noticing for the first time the African vendors, the sadly ineffectual *Propreté de Paris* scooters with their jaunty green flanks, the ageless women in narrow skirts and pumps, exiting the *charcuterie* with a roast chicken and a knowing swing to their walk, three perfect potatoes nestled in the bottom of a string bag. Azher had lived here during his year in France, and he showed me what he referred to with pride as *his* Paris, with its holes in the wall where they served delicious, greasy *merguez* on couscous, and cafés where old men sat smoking hookahs, their eyes far away. "You're just a spoiled rich girl," he teased, and I was transported back to the time when Patrice had said the same.

"*Well*," Astrid whispered when she met him, at Grace's new apartment on the Rue du Roi de Sicile, a little gem with *poutres apparentes* and a vaguely oriental decor that Azher took in with a sardonic smile. Grace, much occupied since her divorce with improving her mind, had started reading Proust, and I think that, in her fantasies, she occupied Odette's plush den, the air heavy with orchids and the lingering scent of departed lovers.

I forgot sometimes how handsome Azher was. "Where did you find *him*?" she asked me with a leer in the kitchen, where she was slicing tempeh for the salad she would bring in a container to dinner at Allard. She now followed a strictly macrobiotic diet, with allowances for the wines of Bordeaux, and was so convinced of its benefits that she touched nothing else, much to the mortification of her friends, who tried to appear innocent as she snuck bites from smuggled Tupperware under the suspicious eyes of Parisian waiters who thought that they had seen it all. Astrid, whom she urged to emulate her, would have none of it. She craved bistro food, duck confits and potatoes and *lardons*, vegetables swooning in butter.

"In Pakistan," Grace declared as we lingered over cocktails, "people hardly ever touch meat—isn't that so, Azher?"

I knew Azher found Grace silly and vain, but because he showed proper deference to Astrid, whom he clearly admired, I forgave him. "Yes, but it's because they can't afford it."

"The problem with the West is that it's rotten," Grace blithely continued. "We feed on carcasses. . . ."

Astrid rolled her eyes and laughed, "Really, Grace . . ."

"No, why do you think you got cancer—" she laid her hand on Astrid's arm. "Not that I'm implying it was your fault, but there's a whole body of research that—"

Astrid cut her off with a smile. "Must we constantly talk about my cancer? I really don't think anyone wants to hear about it. . . ." She was still wearing her wig, but she had confessed to me that it was because her hair was growing back gray. She was going to get it colored as soon as it was long enough. Jason swore it would look natural.

But Grace prattled on undeterred about taking responsibility for your body, and Azher shot me a secret, mirthful glance. Without thinking about it, I put my hand over his. He let me keep it there.

Astrid was thrilled to be back in Paris. She wanted to do everything, go everywhere. She took Maybelle shopping on the Rue du Faubourg Saint-Honoré—though she couldn't resist whispering to me that the only thing they'd find to fit her would be an Hermès scarf—and then for lunch at Dalloyau, in the candy-colored room that Maybelle loved. Przemek's construction business was doing so well that they had decided to turn the trip into a belated honeymoon, and it struck me as a kind of redress that we should all have come to Paris with a lover, for Harold, too, would be joining us shortly. Astrid went out of her way to be charming to Przemek. She flirted and laughed at his stories, and Maybelle joked that she might as well not be there.

"Come on, Maybelle, he only has eyes for you."

"Your mother's a dangerous woman. Best keep an eye on that boyfriend of yours. . . ."

We were all gilded; by desire, relief, hope. We moved in a golden nimbus of anticipation. Astrid had never felt so well, she told me as we dressed for the wedding, and indeed she seemed, in a supple dress the color of rubies that clung amorously to her healed body, to literally glow from within. I, too, dressed extravagantly, in a sea-green sheath I had borrowed from her, with high-heeled red sandals I could barely walk in. I was reading Kristeva's *About Chinese Women* for a class, and as Azher's eyes lingered on my feet, which were already forming blisters, I savored the fetishistic power of my self-crippling, a notion that, when I shared it with Nahid, reduced her to peals of laughter.

I hadn't seen Nahid since Frank's wedding. She loved California and her college, which was right outside Los Angeles and was full, she happily reported, of rich dummies. Delphine, who hadn't been able to make it, was in Los Angeles, too, at USC, and they were still an item, though Nahid was rather more discreet about her leanings.

Released into America's wide horizons, Delphine had embraced being gay with the same verve she had once applied to the pursuit of unattainable love objects. Nahid took it all in good-humored stride but, for the sake of appearances, she showed up on the day of Lea's wedding with a gorgeous Iranian whom she introduced as her fiancé. Azher disliked her instantly. A look of barely concealed distaste came over him when I introduced them, and Nahid eyed him with regal disdain. I paid them no mind. We were waiting outside the church before the service, and Harold, who had flown in the day before, had just arrived with my mother. Frank, who would be giving Lea away, was expected any second. I awaited him anxiously. It would be the first time he had laid eyes on Astrid since she had left for Poland. He had no idea she had been sick; we'd kept it from him, even Lea finally agreeing that there was no point, since the treatment had been a success. He didn't know that Astrid's presence was a miracle, a miracle that I knew she regarded as an exoneration, for she had told me in the hospital, on a day when she was feeling particularly awful: *"No one can say now that I haven't paid for my sins."*

And so I held my breath when his car pulled up, hoping he would perceive that the balance had been restored. Inge emerged with the baby first, a triumphant look in her eye that struck me as half defiance. It only occurred to me later that she must have been terrified. Frank followed, and when Inge handed him the baby, so that she could adjust her jacket, he shot me a look of such naked desperation that I went over and took my half sister from him, causing her to let out a howl that resulted in a hasty clearing of the space around us. Thankfully, Maybelle had just arrived. She plucked the child from my arms and somehow managed to soothe her, while Astrid, who had been eyeing the scene with an inscrutable expression, introduced herself to Inge as if they had never met, complimented her on the baby, and then, with infinite delicacy, kissed Frank on the cheek. I watched him nervously for signs of distress, but, the baby pacified, he had recovered his composure, and he shook Harold's hand with equanimity. When I introduced him to

Azher, he was at his most gracious, and seemed impressed, I
thought, by his formal manners. I had wanted them to have a
chance to get acquainted, to chat about Montaigne or Erasmus, or
any other subject in which Frank would shine, but there was no
time; we had to go into the church.

I was surprised at how moved I was by the ceremony. I had
expected it to be formal and interminable, which it was, but the
Catholic mass had a somber beauty that conferred on Serge and
Lea's marriage the dignity my father's and Inge's had so conspicuously lacked. Frank walked my sister down the aisle with the calm
bearing of a man restored to grace. Lea had converted the month
before, and as she knelt at the altar to receive communion, her veil
flowing behind her, a beam of light from the stained-glass window
overhead fell across her raised face, casting over it an unearthly glow
that mirrored her rapt expression. It seemed a mad and beautiful act
of faith, and as Serge and my sister were united, by an ancient
bishop dripping with lace and jewels like an old courtesan, I, like
everyone else in the church, high on incense, my feet killing me, my
ambivalent lover at my side, believed that they would trump the
odds and love and honor each other for the rest of their lives.

The reception was held at the Lubomirski home, where adjoining salons had been cleared to accommodate two hundred and fifty
people. Serge's mother had tackled the seating conundrum with
brisk efficiency: Astrid, Harold, Frank, and Inge were all placed at
the head table, and Maybelle and Przemek were put with what Lea
referred to as "the weirder Polish relatives," where they seemed
very much at home. Azher and I ended up with an École Colbert
contingent that included Boris Sarkozy, Chiara, Nahid, and her gorgeous fiancé, Faraz, who seemed rather more interested in checking out Azher. The champagne flowed, and before long we were all
gigglingly reminiscing about some of Chiara's more outrageous
exploits while Azher sat moodily drinking mineral water. At the
head table, Inge popped out a swollen white breast and nursed her

baby—to the immense delight of Lea, who reported to me afterward that Serge's mother had nearly swallowed her dentures.

Nahid cornered me in the bathroom. California suited her; her skin glowed with a coppery sheen, as did her hair, which she still had done in Paris because the L.A. colorists made you too blond. She was wearing one of the newly fashionable suits that Astrid abhorred, with big shoulders and a skinny short skirt, and huge diamond earrings in the shape of hearts.

"*What* are you doing with that man?"

I assumed an air of puzzled innocence. "What man?"

"That Paki you brought with you."

"That's not the most culturally sensitive description of a distinguished Pakistani-American scholar that I've ever heard," I remarked as I applied a fresh coat of lipstick. Astrid had pressed it on me, and I was seduced by the lascivious sheen it gave my lips, as was Boris Sarkozy, who had been checking me out all evening. I hoped Azher had noticed. I knew he wasn't having a good time, and I wished that, for once, he would loosen up. I had had several glasses of champagne by then, and was feeling mutinous.

"A what scholar?" said Nahid, who was majoring in the history of pop music. With a long, manicured nail, she popped open the gold Chanel pendant that hung from a chain between her breasts and, with the same nail, scooped out a tiny mound of cocaine, which she delicately inhaled through her regal nostril. "Want some?"

"Sure," I said. As I breathed in, I wondered gleefully what Azher would have to say about my snorting coke in the toilet with this gorgeous bisexual Persian slut. Azher needed to relax. What was the point of living if you couldn't have a little fun?

"I don't get it—what on earth do you see in him?"

"He's brilliant—and under all the sanctimony, quite the hot lover," I said coyly, the thought of Azher's reaction, were he to hear himself so described, only egging me on, even as I felt the first stirrings of remorse.

"I'll bet; he looks like a regular panty ripper."

I blushed. Azher *had* once ripped my underwear, in a frenzied moment that had disconcerted us both; but Nahid misunderstood the cause of my unease. Her face fell.

"Oh, *baby*, don't tell me you've fallen for *that* old trick? Out with it, tell Aunt Nahid everything!"

"There's nothing to tell," I said, harnessing my dignity.

"You'll never get anywhere with him, you do know that?"

I shrugged. "I'm not planning to marry him," I said dismissively, though during the wedding service, all sorts of mad thoughts had run through my mind. "Speaking of which, what's with the fiancé?"

Nahid laughed. "Faraz? He's my cousin, and he's gay as a blade. It's just to keep our parents off our backs."

"Oh yeah? What happens when they start planning the wedding?"

"I wouldn't mind marrying Faraz—he's a sweetie, and a man of the world, unlike your backward Paki."

"My backward Paki, as you charmingly put it, is better-read than most of the people at this party."

Nahid gave me a pitying look. "You've got it bad, don't you?"

It was my turn to laugh. "You make it sound like a bad disco song."

"Sweetie, life *is* a bad disco song—look at your poor father."

"Don't let appearances fool you," I said sharply, my protective instincts surging. "Inge isn't quite the Circe she imagines herself to be."

Nahid looked puzzled. "Inge? Oh, the secretary—I didn't mean her. Haven't you noticed the way he keeps stealing looks at your mother?"

"I'm sure you're mistaken," I said coldly. Who was this Persian glamour doll to tread on our family's fragile ghosts? I began to turn away, the false intimacy of our surroundings suddenly oppressive. Nahid didn't notice. She was following her coked-up train of thought, her eyes entranced with their reflection in the mirror.

"No I'm not; he can't keep his eyes off her. It's driving the Swedish girl crazy."

But my hand was already on the doorknob. "It's the saddest thing I've ever seen in my life" was the last thing I heard Nahid say, her voice wistful, as if this descendant of fallen kings had only then discovered that some wounds never heal; that every loss leaves its mark, that fissures grow and spread, and topple the mightiest walls.

47

S HORTLY AFTER WE GOT BACK, Azher told me that he was getting engaged, to a girl his parents had picked out for him in Lahore. I had known something was coming: Since our return, he had grown distant, as if he were laying the ground for his departure. I read the truth in his eyes and, although I told myself afterward that, had I realized I was being tested, I might have behaved differently—not gotten drunk at the wedding, not flirted with Boris, not introduced him to Nahid, not told him the truth, as I finally had, in a moment of inebriated candor, about the circumstances of my parents' divorce—I knew with the dumb certainty of the abandoned that I had started losing him the minute we arrived in Paris. He tried to be kind. He implored me to regard our relationship through the lucid lens of intellect; but the more he entreated, the more fiercely I clung to my misery, which, unlike the prospect of his leaving me, felt immediate and real.

I tried to be dignified, but the moral high ground proved unsteady. I toppled. I behaved like one of those hysterical women on TV shows I didn't even watch. I cried; I begged; I groveled; and finally, I got nasty.

"Of course I understand: You're going off to a Third World country to marry a sixteen-year-old virgin you've never met."

He *had* met her. She wasn't sixteen; she was twenty. Her name was Binesh, and she was the daughter of an old family friend. It was the most I could get out of him. There is nothing worse, I discovered, than being reasoned with by your tormentor.

"Please stop."

"Why should I stop?"

"Because you are demeaning yourself. I never pretended that this was anything more than it was."

I could tell that he regretted the phrasing the minute it was out of his mouth, but I pounced. "And what was that? A cheap fuck? A last fling?"

He looked pained. "Surely you can see that there are unbridgeable differences between us. You would soon tire of me."

"Why did you come to Paris?"

It was the only time he looked unsure. "It was meant as a gift."

I had him. "Liar." I wanted him to admit I had been in the running, and had failed. That he had considered me.

He soon grew weary. "I am sorry. I don't believe that I ever misled you."

He hadn't. He had never told me that he loved me. When he kissed me, it was with the lightness of a moth. I had put it down to delicacy. I had taken all the signs of his reticence and fashioned them into sentiments so rare and precious that they had no name. I hadn't yet learned to beware of that which defies categorization.

"Bastard!" I hissed. I'd never called a man a name before.

At the end of the term, Azher left for Pakistan. He and Binesh were to be married in Lahore, and she would move to New Haven in the fall to join him. She was not only beautiful, but intelligent, and had been accepted in the premed program. She wanted to be a pediatrician. Since it brought me no relief to learn that she was accomplished, I consoled myself with the certainty that he wasn't in love with her. It was, after all, an arranged marriage.

I packed my bags and went home for the summer. I had an internship at *Semiotext(e)*, a journal that Azher abhorred and that now seemed the only fitting place in which to exorcise him. At night I hung out at the Pyramid Club, where the transvestites on the bar mocked the sham of romance. I cut off my hair and made myself look tough. Astrid wasn't fooled. "Poor baby," she said.

"Mom, I'm okay."

But she looked bereft. "No you're not; you're never okay. Every time it happens, it takes another piece out of you."

Lea's daughter, Clothilde Jadwiga, was born in August at the Salpêtrière, where they used to lock up madwomen and whores, a fact that I pointed out to my sister. I didn't go to Paris; I said I was too busy. It wasn't true. I didn't think I could stand the sight of Lea's happiness, nor that of my father's grotesque ménage. Marriage was a con, childbearing an indignity. Lea and I talked on the phone. The baby, she reported, was not a howler like Marguerite, though she was quite bald, too, poor thing. I was silly enough to ask her if she planned to breast-feed, to which she retorted that she wasn't a cow, thank you very much, and poor Serge had witnessed quite enough female plumbing during the birth, which he had attended after all, the doctors having made disapproving faces when he tried to sneak off. When I related this to my fellow interns at *Semiotext(e)*, hard-nosed New York girls with multiply pierced ears who wore leather jackets in August, they bemoaned Lea's unquestioning internalization of misogyny, though I assured them that, in fact, she just didn't want to have droopy breasts at forty. Nobody thought it was funny.

In the fall, right after classes started, I saw Azher and his bride on the street. She was lovely. She wore an aquamarine shalwar kameez that was at once diaphanous and utterly modest, and had inky-black hair that streamed down her back. Her eyes were as green as Azher's, and when she raised them shyly to meet mine, I felt a completely unexpected urge to protect her. But there was no need; Azher would never tell. He introduced me as a colleague, and I shook her hand and congratulated her. After we said good-bye, I watched them walk down Chapel Street, hand in hand, and I thought, my God, they're in love, and understood at the same moment that Azher and I had never been. Because it hadn't been grounded in anything, our affair had ultimately been inconsequential. It should have made me bitter, but it only made me sad, and even then just a little. It was over. Nobody had been hurt, not really. And I was free.

48

N O ONE WAS PREPARED when Astrid's cancer returned. No one except her doctor, who revealed that he had been surprised at how long her remission had lasted.

"But you said she was cured!"

He looked at me sorrowfully. He had never said such a thing. She had been cured only in our minds.

"At least I made it to the wedding," Astrid said, and then, "I'm not going back to the hospital."

Not going back to the hospital was not an option. I had asked the doctor what would happen if we did nothing and he said bluntly, "Slow death by suffocation." There was no longer time for pretending.

"Just another round of chemo," I pleaded. "It worked the last time."

"Then why am I sick again?"

"You don't have a choice," Maybelle said.

We went back. The nurses were brisk and cheerful. They acted like they were happy to see her. They told her she looked great. They pumped her up with more drugs. Her hair fell out again; this time she didn't bother with Jason; it sloughed onto the pillow in gray strands. I sat with her. Maybelle sat with her. She wouldn't talk to us. When she submitted to Harold's presence, I knew she was broken, for my mother didn't believe in letting a man see you down. Someone suggested an antidepressant.

"You've got to be kidding," Astrid said.

The treatment didn't go well this time. She retched, she froze, she broke into dizzying fevers. They had to use the shake 'n' bake. It was aptly named.

There was no keeping anyone away now. Lea and Grace flew in. The apartment felt like a dorm, a dorm in purgatory, but we only slept there, when we slept at all. This time around, the ward seemed to be full of much sicker people. There were cries in the night. An old woman kept calling, "Morris! Morris!" from her room, and the nurses first looked sympathetic, then aggravated. The man in the next room was in the terminal stages of liver cancer. His wife told me. She drove in every day from New Jersey and sat in the hallway with dead eyes as they got him ready for transfer to the ICU. They took him away and we never saw them again. The young man was back. Again he walked around with his father, but his gait seemed slower.

"The poor boy," Maybelle said with tears in her eyes. It turned out they were from Kansas, and he was a student at NYU. He had leukemia, too. His parents and sister had come up; they'd rented an apartment. They couldn't believe how expensive New York hotels were. The sister wore jeans and pink sweaters like a cheerleader, but her eyes were wide with fright. Whenever the mother went down to the cafeteria, she asked us if we wanted anything. She and Maybelle chatted a lot. Maybelle comforted her. I heard her say, "You know, at his age, the numbers are great."

"Yes," the mother said. "But I'm so scared."

Her guilelessness horrified me. Her son would get well, because she was good and I wasn't.

"Of course you're scared, honey, but I'm a nurse, and I'm telling you, I've seen kids like him do great."

I didn't know how to comfort people. I avoided them. Lea knitted baby sweaters. She was pregnant again. When had she gotten pregnant? When had she learned how to knit?

Things started going wrong. Astrid had a bad reaction to a transfusion. Her windpipe closed up; she couldn't breathe. The room

filled with doctors and we were hustled out. She had to go to the
ICU. Doctor Rosen showed up. "She'll get better care there."

Harold nodded. He was now Doctor Rosen's preferred audience
for bad news, because his eyes didn't get ominously glittery. He took
every blow with the air of one tackling an analytical problem. This
is what happened, these are our options. I don't think he knew any
other way. Lea ran to the waiting room and burst into sobs. She was
comforted by one of the West Indian nursing aides. Astrid had sent
them all chocolates after her first stay, and thank-you notes. I hadn't
even thought of it. Maybelle kept getting more and more busi-
nesslike. "We'll deal with it," she said. "Charlotte, get her stuff."

"I think it's time we considered alternative treatment," Grace
said. "There's a place in Germany—"

"Grace, shut up."

"*Can't you see this isn't working!*" She screamed. She ran into the
waiting room and burst into tears. The waiting room was the desig-
nated place for bursting into tears, though some people didn't quite
make it in time. Once I saw one of the interns crying, a stern Indian
woman called Doctor Patel whom Astrid had found disagreeable,
back when she still cared about such things. I looked away.

"If you can't get a grip on yourself, I'm not letting you back,"
Maybelle said to Grace.

"I'm sorry, I'm sorry."

Maybelle had grown in stature. She was in charge now; even
Grace deferred to her.

In the ICU, they only let you visit every two hours. We sat in the
waiting room, where a TV that no one watched was set on a never-
ending talk show. Some stared at the wall. Others, unhinged by grief
and anxiety, or bored, or angry, would talk to anyone. There was a
woman who complained to all who would listen about the incom-
petence of the nurses. She had a bad leg, but still she came in every
day, all the way from Queens, to see her mother. She would prop
the bad leg on the coffee table, where it sat supported by a pile of

abandoned magazines. When it wasn't the nurses, it was the doctors. You had to keep an eye on them, she said; everyone knew they took better care of their own. It was only after she glanced meaningfully at a bearded man in a fur hat that I figured out she meant the doctors were all Jews. "I wish she would shut up," Lea said, and, "I bet her mother is as dreadful as she is." There was a woman from Tunisia who discovered I spoke French and gave me her card. She hated New York, so uncultured. She didn't know why her father had had to settle here; it was his third wife who had insisted, the one who had married him for his money. Well, they all had, but what did you expect? Thirty-two years old and him in his eighties. Men were fools, and now, with this Viagra, only more so. The wife hadn't been to the hospital once, of course. Too busy with her lover. . . . She herself had renounced the pleasures of the flesh. She pointed out to me the woman who had come every day for six months to see her daughter. Only sixteen years old and in a coma. To live is to suffer.

Chaplains came and went. This being New York, there was even a Buddhist monk in saffron robes. A nice Episcopalian lady asked me how I was doing.

"Okay," I said.

"Sometimes it's harder on the loved ones."

"We're not religious," I said, but if I had known how, I would have prayed to the God I didn't believe in. Lea had talked to the Catholic priest, who said something about extreme unction.

"I don't think she'd like that," Lea told him.

Astrid had to be forcibly intubated. When we went in, her eyes were wide with panic, and she gripped my hand so hard that her nails dug into my flesh. "You need to leave now," the nurse said. They must have sedated her, because when we were allowed back, she was in a drugged sleep. Tubes and wires snaked out of her in every direction, attached to machines that hummed and beeped. "*No!*" someone shouted from an adjacent cubicle. I saw the priest in the hallway.

People died in the ICU. A doctor would come out to speak to the relatives. There was a family, squat and moon-faced, the kids translating for the mother, who sat sunk in her impenetrable grief like a peasant in a Russian painting. The husband, the one who was dying, had the same blunt features as his wife; I'd seen him wheeled out into the hall. They could have been siblings. The wife had spent most of her time in the ward drawing flowers on a sketchpad; one of the nurses had commented on how talented she was, surprised, perhaps, that such coarseness could yield grace. The woman had just stared back uncomprehendingly, and I had thought, *what do any of us know about anyone?* When the doctor came, she let out a wail like a maenad, a sound so awful that people turned away in embarrassment. I watched her, transfixed. I thought, *you don't have to be beautiful to be loved.* It came as a revelation. Beauty had always been made so much of in our family. And now it turned out that it didn't protect you; it didn't even make you special. It was just an accident.

Astrid didn't die. They pulled her back together and we returned to the ward. We all, with the exception of Astrid, tried to act as if this were a fantastic development. Doctor Rosen drew her bone marrow again. This involved, I now knew from having been typed as a possible and, as it turned out, unsuitable donor, punching a needle into her pelvic bone, and withdrawing a reddish fluid that didn't look at all like the greasy white stuff in the butcher shop. "Good news," he said when he returned the next day. "You're in remission." Astrid stared at the wall. Maybelle and I broke into big fake smiles. I followed the doctor out.

"How long this time?" I said.

"It's hard to say. She's been severely weakened by the treatment."

"What about a bone-marrow transplant?" I pressed him. Maybelle was a fit. I had been reading the literature again. I was full of statistics. There was still hope.

"She's in no shape for that right now.

"What if she gets back in shape?"

"Then we consider our options. For now she has to recover."

"I don't want a transplant," Astrid whispered. "I want to go home."

With every passing day, our expectations mutely shrank. The new plan was to get her home for Christmas. It seemed modest, realistic, not asking for too much.

"That would be nice," Astrid said in the monotone that had become her voice. It was almost worse when she tried. Lea and I went out to buy a tree. The friendly Canadians who came down every year for the season had lined them up at their usual spot on Greenwich Avenue. "Let's get a really big one," I said. Lea gave me a look.

"We have to call Dad."

"When she's better."

"She's not going to get better."

"She's in remission."

"Don't make me say it, Charlotte."

"I'll call him."

We carried the tree home together. It was eight feet high, a truly fine specimen. Christmas lights were strung across the avenue, and snatches of carols drifted out as people went in and out of stores and coffee shops. Anyone seeing us might have thought, two beautiful girls carrying a tree, maybe wondered who we were, reflected on the charmed lives that we must lead. I felt like a spaceman. As we dragged the tree up, Claude and Jasper from upstairs came down to help.

"How is she doing?" The question was ever more cautiously posed.

"Not so great," Lea said.

"We'd love to visit her."

"She won't see anyone. Wait till she gets home."

"If there's *anything* we can do . . ."

We put the tree up and left it there, naked. "Maybelle and Grace can decorate it," Lea said. "If you won't call Dad, I'm going to."

I called. I told him. There was a long silence at the other end of the line. I thought of the Atlantic between us, black and fathomless.

"Does she have a good doctor?"

"The best," I said.

"Thank you for telling me."

I was grateful for his restraint, and hated him for it. I reminded myself that you can't have it both ways.

49

WE GOT ASTRID HOME. This time she didn't protest about the wheelchair. The doctor said, try to get her out of bed as much as possible, but he was just following protocol. He had stopped talking about cure. The new terms were *symptom alleviation* and, that ghastly misnomer, *quality of life*. Even Astrid had a feeble laugh over that one. Still, she did feel a little better at home, and she tried hard, with the awful eagerness to please of the dying, to make a show of holiday spirit. During the day she lay on the couch, and we buzzed around her, baking cookies, watching *It's a Wonderful Life*, and playing Christmas carols. I wrapped silk scarves around her head and we called her The Maharani. Claude and Jasper came down with more cookies, and eggnog, which she wasn't supposed to drink because of the raw eggs. "What's it going to do, kill me?" she said, and had a sip anyway. It made her gag. Maybelle made her famous potatoes with Velveeta and blended them to a cream, and she tried to swallow a few spoonfuls. "Lovely," Astrid said. "Delicious." I read to her; girl things, Nancy Mitford and Colette. Astrid loved Colette—so did I; I'd forgotten all about bratty Claudine and Fanchette, about Claudine's clear, French dispassion. Once I had identified with her, but now I found her shallow, heartless. When the sun came out, I pulled open the curtains so it would stream over Astrid. She slept a lot, and with the light on her, she took on the otherworldly look of a medieval queen on a tombstone. Harold came every day with flowers and held her hand. It was the first time I had ever seen them touch. Lea was beginning to look pregnant. She was getting so big so fast, we thought it might be twins, but it turned out to be Stanislas-Henri, the sweetest and most clunkily named of her children. He was always my favorite, and I used to wonder if maybe he had absorbed his sunny disposition that winter, when we all became kind.

We got through Christmas and the New Year. We made it all the way to February. We began to feel hopeful; it really doesn't take much. And then all hell broke loose. Astrid felt short of breath. She collapsed as Maybelle helped her to the bathroom. We called the visiting nurse and she took one look at her and said, Emergency Room. "I'm not going," Astrid gasped, but her wishes had long been overridden. The cancer had returned with a vengeance. It raged through her like an angry ghost, a spurned lover. The actual term was *blast crisis*. It sounded like a terrorist attack. It was. Her blood, choked by immature white blood cells run amok, turned to sludge. Back in the ICU, where we were immediately dispatched, they hooked her up to a machine the size of a refrigerator that spewed out the mutant invaders and pumped the filtered blood back in. The problem was, they would come back. She revived a little.

"Why can't we just keep her on it?" I asked. Or keep giving her transfusions. But even I knew there wasn't enough blood in the world. We had all donated at the blood center downstairs, several times. A few paltry liters, a drop.

The doctor said, "I don't think she can take another round of chemo."

Astrid heard him. "No more chemo," she said. "Take me home."

They stabilized her. They patched her back together enough to make the trip home in an ambulance. We drove through wintry streets, Astrid dozing. When she opened her eyes, they were huge in her impossibly delicate skull.

"I want you to let me die," she whispered to me.

"Okay," I said.

"Thank you." She closed her eyes. Words felt like air.

We began our vigil. The hospice service delivered a hospital bed and oxygen tank, and a supply of painkillers that came with invitingly detailed precautions against overdose. They brought other, more intimate supplies as well. Maybelle handled the delicate moments when Harold had to be sent out of the room. Death, like birth, is women's work: fluids and smells, shit and blood. It's as if the body were giving you one last reminder of its essential grossness. Astrid drifted in and out of consciousness, and we watched her, drinking her in. At first she had patches of lucidity.

"I wonder what it'll be like," she said when I was sitting with her, her eyes open and fixed on me.

"Are you scared?"

"No, not really. I just don't want to fly around with wings."

"Remember when I was little and we were flying to the States, and I asked you why there were no angels sitting on the clouds?"

She smiled. "Yes."

"You said they can't sit on the clouds because they'd fall through, and I said they don't weigh anything, they're spirits."

"Yes, you were always poking holes in things."

Another time she said, "I'm scared. What if I go to hell?"

"You don't believe in hell, Mom."

She didn't answer.

The last words she said to me were, "Be nice to Harold." I doubt she had intended them as such, but she began to fade shortly thereafter.

My mother died on Valentine's Day, a holiday she loved for all its corny kitsch, and for its insane optimism about a condition that had caused her more pain than happiness. Or maybe not. She once told me it was always worth it to fall in love, because if you didn't, you were just another cynic. I had gone out and bought her one of those huge Russell Stover chocolate boxes in the shape of a heart, and maybe she saw it, I can't be sure. Her eyes had clouded over, as if she had retreated to some final anteroom. We never got to say good-bye. There were no Hollywood moments. Her death was the antithesis of her life: She just went quietly away. I watched her draw her last breath, a ragged rattle, and then she was gone forever.

50

W E DIDN'T KNOW what to do about a memorial. Astrid was nominally a Baptist, but she had never said anything about God, even though the hospital was trawled by representatives of every denomination. She *had* once told me that she either wanted to be cremated, or have her body picked clean by vultures on a mountaintop. Grace promptly conceived a vision of smoldering pyres on the Ganges, which was just as promptly extinguished by Maybelle, who said she wasn't having her sister tossed into some Third World sewer. Lea thought we might disperse her ashes from the Eiffel Tower, or the top of Montmartre, but it being France, you probably had to get a permit. Harold said there was a Unitarian minister who did memorials at the University Club, where he was a member, but since Astrid had only set foot there once, to use the ladies' room, that idea was dismissed as well. We had her cremated. Her ashes were returned to us in a surprisingly heavy box, and I discovered that they're not ashes at all, but ground-up bones. In the end, without asking anyone's permission, we scattered one half in the Hudson and the other, more stealthily, from the Pont Neuf. Rivers were alive. They flowed and meandered and had a beginning and a destination. In the ocean, she would have been lost, though I realized later that that was where she would end up.

We had a party. That was what we chose to call it. Astrid had always loved parties. They were at once the most private and public of events, a stage upon which you can shine without revealing your secret heart. People are wrong to dismiss the surface; it is both our

shield and armor. We rented a loft on the Hudson, with soaring ceilings like a cathedral, and invited everyone we could think of who
had ever known her. I was the one who thought of asking Łukasz,
out of the impurest of motives: I wanted him to see what he had
thrown away. Lea thought that Serge's father might be able to get
notice to him through his Solidarity connections, though she
doubted that the authorities would let him out of the country. We
hired a band to play all her favorite songs, "Unforgettable," "These
Foolish Things," "All of Me," and we thought we would let people
speak. Astrid had always loved toasts. In Paris, the Lubomirskis had
a mass for her at the Polish Church. "Think of it as insurance," Lea
said.

Łukasz never showed up but everyone else did, including Candy
de Bethune, who was now on her fourth husband but kept the
name, a matter that was being reviewed by the French courts, who
didn't necessarily agree with Candy's view that, having put up with
the old goat for five years, she was entitled to remain a countess for
life. She clutched us all to her recently enhanced bosom, introduced
herself to Astrid's more prominent clients as her best friend, to the
outrage of Grace, and, after she tearfully told Maybelle that it took
one Southern girl to understand another, Maybelle was heard muttering that it also takes one to know one . . .

Delphine and Nahid came from L.A., tanned and gorgeous and
all over each other. They were both under the thrall of *Flashdance*,
and couldn't *believe* I hadn't met Jennifer Beals at Yale. . . . Everyone
had a few too many, and Delphine, her ripped top sliding off one
shoulder to reveal a tattoo of two linked female symbols, made a
rather incoherent if well-intentioned speech about how Astrid had
totally influenced her as a woman, to which Lea remarked that it
was a shame she hadn't influenced her fashion sense as well. When
she bore down on Serge, now a father of almost two, he looked
absolutely horrified, but Delphine only sweetly pecked him on the
cheek, and said it was nice to see him after all these years. She then
came out to him, which left him perplexed, as anyone who wasn't

clear by then on Delphine's proclaimed sexual orientation lived on Mars.

Astrid's clients all came to pay tribute, and I saw them suddenly through her eyes; not vain and shallow, but brave and undaunted, with their heartbreaks and abortions and divorces, their disappointing children, their big and small victories, and their determination to be noticed, to leave their mark. Unlike me, Astrid was never mean. She really believed that she could bring out the beauty in anyone. "Oh, sweetie, that looks gorgeous," she would say or, shaking her head with a worried frown, "No, that doesn't suit you at all. . . ."The women who shopped at her store knew that she wasn't going to make them look freakish, that she had their best interests at heart. And so they came in droves, the trophy wives and fashion editors, the lawyers and doctors and advertising executives, and a fabulously glamorous Chinese gynecologist called Francine Feng, who told me that *no* one understood the middle-aged woman's derrière like my mother. I wished she had mentioned that in her eulogy, because it would have been just the kind of thing Astrid would have loved, to be remembered for making women's asses look better.

The women by far outnumbered the men. For all her reputation as a great beauty, Astrid's world had been mostly female. And solitary. She had many clients and acquaintances, but only Grace had been her friend. Grace, whose silliness was surpassed only by her loyalty. Most of the men I recognized, from Paris or New York, a few I didn't. One in particular caught my attention, an Italian, who kept glancing my way, a fine smile on his lips as if he were savoring some exquisite recollection. When he came and spoke to me, I knew he had been her lover. His gaze brought her back to life, she seemed to hover between us, and I wished we could stay thus suspended, but he vanished shortly thereafter, and I wondered what it was about him that had touched her, for she would have had, I knew, to have been touched. My mother did not give herself lightly.

At first I didn't notice that Frank had arrived. He hovered by the bar, looking uncomfortable, just as he had hovered at so many parties in Paris, wishing he were home with his books and music. I had to cross the room to reach him, stopped every few feet by a kind word, a reminiscence, an awkward expression of regret. As I drew near, a disoriented look came over his face. I raised my hand and his eyes cleared, but for a second I glimpsed in them a flash of pure happiness: the acute, almost unbearable joy of watching the woman you love walk toward you through a sea of strangers.

51

SOMETIMES, IN MY DREAMS, I walk the hallways of our Paris apartment. Over the years they've stretched and meandered, and in my wanderings, I uncover whole wings whose existence I never knew of: bedrooms and bathrooms and kitchens and attics, and miles and miles of labyrinthine corridors that are at once familiar and utterly strange. Sometimes I dream that I'm allowed to go back. There's been a reprieve, a special dispensation from some mysterious authority, and I have been given leave to reinhabit my childhood home. But there's always something missing, a detail wrong: a door where there never was one, a picture askew, stairs leading nowhere, all suffused with the melancholy perfume of loss. What lingers when I wake is not the unfamiliarity of these rooms but their oppressive clutter, the sheer number of *things* that crowd them: tables and armchairs and consoles, sofas and loveseats, pictures and vases, and framed photographs, thickets of them on every surface, though I can never make out their subjects. It makes me think of a phrase from a book I read years ago, something about the dumb sorrow of objects. Things, like people, require care, and it turns out there's only so much we can care for, that we have only so much of ourselves to give.

Astrid's death turned me into an ascetic. I moved out of my dorm into an apartment that I kept scrupulously bare, and took no lovers. Renunciation was the only way I could find to mourn, and relentless study. Thus liberated, I threw myself into the esoteric French theories that were sweeping through once-staid literature departments. The scientific cast of their abstruse jargon, the disincarnate focus on theory, the sheer (some said willful) difficulty of the language both soothed and fascinated me. There was no author, there was no story, there were just words. That Balzac had lived in the nineteenth, and Voltaire in the eighteenth century was immaterial. Whether you found Emma Bovary admirable or pathetic was beside the point. It was all text. I went to class. I read. I ate when I remembered to. Sometimes Astrid visited me in my dreams, and I woke up happy. I carried her with me through the day, but like Persephone, she could only stay so long. The shades always reclaimed her. I wrote my thesis, on neurosis and narrative in Proust. It sounded awfully clever, but the truth was that what drew me to Proust was his sadness. The only people I felt connected to at that time were Maybelle, Grace, and my sister, and we talked endlessly on the phone, though I couldn't say about what.

I graduated. Frank came and we had lunch at Mory's again. He looked profoundly unhappy. I knew from Lea that his marriage was a disaster, and the fact that he knew that I knew sat like a lump between us. I returned to New York. I temped for a few months and then went to visit Lea, who had just given birth to Pascaline-Amalia. They lived in the country now, and Serge was building up his stables. I was no help with the baby though, and horses made me nervous. I went to Paris and stayed with Frank, but Inge, who kept assuring me that "this is your home," clearly wasn't thrilled about having me around. I went to Berlin, where I cut off all my hair and hung out in Kreutzberg clubs, waking up next to strangers. Maybelle urged me to come to Louisville. I applied to graduate school.

My hair grew back and I immersed myself in metafiction and intertextuality, at Columbia this time. I moved back in to the Jane Street apartment, waitressing at one of the big yuppie mills in SoHo to pay the mortgage. Sometimes I brought a man home. Although I had renounced celibacy, I could only sleep with strangers. I raised the one-night stand to an art form. Astrid had left Grace her business, and she moved to New York to take over, but the magic was gone. Grace had no empathy, and would try to bully women into buying things that made them look ridiculous. I tried to explain this to her, but she only snapped back, "I can't help it that I'm not Astrid!" She was right, she couldn't. She was just silly old Grace, whom I was rather fond of after all.

Lea and Serge and his parents went to Poland with the pope. Lea said it was amazing, millions of people in a field, like Woodstock with nuns. Serge's father had known the pope as a student, and they were still friends, and that spring, when strikes broke out again, he was back in Rome for mysterious consultations at the Vatican. Lea said he really thought they were going to bring the Communists down; it was only a matter of time. She had even met Lech Wałęsa, whom she declared to be quite sexy in an unsexy sort of way. It still bemused me that Lea had any interest in striking workers, but I'd forgotten how doggedly loyal she was. Living with the Lubomirskis, she naturally adopted their outlook, even as she remained the old Lea with me. She was pregnant again, for the fourth time, and when I asked her if she was ever going to slow down, she said, what's the point of being a Catholic if not to have twelve children? I wouldn't have put it past her: Lea approached motherhood with the same obdurate pragmatism she brought to most things; it just wasn't a big deal to her. She never read a manual, never breast-fed, thought Lamaze was silly (*horses manage just fine without it*), and often got the hyphenated French-Polish names of her towheaded brood mixed up, but she kept popping them out with a cheerful unflappability that Grace found appalling but that I secretly admired.

"What is it again you're studying?" she asked me on the phone.

"Poststructural feminist theory," I patiently repeated. I had told Lea thousands of times what I was studying, and she continued to affect complete and total ignorance of my scholarly endeavors, even though I had sent her the article I had published in *The Yale Review* on clitoral metaphors in *Nana*.

"I don't really think of you as a man-hater."

"It has nothing to do with man-hating. Think of it as gender-aware linguistics."

"I didn't know you were interested in linguistics. Are you going to become a professor?"

"No," I said. If there was one thing I knew, it was that I didn't want to teach. I had no interest in shaping young minds.

"Then what's the point?"

"What about knowledge for the sake of knowledge?" I said testily. I thought I heard her yawning on the other end of the line, but I couldn't be sure. It might have been the baby making a noise.

"You're in a rut," my sister informed me. "It's not healthy. You're studying something completely useless, and you're still living in Mom's apartment. I bet you haven't even thrown her things out."

It was true, I hadn't. That they were hers and not mine made them bearable. In fact, I was becoming attached to them. "Why should I? They're beautiful things."

"Give them away. Grace has been eyeing her Lacroix coat for years."

I told her to mind her own business, but she was right. I *was* in a rut. I hated Columbia, was living in a shrine to my dead mother, and had even had dinner twice with Harold, whose delicacy only goaded me into making outrageous statements about penis fetishism in the nineteenth-century novel, which made him blink rapidly and hastily ask for the bill.

I was working on an article on the encoding of the female body in Renée's dressing room in *La Curée* and had been invited to speak at a Zola symposium at Paris VII—Zola was big with the poststructuralist crowd for the same reason he was unpopular with Henry James. I had slept with three people in the past two weeks—an investment banker who urged me to get into real estate, and, for the sake of variety, two NYU girls I had picked up at the Cubby Hole—and I felt hungover and listless. With increasing frequency, I found myself looking up from my computer and muttering *blablabla* to the convivial, if rather dull-witted pigeon who had taken up residence on the windowsill. The symposium, which would be full of chain-smoking women in leather pants, held little appeal, but maybe a change of air was what I needed. The university was going to pay for my ticket. I booked the flight.

I arrived on the kind of lugubrious October morning that makes you wonder why anyone associates Paris with springtime. Frank had offered to pick me up at the airport, but I was afraid that Inge would take this small solicitude as a slight, so I took the RER. Inertia, at least on Frank's part, was now the sole force that kept them together, but Inge still went doggedly through the motions, renovating bathrooms and picking out new curtains for the living room, whose furnishings kept shifting restlessly, as if set in motion by her unease. No longer having any real reason to dislike her, I began to pity her. Inge was fundamentally a decent person; and the discovery that Frank still loved Astrid must have laid waste to her sense of propriety. What tormented her the most, however, was the belief that he hadn't bonded with Marguerite—"As if poor old Dad had ever *bonded* with us," Lea scornfully remarked, for she had been the recipient of this hapless confidence, motherhood having finally given them something in common. The truth was that Marguerite, now six, was sadly lacking in enchantments. Stolid and blond like her mother, she had the plodding gait of a Scandinavian peasant, and an incurious blue gaze that was often fixed on a wall or a door. Inge was besotted with her, but Frank treated her the way he treated all small children, with a distracted tolerance that bordered on indifference. Even I couldn't remember him speaking to me before I was at least eight, but poor Inge was convinced, undoubtedly correctly, that he loved her child less.

I felt for my father. It came to me that, in my Jane Street cocoon, I, too, had been trapped in someone else's life. Now that I was unmoored, however, the truth I had always suspected reared up with the stark simplicity of the obvious: I didn't want to be a deconstructionist critic. I didn't want to spend the rest of my days writing impenetrable essays about things that didn't exist. As I emerged from the metro at Place de l'Alma to a sky the color of oysters, I caught a morning whiff of warm bread and detergent, and

I remembered with a sharp pang that real sensations had once mattered to me: the taste of chocolate, the sharp fizz of lemonade, the smell of my skin at the beach, Astrid's perfume, which, in a disorienting moment, I thought I detected as a woman hurried by in a jacket of a color known in French as *pervenche*, one of those infinitesimally subtle gradations of blue for which there is no word in any other language. It was a color Zola might have used to describe a girl's eyes, or the elegant *tournure* of a courtesan's peignoir, and suddenly it came back to me why I had always loved him; and Stendhal and Balzac and all the other Dead White Men it had become fashionable to mock: because they possessed the magical quality of real writers to summon worlds—worlds full of people you actually cared about, as opposed to the ambivalent wraiths of postmodern literature.

As I walked along the Rue de La Trémoille's sandstone façades, and turned into the Rue du Boccador, I knew that I would not deliver my paper at the conference. I couldn't have cared less about whether the crown on the ceiling of Renée's flesh-colored boudoir represented her clitoris or her belly button. It was just a stupid architectural detail, like the plaster rosettes on the ceiling of Frank's lobby, the gilded birdcage I rode up in, or the pale gray double doors that opened to reveal not Inge, as I had expected, but my father, who had stayed home to wait for me.

"Charlotte," he said.

"Hi, Dad," I said, and we hugged self-consciously. A shower smell still hung in the hallway. He told me that Inge had taken Marguerite to school. She had just started the first grade, he added, and then paused, as if trying to extract significance from this fact. "I have to go to a meeting," he said apologetically, "otherwise I would have taken the day off."

"That's all right, Dad, I didn't get much sleep. I'll probably take a nap."

He brightened. "Ah, yes, excellent idea." Then he paused again. Everything about him had slowed down. I longed to tell him that I, too, felt the weight of existence, but we lacked the vocabulary for such an exchange. "I thought we might go out for dinner, but Inge is cooking a special meal."

"That's great, Dad," I said.

I went to Lea's old room and lay down on the cool white coverlet. I felt the pleasant light-headedness of jet lag, the slight chill of foreign air. From the open window, courtyard sounds drifted in: the clang of a metal bucket, the concierge calling to the mailman. I closed my eyes and fell asleep.

A month later, I was still there. At first I thought Inge had resigned herself to my presence, but I came to perceive that she was grateful to have me there as a buffer. I wrote to my department head at Columbia and told him that I wasn't coming back, and I sent a check for the ticket they had paid for. I tore up my paper and went out and bought the collected works of Colette. I slept and read and played Scrabble with Frank in the evening. We listened to Vladimir Horowitz playing Schumann's *Kinderszenen*, and I pretended to be as enthralled as he was, though what really caught my attention was the guy coughing in the audience. Inge suffered from migraines, so sometimes I would take Marguerite to school, her fat little hand in mine. When her teacher asked me who I was, I said her sister, and she raised her eyebrows in the way of French functionaries confronted with a potential irregularity.

"*Un remariage,*" I explained.

"*Ah bon.*"

I went to visit Lea in Normandy and we made bets on when Inge would leave. I said a year, she said two. Serge, who was growing thick around the middle from all the Camembert and calvados, retreated behind his newspaper. Lea, too, was filling out, in the comfortable way of women who know they will always be lovely. Her haunches had grown heavier, as if childbirth had rooted her in the earth, and there was a ripe fullness to her face. We put on rubber boots and walked in the forest, their Hungarian vizslas skidding ahead of us over the wet leaves. They were the most beautiful dogs I had ever seen, tawny and muscular, with soulful brown eyes, and Lea laughed that Serge loved them more than the children. It was the height of the hunting season, and the dogs were restive, their damp noses sniffing at the air. The house, an old stone manor, smelled of dog and damp and the milk and bath odors that accompany small children. It was not my world, but I saw its charms.

I went back to Paris. I needed to make a decision: either stay or go back to New York; get on with my life. I stayed, and took Frank's suggestion that I try my hand at journalism. He knew someone at the *Tribune* who offered to read anything I might care to send in. I didn't like to take advantage of my father's connections, but the idea of writing about something real had a seductive appeal. I sat in cafés and scribbled down ideas for stories, most of which ended up in the wastebasket. I had no idea what people might want to read. I felt as if I had spent the past few years on an island, and now that I was back among the living, I needed to relearn their language; the foods they ate, and the movies they saw, the way they talked to their children. I devoured magazines. I bought *Elle* and *Le Nouvel Observateur* and *Paris Match*, where I caught up on Chiara Grzebine's acting career.

Grace took over the Jane Street apartment. She needed a change, too. She had let her latest boyfriend, a Brazilian waiter, move in with her, and it hadn't worked out. I told her to go through Astrid's clothes and take what she wanted, and when she choked up, I wished I had made the offer a long time ago. Shedding was clearly my vocation. I didn't really know anyone in Paris anymore, and felt as if I were in a suspended state of being home and not home. It wasn't unpleasant. I did things I never would have done when I lived there, tourist things: I wandered through the Picasso museum, had a glass of wine at La Cloche des Halles, and took a tour of the Conciergerie, where Marie Antoinette had been imprisoned. I could easily have had a lover—in Paris, if you spend enough time alone in cafés, you can't really help it—but I didn't return the playful looks.

I was coming out of the FNAC when I saw Łukasz on the street. He almost walked right into me. I must have looked as dumbfounded as he did, though I detected in his gaze an uncertainty that was absent in mine. The last time he'd seen me, I had been a teenager in a party dress, my legs too long, my teeth too big for my mouth. Łukasz, however, looked more youthful than I remembered, and it was only then I realized that he must have been several years younger than my mother. "It's me, Charlotte," I said foolishly. Why would he remember me? But he smiled, the same self-effacing smile that had inspired my childish trust.

"Charlotte. Of course I remember you."

Please don't say, "you're all grown up now," I thought, but small talk, I recalled, had not been his strong suit. He looked the same: rumpled and drawn, a man too occupied with important things to pay attention to what he wore. I wondered what he was doing in Paris. Shouldn't he have been in Poland, busy with all the life-or-death matters that had kept him from my mother? I pushed away the bitter thought; it had all happened such a long time ago. We stood awkwardly, looking at each other, and it was only then it dawned on me that he had no idea.

"There's something I have to tell you," I blurted out. I pointed at a café across the street. He seemed puzzled, but he followed me. We sat on the terrace. It was a bright November afternoon, and a weak sun warmed the glassed-in enclosure. His hair, I now saw, was grayer, but his eyes were sharp and blue. I thought of the sleek Italian at the memorial. I thought of how little I knew or understood.

"I didn't know," he said when I was done. That was all. He made no excuses, no apologies. I appreciated the decency of not pretending, but outrage rose within me.

"She went to jail for you. She thought you'd abandoned her." My eyes drifted down to his feet, which were clad in the shoddy shoes all Eastern Europeans seemed to wear. My mother with a man in cheap shoes!

He looked pained. He was clearly not accustomed to discussing private matters, to being confronted by young girls. But I wasn't a young girl anymore. I stared at him hard, willing him to waver.

"I am sorry," he said. I searched for sorrow in his eyes, but they were impenetrable.

"Are you still with your wife?"

He held my gaze. "No. We are divorced. But we still work together."

"Why are you in Paris?" I was having trouble modulating my voice. He probably found me shrill and hysterical; or perhaps he was just indifferent. He probably hadn't even been in love with her. She'd made up the whole thing, the fantasy of a bored wife. He picked up his coffee. There was something deliberate about the gesture, and I remembered that he had been in jail, that far greater matters had been at stake. *Who cares about your stupid country?* I thought. He drank the coffee in one gulp, and set the cup carefully down. Maybe he was afraid to break it. "That I am not at liberty to tell you."

I was confounded, until I realized that he wasn't trying to be funny. He got up, his expression apologetic, and fumbled for change in his pocket, throwing down much more than our two coffees cost. "I am sorry, I really must go." Considering his certain poverty, it seemed a reckless extravagance. I gazed at him dumbly and, for the first time, he seemed unsettled. He reached into his pocket again and pulled out a pen, with which he scribbled something on a napkin, pushing it hastily toward me.

"You can reach me here if you need to," he said.

I nodded. It was more in acknowledgment than agreement, but before I could wonder why he would think that I might ever need him, he was gone.

52

LEA AND I WERE BOTH WRONG ABOUT INGE. She left after three months. I would make noises about moving out, and Frank would say, "No, no, there's plenty of room for all of us." One morning Inge got up and announced, "I'm going back to Sweden."

"I'm sorry," my father said.

When she was gone, he said, "I never cared for this apartment."

We moved back to Saint-Germain, to an eighteenth-century building with a courtyard on the Rue Mazarine, just a few blocks from our old place, which, as the concierge had revealed when I stopped by, was now occupied by another American family. Nobody else could afford it. It had never occurred to me that my childhood home was a way station. It belonged, I found out from Frank, to an impoverished aristocrat who had made a profitable arrangement with a relocation agency catering to expatriates. French people didn't rent. They were as rooted as trees, and could only regard with bemused pity those of us who, like the souls of Dante's lovers, were condemned to eternal restlessness.

I pretended that I was just staying for a while. We had a quiet Christmas, dining at Lipp with the tourists, and we rang in the New Year at Lea's, where Frank seemed baffled at the ever-increasing number of his grandchildren. Serge was glued to the television. The cascading developments in Poland were being covered by all the networks, and there was a general feeling of history in the making. In February, the government started negotiations with Solidarity. The Hungarian opposition was pressing for reforms, and the Czechs were getting restless as well. The whole of Eastern Europe was beginning to look like a big domino game, with everyone waiting for the first tile to fall. Serge's father rushed off to the Vatican, and on the phone, Maybelle crowed, "This time Przemek thinks it's for real!" I wondered if Łukasz's presence in Paris had had something to do with the upcoming negotiations. I had kept the napkin with his number in a box with other objects I didn't know what to do with.

I had finally published two small pieces: one on why Americans don't read Zola (with an acknowledgment to Azher), and another, based on my failed attempt at recapturing Astrid's mystical experience of the Deux Magots, on the decline of café culture. Frank had found them both very clever, but it was 1989, and the world was being turned upside down. I wanted to write about events, not impressions; about things that mattered. I got the idea for my first real article from Lea. It was about the behind-the-scenes role of the Knights of Malta, the obscure medieval order to which Serge's father belonged, in the Polish democracy movement. I wrote about the émigré aristocrats hovering at the sidelines, their hopes of one day reclaiming their heritage rekindled by the vision of a shipyard worker. Even my normally sane sister had begun to fantasize about the Lubomirski estates. "Wouldn't it be nice, a castle to raise the children in?" I didn't quote her—privately I thought they were all mad—but my piece was just Gothic enough, with its evocations of anachronistic secret societies and allusions to Vatican involvement, to stand out from the more mundane political reporting of a situation that increasingly had the world on edge. It got published, and the next thing I knew, people were calling to solicit more.

In April, the Polish government legalized Solidarity and agreed to hold free elections. Łukasz, who spoke both French and English, was constantly on TV. With his good looks and professorial manner, he appeared to have become a kind of poster boy for Solidarity, some of whose members were decidedly lacking in social graces. One night I was watching the news with Frank, and Łukasz appeared in the frame. I glanced at my father, but he just watched the program and, when it was over, remarked that he'd never thought he would live to see the Iron Curtain torn down, that these were truly amazing times. Maybe he hadn't recognized Łukasz; he had after all only spoken to him briefly at Grace's party years ago. Maybe Frank really could dissociate the personal from the historic. And yet I felt sure he *had* recognized him.

Łukasz had been one of the participants in the Round Table talks, and it was widely expected that he would have a position in the new government. He looked tired but elated. The Russians hadn't lifted a finger, and people were finally beginning to believe that it was true, that they weren't going to interfere. Elections were scheduled for June. It was then it dawned on me that this could be my big break. On the napkin was a six-digit phone number, and a Warsaw address on a street called Długa. I called the number. It rang and rang, but finally an answering machine picked up. I recognized his voice. I left a message, asking if I could interview him. I didn't think he would call back, but a week later, he did, and said yes, but it would have to be over the phone, as he couldn't possibly leave Poland right now. I asked, "What if I came to Warsaw?"

Łukasz was enough of a catch that the *New York Times*, whom I hastily pitched the piece to, said they would give it serious consideration. This time I flew. The plane was full of journalists and political consultants, all availing themselves freely of the bar cart. The festive atmosphere even rubbed off on the Air France stewardesses, who looked the other way at the people talking in the aisles with plastic cups in hand, even when the seat-belt sign flashed on. An Italian photographer from *Il Manifesto*, the Communist paper, chatted me up outside the bathroom, and I remarked slyly, "I guess this is kind of a bummer for you guys," but he cried, "No, no, it is a revolution of the people!" and asked me to have dinner with him that night.

Warsaw that May bore little resemblance to the wintry wasteland I remembered. Lipstick-colored petunias cascaded from balconies, and the sidewalk cafés were full of pretty girls tilting their faces toward the sun. Even Stalin's Palace of Culture had a jaunty appearance. The streets were plastered with election posters, and there was a nervous buzz in the air. I was staying at the Hotel Victoria, opposite the Saxon Gardens that Maybelle and I had traversed with Przemek in his horse-drawn carriage, and around the corner from the Opera, where the mysterious woman had passed me the note. I checked in and rode up to my room in the elevator with two guys from *Newsweek* who said that even the hookers in the lobby had gotten better-looking.

Łukasz had told me to call him when I arrived, but once again it proved impossible to get hold of him. I left a message, waited an hour, left another message and finally went for a walk. To my surprise, I was quickly able to orient myself, as if the topography of the city had imprinted itself on me that awful winter. I headed toward the Old Town, past the Hotel Europejski and onto the shopping street that led to Sigismund's Column, which I remembered Przemek pointing out to us. The horse-drawn carts still stood in the middle of the Market Square, hemmed in now by a sea of café terraces and flower vendors, who seemed to be doing a brisk trade in lilacs and lilies of the valley. Several women I passed clutched bunches of them, their languid scent wafting by. Couples held hands and kissed, or nuzzled over Pepsis in glass bottles. I ordered ice cream from a waitress in orthopedic shoes who beamed as if I had picked the best thing on the menu.

That evening I hung out in the bar with the journalists. Maurizio, the *Il Manifesto* photographer, turned up and said, "Ah, I knew I would find you!" He had sexy eyes and a bandanna around his neck, and I flirted with him. He took me to a night club with a disco ball where he ordered Soviet champagne and a tin of Beluga caviar. In a swirling spray of refracted light, we danced to James Brown and some awful Europop, and then went back to my room and had the kind of brisk, cheerful sex that is only possible with Italians. "See you," he called out the next morning, as he rushed off to a press conference at the Ministry of Exterior Affairs. "Okay," I said. I felt invigorated and giddy. I grinned at myself in the mirror while I brushed my teeth in the socialist *luxe* bathroom. I could have it both ways, be a serious journalist and bed Italian photographers. Maurizio was clearly a playboy, but I didn't have to fall in love with him. The evidence of anything being possible was all around me.

There was a message from Łukasz at the desk. He would see me at seven that evening, at the Solidarity headquarters. Maurizio called and asked me out again and I said I couldn't, I was busy. "Ah, you will break my heart—can you hear it breaking into pieces?" He made a rattling sound, as if he were shaking a can of peanuts. I laughed. "Don't be silly," I said. I took a shower and washed my hair, and sat by the open window to dry it in the late afternoon sun.

I arrived at the Solidarity headquarters ten minutes early, notebook and tape recorder in hand. It was a madhouse—people huddled over computer screens, talking on the phone, rushing by with stacks of files, shouting imprecations, and smoking, smoking, smoking until the air was gray. I managed to catch someone's attention—a woman with her hair knotted hastily back, as if she just couldn't be bothered—and she said Łukasz might be upstairs, honestly she had no idea, and rushed off to wherever she had been going. Phones pealed everywhere, and in a corner, a clutch of men who looked as if they hadn't slept in three nights stood listening to a tape recorder. No one paid any attention to me. I went upstairs and down a hallway and thought I saw Ania, Łukasz's wife, coming out of a room, but I couldn't be sure. Everyone appeared hyperanimated, like characters in a cartoon, their skin turned sallow by the fluorescent light. A midwestern voice shouted, "Jesus! I need them yesterday!" probably one of the American consultants that Maurizio had told me were working with Solidarity, much to the disapproval of the Europeans.

On the third floor, by a gigantic Xerox machine that still had the factory stickers on it, I found another harassed-looking woman. I asked for Łukasz again. I had taken care to dress professionally, in a stern skirt and jacket and blunt-toed navy pumps, but the way she took me in made me wonder if the scent of my Italian Communist still clung to me, or if she just thought I was too young or too pretty to be taken seriously. In desperation, I invoked the *New York Times*, and only then did she, grudgingly, lead me to a closed door upon which she briskly knocked. As we waited for a response, my nerve deserted me. Whom did I think I was fooling? By then, however, the door had been flung open, to reveal an improvised conference room at which Łukasz and several men sat hunched in intense conversation. The woman said something and Łukasz looked up. He seemed surprised to see me, and then appeared to remember that I was there at his invitation. The others barely glanced at me. Łukasz got up and motioned to me to follow him out. We didn't shake hands, and I wondered if he had had second thoughts. He showed me into a room at the end of the hallway that held a sink and refrigerator, a table, and four chairs. From the wall, a girl in a bikini smiled from a German calendar advertising cars, next to a picture, slightly askew, of Lech Wałęsa with the pope. I sat in one of the chairs, and he took another across from me. There was a coffee machine on a counter by the sink, but he didn't offer me any. I guessed he was used to having sustenance brought to him, by the tired women who flock around heroes and revolutionaries.

"Well," he said, and the interview began. It wasn't so hard. I had notes, and I had done my research. I asked him about the elections, about whether he thought the Solidarity party could really win, given that the Communists had allocated themselves 60 percent of the seats in parliament. He said that the voters would decide. I asked about the Hungarians and the Czechs. I asked whether he really thought Gorbachev would let the East Bloc slip through his fingers. I asked him all the questions anyone would have asked, and his answers were smooth and assured, somewhat banal. He was learning fast. They all were: They were becoming politicians. Maurizio said that as soon as they came to power, it would go to their heads, but here we were at the dawn of the era, and who knew? Maybe these guys would trump the odds. For now I had an exclusive interview with my name on it.

I was getting up to leave when Łukasz held me back with a hand motion. I thought of pretending I hadn't seen it—I didn't need to know any more. But Łukasz, by now, was accustomed to getting his way. A tinge of imperiousness had crept into his manner.

"Your mother was an extraordinary woman," he said.

"I know," I said, accepting his gesture in all its well-meant hollowness. He hadn't understood her at all. But then passion, unlike love, doesn't require understanding.

53

THE *TIMES* BOUGHT MY PIECE, and Maurizio said, "You can't go back to Paris: This is where history is happening!" It was hard to argue with him, especially after his paper rented him an apartment and he offered to share it with me.

"Won't it cramp your style?" I teased.

"I am an Italian; nothing cramps my style."

I stayed. Solidarity won the elections, and Łukasz became the spokesman for Tadeusz Mazowiecki's government. He started to wear suits: first the cheap ones that had made the Polish dissidents so poignant, then Hugo Bosses with sharp ties. Maurizio had heard that the Americans, who everyone knew had bankrolled the election, had brought in fashion consultants to spruce up the Solidarity guys. I pointed out that no red-blooded American male would be caught dead in a double-breasted jacket; the suits clearly had Vatican Involvement written all over them. We bantered back and forth in this manner on the Hotel Victoria's shag-carpeted barstools. Maurizio was on the staff of a major daily, and I was only a freelancer, but there was plenty of work to go around, and being with him gave me an in, since he knew and was liked by everyone, a character trait that both mystified and fascinated me. He was always buying rounds of drinks, flirting with men and women alike—though the men usually had no idea they were being flirted with, as this seduction took place under the guise of sports talk—and practicing his atrocious Polish on the hookers at the other end of the bar. Nobody takes photographers, or Italian Communists, seriously. People dropped their guard around him, and so he heard things, got scoops. I might have made use of my connection to Łukasz as well, but he wasn't so easy to get at now that everyone wanted a piece of him. I did attend a couple of press conferences, where he made a point of smiling at me, but it was a stiff smile, and I realized he might think I was shadowing him. I stopped going. His, in any case, had now become the official line.

When the Round Table talks began in Hungary, we headed to Budapest along with everyone else. Unlike Warsaw, it was a beautiful city, with sweeping bridges and wide boulevards lined with graceful Belle Epoque buildings. It had real cafés, like Vienna, which pleased Maurizio immensely, even as he turned up his nose at the coffee, which he drank with a sad grimace. During the day we followed demonstrations and attended raucous press conferences, and in the evening we strolled along the Danube, whose polluted waters turned sumptuous oily shades at dusk. I discovered the old Turkish baths on the other side of the river, and spent an afternoon bobbing in the sulfurous waters of the central pool, my eyes focused dreamily on the clouded bits of colored glass in the dome overhead, which bathed us in a shifting, subaqueous light. That and a vigorous massage only cost two dollars. When I mentioned this in shock to Maurizio, he shrugged.

"Why don't you look on the bright side? Everyone can afford it."

I confessed that I'd given the attendant a twenty. She'd pocketed it with a furtive smile.

"Well, then, you evened things out."

I knew I'd done nothing of the sort, but I envied him his clear view of the world, which sometimes reminded me of Lea's. What I had done was perpetuate a corrupt system, another quaint notion to Maurizio, who had worked the Eastern Europe beat long enough to take bribes for granted.

"A guilt offering is not a bribe," he pointed out.

"It sort of is, in reverse."

"You worry too much for a beautiful girl. Come here. If I tell you I am madly in love with you, will you stop worrying?"

"How many times have you been madly in love?"

"Hundreds."

"I thought so." But who could resist him? This was what distinguished Maurizio from your garden-variety skirt chaser: He wasn't cynical. He really *liked* women; liked talking to them, being with them, exploring the folds and crevices of their bodies, inhaling their scent. He enjoyed being in love like he enjoyed wine, or sex, or arguing about sports, and being loved in this generic way was an experience that I found at once utterly ridiculous and insanely compelling. I told myself I was mad. Finally I relaxed. I wasn't an emotionally stunted clod: I, too, could live in the moment, especially that summer, when everyone else was.

And so August found us at the famous picnic on the Austrian-Hungarian border, when it was stormed by East German vacationers and the guards stood by and let them through. By September we were in Prague, where so many thousands came out in the streets that the police just gave up. There was talk of Dubček returning from exile, of Havel running for president. Even Bulgaria and Romania were stirring. We kept moving, following the collapsing dominoes all the way to Berlin. As we watched the people pour through the wall, Maurizio clicked away, roll after roll of film, and I wiped away tears as Maurizio wondered out loud how many of them had been Stasi informers.

In Kreutzberg, we ran into Nahid, who was veejaying an MTV special. We sat in a bar surrounded by German punks with green hair and she told me that Delphine had had a *crise* (Delphine had called it an epiphany) and joined the Peace Corps. Her father had finally died, and Candy de Bethune had promptly circulated the rumor that the poor man had expired after seeing a picture of Delphine in *Paris Match*, marching topless in an ACT UP demonstration with the words CORPORATE GREED scrawled in lipstick across her stomach. Rather more commentary had been generated by her pierced nipples, Candy wondering specifically if they wouldn't be hell on one's *soutien-gorge*.

"So what do you make of all this, as an Iranian?" Maurizio asked.

"And a tool of American cultural hegemony," I added.

Nahid grandly shrugged. Her latest lover, a statuesque girl from East Berlin, nuzzled her. "Nothing. When their twenty marks run out, they'll all have to go back. Do you think everyone's going to get a job at Volkswagen overnight?"

"*I* want to work for MTV," said the East German girlfriend, who looked to be about seventeen.

"So much for American cultural hegemony."

"Let me tell you the secret about American cultural hegemony," Nahid drawled. "It works. How's Lea? I never hear from her anymore."

"Doing her bit for world overpopulation. She's pregnant again."

"I always knew she and Serge would end up together—the bad boys always settle down first."

"She might get to be a châtelaine after all. Serge has been checking out the old estates."

"How sad," Nahid said.

"I would have thought you would sympathize. What if you could get your palace back in Tehran?"

Nahid fixed me with a cool eye. "Only fools live in the past. Fools and fanatics."

"Terrifying girl," Maurizio remarked as we walked back to our hotel.

"Is she? I don't know; she just doesn't have any illusions."

"Yes, that is what is terrifying."

"Underneath it all, she has a good heart," I said.

"That, I doubt."

I had expressed myself awkwardly. I was pretty sure that Nahid was completely amoral, but she was neither mean nor vindictive, which counted for something. And she was a loyal friend. I sometimes wished Maurizio were more subtle. He laced his arm around my waist. "Let's go home and make love." He always called it *making love*, never *fucking*. He was a real romantic, though not in the tragic nineteenth-century sense, which, I guess, didn't make him one at all. Maybe I was the real romantic.

"Come to Rome," he said.

"I have to get back to Paris. I haven't been home in months."

"Okay, then go to Paris, and then come to Rome."

"All right," I laughed.

Maurizio grinned. "Excellent! Rome is full of American girls who came for a visit and never left!"

"Isabel Archer isn't exactly one of my role models," I said, and received a blank look in return.

"Inside joke," I said. "Come on, let's go."

54

I WENT BACK TO PARIS. Frank opened the door before I could fish my keys out of the bottom of my bag. I knew the minute I set eyes on him that something was in the air.

"Hey, Dad," I said after I'd kissed him. "What's up?"

"Oh, nothing much. How was Berlin?"

"Amazing—you would've loved it! We—" I prepared to recount all the world-shattering events I had witnessed when I noticed a look of slight discomfort on Frank's face, and that he was wearing his hat and overcoat.

"Sorry, were you on your way out?"

"Er, yes—I'm afraid I wasn't expecting you. I have a dinner engagement."

I smiled forgivingly. I hadn't told him what time I was arriving, and had by chance caught an earlier flight. "Dad, it's okay, I'll tell you all about it later."

"Yes, I very much look forward to it. You look well." Now he was lingering out of politeness.

"Dad, go—I'll see you later." I practically pushed him out the door.

Dinner engagement? When Frank went out to dinner, it was usually with me or on business. This, however, was Saturday. I smiled to myself: My father had a date. I called Lea.

"Why shouldn't he have a date? I bet you'll never guess who it's with."

I racked my brain. The cocktail party invitations had dwindled to a trickle, fashionable Paris having only so much patience for the recalcitrant. Had someone gotten to Frank in my absence?

"I give up."

"It's Sylvia Fauché."

"What?"

"Your old best friend's mother. They've been going to the ballet together, and the opera."

"How come I'm the last to hear about it?" I said. I was, in fact, rather wounded.

"Because you're too busy becoming the next Oriana Fallaci. I, for one, am delighted. They're perfectly suited to each other; I can't believe we didn't think of it earlier."

"I can: They were both married, to other people."

"Well, now they're not."

"I can't believe he told you and not me," I peevishly owned up.

"He didn't tell me anything. Candy de Bethune saw them at *Orphée*, and now the world knows. Anyway, what's the big deal? You used to adore Sylvia. I remember you telling me once that you wished Mom were more like her."

I had, I remembered guiltily, around the time of the hash-smuggling fiasco. It stood to reason that Sylvia would love the ballet, and opera, too. Gentle, sad Sylvia, of the velvet headbands and American Church committees.

"How on earth did they meet?"

"How do you think? She needed a lawyer after her husband died. Did you know that Dad is a specialist in French estate law? That's what he spends most of his time on, sorting out estate issues for Americans who marry French people. Of course, if they get married, you'll have to move out, but you ought to be able to afford your own apartment, now that you're a famous journalist. Speaking of which, I read your interview with the 'Rising Star of Solidarity.'"

The sarcasm should have tipped me off, but I was too full of myself. "Really? What did you think?"

"The same everyone else did: What on earth possessed you? Dad read it, too, by the way."

An uncomfortable warmth crept up the back of my neck. Of

course Frank had read it; what would make me think that he
wouldn't? What, indeed, *had* I been thinking?

"Did it ever occur to you that he has feelings?"

"Oh God," I moaned.

"Yes, well, it's a bit late for second thoughts."

"Does he hate my guts?" Even I couldn't believe I'd said it. Was
this really my biggest concern, that having regained my star status, I
had tumbled again?

"I have a stunning revelation for you: You are just about the last
thing on his mind right now. I would say, in fact, that he took your
bizarre decision to track down Mom's lover with remarkable equanimity. I'm not sure he can take much more opening up of old
wounds, though, so maybe it's time you moved on."

"I'm so sorry," I said.

"Tell that to Dad."

I did. I tried. I waited up for him, and when I heard his key in the
door, I was standing, shame-faced in the vestibule. I hoped Sylvia
wouldn't be with him, but of course he wouldn't bring her home
with me back in residence. He was too much of a gentleman. Not
only had I fallen from grace, I was in the way.

"Dad, I—"

"It's all right, Charlotte," he said. I hated that he was more
embarrassed than I was. I hated that he had already forgiven me.

"I'm going to look for my own place," I said.

"Charlotte, you're always welcome here."

But you're only welcome where you don't live. I wasn't the only
one who needed to move on.

Absolution came a few days later in the form of an invitation, to
dinner at L'Assiette, Frank only mentioning in the taxi that Sylvia
Fauché would be joining us.

"Dad, you're a lousy obfuscator," I teased him.

"Really? I've been told I'm quite good at it."

That the first great restaurants looked like bordellos was no accident. Eating is the only intimate act that most of us are willing to

perform in public, and even in the most modest bistro, you can tell at a glance the couples who are undressing each other in their minds; the ones who are bored, or simmering with resentment; the ones who've run out of things to say, and those few who are at ease in the moment, who have just lapsed into convivial silence. Were it not for my presence, Frank and Sylvia would have been among the latter. When had this happened? How had they become so familiar that I felt like the third wheel? But Sylvia was too gracious not to pull me in.

"I think it's so wonderful that you've become a journalist," she said warmly. "It suits you." Did it? How did she know? How many words had Sylvia Fauché and I actually exchanged in our lifetime? Her cashmere sweater brought out the blue eyes that, through some felicitous alliance of literature and heredity, seemed to have flown straight off the pages of Proust. I'd forgotten how pretty she was. No, beautiful. A beautiful woman in her fifties, the same age Astrid would have been.

"How is Delphine enjoying the Peace Corps?" I asked. It seemed the most neutral of any topic relating to Sylvia's daughter, and, though I had no idea how things currently stood between them, I couldn't very well pretend that we hadn't been childhood friends, that Delphine wasn't yet another link between us.

Sylvia looked almost relieved. "Do you know, I think she's finally found herself. She loves Tanzania, and her colleagues seem to adore her. It's a shame you haven't stayed in touch," she said wistfully, and a taste of the old smugness came back to me, of the days when I was considered a good influence, as well as a recollection of what Nahid had told me, that Delphine was working on a condom-distribution project. Poor Sylvia . . . Since feeling sorry for her was an altogether more comfortable state than wondering if, were I not there, she and my father would be eyeing each other hungrily over the oysters, I clung to it. "But now that you travel so much, maybe you'll see more of each other."

I'd see more of her if you married my father, I thought. "I don't really get to Africa," I said, "but of course I'd love to see her."

The food was delicious, the wine superb. I let the oysters slide down my throat, the *foie gras poêlé* deliquesce onto my tongue. A few tables over, a government official sat with his mistress. L'Assiette was that kind of restaurant: discreet, understated, the kind of place Astrid had hated, and that Sylvia had undoubtedly chosen as the backdrop of my seduction. I succumbed, and her gratitude at my compliance smoothed over any misgivings I might have harbored about being such an easy lay. How well things had turned out. After a few glasses of Pomerol, I found myself regarding them through misty eyes. Gone was Frank's look of wishing he were home in his study. Gone was Sylvia's sadness, which I'd found so alluring as a child, ascribed to a romantically melancholic disposition, and suddenly saw for what it was: the dreary oppression of an unhappy marriage. It was only later, after the Pomerol had worn off, that I was visited by the unsettling corollary to this discovery, that my father might have been unhappy in his marriage as well.

"So what are your plans now?" Sylvia asked.

"I'm going to Italy."

"Italy, how lovely!"

"Yes, I've always wanted to see Rome in the winter."

Frank looked at me askance but I smiled reassuringly. This was the new me, the one he could take to dinner at L'Assiette with his lover. The one who looked forward to future pleasures rather than mull on distant grievances. The one who behaved.

"You're not going to take on Italian politics, are you?" he asked nonetheless with a slight look of alarm.

"No," I said. "I'm going on vacation."

55

I WENT TO ROME. I'd only been once, as a child, with my parents, and all I really remembered was the Coliseum, which had made a big impression on me thanks to Lea's enthusiastically gory description of what the ancient Romans had used it for, and the Christmas bazaar in Piazza Navona. Maurizio lived in Testaccio, which was out beyond the pyramid you pass on the way in from the airport. People had started opening clubs there, but it wasn't yet the fashionable destination it is today, and the neighborhood retained an authentic working-class flavor, much trumpeted by Maurizio. It wasn't as beautiful as the Rome I remembered, but beautiful is for tourists. I, Maurizio explained, was seeing the real Rome, the Rome of working people.

"Remind me why we're supposed to love the working classes unconditionally," I teased him, as we sat in a local trattoria slurping our way through a platter of oxtails. On his home turf, Maurizio went unabashedly native. A scarf in the colors of his soccer team looped around his neck against the November chill, he stopped in every coffee bar for the obligatory political or sports debate, joked around with kids on the street, and flirted shamelessly with the counter girl at the *panificio*, whose breasts were said to be the exact shape of a particular kind of bun sold by this establishment. I supposed that was what kept him centered, having a place to go back to where all the shopkeepers and trattoria owners knew him. We never saw a menu in the restaurants he patronized; they just brought food to the table and slapped him on the back. It was easy. It was also a little unsettling, especially when the evening's offering was pasta with lamb intestines.

"Because they are more deserving—anyway, who are you going to side with, the plutocrats?"

"My grandmother is a plutocrat," I said. Actually, I guessed Frank was a plutocrat, too, but there was something about my father that defied easy categorization. Indeed, there was something about most people that defied easy categorization, even if I doubted Maurizio would have concurred. His world was, on the whole, a self-evident one. "My mother's mother, on the other hand, was a waitress."

"You see, I knew you were a woman of the people."

"And your parents, naturally, were both oppressed factory workers."

"Are you kidding? My father is a big shot at the EU."

"Then how on earth did you end up at *Il Manifesto?*"

Maurizio, never one to dwell on contradictions, winked. "Who do you think got me the job?"

That was the thing about Maurizio: With the exception of a ferocious devotion to his soccer team, his convictions sat light as air. He lacked the indignation that fuels true passion; as he said himself, he was just a photographer. And so we chatted in the buoyant manner of those who have nothing at stake. We ate, we made love—I didn't mind calling it that, even though it was curiously free of the anxiety that, in my mind, came hand in hand with that state. Not that I hadn't slept with plenty of men I didn't love, but this was different; there was a convivial quality to our coupling, as there was to most everything we did, from tooling around on his Vespa to playing pinball, about which we were rather more competitive. He took pictures of me. I still have them, and in these prints, I look like a girl in love, an illusion that puzzled me until I figured out that the photographs were really an expression of Maurizio. Seen through the filter of his desire, I took on a generic glow that said everything about him and nothing about me. Maurizio loved women in a generous but ultimately undiscriminating way. He'd loved many before me and would love more when I was gone, and the ghost of our inevitable parting did not hang heavy over me. In fact, the knowledge that I wasn't going to get my heart broken, that this would just die of natural causes, was not only exhilarating in its novelty, but made me like him all the more. There was a lot to like about Maurizio: that he was generous and kind, that he was smart but not arrogant, that he didn't pick fights, and that he called his mother every day, but real intimacy eluded us. I wasn't sure I believed that love is inextricable from pain, but when I looked at Maurizio, there was no shock of recognition. We were simply too different. It was fun pretending that I, too, could stride through life without a care, but I was too conscious of the feeling that I was playing a game.

And so, when people started massing on the streets of Bucharest, I watched Maurizio pack his bag.

"Aren't you coming?"

"Not this time."

"But this is it! They're going to string that bastard Ceauşescu up by his balls."

"Send me a postcard."

"You can stay here as long as you want," he offered. He really was a nice guy.

"Thanks, but I have some things I need to take care of."

"In Paris?"

"No, in New York."

"I'll see you in New York, then."

"Sure," I said, and who knew, he might even show up, and I would be happy if he did, but I was glad my life didn't hang on it.

56

PARIS CREEPS UP ON YOU. New York catches you by surprise. When Manhattan's skyline popped up ahead after that particular bend on the Long Island Expressway, I felt the thrill that always grips me at this vision at once preposterous and familiar, and I asked the cab driver to take the Fifty-ninth Street bridge, rather than the tunnel, just to draw out the sensation of approaching a place that seems designed to be seen only from afar. It was still a shock to have Grace open the door. She was wearing an old sweater of Astrid's, an orange angora with an asymmetrical ruffle that she had bought on a whim and then decided was a bit much—undoubtedly the reason, I told myself in the uncharitable impulse that she never failed to arouse in me, that Grace had picked it out—but I still felt a surge of indignation, even though I had told her several times to take anything she wanted.

"Champagne's on ice!" she cried. She hadn't changed anything in the apartment, and my sense of having stepped into a time warp was only exacerbated by this familiar ritual. "Tell all! Were you really there when the Berlin wall went down? I watched the whole thing with Claude and Jasper—he's not well, you know," she added, in the lowered voice that, when referring to a gay man, had come to signify AIDS.

I remembered that Lea, who spoke more often to Grace these days, had mentioned something about it, but Claude and Jasper had been Astrid's friends; I had never really cultivated them, even when I lived in the apartment after her death, and I had felt only the inadequate regret one does at the news of a mudslide in Guatemala, or the death in a car crash of someone you went to high school with but didn't know. Grace, however, had become close to them. Much of her time, she told me, was now spent nursing Jasper, so that Claude could get out and tend to their flower shop on Greenwich Avenue. Jasper may have been dying, but people were still having weddings, and funerals. What everyone said about life going on, it was true, and you really couldn't be angry at them for it. I glanced at the huge arrangement on the mantel: calla lilies and mimosa and something twiglike and vaguely Japanese-looking. It wasn't just Astrid who was entombed in this frozen interior; so was the part of me that knew the names of flowers.

"Yes, aren't they gorgeous? Claude brings me a new one every week; he says it's the least he can do." Grace smiled wryly. "Who would've thought I'd end up being so good at helping people die? I should get a medal."

"I'll contact the Sisters of Mercy," I said, relieved that Grace's narcissism hadn't been entirely vanquished by good works. We grinned at each other, but there was a lingering sadness in her eyes, one that, it came to me with a pang, had once lived in mine but was now more of an occasional visitor. I could almost identify the moment when I had felt it lift. I had woken up to find Maurizio's arm flung across me, an oblong of winter sun stretching across the bed and the smell of baking bread rising from the *panificio* downstairs, and I had thought: *I am on the other side.* Grace's grief had settled in; it had become a part of her. Surrounded by Astrid's things, there was something of the priestess about her, the keeper of the shrine, the one who would remember when everyone else had forgotten.

"Grace, was Astrid ever happy?" It was an odd question to ask with a glass of champagne in my hand, not to mention a ham-handed one, but it was only then it hit me, with the uncannily revelatory power of the completely obvious, that Grace was the only one who knew.

"Of course she was," she said, but the sentence hung incomplete.

Was she going to let me in, or would I be six years old forever? "Astrid was a complicated woman," she relented. "The things that satisfy most people weren't enough for her."

I knew that this conversation rested on my ability not to take any of it personally, but it was hard not to. "You mean, like an adoring husband and two daughters and a fabulous life in Paris?"

Grace regarded me with a sort of exasperated pity. "Do you have any idea how bored she was?"

I glared at her. For all my good intentions, the old adolescent truculence was flaring right back up, even though I knew that whatever mercy Grace had intended to show me would be proportionately diminished.

"Yes, bored. So was I, but I was more easily distracted. Astrid was smarter than me, I always knew that, and so did you—don't think I don't know you always thought I was a dim bulb—but we had one thing in common, your mother and I: Do you have any idea what it was like to be a kept woman, even in Paris—especially in Paris—in the middle of the seventies? To know that no one would ever take you seriously? Nobody did, you know? It didn't matter how many lectures or demonstrations we went to, or how much we got psychoanalyzed, or that we both honestly did slog our way through *The Gulag Archipelago* and Simone de Beauvoir—the crap *she* put up with, by the way, some feminist icon. . . . In most people's eyes, we were indistinguishable from Candy de Bethune. Don't ask me how, but they could sniff you out even under fifteen thousand dollars worth of Chanel couture—*especially* under fifteen thousand dollars worth of couture. There were the Smith girls like Sylvia Fauché, and then there was us, one notch above *poules de luxe*.

"My mother was one of the most elegant women in Paris!"

"Honey, your mother was the illegitimate daughter of a cocktail waitress, and I was a Jewish girl from Brooklyn."

"Oh, for God's sake, Grace."

"Easy for you to say with your fancy degree and your career. And don't think it helped that we were respectably married. Most people assumed we'd ensnared our husbands with sexual wiles. It's funny how no one ever minded all those scrofulous aristocrats marrying Americans for their money . . ."

"Grace, you're being completely Gothic."

"Yeah, well, life in France had its medieval side. Believe me, you're lucky you ended up back here. You're an American—your sister, that's another story, but you belong in New York, and so did Astrid."

"I'm sorry, Grace," I said. "I just don't believe that Astrid cared that much what people thought about her."

"You're right; I cared more. But it bothered her, too. Why do you think she was so happy you got into Yale?"

"She didn't seem to mind Lea dropping out of the Sorbonne."

"That's because she knew Lea was set for life. You, she always worried about."

"Could've fooled me" was on the tip of my tongue, until I remembered that, at the time I required worrying about, I had shut Astrid out. We sat for a moment as I let it all sink in.

"And this is supposed to explain why she betrayed my dad for Łukasz?" I finally said.

Grace looked disappointed. "Oh, so *that's* what you want to know about?"

I grew defensive. "Yes, I would, because I still don't get it. Especially after meeting him. He's a complete narcissist."

Grace shrugged. "Astrid was always looking for something bigger than herself. You think it was *my* idea to go to India? We both got ringworm, and the swami smelled like a goat. That was the big difference between us: Astrid came out of the ashram wanting meaning, and I came out wanting a bath." She took a philosophical swig of champagne. "Sometimes I credit my endurance to a complete incapacity for enlightenment."

"So Łukasz provided meaning?"

"He sure as hell didn't provide sex. I sometimes wonder if they slept together at all. Astrid was an odd bird; she'd get these notions

and cling to them. She was really fired up about those Polish pro-
testers. Me, I just saw a bunch of badly dressed guys in mustaches.
You know, your mom was one person who really would have benefited from an education; it might have helped her put some order
into all her crazy ideas."

"But the crazy ideas were always yours," I said, though all of a
sudden, I wondered.

Grace regarded me with the same exasperated sympathy. "Ask
yourself this: Who ended up in jail? Me or Astrid?" Her eyes filled
with tears. "Do you know that I still miss her?"

"I do, too," I said, and I took Grace's bony hand, but it wasn't
exactly true. I didn't miss her the way Grace did; I couldn't. She had
never revealed herself to me.

"Some job I'm doing of welcoming you home. . . . I know, let's go
to Max's!"

"All right," I said, though I wasn't all that hungry, but I was
moved to generosity, which was probably why I told her about
Maurizio over a meal that I ate and she picked at. I wondered why
she still bothered to deprive herself; maybe it had become second
nature.

"Good for you: Every woman should have at least one Italian
lover! I wasted way too much time with Russians. . . ." She grew suddenly wistful. "It's an odd feeling, you know, that you'll never be
made love to again."

I wondered if she wanted me to argue with her, but we both
knew that Grace, too, had crossed one of life's invisible lines.

"I guess you'll want the apartment back."

"No, you stay there. I'm thinking of trying a new neighborhood."
This was a complete lie; I had made no plans whatsoever, but it was
suddenly clear that I would stay in New York, and that Jane Street
was the last place I wanted to live. Grace belonged there. I didn't. It
was that simple.

"At least take some of her things."

"No, you'll take better care of them."

Grace reached for a cigarette. "Filthy habit," she said, "but everyone seems to end up dying of something else."

I hadn't smoked in a long time, but I took one, too, to keep her company.

"Grace," I said, "did you *really* read The Gulag Archipelago?"

"Well, I did skim over a couple of the more boring parts."

"I skipped most of the battle scenes in War and Peace."

We smiled at each other.

"Funny, isn't it, how in the end, it's just you and me?"

To this day, I'm not sure what she meant, but sometimes, it's the things you don't understand that make the most sense.

57

SYLVIA AND FRANK were married that July in a quiet ceremony at the American Church. It may have been the only wedding in Paris history that Candy de Bethune didn't crash, but there was no official announcement, and everyone was out of town for the summer. Frank and Sylvia would shortly be following suit, their destination the château near Bourges, which had been mired since Sylvia's husband's death in an inheritance dispute involving his sister's children. Frank, his Strether-like proclivities now unhindered, had acquired a taste for meditative walks along the river, and had announced gaily that they would just buy another castle—France was full of moth-eaten old piles no one wanted—and to hell with the Napoleonic Code!

I wondered how much this sudden extravagance had to do with his mother's death that spring. He and Lea had come over for the service, which had been arranged by the family solicitors at Saint James' Episcopal Church on Madison Avenue, and we had stood self-consciously at our assigned places at the front, my father's face a blank mask, Lea and I glancing curiously around at all the equally expressionless mourners. You would have thought from the packed pews that my grandmother had been popular and beloved, but there was a chill formality to the whole affair that lent a certain weirdness to the numbers. Who were these people? Business associates? Friends? A few of them were introduced as relatives—cousins, for Frank had been an only child; an aunt, but he obviously had no relationship with them. They filed past us and shook our hands with the mournful solemnity one assumes on such occasions, and then they disappeared into taxis and town cars. There was no reception, no gathering, no opportunity to share memories. My grandmother hadn't wanted one, and since she'd already been cremated, there was no trip to the cemetery, either. All the details had been handled by her solicitors, again as per her instructions, and I was left with an unfocused sadness that, having nowhere to land, hovered uneasily until it dissipated.

As for Frank, Lea said that he was now disgustingly rich, but I doubted that was the reason for the subtle change that came over him. My father seemed to have been liberated by his mother's death, and I could only wonder again at this woman who had inspired so little love in her long life. Lea and I had also received sizeable inheritances, in the form of trusts that were clearly designed to ward off fortune hunters. We joked about it, but it made us both uneasy, that a gift should come tainted with suspicion. It was hard in the end not to compare her to Astrid, who had left no great riches, but whom everyone missed.

Delphine surprised us all by showing up hugely pregnant, a gorgeous Tanzanian called, implausibly, Bruce (it turned out his real name was Zawadi) in tow. Sylvia didn't bat an eyelid, and expressed delight at the prospect of a lovely caramel-colored baby. "She doesn't even *realize* how racist she is!" Delphine exclaimed to me in exasperation.

"I don't see how she's being racist," I remarked. "It probably *is* going to be caramel-colored—assuming that hunk on your arm is the father?" You never did know with Delphine . . .

"Bruce is one of the top hip-hop artists in Tanzania," Delphine grandly informed me. "We're working together on an AIDS prevention project—it's really exciting; you should write about it. We could use the publicity."

"I might be able to do something," I said, "but you know, I'm working for *Glamour* these days."

Delphine's eyes grew round with horror. "What!"

It was true. Shortly after moving into my new place in Brooklyn

Heights, funded by my unexpected inheritance, I had run into Francine Feng, the Chinese gynecologist who had so wittily eulogized Astrid. She had asked me what I was up to and, when I had mentioned that I was unemployed, the prospect of chasing trouble around the world having lost its luster, she had remembered that Clarissa Temple, one of Astrid's oldest and most devoted clients, was looking for an assistant editor for the culture section.

"I'm not an editor," I said.

"Honey, who cares? Clarissa thought the world of your mother; such a sense of style! I'm sure she'd be willing to at least talk to you."

Not only had Clarissa been willing to talk to me, she'd offered me the job on a trial basis—it seemed that my journalistic credentials made up for my lack of editing experience, and I might also have the opportunity to write. I accepted gratefully.

Delphine, however, looked as if I had just announced that I'd taken a desk job at *Soldier of Fortune.*

"Relax," I said, "I'm doing culture, not underwear. Anyway, you're a fine one to talk about switching sides: Last time I checked, you were gay."

"Human sexuality is fluid," Delphine said with great seriousness. "God, I can't believe we're going to have the same mother. She always liked you better."

"I think we're both out of the running," I said, pointing to Marguerite, whose French braids Sylvia was just then fussing with.

My half sister—it was still something of a shock to think of her that way—had arrived in June for a summer visit meant to improve her French and maintain what Inge, ever family-conscious, worried were her tenuous ties with her father. She was in fact a nice kid, with her mother's open Scandinavian face, but Frank regarded her with the bemusement of a man who has suddenly found, in the back of his closet, a turquoise sweater given him years ago by a girlfriend. He tried very hard to be nice, but my father really did have no idea about children, even such a placid and well-behaved one, and so Sylvia had taken her in hand, a development that had benefited them both, since it gave Sylvia a project, and Marguerite the kind of fairy-tale mother that any girl but Delphine would want. Sylvia was genuinely fond of Marguerite, who followed her obediently to the ballet, and submitted with good grace to being dressed up in Jacadi frocks and Mary Janes. And Marguerite in turn adored Sylvia, a betrayal that Inge must have sniffed out, because when she returned from Stockholm the following year with a suitcase full of sensible Scandinavian clothes, Marguerite shamefacedly confessed that Inge had given all the lovely dresses to Oxfam. "That's all right," Sylvia gently retorted. "We'll just buy you new ones and you can leave them here."

If I did not feel treasonous in rejoicing at my father's happiness, it was because I had a feeling that Astrid would have approved. Hadn't she once told me that he should have married a Smith girl? His marriage to Inge had been ill-fated from day one; this one had the feeling of things falling into place. And theirs, it turned out, weren't the only nuptials in the cards. During the lunch that followed, Delphine pulled me aside and whispered hastily, "Listen, Bruce and I are getting married next week and we need a witness."

I assumed the same expression she had when I announced that I was working for *Glamour.*

"Look, it's just for the papers, okay? The French are such fucking racists."

"Oh well," I said with a grave expression, "if it's just for the papers . . ."

"Don't you dare tell my mom!"

That Delphine and Bruce, who ended up enjoying a modest success in New York's downtown music scene, are happily married to this day will surprise no one who saw them together at her mother's wedding. As Lea put it, Delphine just needed the right East African hip-hop artist to make her life complete.

58

THOUGH I NO LONGER covered Eastern Europe, I followed Łukasz's ascent with a certain proprietary interest. As he grew more powerful, he mastered spin and became elliptical. The government kept changing, scandals bubbled and burst, but Łukasz weathered most of them, and even had a turn at minister of foreign affairs (Lea and Serge had moved to Poland by then, so I got an earful on that one). He became involved with a French actress and eventually married her. It didn't last. But that was much later, around the same time it surfaced that, in the course of one of his arrests, he might have provided information to the police about some of his Solidarity colleagues. Similar allegations were made about Adam Michnik, another iconic figure, and even Lech Wałęsa. They were never proved, but the worm had been planted.

Maurizio was right: It had gone to their heads. He and I had lunch, and sometimes more, when he came through New York. Astrid had once told me that some men make better friends than lovers, and, when I wondered why she hadn't always shown such sagacity, I reminded myself that people rarely follow their own advice. Nobody bothered enquiring anymore if I was ever going to settle down, at least in the pairing-off sense that is commonly meant by that expression. Lea had long dismissed me as a hopeless case, one of those women, she grimly prophesied, who would die alone and be found eaten by her Siamese cats. That I had no cats did not disturb her vision in the least. As for Sylvia and my father, they had retreated into the self-absorption of happy couples, and would, in any case, have been too discreet to ask.

The fact was, I *had* settled down. Having a steady job rooted me, and I liked working at *Glamour.* I liked dressing and going to work, my heels tapping firmly on the sidewalk, my tote bag reassuringly heavy, an air of purpose in my stride. I felt at home among the smart, stylish women in the editorial office—much more than I had among the urban guerrillas at *Semiotext(e).* I even effortlessly assumed the tone of sophisticated and slightly arch ebullience that was expected by my readers. Delphine, now living in New York with Bruce and their caramel-colored daughter, Nico, never lost an opportunity to complain that we were perpetuating an unrealistic model of femininity, but I think we were all aware that it was an essentially harmless, and, at times, possibly essential enterprise. Grace put it perfectly: Sometimes all you can do is try to look your best. I wasn't, in any case, writing about fashion—I lacked that particular talent—but I was writing, about books and art and movies, for women who cared about looking good, and often, in doing so, I would mentally address Astrid.

The most dramatic changes by far took place in the lives of Lea and Maybelle. Either Nahid was wrong, or the world was full of fools. With the Communists gone, an awful lot of people, Serge and his father included, had started revisiting the past: factory owners and doddering countesses, Jews and priests, descendants of descendants—the great ragged patchwork of exile that had blanketed Europe for decades with its melancholy ghosts. Deeds and documents were dusted off, old photo albums pulled out of closets. Since Serge's family had once owned half of southeastern Poland, full restitution was deemed unlikely, not to mention impractical, but several possibilities were raised, including a ruined castle by the Ukrainian border with a garbage-choked moat adjoining a failed agricultural collective.

Serge went on a reconnaissance tour with Przemek, with whom he had become friendly over the years. It had come out at one of the family functions that he and Maybelle attended much more sedulously than I did, that not only was Przemek from the very corner of southeastern Poland that had once held the Lubomirski family seat, which implied that his ancestors had once been owned by Serge's, he was a horseman, too—in his youth, he had worked on one of the nationalized stud farms that had tried to keep Poland's Arabian breeding tradition alive after the war. Unlike Serge, though, he had a head for numbers and the practical outlook of a man who had had to make his own way in the world. Together they dreamed up a plan of reviving the legendary Lubomirski stables, which had been decimated by two world wars and forty years of Communist rule. It was the kind of crazy fantasy that all of a sudden seemed possible, and they became consumed by it, Lea and Maybelle sighing, "You know men. . . ."

Eventually they would succeed, thanks in great part to Przemek's business acumen. They accepted the castle, the fabled Lubomirski family seat being out of the running. The rambling Renaissance folly had long ago been turned into a museum, and defaced by such necessities as linoleum and public toilets on every floor. A scandal, Lea declared, even as she had to concede that the heating bills alone would have put them in the poorhouse. The ruined castle nearly did. It was full of rats and rusted tractor parts and pronounced too expensive to restore by a series of architects who shook their heads at this madness. Przemek wasn't put off. He brought in an endless supply of cousins, many of whom had worked in construction in America and had now come home to roost, and they went to work. They refurbished the main dwelling, built paddocks and runs and breeding sheds, and, in an experiment, planted a few acres of Kentucky grass. Lea said, "I can't believe we're doing this!" but when the local peasantry (and the pharmacist) started addressing her as "Princess," she had to concede that there was a certain logic to the whole enterprise. Such sweet people, she assured me, and they'd been so miserable on the collective farm.

Maybelle, too, began to pack. Przemek was to be the manager of the stud farm and had bought a place for them nearby. Maybelle was adored by Lea's children, and she and my sister, brought

together by their husbands' linked fortunes, had become insepara-
ble. As she shed her youthful vanity, Lea had come to appreciate in
our aunt the very virtues that had driven a subtle wedge between
us. It was I, now, who was the outsider. Single and childless, I had
become a tourist in their lives, one whom they regarded with a sort
of benevolent pity, for surely I, too, must long for domestic bliss.

I didn't. I had lovers, boyfriends. Some lasted, some didn't. "Take
your time," Grace advised. We had dinner together every Thursday;
it was a ritual we fell into naturally. I ended up taking only three
things from the apartment on Jane Street: my favorite portrait of
Astrid, a chaise that she and I had picked out together at the
Chelsea flea market, and the turquoise Fortuny dress that made her
look like a mermaid. I didn't want to be hemmed in by objects,
responsible for their care, bereft at their loss. I had just turned thirty,
a birthday that I had celebrated quietly with Grace. It felt like a fine
age for a woman, an age of dignity and possibility. It had happened
almost by stealth, this assumption of womanhood, like a mantle
falling gently but firmly about my shoulders. And so I wore it, even
as I knew every woman's secret, that the girl still lives inside you,
surprising you at odd moments; in the middle of the night, when
you wake up and wonder if your mother has come home yet, or at
a party, as you stand, a little self-conscious at the edge of the floor,
your foot tapping to the music, hoping that you look all right, that
no one can tell you're nervous, that someone will notice you and ask
you to dance.